PENGUIN BOOKS

BACKCLOTH

Since 1947 Dirk Bogarde has starred in more than sixty films. His popularity as a teenage idol brought him vast amounts of fanmail and an enormous box-office success, which was to continue through the fifties and the sixties. Later he achieved a different kind of success with such films as *The Servant*, *King and Country*, *Accident*, *Death in Venice*, *The Night Porter*, *Providence* and *Despair*.

In recent years he has become well known as a writer with the publication of his first three volumes of autobiography, *A Postillion Struck by Lightning*, *Snakes and Ladders* and *An Orderly Man*, and three novels, *A Gentle Occupation*, *Voices in the Garden* and *West of Sunset*, all of which reached the bestseller lists and have been translated into a number of languages.

He lived in France for many years, and was made a Chevalier de l'Ordre des Arts et des Lettres by the French Government in 1982. In 1985 he was made an Honorary Doctor of Letters at the University of St Andrews.

D0964344

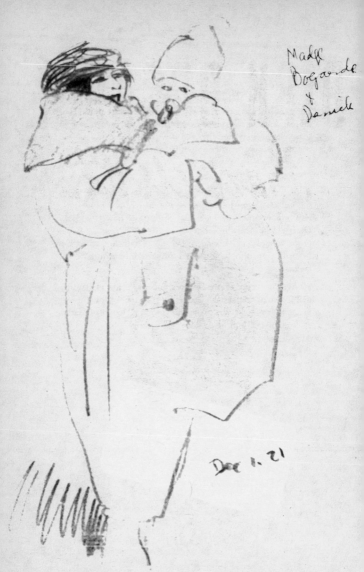

Madge
Bogaerde
& Derick

Dec 1. 21

My mother and myself. Unsigned drawing attributed to J. H. Dowd,
1921

DIRK BOGARDE

Backcloth

PENGUIN BOOKS

PENGUIN BOOKS

Published by the Penguin Group
27 Wrights Lane, London w8 5tz, England
Viking Penguin Inc., 40 West 23rd Street, New York, New York 10010, USA
Penguin Books Australia Ltd, Ringwood, Victoria, Australia
Penguin Books Canada Ltd, 2801 John Street, Markham, Ontario, Canada l3r 1b4
Penguin Books (NZ) Ltd, 182–190 Wairau Road, Auckland 10, New Zealand

Penguin Books Ltd, Registered Offices: Harmondsworth, Middlesex, England

First published by Viking 1986
Published in Penguin Books 1987
7 9 10 8
Copyright © Labofilms S.A., 1986
All rights reserved

Acknowledgement is gratefully made by the author and publishers to Belwin Mills Music Ltd
for permission to reproduce lines from 'Chattanooga Choo-Choo'

Made and printed in Great Britain by
Richard Clay Ltd, Bungay, Suffolk
Typeset in Bembo

Except in the United States of America,
this book is sold subject to the condition
that it shall not, by way of trade or otherwise,
be lent, re-sold, hired out, or otherwise circulated
without the publisher's prior consent in any form of
binding or cover other than that in which it is
published and without a similar condition
including this condition being imposed
on the subsequent purchaser

This book is for Glenda Jackson,
with my love.

SOURCES
AND ACKNOWLEDGEMENTS

My principal sources have been the notebooks and diaries kept from 1940 until the present day, plus some letters to my father written between 1940 and 1946. I have also made use of material in many of the letters which I wrote over some years to 'Mrs X' in America. Her constant questioning and interest forced me to remember a great many details with which I attempted to amuse and distract her during her final illness.

All these letters, postcards, and some of the notebooks, will be destroyed after the final editing of this book, for I have no wish that they should perhaps fall into the hands of un-comprehending strangers.

They have served their purpose well.

I have made no efforts to correct these 'pieces', or to alter their 'style': they remain exactly as written at the time. In the diaries I have excised portions which were repetitive or of no interest to the progress of the book.

The spelling of all the place names in the section on Java is correct. These are how the towns were named in the years before Indonesian Independence.

Where necessary I have used, to avoid distress, pseudonyms.

I am particularly grateful to Hélène Bordes, *maître de conférences* at Limoges University, who when I had reached a particularly despairing period in my work threw, as it were, a 'plank' across the ravine and encouraged me to continue.

My gratitude, as always, to Mrs Sally Betts who, after ten

years, still manages to cope effortlessly, it would seem, with the trials and tribulations which my untidy typescripts must cause her, and for making sense and order out of my many corrections and sudden additions.

D.v.d.B.

PART ONE

CHAPTER

I

Memory: I scratch about like a hen in chaff.

The first thing that I can recall is light.

Pale, opaque green, white spots drifting. Near my right eye long black shapes curling down and tickling gently.

Years later when I reported this memory to my parents they confirmed it. There had, apparently, been an extraordinary pea-soup fog; it had snowed at the same time. My mother had lifted me up to observe the phenomenon; the black feathers which wreathed her hat irritated my eyes and I tried to pull them away. I was nine months old.

When I was two, I remember lying on my back on the lawn behind the house in St Georges Road. It was a brilliant day of high wind and scudding cloud. The tall house reeled away from me as the clouds whipped across the blue sky and I was afraid that it would fall down and crush me.

And later I saw our giant ginger cat – well, giant to me then – nailed alive to the tall wooden fence which separated us from an unfriendly neighbour. I remember my mother weeping: which frightened me far more than the sight of the dying cat for I had not yet learned to recognize cruelty or death, but I was recognizing pain and distress on a human face for the first time.

It would not be the last.

The house in St Georges Road was tall, ugly, built of grey-yellow bricks with a slate roof. It had the great advantage for my father, who was an artist, of a number of high-ceilinged rooms with a perfect north light. It also had a long narrow garden with ancient trees.

An Irish woman lived in the basement with two children

and cleaned the house from time to time. She had once been a maid to the Chesterfields, who lived in a very grand house not far away called The Lodge.

Sometimes I would see her crouching on a landing with a mop or a brush. There was an almost constant smell of cooking from the basement, and my father said it was Irish stew because that's what the Irish ate.

I suppose that made sense to me – at least, I have remembered it.

My father was a prudent man, with little fortune, and he let off most of the rooms in the house to artist friends, so that (apart from the prevailing smell of Irish stew) the place reeked of turpentine and linseed oil, and the mixed scent of those two is the one that I remember best and with which, anywhere I go, if I smell it, I am instantly at ease, familiar and secure.

One of his lodgers was, in fact, an artists' model who had been left behind, in a rather careless manner, by an artist who had wandered off to Italy to paint. I knew her as Aunt Kitty.

Tiny, vivid, a shock of bright red hair brushed high up from her forehead, brilliant green eyes heavily lined with kohl, she was loving, warm and exceptionally noisy. For some reason, which I can no longer recall, I always seemed to see her carrying a tall glass of Russian tea in a silver holder. I never knew why – or even what it was, then; and I never asked. She just did.

She had a powder puff in a red leather bag which I found interesting, for it looked exactly like a fat little bun with an ivory ring in its middle. If you pulled the ring, out came the powder puff, of softest swansdown, and the powder never spilled. It smelled sweet and sickly. I liked it.

Her room was dark nearly all the time for she hated daylight, which, she said, gave her terrible headaches. So the room was lighted here and there with small lamps draped with coloured handkerchiefs; each had a stick of incense burning beside it. The handkerchiefs cast strange and beautiful patterns on the ceiling.

There was a gold and black striped divan. Cushions in profusion tumbled all about the floor for one to sit on or lie upon. She had no chairs. I found that exceptionally curious. As

I did the polar bear rug with roaring head, fearful teeth, glassy eyes and a pink plaster tongue, and the tall jars stuffed with the feathers from peacocks' tails.

It was the most exciting room in the house. She also had a portable gramophone which stood on a table with a broken leg that she had supported with a pile of books. She would wind it up after each record, a cigarette hanging from her lips, hoop earrings swinging from her ears, dressed as I only ever remember her dressed: in long, rustling dressing-gowns, covered with flowers and blue-birds, bound around her waist with a wide tasselled sash. The tassels swung and danced as she moved.

On occasion she was distressed and wept hopelessly: then my mother had to go down to the scented room and comfort her. Sometimes, too, she was rather strange. Leaning across to caress my cheek, for example, she would quite often miss me and crash to the floor in a heap. I found this worrying at first. However, she usually laughed and dragged herself upright by holding on to the nearest piece of furniture.

She once told me, leaning close to my face, that she had had 'one over the eight', but I didn't know what she meant, and when I asked my father he bit his lower lip, a sign I knew to indicate anger, and said he didn't know.

But I was pretty certain that he did.

Her dazzling eyes, the henna'd hair frizzed out about the pale, oval face, the coarse laughter, the tassels and the peacocks' feathers are still, after so many years, before me – and remain indelibly a part of my life.

She offered me, in that crammed room, a sense of colour and beauty, and even, although I was almost unaware of it at the time, excitement. I was uncomprehending of nearly all that she said but I did realize that she was offering riches beyond price.

First had come light; after light, scent, originally of turpentine and linseed oil (hardly romantic one might think), and now I was shown colour and, above all, made aware of texture.

'Touch it!' she would say. 'Touch the silk, it's so beautiful. Do you know that a million little worms worked to make this single piece?'

I didn't, of course, but the idea fascinated me. That something so fine, so sheer, so glorious should come from 'a million little worms' filled me with amazement, and I liked worms from then on.

Sometimes she would go away, and when I asked Mrs O'Connell where she had gone to she would only reply, 'A-voyagin'.' Which was no help. My parents when questioned said that she had gone on her holidays. I had an instant vision of buckets and spades, shrimping nets and long stretches of sand with the tide far out. And in consequence, knowing that she would be having a lovely time, put her from my mind.

When she returned she came bearing amazing gifts. Silver rings for my mother, a basket of brilliant shells of all kinds and shapes for me, French cigarettes for my father who, I knew instinctively, liked them better than he liked Aunt Kitty.

She brought for herself rolls of coloured cloth. Silks, voiles, cottons of every hue and design. These she would throw about her room in armfuls, so that they fell and covered the ugly furniture, then with the cigarette hanging from her lip she would wind up the gramophone, drape a length of cloth about her body, and dance. Barefoot, her nails painted gold.

Mesmerized I would sit and watch the small feet with golden-tipped toes twist and spin among tumbles of brilliant silks and the spilled shells from my palm-leaf basket.

'And when I tell them
How wonderful you are,
They'll never believe me-e . . .'

She told me, winding up the gramophone for the second side of the record, that the silks had come across the sands of Araby on the backs of camels, that she had seen monkeys swing among the branches of jacaranda trees, and flights of scarlet birds sweep across opal skies.

I hadn't the least idea what she meant. But somewhere in

14

Aunt Kitty's room

my struggling mind the awareness was growing, from her words, that far beyond the confines of St Georges Road, West End Lane, Hampstead, lay a world of magic and beauty.

Once I heard my father say that one day Aunt Kitty wouldn't return from one of her 'voyages'.

And one day that's exactly what happened. She never came back again: the Ground Floor Front was locked. I asked where she had gone. My father said possibly into the belly of a crocodile. It distressed me for a whole morning.

Years later I was to discover that no crocodile had taken Aunt Kitty: she had gone off, perfectly willingly, with a rich sultan from the East Indies.

When her room was opened it was exactly as she had left it, she had taken nothing with her, not even the silks. There were the gramophone, the draped lamps, the gold-striped divan, the bear-skin and the little red leather powder puff wrapped in letter paper on which she had printed a message to my mother, begging her to keep it always as a remembrance of her.

And she did. For many years it lay at the bottom of her jewel case and sometimes I would take it out, with permission, pull the little ivory ring, release the swansdown puff and the strange, musky scent. Naturally, over years, the scent grew fainter and fainter until, finally, there was only a ghostly odour, and the swansdown puff grew thin, grey, and moulted. But Aunt Kitty remains in my mind today, as clear and as vibrant as she was in the days when she wound up her gramophone for me.

'We'll have a little dancy, ducky, shall we? Would that be lovely?'

> 'And when I tell them
> How wonderful you are,
> They'll never believe me-e . . .'

★   ★   ★

Sometime after Aunt Kitty had left us, my sister Elizabeth was born. I was taken off to Scotland by my maternal grandmother Nelson, a friendly, firm, warm, straight-backed woman in black, to keep me 'out of the way'. I can only remember a new tweed coat with a velvet collar, of which I was inordinately proud, a railway compartment and on my lap a round, black lacquered wicker basket, painted with pink roses, which contained my sandwiches for the journey. It is a fragment of memory; that's all there is, but I see it sharply.

When I returned to the ugly house in St Georges Road, an enormous pram, with wheels like dustbin lids, stood in the front drive and Mrs O'Connell said that I had a baby sister and that, if they weren't careful (they apparently being my parents), a cat would sit on the baby's face and smother it. Faithfully, I reported this piece of information and my squalling sister was draped in netting.

With another member in the family, my personal discipline was relaxed, and I was left free to wander from studio to studio, squashing tubes of paint, watching the 'uncles' (they were all called 'Uncle', the resident artists who rented my father's rooms) painting their canvases, and being as tiresome as any child of four could be in a cluttered room full of sights and smells and bottles.

Bottles had a great attraction for me. I wonder why? I can remember, very clearly, taking down a full bottle of Owbridges Lung Tonic and swallowing its contents. I liked the taste of, I suppose, laudanum or whatever the soothing drug was which it contained. Though I well remember performing this wicked act, the time following it is obliterated. I went into a coma for four days, and nothing, not even salt and water, mustard and water, or being given my father's pipe to smoke apparently made any impression on me. No one was able to accomplish the essential task of forcing me to vomit up my stolen delight. I lay as for dead, heavily drugged.

I recovered – and later drank a bottle of rose-water and glycerine to the dregs. I was thrashed for this by my father, who always did it rather badly and apologetically with one of his paintbrushes.

But it didn't stop me. I stole from every bottle set high on shelves or left, carelessly, standing about. The studios were forbidden territory. Not only did I squash the artists' paint tubes empty, I was obviously quite capable of scoffing their linseed oil and turpentine.

A 'handful' is what I was considered, and handfuls such as I had to be dealt with firmly.

But no one had much time to deal with me, so, apart from being locked out of all the uncles' rooms, I was pretty well left on my own to play about in the garden and feed my sister with pebbles or anything else which came to hand. And, of course, got another walloping. People simply didn't understand that I was being kind.

Some of these fragments I remember with intense clarity. Others less well. Memory, as far back as this, is rather like archaeology. Little scraps and shards are collected from the dust of time and put together to form a whole by dedicated people, in this case my parents, who filled in the sprawling design of my life at that early age, and made real the pattern.

Aunt Kitty's room, for example, I can only see as a vague, shadowy place, filled with sweet scents and the trembling shapes of feathers and handkerchiefs flickering high on the ceiling. And I remember the gold and black striped divan, for it was to become my own, many years later, when we moved to the cottage. Equally I remember the polar bear rug. It was the first time that I had dared to place a timid hand within the roaring mouth; for the simple reason that Aunt Kitty had assured me that it would not bite.

It didn't. I trusted her from then on implicitly.

I trusted everyone in sight. Unwisely.

I can remember the great spills of cloth, but not the stories of camels and Araby or the scarlet birds swooping across opal skies. These items were added by my parents much later, who had, doubtless, heard her recount them and she told stories all day long to enthral me. But I do remember the worms; and the million it took to make a tiny scrap of glowing material. However, most of those very early years are simply the shards and scraps. Vivid none the less.

18

But from five years old onwards I have almost total recall – although I rather think that Elizabeth, with a feminine mind, has a far greater memory for detail than I.

*   *   *

My father grew restless in the grey-yellow brick house and decided that he wanted to move out to a quieter area: he suffered from catarrh, and also from hideous nightmares which his experiences, a few years before, in the Somme and at Passchendaele had engendered.

These of course I knew nothing about. Sudden shouts in the night perhaps, I can remember those, and my mother's anxious, caring face the following morning as he set off to his work at *The Times*, where he had become Northcliffe's golden-boy, and the first Art Editor at an absurdly young age.

So we moved away from the grey street off West End Lane into a small, but pleasant, house among abandoned fields just outside Twickenham. It was the talk of the family, and of its friends, that the sale was a 'snip'. He had bought it extremely cheaply for some reason, and everyone was amazed. The reason was soon to become apparent.

But for the moment we had a muddy road running through fields before us which trickled off into a path between high summer grasses, elderberry bushes and past a great rubbish tip buried deep in a quarry.

Behind our house ran an immense rose-pink brick wall, and behind that lay a park of great beauty and a square, complacent Georgian house burrowing away among chestnuts and elms. The people who lived there were exceedingly pleasant, and had children of about our age, and there was a green paint-peeling wooden door in the wall through which we were allowed to enter and join them at play on their smooth lawns among the croquet hoops.

We also had a garden, but, naturally, far more modest, in which my mother started to grow herbs and exotic vegetables which were, at that time, not easy to find in England. We had a huge cherry tree, some apple trees at the far end and a mass of climbing roses. Nothing could have been a greater change from the long narrow garden near West End Lane and the continuous smell of Irish stew.

We, Elizabeth and I, were in a paradise: but as in Paradise itself there was a serpent.

One morning the dirt track in front of the house began shuddering with trucks and lorries of all descriptions; they droned and rumbled all day long, and when they left, in the late evening, we discovered the fields before us, and around us, stuck with scarlet wooden stakes and draped about with sagging ropes. My anguished father discovered, too late, that he had purchased his house in the exact centre of an enormous building development; which was the reason that it had been, as everyone said, 'so ridiculously' cheap. 'A snip.'

We were buried among bricks, lime, cement and piles of glossy scarlet tiles. The road was churned into a mud-slide and the windows rattled all day with thudding trucks.

Within a year the fields in front had yielded up a row of semi-detached villas, with bay windows and tudor gables, their roofs, as yet untiled, looking like the pale yellow bones of a smoked haddock.

My father was in despair.

I was fascinated by all the work and upheaval and spent as much of my time as I possibly could clambering about in the unfinished foundations of suburbia. Although the workmen were friendly, and seemed not to mind me being among them, there came a time when they shouted at me to 'bugger orf!', and once someone threw a half-brick which sent me scurrying.

Another time I got a hod-load of lime full in the face; rather like a custard pie. It was, of course, quite accidental, and all I can remember is that it burned appallingly and I fled, blinded, from the half-built house, screaming at the top of my lungs, across the battered field and the rutted road. My distracted mother could not understand what had happened, naturally, and I was unable to tell her because I was yelling. She washed my face and hair and tried to get me to explain what had occurred, to no avail.

At that moment, an enormous man burst into the kitchen, pulled me on to his lap, and licked, with naked tongue, the lime from my eyes. Had he not done so, I have been assured, I would in all probability have been blinded for good. Counselling my distraught mother to bathe my eyes with milk and not to let me out of her sight ever again, he left. I wondered who he was, and have often thought of him with gratitude.

I only stopped going to the half-built houses because I was warned that I'd be given a thrashing I'd never forget if I did. So I wandered off up the little path towards the deep rubbish tip in the quarry. It was quieter there, no one came near, and I could explore the tumbled rubbish of Twickenham with complete freedom. Boxes and crates, broken chimney pots, old tin cans, a battered pram; pieces of wood, quantities of smashed tiles and earthen drainpipes. Nothing smelly.

I remained always just at the edge, for it was very deep, and I had a fear of falling in – which, one day, I did. Because I heard a kitten crying down at the bottom. Leaning too far over the slippery edge of broken tiles and chimney pots I slid rapidly to the bottom, found the kitten, a skinny creature which had managed to get out of a sack, leaving the dead bodies of its companions, and sat down cradling my find, confident that someone would collect me.

I had tried to clamber up but had found that impossible: each step I took up the jagged slope of rubbish sent me slithering backwards, and there was no possibility of climbing the, to me at that time anyway, sheer sides with a frantic kitten. So I just sat quietly.

Calling had no effect either, I was soon to discover, for my thin voice never reached the lip of the pit, and my wretched mother, who had quickly discovered my absence, passed and repassed my prison without having the very least idea that her first-born was sitting below among the debris. Eventually a search-party was formed from the builders and masons on the swiftly growing estate; I was discovered and dragged to the surface with the kitten. I think that my mother had been so frightened that she forgot to punish or even scold, and I was permitted to keep the kitten, who grew into a fine creature which we called 'Minnehaha'. Unknowingly getting his sex wrong.

The little path through the grasses was not exactly out of bounds, although now the quarry was. But along the path a jungle of most attractive plants and grasses grew, and tiny green crickets scissored in the sun. I picked handfuls of bright black fruits from a small bush, ate them, and stuffed my unprotesting sister. Full. With deadly nightshade.

Both of us, this time, went into a coma. There had been a nurse and a doctor and enemas and thermometers and the moment I was well enough to do so I up-ended the nursery fire-guard, shoved my sister into it as a patient, and we played 'hospitals'. It was very exciting, but pretty dull without 'pills' or 'medicines'.

I consumed, because it was my 'turn' to be a patient, a full bottle of aspirin. Another coma.

My mother was told that nothing could be done – I had taken such a massive overdose that I'd either die or recover. All that she could do was lie with me, her hand on my heart, and if she felt the least change of rhythm she was to call the doctor instantly.

I slept like a lamb, my heart beating contentedly.

I do not think that I had suicidal tendencies. Certainly I had no murderous ones. Then. However, my parents decided that the time was ready for me to have some kind of supervision and discipline in life: I had been altogether far too spoiled.

To this effect, early one morning, my sister and I, peering down into the hall through the white-painted banisters from the upper landing, saw our mother (elegant even at that hour, in a coffee-lace morning-gown and boudoir cap) engaged in earnest conversation with a Girl Guide. The latter smart and upright as a ninepin. Trim in her uniform with a bright white lanyard at her shoulder, a whistle at her neck.

Miss Ellen Jane, of Walnut Cottages, Twickenham, had just entered our lives. She has stayed part of it ever since.

'Ellen is my given name,' she said. 'At home I'm called

"Nelly", but you'd better call me "Nanny", that's what I'm supposed to be, and that's that. It's more fitting.'

Elizabeth couldn't come to grips with 'Nanny', so she compromised and called her 'Lally'; and that is what she has always been.

It was a curious feeling having someone literally 'in charge' of one at all hours of the day, and even night. I began to enjoy it quite. I lost any suicidal tendencies I might have had because all bottles, knives, pills or potions were removed from my reach, and I willingly gave in to this cheerful creature who would stand no nonsense, as she said (and clearly meant it), and who looked a little less daunting in her new uniform of blue cotton and long white apron with celluloid cuffs.

It was rather interesting, I found, to be forced to sit upright at table and not to 'slouch about'. To replace my napkin in its linen envelope, to stop swinging my legs, to ask permission to leave the table (and often be refused until we were all satisfied), to have to wash my hands every two minutes (so it seemed), and above all to be read to in bed – a great change from 'Gentle Jesus', which we had to mumble in a hideous mono-tone, kneeling, with one eye on *The Water Babies*. But perhaps most interesting of all was the morning journey to the lavatory, the details of which operation had to be reported in full. If they were unsatisfactory one was sent back again.

But after a while I became less interested. I am easily bored. The novelty wore off, and I began to resent the routine and having my neck examined each morning to make certain that I had, in fact, washed 'round the back'.

My sister didn't seem to have to undergo quite so many humiliations, I began to realize, and she was far more cosseted and fussed over because she was younger. And prettier. Jealousy started to sprout like a bean shoot in the darkness of my heart – it also began to show.

And that was the start.

Miss Harris and her sister ran a genteel school for young children in a square Victorian house overlooking the Green. In their back garden, down among the laurels, and where the teachers parked their bikes, there was a long tin shed, painted dark red; this was the kindergarten.

I landed up there.

A blackboard, a big iron stove, tables. I remember nothing else. I imagine that one was instructed in the very basics, but I never bothered to learn them. This has had serious consequences for me throughout my life.

Jealousy seething, anger mounting, I sat and thought only about Minnehaha or how best to build an aquarium, or when we would next go down to Teddington Lock with net and jam jar to fish for sticklebacks.

I simply didn't bother with Miss Harris and her silly kindergarten; my brain absolutely refused to see the connection between 'CAT' and 'MAT' and I frankly didn't give a damn which sat on which. As far as I was concerned it was a wasted morning.

My parents found it to be the same thing after one caustic report from Miss Harris herself: 'He doesn't try. Won't put himself out at all.'

He was not about to.

Stronger medicine was needed, and it was found in the form of a tall red building along the river, almost next door to Radnor Park. A convent-school a-flutter with smiling nuns.

I was captivated by their swirling grey habits, by the glitter and splendour of the modest, but theatrically ravishing, chapel, the flickering lamps beneath the statues of the Virgin Mary and Joseph. It went to my head in a trice and I fell passionately in love with convent life.

I liked, above all, our classroom, a high-ceilinged, white-painted room with great mirrored doors which reflected the river, the trees beyond and the boats; I worshipped Sister Veronica with her gentle hands and the modest mole from which sprouted, fascinatingly, a single hair, and Sister Marie Joseph who was fat, and bustled, and stood no nonsense, but taught me my catechism and let me come into the chapel whenever I felt the need, which was often.

Not to pray, you understand, but to drown in the splendours

of lamps, candles, colours, a glowing Christ and the smell of something in the stuffy air which reminded me of Aunt Kitty.

The colours, the singing of the choir, the altarcloths shimmering with gold thread filled my heart and my head with delight. I was lost: and decided, there and then, to be a priest.

Religion, certainly the Catholic religion, was not taught in our house. My father was born into a strongly Catholic family, with a staunch Catholic convert mother, and it was as a Catholic, firm in his belief, that he went to war in 1914. His belief, like that of so many other young men of that time, was shattered on the Somme, in Passchendaele, and finally for all time when he pulled open the doors of a chapel, after the battle of Caparetto in Italy, and was smothered in the rotting corpses of soldiers and civilians who had been massacred and stuffed high to the roof.

'Jesus,' he once told me, many years after, 'does *not* have his eye on the sparrows. But you follow whatever faith you wish; it is your life, not mine.'

And so Elizabeth and I grew up and flourished in a vaguely ambiguous atmosphere. We were sent to the convent on the riverside, I was allowed to have my own altar, which I built with intense care in a corner of the nursery, and we mumbled our 'Gentle Jesus' and The Lord's Prayer without interference. We were left to make up our own minds about God and Jesus, Joseph and The Virgin Mary.

It was not a difficult process for me because I had fallen quite in love with everything that Catholic teaching had to offer. Without, of course, realizing that what I had *actually* fallen in love with was the Theatre. Not religion at all. The ritual, the singing, the light, the mystery, the glowing candles: all these were Theatre, and Theatre emerged from these things and engulfed me for the rest of my life. Learning my catechism was, after all, merely the prelude to learning my 'lines'.

Like my father before me, I laid aside my belief, not that it had ever been very strong to be sure, for ever in my war.

Whenever I make a declaration of this kind I am inevitably

swamped with letters from well-meaning people, usually women, who want to convert me to 'believing' again. I am bombarded, literally, with religious books, usually American paperbacks, of all possible permutations and persuasions. One which turns up regularly is called *Wrestling with Christ*, which appears to be an enormous best-seller but fails to answer any of the questions which have concerned me over the years. I have absolutely no wish to wrestle with anyone – especially with Christ.

It is particularly hard to retain a shred of 'belief' standing in the middle of a battlefield, at the age of twenty-three, watching piles of dead, frequently mutilated, soldiers, their bellies bloated with the gases of decomposition, being bulldozed into a mass grave. I watched them tumble, spill, slither like old shirts in a spin-drier, and as I walked away, retching in the stench of death, I knew that, at last, I had come of age, and that I could never recover the happy platitudes of immortality and 'Jesus Loves You'.

Where I wondered, on another occasion when I tripped over a row of what I took to be dusty footballs, but which were, in fact, the maggot-ridden heads of a file of small children who had sought shelter from our *own* bombing in a French village, what ever happened to that loving, comforting phrase, 'Suffer Little Children to Come unto Me'?

Something was not quite right. It was not what I'd been taught, and my first, appalled, uncomprehending sight of a concentration camp, two of the women guards smiling brightly and wearing scarlet nail-varnish among the decaying mounds of bodies, shred whatever belief I had had to tatters and dispersed it in the winds of fact, and hideous truth.

I would always, however, say my prayers. I still do to this day. But it is a prayer to a greater force than the simpering plaster figures to which I prayed so ardently all those years ago.

However, to return to Twickenham and innocence: a priest I decided to be, and that was that. The fact that no one took my decision seriously, even beloved Sister Veronica herself, did not trouble me. I had time before me, and I was exceptionally happy.

There were other moments of happiness which I recall during the Twickenham years. Days on the river in a punt. My father in white flannels and shirt, poling us along, my mother lying among cushions, a Japanese parasol shielding her face from the sun, Layton and Johnstone on the portable gramophone, a picnic hamper among the bathing-towels, the smell of boat varnish, and the excitement of getting to one of the locks and watching the rise and fall of the water.

In Church Street there was a small toy-shop filled with treasures, and every Saturday I went there with my 'Saturday penny' (actually I was given two) to buy a celluloid animal from a huge cardboard box to add to my growing 'zoo'. I, the budding priest, thieved one or two occasionally when the elderly woman who ran the shop was not looking. Twopence only bought one creature. Sometimes the desire to have another was too great and wickedness overcame me. With horrifying facility.

I knew perfectly well, for Sister Veronica had told me, that if I had done some 'really bad' thing I could one day go to confession and all would be forgiven. Catholicism, I figured, was a convenient affair.

The General Strike was something which threw a mild spanner in the works of this halcyon life; no amount of prayer, and I did a good deal of it both at home and in the chapel, seemed to help. My father drove an omnibus in a tweed cap and plus-fours and my mother joined some ladies and handed out soup. Otherwise it had little effect on my life or Elizabeth's. We were still marched off to the lavatory each morning and I still had my neck examined to make certain I had not 'skimped things', as Lally said. The days were fairly calm apart from the fact that we saw less of our parents, who were busily engaged. But there was a vague sense of unease about, and I didn't much care for that.

I never have.

All around us the terrible red brick houses with Tudor gables

continued to spring up: the deep quarry into which I had fallen, and in which I had found Minnehaha, was filled in and a road laid across it; the pale rose-pink wall which surrounded the splendid park behind us was demolished; the great trees were felled; the Georgian house lost its complacency and crumbled into dust beneath a huge metal ball swung on a chain, and a cinema, with Egyptian suggestions in its architecture, arose slowly on the site, the gentle croquet-hooped lawns were buried under asphalt for a car park.

My father decided that it was time to leave.

The fields had gone and in their place we now had lamp-posts and neighbours whom we really had not expected. I minded less than my parents, who were sunk in gloom. For who, in their right minds, would purchase a house, pretty if shabby, surrounded by fences, gates and tudor gables? As a matter of fact, I found neighbours rather interesting.

Immediately opposite us a Mrs Rance had moved into the first of the houses to be finished. She was a small, thin woman, her hair in curlers under a hairnet; she spent a good deal of her time coming across the still muddy road to borrow a cup of sugar or a 'small jug of milk, I've run out dearie'.

Lally disliked her intensely. She knew *her* position and *her* class. Mrs Rance obviously did not, we gathered. But what made her interesting was that on one or two occasions she would come staggering to our front gate screaming and waving a blue glass bottle in the air; then she would fall down in a fit and our mother would have to telephone a doctor.

'Been at the iodine again,' said Lally with satisfaction. 'If she wants to do away with herself, and this is the third time she's tried it, why come and trouble innocent, law-abiding people, I'd very much like to know?'

I took a deep interest in Mrs Rance and her well-being, and with vague notions of the priesthood looming in my mind I felt impelled to go to her assistance, as she was often lying, writhing about, outside our front gate. But there was little chance of that with Lally. I was carted off to our nursery, or room, and as it looked out over the back garden and the cherry tree I never saw what happened to Mrs Rance. I can't remember seeing her ever again – maybe the iodine did the trick.

The next people to move in opposite were the Hammonds. A family of four, three boys and one girl called Jessie. Jessie was one year older than I was and I liked her because she had a small tent in their back garden, a wilderness still of rutted mud and cement dust, and invited me to come and play with her.

It made a change from my sister, because Jessie was really pretty daring. She showed me a secret box in which she kept cigarette butts, and we sucked away at these for a time; without, of course, lighting them. They made me feel sick. So she rustled about and produced another tin box, battered but secure, in which she had a hoard of rotten apples, bits of cake and a whole tin of baked beans, which, with an opener in the shape of a bull's-head (which I coveted instantly), we opened and ate cold, in handfuls.

I felt a little more sick, but felt better after a bit of mouldy cake. Then she pulled down her knickers and said that she would show me her 'thingy' on condition that I showed her mine. This surprised me slightly – we had only known each other for an afternoon. Also I was still feeling a certain unease in my stomach and anyway I'd seen Elizabeth naked in the bath every night, just as she, indeed, had seen me: so I was not fearfully interested for I could hardly believe that I was about to witness something extraordinary or amazing.

I complied willingly.

We regarded each other in silence, standing in a half crouch in the sagging tent. I was quite unamazed.

'My brothers have got one like yours,' she said.

'My sister has one the same as yours, so there.'

'Girls have to sit down if they want to have a pee-pee; it's easier for boys.'

'I think I'll go home now,' I said.

Later I was extremely sick, and couldn't eat supper, which alerted Lally to the fact that perhaps all was not well. She told my father that I had spent the afternoon with 'those dreadful

30

people in the new houses. It's not fitting. They'll spoil his ways, and there is nothing that I can do on account of the fact that I have only one pair of hands and no eyes in the back of my head. He wanders.'

My father was a just and kind man; he followed my anxious mother down to my room and asked me what had happened that day. 'We only want to know what has made you so ill, and then we can get it set to rights,' he said reasonably.

So I told him in detail, from sucking cigarette butts to eating mouldy cake and cold tinned beans, and examining each other's 'thingys'.

He looked grim but said nothing; my mother took my temperature, found that it was normal; they said goodnight and went away.

A few weeks later we moved to Hampstead.

$$\star \quad \star \quad \star$$

And that is that. The first seven years of my life recalled as faithfully as I can remember, aided by others who have filled in the gaps.

The years of innocence. These, I am told, are the impressionable years, the formative ones during which all the things which one discovers, or is shown, stay with one for the rest of life and, as it were, one is moulded. One sets like a jelly. Perhaps not quite the right word? Cement? That sounds too heavy. Moulded, or fixed, must suffice.

I discovered light and scent, and, through Aunt Kitty, was made aware of colour and texture. Enduring sensations for me all these years later.

I have, it would seem, left out a fifth most important one. Music.

Music was a constant part of my life in those years: my father's passion was music. Not always the kind that I particularly cared for, it must be said. His studio at the top of the house was filled with what I grew to know, and detest, as chamber music. It was the music to which he painted. We called it, naturally enough, 'po music', and I always had a vague idea that it was played in lavatories – for where else on earth could anyone be forced to sit still long enough to hear those sombre cellos and skinny violins?

But there was opera too. Great ballooning sounds soared through the house, voices swept us from corner to corner, subliminally reached us in sleep; we were aware of music from our earliest moments, and in time, as is right and proper, the sounds which were incomprehensible between four and seven years, for example, began to take their own forms and one responded, or did not, as the case might be.

At the convent, of course, there were songs of praise and sonorous organs and those too became a part of the whole pattern of one's existence.

Music was everywhere; but I agreed with Lally, fervently, when she said that she 'did like a nice tune, something you can hum. And you can't hum much of your father's music I can tell you. No tunes there.'

But, anyway, music.

Light, scent, colour, texture, music. I entered the next phase of life with a rich haul.

But I was equally alert to grief and distress. My mother's face and the nailed-up cat; Mrs Rance with her blue glass bottle writhing about in the dirt of the street. There were distressing things in life which had little to do with colour or music and texture, or any of those things, and pain took its place in the pattern, inevitably, for I would always remember my near-blinding and the intense bewilderment of pain without sight.

A warning, an alerting to things. Childhood was not all halcyon days.

Nevertheless, it was a radiantly happy one for me. For one thing, we were very close, and we loved each other. We also touched each other, and were emotionally demonstrative in public, this at a time when such a thing was not encouraged generally.

Nudity was perfectly normal, and all the natural functions were discussed openly. There were no sniggers, blushes, nudges or, later on, dirty jokes in corners of school playgrounds.

We knew, at an early age, all the facts of birth, had watched countless kittens, guinea pigs and white mice being born, and, on one momentous occasion, had even seen a foal dropped. There were no secrets there for us, which is very possibly why poor Jessie was such a 'dud' that day in her tent. I suppose it might have been a different thing had she possessed two or three anatomical necessities – or even one made of Meccano; but poor Jessie's 'thingy' was just like any other old 'thingy' as far as I was concerned, and I was splendidly unimpressed. I was also, at the time, we must remember, about to throw up.

Another thing which was of vital importance to those early years was the fact that our parents, and Lally too, *talked* to us. Which is not the same thing as being spoken to. By 'talked to' I mean that things were discussed, analysed, argued about (within reason), and that all questions were answered. No one said 'I don't know, dear', or 'Do go away, I'm busy', or 'Go and play'. We were encouraged at all times to observe, and were questioned on the things which we had seen: a sunset, a tree root, a full moon, a half moon, dust motes in a beam of sunlight, the colour of an apple, anything. Everything.

I was fortunate in speaking coherently at a very early age. It must have been pretty excruciating for people most of the time, especially the 'uncles' in their studios who had other things on their minds, but I questioned and I was always given an answer which would satisfy me. For the time.

Lally had the patience of Job, my mother, an ex-actress, had most enviable sources of invention, my father had a calm, considering and very deliberate sense of reason: from the three of them one attained interest and satisfaction. So, naturally, I found life at home far more stimulating than life in Miss Harris's tin shed down among the laurels, where everyone seemed to me to be very young and deadly dull. If I decided to ignore, absolutely, the very basics which the poor woman, and her wretched assistants, tried, despairingly, to drum into my head, that was entirely my choice.

I have already said that I get bored easily. Well, Miss Harris and her 'CAT' and 'MAT' business, or making Christmas decorations with flour-paste and strips of coloured paper, or shoving round pieces of wood into round holes in other pieces of wood, seemed to me to be the ultimate in idiocy and tedium. I was bored witless. No one answered my questions; or else they looked anxious if they did because, as my mother was told, some of the questions were considered 'not quite suitable' for a child of such 'tender years'.

So I packed it in. It was all a waste of time. I was quite wrong of course. It took me a long time to latch on to that fact, and much longer to catch up, as indeed I had to eventually.

I imagined that family love and family life were sufficient, but you can't do without 'the basics', alas. A little bit of learning *can* be a dangerous thing, but it doesn't come amiss if it is used sensibly. I wish that I could say that all this bounty and love turned me into a child of an adorable disposition. By all the rules it should have done.

But it did not.

As you have discovered, I was an embryonic, if not an actual, thief. You could also say that I was a drunk: if you consider rose-water and glycerine or Owbridges Lung Tonic. It's a moot point.

But, naturally, I did not consider thieving in the toy-shop in Church Street as a crime. The shop-keeper had far more celluloid animals than I did; she very probably didn't care for them as much as I. So I took from the rich to assist the poor. The poor, in this instance, being myself. I reckoned that it made perfect sense.

After all, it is a widely held belief even to this day.

'A giraffe!' said Lally. 'Goodness me. I didn't know we had a giraffe in your zoo.'

'Ummmm.'

'Now, when did you get that? I don't remember it, do I?'

'No. I don't know . . .'

'With Mummy was it? Perhaps with her, eh?'

'Well . . . ummm, well, you know . . .'

'No I do *not* know! What I *do* know is that a giraffe costs much more than your Saturday penny, that's what I know.'

'They cost fourpence. Because they are bigger.'

'So?'

'I took it. When she wasn't looking.'

'You thieved it!'

Dry-mouthed, tear-flecked, I was dragged by my mother to Church Street and the toy-shop, where I was forced to return the giraffe and, what was even worse, made to apologize to the woman before two strangers who happened to be present at the time.

The woman folded her arms slowly. I can see her now. 'You want me to call a copper, then?'

My heart ceased to beat.

'It is entirely up to you, Miss Pratt,' I heard my mother say as if I was far below ground at the end of a drain somewhere. 'You do as you see fit: you are the one from whom he stole.'

I couldn't believe it! Such heartlessness! My own mother! Prison!

'By the looks of him, I'd say he'd had a good fright, so I'll let him off this once. But I don't never want to see you in this shop again, my boy.'

I emerged from my drain. Enraged at the humiliation. Furious that I had been caught.

I never stole again. Without being absolutely certain that I'd get away with it. I pinched the 'tips' from under the plates when I was, briefly, a waiter; took bottles of milk from doorsteps on many a grey winter morning when, foodless, I went off to start the little boiler at the 'Q' Theatre, and like everyone else scrounged, or 'swanned' as we called it, in the army during the war. Very modestly indeed.

However, the scar made in the toy-shop that day remained, and remains. Once in 1945, in Germany, we were in urgent need of a coffee-pot – our old one had been hit by shell splinters – so I broke into a cottage on the edge of a wood to see if I could find a replacement. Which I did. A fine grey enamel one with blue flowers and a hinged lid.

All the time I was aware that eyes were watching me.

Guilt flooded. Church Street came back in the shattered cottage kitchen with the clarity of immediacy. I set the pot back on the dead stove and left, just in time to see the vague shadow of a woman dragging two small, terrified boys to safety behind a row of blackcurrant bushes.

My shame was as acute as, under the circumstances of a war of Occupation, it was absurd.

But, once upon a time, I had been as small as they were.

CHAPTER

2

If Aunt Kitty was the first of my surrogate aunts, as she undoubtedly was, and the artists who crouched earnestly before their easels in the grey-yellow brick house in St Georges Road were my first surrogate uncles, they were not to be the last. I collected relations assiduously in much the same way that any other child collected birds' eggs, or coloured shells, cigarette cards and marbles.

However, I was extremely prudent: one has to be selective, and especially so with uncles and aunts. Children are instantly aware of, and alerted to, people who do not particularly like them, or who feel uneasy and discomforted by their presence. In much the same way that a dog senses this antipathy, so does a child, and he is careful to avoid them: they are not usually people one can trust. So I chose with caution. It was really not very difficult because I picked them only from the tight-knit group of my parents' friends, who were all considered to be 'rather good with children'.

Certainly they did not patronize, or dismiss, or talk down. They were often fun, and always patient with questions which I rattled at them with the speed of a sub-machine-gun, and on occasion they offered splendid gifts. That was a particularly important requirement. Rather like awarding stars to restaurants. Thus the aunts and uncles who were the most prodigal, or imaginative, were awarded the highest marks. But, generally, they were chosen to flesh out our exceptionally happy family life, and to rectify an apparently serious omission.

We had all the love that we could possibly require from our parents, and in the comforting presence of Lally. But what we seemed urgently to lack were kith and kin, as she called them. It worried me greatly even though, until it was mentioned one day in the ironing-room, it had not really occurred to me that kith and kin were necessary. We had moved away from the river-mud of beloved Twickenham, to the gravel hills of Hampstead, which I hated.

Twickenham, even though the trees and fields in which I had started to grow up were vanishing under bricks and pebbledash, still had a vague village charm about it, and the river provided constant magic. Just the muddy smell of it satisfied me, or the trailing lengths of willow on Eel Pie Island, the punts swinging idly about at their moorings in the boat-yards, the lush grasses across the river in Ham Fields. All these gave me the (inaccurate) illusion of the country. Hampstead was far less attractive, and the late Edwardian house into which we moved was not a patch on the shabby, but embracing, house we had left behind. The Hampstead one had a long garden at the back with apple and pear trees and a monstrous castor oil plant, or bush, plus an abandoned patch at the far end, overgrown with docks and nettles, which was allocated to Elizabeth and me as our 'place'.

The house was solid and ugly, and, apart from an immense stained-glass window, staccato with bulrushes, dragonflies and waterlilies which I liked above all else, it was gloomy and unloving. Even though I was, after a couple of years, removed from the pink and white-daisied nursery which I shared with my sister, and given the precious privacy of a room of my own, I was always ill at ease there. Except in my room. Very small, but overlooking the back garden and the branches of a tall pear. I was allowed to choose my own wallpaper (blue-tits in wistaria), and rebuild my altar to Jesus in a corner, and grieved privately when the splendid stained-glass window, which rose from the first floor to the second landing in shimmering glory, was covered by long net curtains and thus banished from sight.

The only place left which had any relics of Twickenham-remembered was Lally's area – the ironing-room and her

38

sewing-room – and we spent a good deal of time there with her. The rest of the house had taken on a strange formality, under my father's exuberant hand, which hindered our carefree existences.

We had a drawing-room now. Rose and black panels with gold Chinese dragons, and Aunt Kitty's black and gold striped divan. Immense cushions were strewn about the floor, and great bowls of philadelphus or peonies, according to the season, stood on low tables and blackamoor pedestals. It was out of bounds to us, except on Christmas Day. And as that only arrived once a year, we really hardly ever saw it.

So to Lally we gravitated willingly. To the room with the sheet-covered table, the comforting smell of warm linen and the curious damp scent of Robin starch. And while she cheerfully folded table napkins, pillowcases and our striped pyjamas we sang the songs which she had heard at the local cinema – still more or less forbidden to us, unless Charlie Chaplin or Jackie Coogan were in the film; but as I liked neither very much (Mr Chaplin never made me smile once, and often scared me out of my wits, and still, I regret to say, does; and Jackie Coogan I considered a bit soppy), I did not feel deprived in the least. Lally told us, in great detail, the story of every film she went to, and she went often, and sang us all the songs, la-la'ing when she couldn't remember the words.

My job in the ironing-room was to take the piles of warm ironing and stack them on the shelves in the linen cupboard, where Minnehaha spent a great deal of time when he was not lying stretched out under the castor oil bush like a Rousseau tiger. One day I had arranged the yellow damask table napkins tidily away when Lally set down her iron and sighed.

'Funerals,' she said. 'Sad business at the best of times, but yesterday's was sadder than many, I won't deny. I don't like them, not as a rule, not funerals. But I felt it was my duty so I just had to go. Poor Edna Stannard dead, with no kith and kin to see her off! All by herself.'

Unease pricked me.

'What's kith and kin?'

39

'Relations. Aunts and uncles, cousins. Family and all that, and so forth.'

'Well, we haven't many of those either. Do you *have* to have them?'

'It's usual,' said Lally, taking up her iron once more and spitting lightly on it to see if it fizzled. Which it did.

'What do you have to have them for?'

'Things like yesterday. Funerals . . . birthdays, holidays. All sorts of things. Nice to have your kith and kin about you. Your own flesh and blood.'

'Have you got them?'

''Course I have! There's brother Harold, and Ruby, and baby Dennis, and others – remember I told you? We had a lovely time together last Christmas with Mr and Mrs Jane [her parents], and a goose and a bottle of tonic wine, and brother Harold played "Come All Ye Faithful" on his clarinet. A *lovely* time we had.'

I was silent with mild dismay. I remembered our Christmas in the black and rose drawing-room. The tree in the corner, and all our 'uncles' and 'aunts' laughing and talking. Aunt Coggley, Uncle John, Aunt Celestia, Uncle Salmon, Uncle Bertie and Aunt Gladys . . . a host of kith and kin, but, I realized now, they were not *real*, they were just pretend ones. Ones whom Elizabeth and I had collected. They had nothing to do with our own flesh and blood. It was extremely disturbing.

'What's the matter now? Cat got your tongue, young man?'

'No. I was thinking, that's all.'

'Well I declare! We don't do very much of that; do we now?'

'We don't seem to have any kith and kin, do we? Not really. Only pretend ones, like Aunt Celestia, or Uncle Bertie . . .'

'What a lot of tommy-rot indeed! What about all your mother's family in Scotland then? They are your kith and kin and no arguing. Not to mention Granny Nutt.'

'But Granny Nutt isn't really our grandmother. She's our real grandmother's sister. Only she died, so Granny Nutt took her place, sort of.'

'Your English! I declare! Well, if you are a bit thin on your father's side, and no blame to him I hasten to add, you've got plenty on your mother's side, nine in family she was, so don't you start getting into one of your moods about no kith and kin, goodness-me-today! You've got more than I have, and hand over that bundle of handkerchiefs, if it won't break your arm.'

She was right, of course. But however much I considered the truth of what she said, I simply couldn't put it all together or reconcile myself to an enormous tribe of Scots relations glowering away in the gloomy north. I had only been there, to my knowledge, once in my life when my sister was born, and that was five or six years ago. Apart from a hazy memory of my straight-backed, black-garbed Granny Nelson, and a white-haired man who sat alone with a small dog by the big stove in the kitchen (who was, I was told, my grandfather: banished for some unspeakable misdemeanours), I remembered little else.

Apart from the fact that I had to put pepper and salt on my porridge. I remembered *that* with shock. But no face came back to me, no suggestion of 'nine in family'. I suppose that the sheer distance between us all, and the fact that none of them sallied forth, or ventured south, made them impossible to visualize. I had therefore dismissed them swiftly. In a few years' time they were to swamp me; but as yet, in the happy warmth of the ironing-room, I was blithely unaware of unhappiness ahead. However, I decided, there and then, that kith and kin must be collected diligently from now on. I had no intention of dying suddenly and finding no one loving and kind at my graveside. That was absolutely out of the question.

Granny Nutt (Nutt because she had married a jovial solicitor of that name) was of 'the blood'. That could not be denied because she was my father's aunt. She was also 'good with children' in a rather timid way; but she was all we had as 'family' so we made do with her, and managed very well. She was a small creature, with fine bones and brown eyes, her hair piled tidily on top, fixed by a tortoiseshell-pin through a neat bun, a black velvet ribbon round her throat, silver buckles on her shoes.

We often went to her pretty house by the river at Hampton, where her husband, the jovial solicitor, tended an immaculate garden. We had polite tea, with a good many different kinds of sandwiches and cakes, after which we were allowed to explore Uncle Arthur's domain. I remember that it was desperately ordered, trim and uninteresting, except for a stone bird-bath, a rustic summerhouse and the river Thames which formed the boundary at the far end. This always attracted me, and Uncle Arthur admitted that it was 'Extremely useful. All I have to do when I have finished weeding, or cutting the lawn, is to bung the whole lot over the hedge into the water. The tide bears it all away to the sea. Most useful.'

Apart from the teas and the Thames, which were pleasing, there arrived, every Christmas and on each of our birthdays, a very respectable postal order from our surrogate grandmother. I have an uncomfortable feeling today that Elizabeth and I accepted her for these yearly spasmodic bursts of generosity instead of any deep-felt love of 'family', or loyalty to blood. We really didn't know what those meant, anyway, but we did know what a postal order meant.

Granny Nutt was warm and gentle, and Uncle Arthur patient. He taught us to play croquet on his smooth lawns, which bored us witless, but seemed to amuse him. And I played attentively; pretending passion almost, because I felt certain that to do so could remind him, when the time was due, that our postal orders might be bumped up a bit. Surely he would say to his wife, at the end of our visit: 'Charming children! Most interested and enthusiastic about croquet. Perfect manners; they even allowed me to win a couple of games. I think that perhaps at Christmas we could increase the amount from seven and six-pence to, say *ten* shillings, don't you?'

Of course he never said anything of the sort. The postal orders stuck implacably at seven and sixpence for all time, and I can't even be certain that he wasn't as bored as we were with his wretched game, even though we did, on occasion, let him win deliberately. To no avail.

But Granny Nutt was our only tangible piece of kith and kin, of blood, I now realized. One moved with caution therefore.

I last saw her in the early fifties sitting on a metal chair in the front garden of a hideous hotel in Bournemouth to which she had retreated at the death of Uncle Arthur. Upright still, a furled umbrella tightly held in gloved hands, a toque with a stiff black feather, her skirts, even then, to the ground, the velvet ribbon round her throat, silver buckles – or were they steel? – on her shoes. I kissed her goodbye – I was off to London – and I can still recall the light scent of her cologne, the tickle of the spiky fur collar on her coat.

'It was so good of you to come and see me. So good . . .'

'I'll send you a postcard from Abbeville, when I get there next month.'

She barely smiled, nodded, clasped the umbrella to her knees.

'I would imagine that it would be difficult for you to send it *before* you got there, wouldn't it? But please do. I shall so look forward to it.'

'I will. I promise.'

'I can't think why you want to go to that sad, sad place in France.'

'To see the war graves and the old battlefields.'

'Your father had a most unpleasant time there, you know? And Grace, your grandmother, died while he was fighting there in 1916. He was left quite an orphan.'

'I know.'

'I'm getting old and repeating myself. A fault in solitary people. You'll place some flowers, won't you, on a grave?'

'A grave?'

'I shall set you an errand. Will you do it for me? Place them

43

on one of the Unknowns. There are very many. They are forgotten easily: known only to God. Put some flowers on one, will you? For me?'

I said that I would and drove away to London, leaving my kith and kin, the nearest and, finally, dearest, sitting on her tin chair in the thin spring Bournemouth light. She died before I remembered to send the card from Abbeville to tell her that I had indeed put some wild flowers on an unknown grave, and that I had kept my word.

So although I did have the Nutts for real kith and kin (Uncle Arthur just scraped in because, after all, he was not of the blood), the pretend uncles and aunts were always the more amusing and gave infinitely more pleasure. This was mainly so because they had been hand-picked, so to speak, and had had to undergo extremely stringent tests before they could be elevated to the august ranks of the chosen. Also, they were younger.

These tests were naturally changed conveniently from person to person, but in the main they were basic, and remained the same. First of all a prospective mourner had to like children. That was the essential, and main, requirement.

They must not patronize, ignore, or belittle. They had to have the vitally important qualities of humour and, above all, laughter. Without those they couldn't possibly be accepted. They must also like animals: if they couldn't quite *adore* them as I did, then they had to show, at least, a warm interest and not, as some, pale with terror at the sight of a harvest mouse, or cry out in horror at the presence of a cheerful old toad or even, silliest of all, a harmless bat.

People like that simply couldn't pass. It was not essential, but of course greatly to be desired, for them to come fishing for efts or sticklebacks, or even to assist at the delivery of a family of white rats or a litter of rabbits, but it was perfectly all right if they merely showed interest in the business, and more so if they offered (as many did rather than actually look at the messy business) a piece of silver money with which to defray the cost of feeding them, or for the purchase of a larger cage or a better aquarium in which to house them.

But it was not absolutely essential. Laughter and kindness was all that really mattered, for after all I was making sure that there would be a cheerful assortment of loving kith and kin at my graveside. I had no intention of being sent off quite alone like poor Edna Stannard. My parents and Lally, I was certain, would be *far* too distressed at my demise to do more than just stand sobbing. I wanted jollity and love at such a moment, and people to comfort the bereft members of my family.

I had it all arranged.

How easy it was in those distant days! How simple life, or even, on this occasion, death, appeared to be.

Now that I am well down my personal corridor, I have made firm rules that there will be absolutely no one to mourn my going: no flowers, no music, no loving pretend aunts and uncles – they've all gone already anyway. When I go, I go as I came in; if I'm lucky. Quietly, and alone, and absolutely without fuss. During the intervening years I have learned a great deal – but then, in the crystal-clear days of early childhood, nothing had as yet cast any ugly shadows across my path.

The shadows were to come of course; but fortunately one doesn't know that at eight or nine, and I, for one, lived in Cloud-cuckoo-land, unaware of mortality in its true sense. Except that it came to white mice or goldfish. And Edna Stannard.

I have said that we were seldom permitted to go into the rose and black panelled drawing-room, but that is not strictly true. Certainly Christmas Day was the time when we were given absolute freedom among the blackamoor pedestals and fat scattered cushions.

But there were evenings too, during the year, when, dressed in our best, we were allowed to come down to join our parents in welcoming their guests for half an hour. This happened really fairly often, because they entertained a good deal, and it was on these formal occasions that I would spy out a possible member for kith and kin. It was a useful pastime. While handing round olives, or little biscuits, and cheese straws, in my white silk shirt, grey flannel shorts and patent leather pumps with shiny buckles, I sized up likely mourners for the churchyard.

Aunt Coggley was the very first member of the chosen: Irish, with a long nose and beautiful hands clustered with rings, she laughed with a warm, private sound and did her very best to teach me the basics of spelling at which I was, and still am, appallingly bad.

'There is no "e" at the end of "potato", darling. You keep sticking in "e's" where there are none. Try again, and how many "s's" are there in "necessary"?'

I would struggle to please her, because she was so nice, but I still, to this day, shove in 'e's' with the abandon of a best man throwing rice at a wedding, and scatter 's's' about like salt. But I can still hear her patient voice in mild reprimand every time that I do so.

Uncle Bertie was jolly, fat and also Irish. He was a highly considered surgeon at the Ear, Nose and Throat Hospital, and so he had double uses. He was always full of cheer and delightedly dressed up as Father Christmas every year. He also removed my tonsils and adenoids perfectly, assuring me that it was most unlikely that I should die in the process. I did not. His stock was therefore gilt-edged.

Aunt Celestia I chose because she was extremely interesting and often went mad. From time to time she was sent away to a home where, she told me, they did quite terrible things to her with electric shocks. Celestia was short, with grey cropped hair and hands like a bricklayer's. She was a sculptor and potter of some renown, and smoked by holding the packet in one hand and lighting a new cigarette from the butt of the old one as soon as it had burnt her fingers. Which were amber-coloured, as was the long streak which ran through her boy's hair. She used to give me the dead butts, wet at the end, to put in the fire.

'Don't put them in ashtrays, boy,' she would say. 'They'll start counting them, and then they'll try to stop me. But I do need my nicotine, you see.'

I didn't, and burnt the stubs secretly, in the fire, once holding a hot, and smelly, handful for a long time while she told me, in a low, whispering voice, full of conspiratorial laughter, how she had unscrewed the keyhole cover from the door of her room at the home, and swallowed it.

'There!' she said triumphantly. 'Wasn't that a sensible thing to do?'

'Was it?'

'Of course it was, boy! Then, you see, they had to take me to a *real* hospital and I was able to prove that I wasn't mad at all!' Her voice was like gravel shaken in a box.

'How did you unscrew the keyhole thing?'

'A nail file. Had it in the lining of my handbag. You must always carry a nail file about with you; can't ever be sure when you'll need it. And of course,' she added, lighting a new cigarette from the wet, glowing butt, coughing a good deal, 'of course you can always stick it in their eyes, the nurses, when they get unpleasant. Here's another butt! Off to the fire, heigh ho! *What* a good fellow you are!'

No patronage from Aunt Celestia; she took one splendidly into her confidence and made one feel extremely important.

But it was, perhaps, Uncle Salmon who had almost the biggest effect on my life at that time. He was something very important at *The Times*. Foreign News Editor? I forget. A big, burly, tweedy man, who smoked a stubby pipe and enjoyed his claret. It was he who, one evening, suggested to my father that we should take over the lease which he held on a ramshackle cottage in the middle of the Sussex Downs. He had lived in it, at weekends, for some years, but the place was too isolated for him finally, and he was moving to another cottage near Hailsham. The rent was seven and six a week, there was a well, no electric light or telephone, an outside privy, and nothing but sheep and larks to disturb the peace.

'Excellent place for the children, they can go wild there. Most important to do that in your early years, Ulric. They shouldn't be cooped up in Town all day.'

We took the cottage, which altered all our lives in various ways.

47

'. . . a ramshackle cottage in the middle of the Sussex Downs . . .' Lullington, 1929

Uncle Salmon came down to stay during our first weeks there, bringing with him a case of excellent claret and a tortoise for Elizabeth and me. We called it George; after the donor, although his name was William.

However, Uncle Salmon was warmly accepted to see me off at the graveside: there would have been no better uncle for the job.

But of all the aunts and uncles, the one who had the profoundest effect on the whole of my life was Aunt Yvonne.

I chose her from the group of friends who were closest, and therefore more frequently met, to my parents. She was Belgian (but insisted on being French), and an actress of great renown. She had all the right qualifications for a mourner: she was exceedingly pretty in a plump, sparkling-eyed way, she laughed a great deal, she never condescended, she adored children, supplied extravagant and greatly imaginative presents regularly, was curious and interested in slow-worms, lizards and my jar of snails – which, she assured me, were delicious baked in garlic and butter – taught my mother how to cook, and, eventually, introduced me to the theatre one afternoon in Glasgow when I had gone to see her in a matinée of a play she was touring.

For thirty glorious minutes I was on a real stage in a real theatre, and almost from that moment I set aside the idea of graveyards and mourners, of kith and kin, of practically everything except a blinding determination to become an actor myself one day: in the then quite short corridor of my life, Yvonne Arnaud took me by an eager hand and pushed me, willingly, through the door which was to lead me towards the theatre and my future. I never looked back.

* * *

But I am looking back now, so many years later, with amused wryness. What nonsense it all was.

How seriously I searched for kith and kin to mourn my departure from a life which I had hardly begun! But how well I chose; for many of them added enormously to that life, not only to the pleasure of living it, but to my awareness of what it actually means to *be* alive.

In those smugly happy early years I thought, if I thought at all, that nothing would change. But of course it did, inevitably, and caught me on the hop. Idling my way through life with the complacency of a well-fed cat, avoiding any kind of responsibility to anyone but myself, wandering through my schooling with the uninterest of a sloth, I was disagreeably shocked when, at the age of thirteen, a completely unexpected brother was born, throwing me into a turmoil of appalled jealousy and almost speechless self-pity, and my sister and the rest of the family into twittering delight. I had not planned on this hideous arrival. It was unthinkable; and because of that I literally *hadn't* thought. Fatal error.

Suddenly I, and my self-centred little existence, were brutally set aside (as I saw it at that time). Within days a whole raft of carefully cherished aunts and uncles turned, as one, with happy cries of joy and welcome to the red, wrinkled creature howling up in the daisied nursery.

To my stricken dismay Aunt Celestia, my closest friend, the one for whom I had toiled so hard to hide the soggy evidence of her shameful vice, even went so far as to design, and make personally, a magnificent silver christening goblet for the intruder. I was horrified at the treachery.

In the rose-pink and black panelled drawing-room my brother, carried by an adoring Lally, was the centre of an admiring crowd (of the very people whom I had personally chosen for my *own*!) and, swathed in a billow of lace and fine wool, bubbled and smirked as they drank his health in champagne from a traitor's-cup, fashioned by the disloyal hands of my cherished, up until then, Aunt Celestia.

It was almost more than I could bear. My mourners had reneged on me! But worse was to follow.

My real kith and kin, my mother's 'family of nine', were still glowering away in the dark north: spectral figures of my future doom, unremembered, unloved, hovering in the gathering gloom of Scotland and my own suffocating misery.

Shortly I was thrust among them. Bewildered, astonished; an astounded stranger. The apparent object of this vile action, being sent far away to join exactly what I had always felt bereft of since Lally's conversation in the ironing-room, was school.

As I had long ago detested poor Miss Harris and her teachers in Twickenham, so I had idled or ignored the excellent facilities offered me in Hampstead to improve my mind. I had even drifted in a haze of happy, and determined, ignorance through the veined hands of a black-booted and wing-collared tutor. In a stifling room in a mouldering villa in Willow Road. To no avail.

So, a good Scots education was deemed essential. No slacking; nose to the grindstone; hard slog.

To soften the blow, for after all my parents were not monsters and I adored them even if they had deliberately upset my house of cards, and because I had already reached the advanced age of thirteen (too old it was felt to hurl me into boarding school), the evil deed was to be made more palatable, if that word can possibly be applied to such a measure, by sending me to my real kith and kin. Kith and kin who would cherish, console, counsel, feed, and water me while I worked away at logarithms, algebra and the Divine Right of Kings.

I found that real kith and kin were very different indeed to my carefully hand-picked assortment of happy, carefree aunts and uncles in the south who had no blood ties whatsoever. These were creatures of happiness and gaiety. Now I was surrounded by serious, flannelled, kind, restrained, unlaughing, colourless – to me at any rate – people who played bridge and tennis, went weekly to church (a long walk each Sunday), and visited the ageing members of the family on regular days each month.

There was never, at any time, music in the houses of my kith and kin. For that one was hauled, reverently, to a concert hall. And then very rarely: it was expensive.

Aunt Kitty's colours, scents, textures, simply did not exist in the porridge-and-beige 'living-rooms' (as they were called, as opposed to 'drawing-rooms'), and the nearest I ever got to 'flights of scarlet birds swooping across opal skies' were flocks of moulting pigeons feathering through the drizzling rain above the oily cobbles of Glasgow's streets. 'Imagination and breathless wonders' were occasionally suggested by dreary performances every year of the D'Oyly Carte Operatic Company. The tragedy was that, by the time they reached Glasgow, most of the lustre seemed to have faded, and there was precious little 'breathless wonder' to be seen.

My aunt and uncle, with whom at that time I lodged, had a deep affection for the Company. They knew every show and song by heart, and never missed a chance to see them *all* when they came to town. Seats were booked, for the entire season, months ahead. It was a deathly business, I thought.

Nightly I sat in sullen despair, unmoved, uncomprehending; hating the pouting, the winking, the gymnastic movement, the posturing and the words. Few of which I could understand, however loudly they were sung. 'Poor Wandering One' or 'The Lord High Executioner' were nothing in comparison to the songs to which my mother and Aunt Coggley danced the Charleston, with beads and skirts flying:

> 'Who's wonderful! Who's marvellous!
> Miss Annabel Lee!'

Of all the shows, I think that perhaps I disliked *The Mikado* most. I can't remember how many times I had to sit through it, numb with misery. I only know that today the merest echo of 'Titwillow' is enough to fill me with terror and a sense of dreadful claustrophobia. Everything comes instantly back: the Circle Stalls, the shabby red plush, the gradual, terrifying dimming of the great chandelier above me, and the image of Uncle Duff doubled up with gleeful laughter at those bloody three-little-girls-from-school, the tears coursing down his cheeks and the side of his nose, until he would reach for my aunt's handkerchief (never his own, I wonder why?) to dry them. Hiccuping with pleasure. 'Titwillow' had them both rocking with refined delight.

'Yon's a comical song!' Uncle Duff would say. 'A very comical song, I tell ye . . .'

I hated 'Titwillow'. I still do.

And then back on the tramcar to the shabby suburb where, owing to straitened circumstances caused by the Depression, we now lived in the porridge-beige house: antimacassars on each chair, framed covers of *Nash's Magazine* on the walls, and lazy-daisy-worked table-centres.

With cocoa and biscuits before bed.

It is strange, looking back from here, that these Special Treats, for that is what they were known as, never, for one moment, kindled the remotest desire within me for the theatre. I was unmoved. I, who had written my own plays from the age of five, who had dressed up as an actor at the drop of a hat, and recited pages of home-made poetry to silently suffering kith and kin in the south, was left absolutely cold by D'Oyly Carte and his Company.

If I seem to be ungenerous, and I do, then I can only say that I am. There was great kindness on offer from my real kith and kin on all sides; they did everything possible to make my life tolerable, amusing, instructive and pleasing. Within the strict limits, of course, of what was tolerable, amusing, instructive and pleasing to themselves. They couldn't move out of the restricting frame of their traditional behaviour, and the appalling regularity of their lives depressed me beyond bearing.

Of course it was understood that I was 'difficult' because I had come from a 'Bohemian background', as they called it. After all, my mother smoked, wore lipstick and nail-varnish ('It's *not* suitable,' my aunt would say distantly, but she wouldn't explain what *was* suitable), and went so far as to dance the Charleston. What, I wondered, was so awful about the Bohemians? In the dictionary I discovered that Bohemians came, reasonably enough, from somewhere called Bohemia. Which didn't seem to me half as bad as, for example, coming from Bishopbriggs. In any case I had not the remotest idea where Bohemia was, or what they did when they were there. I *had* noted an added line in the dictionary which said something

53

about 'unconventional behaviour', but 'unconventional' was too long a word to look up, and my interest, hard to hold at the best of times, had already flagged.

As far as I was concerned, if the life I had been living was Bohemian, then it was absolutely splendid. At least it was a life filled with pleasurable surprises, omitting of course the distressing, and unexpected, arrival of my unfortunate brother, but we didn't live a *single* day in which *every* moment was planned down to the last fragment; I never knew precisely what would happen on the third Sunday in the month, or the last day of the week, or four Tuesdays ahead. Anything could happen, and did. All was wondrously unplanned, and free.

Among my real kith and kin, every single hour, day, week, month had been fully organized in advance, and nothing ever changed anything. I knew exactly what I would eat for my lunch and supper days ahead – the menu would never alter. Mince and sprouts; cod and parsley sauce; finnan haddie and mashed potatoes; black pudding; and so on, all the way through until we got to mince and sprouts again. Usually on Wednesday.

I knew, weekly, to whom I would be taken to Sunday tea. Some aged friend, 'under the weather a wee bittie', or a crumbling member of the kith and kin, and I recall, with numbed awe, those crammed tables piled about with plates of oatcakes, potato pancakes, drop scones and God knows what else, at which they glutted, talking all the while about gallstones, gall-bladders or Aunt Teenie's enemas. I was forced to listen. One was not permitted to leave the feast.

Friday, without fail, was bridge night. The small green-baize table was set up (we ate early for this occasion), pencils were sharpened, score-cards put out, the cards reverently placed in the centre. My aunt wore her 'good blue'. It was during the very first session that I discovered exactly what a bridge roll was, because it was my job, at half-time, to serve them, along with paper napkins, while the tea was poured. Glossy, tasteless, doughy cigars stuffed with fish paste and cress. I found the discovery less than interesting. Merely curious.

On Sunday we walked to church. Two miles there, two miles back, before the terrible teas later.

In the beginning, when it had been explained to me that church parade was absolutely obligatory every Sunday, I felt exceptionally happy. Memories of Sister Veronica, of a smiling Christ, of the heady smell of incense and the mysterious ritual of the Holy Water, crowded back, and I was certain that I would feel less strange and lost among the familiar splendours of crimson and gold, and soaring organ music.

Ah, but no! No. This was not the Church to which I had turned with such joy and passion, and devotion. Here all was sombre and cold. Ash and charcoal. We apologized for our sins (I never knew what sins any of the congregation could have possibly committed, so dull a lot were they) and begged forgiveness repeatedly. It seemed to me that the Scots were very much aware of wickedness and redemption, but no one ever, as far as I could understand things, worshipped Jesus or God or the Holy Ghost or anyone else with whom I had been familiar.

What on earth, I wondered, was there to forgive them for in this sterile, spartan, ordered life? No one *did* anything! I was fully aware that I had, up until then, committed no sin: even masturbation had long since ceased. The effort of trying to conceal a twopenny tin of Vaseline had proved too difficult: I knew that all the drawers and cupboards in my room were 'tidied up' every single Saturday; so I took a vow of celibacy. The only sin to which I could possibly make a claim was that of peeing out of the carriage windows in Queen Street tunnel on the way back from school. But it hardly seemed worth mentioning in the harsh, whitewashed church, among the black overcoats and the tweed-and-fitch costumes of the congregation humped forward in repentance.

So I took no part in the proceedings except to kneel, stand, or sit. And when I did pray it was to a very different Jesus: whom once I had loved, and to whom I had built glittering, if modest, altars. If, for the time being, he had deserted me, I had absolutely no doubt that he'd come back

The Anthracite Years. Near Glasgow, 1934

and rescue me. I have always been optimistic. To the point of being unrealistic.

However, I had to wait a good time for rescue: I eventually returned to my Bohemian family, and my abandoned life among them, triumphantly untutored, but strong, when I was almost sixteen.

They were, I know, the three most important years of my life, the horseshoe-on-the-anvil ones. I could not have done without them. In that time I was forced to reconsider who and what I was. I had never, to be sure, given it much thought: only that I was a pleasant enough fellow, happy, obliging and fond of everyone, or nearly everyone, I met. Causing no trouble that I knew of, and wishing none. It was a simple pattern.

But in the bosom of my real kith and kin I began to realize that to survive I must alter the pattern of behaviour drastically. Being happy and obliging and fond of everyone was a sign of weakness. It was, in fact, considered 'cissie' to behave like that. A boy had to be strong, play games, speak when spoken to, and never idle around with poetry or books, keep frogs and tadpoles, or play the piano. Having a personal opinion was considered impolite, and to ask questions would only make one 'impertinent' or imply disrespect for one's elders.

So I began to construct a private world of my own.

I worked at creating this world of a 'loner' harder than I had ever worked at anything in my life before – which was, one must admit, about time.

I avoided my schoolmates, few of whom liked me because I was a Sassenach and spoke with a 'posh' accent. So I withdrew from their company as often as I could. In time I learned, in self-defence, to speak as they did, with the same ugly accent, so that when I *had* to be a part of their group my failure as a person was not quite so apparent, but this accent brought horrified criticism from my uncle, who said that it was 'vulgar' and was not to be used in his house. I thought that this was rather unfair as it was he who had recommended the school to which I was sent, and he ought, I thought, to have known that it was a fairly tough one. Rather than join my fellows, therefore, I spent most of my time alone, or else walking dogs for the neighbours. For which I often got a sixpence or a cupcake. Solitude became desirable in this world, and I sought it.

I started to isolate myself from people, and to build a strong protecting shell against loneliness and despair, both of which could have been my constant companions had I been weak enough to allow them to come too close. I sometimes felt, cheerfully, that I was rather like a hermit crab. Tight in his borrowed shell, like the ones I had scrabbled about for in rockpools at Cuckmere Haven in the happier days. I was safe from predators; and by predators I meant everyone I met.

There were, of course, times when I was able to leave, for a short time, my self-imposed shell protection, certainly at holiday times when, to my aching relief, I was allowed to return to the south and my family. But I went back into the shell the moment my train left Euston Station for Glasgow, and settled there until the next holiday.

There was, I have to admit, one aunt whom I loved very much. Tall, once pretty, now harassed and impoverished, living in a mean flat with two children and the remains of a 'disastrous marriage', who, it appeared, played whist all day. With her I felt quite secure. We talked about music and about books, she allowed me to play her piano, an out-of-tune upright, jammed into the too small sitting-room, and did not think it ridiculous when, one autumn, I found a red admiral butterfly which I kept in a jam jar in one of her cupboards and fed on jam spread on the tip of my finger. She was as delighted as I that we managed to rear it through a bitter winter and release it in the early sun of the following spring. A triumph indeed! We were both very proud. No need of a shell, therefore, with this splendid woman.

And then there was the time when Aunt Yvonne, my pretend member of kith and kin, arrived in the city with her play. I played truant and raced to the theatre as if she was a life-raft rather than a famous actress: it was at that time that I found my life *could* be altered, and that the theatre was to be my future.

So there were vital compensations, and I made do with the rest of my existence until the time came for it to end; at least, that episode of it. The years were really not harsh. It was simply that I was, as I have said before, an astounded stranger set among people with utterly different standards of behaviour and of living: we simply couldn't understand each other; that's all it truthfully was. We couldn't come to terms or make any compromises. I was the guest, it was up to me to conform to their ways, so I did. But I never compromised.

The hermit crab idea worked very well for us all. I was quiet, well-behaved, polite, and worked, as best I could, at my lessons: I caused no trouble, sat at the dreadful teas, handed round the bridge rolls, walked peacefully to church, helped with the washing-up, and did my best with D'Oyly Carte and Co. All the time I was watching, observing, noting down every little thing which I saw or heard in my more-or-less silent existence: for future use.

It was a vastly important change in my life: I, who had heeded little around me before, was now suddenly obsessed with storing up sights and sounds, and people too, for that matter. I had notebooks filled with coded scribbles (coded because of the Saturday 'tidying'). There was nothing about this new development in me that I was about to give away. I was determined to bring all my treasures with me when the time came, intact. It was impossible to write letters to my family, with any truth, for they were always vetted by my uncle, to ensure that they were correctly spelled . . . and punctuated. So.

But no one discovered the notebooks.

In two years I had discovered the intense joy of observing, recording, and writing. I had also discovered the theatre and planned my future. The third, and thankfully last, year was spent in polishing everything up so that I would be ready to amaze my Bohemian world when the time came for me to regain it.

★　　★　　★

This was much harder to do than I had expected. Three years of offering bridge rolls and paper napkins, of playing constant truant from the unloved school, peeing out of carriage windows, and playing endless games of solitaire in silent rooms while my elders and betters knitted or read the *Glasgow Herald*, hardly prepared me for the sophistication of the Chelsea Polytechnic, to which I was almost instantly despatched, in the Kings Road, Chelsea.

This was, I hasten to add, a very different street to the tacky, glittery place it is today, but even then it was pretty startling after the glumness of Renfrew Street or the dainty refinement of Kelvinside. I was woefully ignorant of everything that happened in the Kings Road, knew nothing of the speech patterns, nothing of the patterns of behaviour, and was overwhelmed by sudden independence.

There were no members of kith or kin here: either of the blood or merely pretend. They had long since vanished, with the last of my childhood. It was a question of starting off again and relearning. A new existence beckoned – and this was a way of life which I had deliberately sought; it was a road which I hoped (in secret for I did not speak of it aloud to my anxious, almost hopeless, parents) would lead me towards the theatre. Eventually.

I knew that I had years of lost time to make up, and set about doing exactly that.

The still-sharp memories of Aunt Kitty and her ground-floor-front room, sweet with the scent of incense, her bright silk kimonos, the spills of cushions, the thick fur of the polar bear rug, raced back and embraced me in many a peeling painted house in Worlds End where students lived in shabby rooms and gathered together (each of us bringing a quart bottle of beer, two if we could afford it) for parties on Saturday nights.

If Aunt Kitty's incense was overwhelmed by the greasy smells of fishy newspaper which had wrapped up twopence worth of fish and chips, or the sour smell of sweat, in these scrofulous habitations, then I hardly noticed. The essence was the same.

There was music, laughter, texture and colour. We lived our lives among these things, they were essentially a part of the work we were trying to accomplish. Or thought that we were trying to accomplish.

The Sunday mornings afterwards were, perhaps, a letdown.

Smelly, stale, snoring people lying in untidy heaps like discarded clothing from a charity sale, crumpled paper, stacked canvases, jars full of browning, cigarette butts (a shade here of wicked Aunt Celestia, but no fire in which to burn them) and empty bottles lying about like tumbled skittles.

But I was absolutely convinced that what I was seeing about me represented Life, with a capital 'L', and my heart beat like that of a soaring lark's.

This innocence could not, of course, last long. The vow of celibacy which I had taken in the yellow-oak bedroom of my uncle's house was, mentally, set aside. It was abruptly broken by an avid girl with earphones and breasts like filled hot-water bottles, who raped me expertly on the floor of her studio in front of the gas fire and sent me reeling on my way.

I'd arrived!

Although I was, privately, a little irritated that she, and not I, had made the majestic move (and *that* while I was afloat on light ale), it did not diminish the slight swagger which I attempted to use on my daily walk to catch the No. 11 bus to Victoria. But I don't think that anyone noticed this subtle demonstration of my manhood: certainly no one did at home.

From then on, as well as doing my best to design bookcovers, shade spheres and pottery jugs (for perspective), and come to terms with the exceptionally complicated human form in life class, I also determinedly set out to be a predator, eyeing every wretched girl with a slavering regard, which I earnestly hoped was suggestive. I didn't get far.

Young women were not as 'easy' then to snare, morals were still, even in the Kings Road, morals, and nothing much happened beyond a smeary kiss in the locker corridors, or a hasty, inept fumble and grope in the Classic cinema.

'Stop it! Oh *do* stop! I'm trying to see what's happening.'

'I love you.'

'Isn't she marvellous! So *svelte* . . .'

'I love you.'

We hissed at each other like adders in the back row of the half-empty afternoon performance. My yearning was desperate.

'What *are* you doing! Stop it! Stop fidgeting!'

'Please, Anthea, let me. Be a sport . . .'

'Stop it! Just stop. It's disgusting.'

'Anthea . . .'

'Ow! That hurt! You're pinching me. People will notice.'

'You are so marvellous, please let me, please . . .'

'Stop it! You're too rough and anyway I've got my knickers on.'

I sulked back to Victoria Station vanquished. Ruined, having spent the last of my weekly allowance on the back stalls. I was very worried. I seemed to be rebuffed by every girl I hauled off to the back stalls with a bar of Toblerone chocolate to watch Bette Davis or George Brent.

Could it be that I had bad breath? I cupped my hands about my mouth and huffed and puffed trying to trace any unpleasant odour. I scraped my teeth to points brushing them with the sharp-tasting Euthymol toothpaste, which almost took the roof off my mouth at the same time. I had no pimples; no dandruff; or acne. I was skinny, I had to admit that, but not all girls liked muscular men, and surely it was apparent that if anyone had kicked sand in my face I'd have fought back? Not *all* skinny men were weaklings. Perhaps I was unattractive? Too boyish? Not rich enough? Always a possibility: I had to manage on a pound a week which, even in those distant days, was pretty tight.

Perhaps they were frightened that I'd give them a baby? That must be the reason for such reluctance. My spirits rose: I was potent! They feared me! But there was something you could do *not* to have a baby, and yet still be allowed the delirium of the search, pursuit and capture. I was certain of it.

I couldn't quite remember what it was.

To my father then, one weekend. The Father and Son discussion which both he and I had always avoided from shyness. We were walking up through the orchard to an oak where the terrier, Rogan, had possibly found a badgers' sett. My father carried a pitchfork, for some reason.

'If you make a mistake, there is always the possibility that you could end up in serious trouble,' he said. 'What if the girl became pregnant?'

'Well, actually that's really why I wanted to talk to you.'

'It's a difficult subject. And today's Sunday.'

I was uncertain why Sunday had anything to do with it.

'Well, the thing is that, of course, I know all about babies. I've known about them all my life. Where they come from. How. So on.'

'Good,' said my father. 'I can't think why that dog keeps on yelping.'

'But what I want to know is what do you have to do so that you *don't* have them?'

'He's probably cornered some wretched cat.'

'Can you tell me? What not to do?'

'Well, it's obvious, isn't it? Don't go too far. You are sixteen and a half, you really ought to know by this time.'

'I didn't have much of a chance in Scotland. They're very funny up there.'

'Well, for heaven's sake, don't get some wretched girl into trouble.'

'I don't want to. That's the whole *point*. Why I'm asking you. I mean it's only fun.'

'Fun can be bloody expensive.'

'Pa, I know there is something one can do.'

'I don't suppose you bothered with that blue book I gave you last year? It's all in there. Simple. Diagrams, everything.'

'I couldn't understand it. And how do you not go "too far"?'

63

'He's still howling away, it can't be a badger . . . a cat up the tree. Have a word with Dr Lovell. He's a good chap, he'll put you right.'

'But I'm not ill!'

My father turned suddenly, the pitchfork over his shoulder.

'You haven't got clap, have you? Is that it?'

I was frozen with shock.

'What's clap?'

'I'll give Lovell a call, ask him to come down for a drink. You can explain it to him then. He's a good chap. Sensible. He'd better have a look at you.'

'But I'm not ill! I told you. I haven't got whatever it is . . . I only want to know how not to have babies, that's all, Pa!'

'Oh for God's sake! I thought your mother had explained all this, years ago. It's her job. I've got enough on my hands with *The Times*.'

I followed him on up the orchard to the oak in perplexed silence. At the tree, the terrier, shuddering and slavering, howling at something in the high branches.

'I knew it couldn't be the badgers. They cleared off ages ago. It's a damned cat.'

'When will you call Dr Lovell then?'

My father cleared his throat a couple of times. 'As soon as we go back to the house.'

We turned and started back down the path.

'Thank you. Could you tell him what it's about, I mean before he comes? It's a bit embarrassing.'

Perhaps I did have clap? What was it? Could you get clap from just kissing a girl or having a bit of a fumble? My mouth was dry.

'That's all it is, is it?'

'Yes. That's all.'

'I mean, be frank. You haven't got someone into trouble have you?'

'God! No!'

'It's rather a liability. Starting a family at sixteen and a half. I'd have said.'

'No. No . . . I haven't. Just . . . about how not to. That's all.'

'I'll ask him in for a drink. He's a good chap.'

We walked on in silence, the dog still yelping far away among the trees. The *last* thing I wanted to do was to start a family, I thought. Families are all very well but they mean kith and kin.

And I'd had quite enough of them to last me a lifetime.

CHAPTER

3

In the first sixteen years of my life I had, by my reckoning anyway, thirteen years of childhood. Which, when all is said and done, wasn't so bad really. From thirteen onwards, an early thirteen too, I was forced into adolescence.

In very much the same way that rhubarb is forced. A flowerpot is placed over the first tender shoots and the stems left to struggle, lightless, leaves uncurling like tight yellow fists, striking up wan, pink, unexposed to the elements.

By the time I had reached sixteen this is really what I felt like. Forced rhubarb. Pink, tender: suitable for tarts and puddings and not much cop in jam – in my opinion anyway. The sturdy, crunchy, healthy green plant has much more bite to it than the pallid forced stuff. Alas! I was the latter, not the former.

In my notebook, now rather torn and battered, for 1934, I see that I have headed the first page 'The Anthracite Years'. I can't, for the life of me at this moment, really think what I meant by this pretentious phrase. I imagine that it was written in hindsight, for precious little of it is in the code I had to use against prying eyes, but I know that it referred to the long, to me then, years I spent in the north. It was meant to imply, I would think, the drabness and blackness, or bleakness anyway, of my life there.

Rather inaccurate as it happens: anthracite is a sharp, glittering substance. Black indeed, but it looks rather like jet. Not dusty and drab like, for example, coke. But at thirteen, if I was thirteen, and I can't be certain because there is no written date beyond the year, and I am not absolutely certain that even *that* is quite accurate, life did seem to me to be grimly, unrelentingly grey.

Perhaps, on the other hand, I used the word 'anthracite' on account of the stove in the sitting-room, which was fed with the stuff from a hod which stood on a neat piece of folded newspaper at its side. (So that no 'mess' would be made.) Was I using the stove and the hod as a symbol for the years? Or was I referring to the 'tips', or 'bingies', as they were called then, which peaked across the ruined countryside surrounding our wretched suburb? I can't be at all sure.

What I am certain of is that those three years caused an extraordinary personality change in me. I was perfectly aware of it even at the time. Far from my 'Bohemian' life, isolated by speech, custom and behaviour, I was forced to assume immediate defence mechanisms: my solitary life (for in spite of being in the heart of my maternal family I never joined them) forced me to become my only friend and partner.

To be sure, I joined in with my cousins as often as I had to; I entered into the gloomy existence of my elders and, as they would have it, betters. But I was always a little way apart, looking at myself, aware of another person who politely and pleasantly went through the motions of meek acceptance.

However, in the heart of me I never accepted at all. I stayed separate. Watching and, as I have said, keeping notes on the, to me, curious behaviour of my relations.

In time I almost grew to enjoy this forced separation from self; I enjoyed being the 'loner', although as far as I was aware there was no such word for that in those days. But the happiest times I ever spent were by myself, or walking those damned dogs across the tussocky, grimy fields among the 'bingies', the detritus of some long worked-out pit.

Instead of sharing everything in an extrovert manner, as I had done before, with my sister, Lally and my parents, I burrowed deeply into a secret life, writing my notes, thinking my own thoughts, and paying far too much attention to myself. The perfect example of an introvert. This has remained with me all my life.

After those years of solitary existence in the midst of an alien community, I rebuffed any advances whatsoever towards the shell I had built around me. The hermit crab syndrome was firmly fixed, and I only quit that shell as I grew older, to find another, more suited to my size. But still a shell. I dreaded, and I still do, possession.

No one was allowed to come too close. I staved off all-comers with a quiet, determined strength. It puzzled a great many people then — it does to this day. I share — up to a point. Not beyond that point. And the limit is fixed by myself. So far and no further. I make the rules in this game of self-preservation. After all, it's my life.

Those first thirteen glorious years of childhood ended almost at the moment that I reached Queen Street Station, Glasgow, and, without my properly being aware of it, adolescence began. Or *had* to begin.

To be firmly crushed, a foot on a beetle, nearly six years later when my call-up papers arrived one morning; and with very little ceremony, in fact absolutely none at all, I bade it goodbye to commence manhood.

It is little wonder to me that I have made some peculiar errors throughout my life, for I have constantly tripped myself by falling into the holes which I have made in my snatched experience. I've always been as green as a frog: I have no one to blame for that except myself, and I do not. I am my 'onlie begetter'.

It is no wonder then that at sixteen, and in the Chelsea Polytechnic, I lost my head to some degree, but never absolutely my 'shell'. The temptations which were strewn across my path were extraordinary. Freedom itself was amazing! Even, at times, alarming.

I often wonder, today, watching a bus-load of Russian tourists plodding through the glittering streets of Cannes in their solid shoes, floral prints and thick suits, what they can possibly be thinking, deep down in their Slavic hearts, as they are confronted by so much bounty, beauty and luxury around them. Very much the same, I would say, as I felt when I got my release from Scotland, School, and Kith and Kin. An hysterical, numb bewilderment.

But perhaps they don't. Perhaps they see it all as vulgar decadence. Perhaps I am merely being romantic – a fault of 'the loner'.

However, I took off, in a cautious way, and even though the excellent Dr Lovell gave me, at my father's urgent request, the 'low-down' (as he had called it) on my sexual proclivity, he only succeeded in dousing desire, failing absolutely to extinguish lust. He was, I recall, distressed that I should spend my time with what he called 'those louche young women in Chelsea'. Although I wasn't absolutely sure what 'louche' meant, I got a pretty good idea. He suggested, in vain, poor man, that I should spend more of my time with 'clean, healthy girls' and actually named a mutual acquaintance in the area as an example. To my horror.

Pam Wimborne looked like a younger version of my Scottish aunts. Neat, scrubbed, tweed skirts, flat-heeled shoes, pursed lips, a kirby-grip in her hair. She played a daunting game of tennis, and used words like 'actually' or 'frightfully' all the time, and everything she encountered in life was either 'top hole' or 'too ghastly for words'. She had the sex appeal of a vegetable marrow and was destined, I knew instinctively, to grow to look like one in the years ahead. Quite apart from all these unhappy faults, she was what I privately called 'a broody'. That is to say she was ready to settle down, and lay. Possession!

So Pam Wimborne was out, and I returned to my louche ladies in Worlds End. They hadn't the least intention of settling and spawning. Sex, to most of them, was as casual and as intimate as a handshake in a crowded room. It suited me very well indeed.

But naturally the summer holidays from the Poly were rather long, and it was during this period of time that I was at my most vulnerable. There were any amount of 'broodies' in my part of the world; all cheerfully ready to own me. Or so I liked to think. I was always a little too certain of my irresistibility.

It seemed that one only had to go out with a girl for a few cycle rides in a week, to walk through Rotherfield Woods twice, or go to the cinema in Haywards Heath for their families to start to vibrate with interest about one's intentions. Mine were perfectly clear to me; theirs, the girls', were perfectly clear to them. But we were poles apart – as I was frequently to discover.

If one of them expressed mild interest in, say, nature generally, I would have ready, almost at hand, a fascinating colony of ants in Rotherfield Woods. In those woods I knew that the bracken was dense, shoulder high and secluded. One lady (by courtesy of the Gas Light and Coke Company, where she worked) so overwhelmed me with her physical splendours that I made desperate plans to go and see ants' nests daily. But she had little interest in ants or their habits. She also pointed out, on the only occasion that I managed actually to lure her in their direction, that she was wearing (as if I was not alert to the fact; slavering almost) a new white pleated skirt, that she wanted no sort of 'funny business', if that is what I had in mind, and that in any case bracken stained things green, and it would never come out. She added that she didn't give a fig for ants and *hated* nature.

So I gave up and returned to the difficult task of building a studio up in our orchard where I had a vivarium full of grass snakes and tree-frogs (which were devoured by the snakes with amazing speed), a marionette theatre, four bound volumes of *Theatre World*, a heap of windfall apples in a box and a number of *Health and Efficiency* magazines hidden beneath the floorboards.

Thwarted, I turned to Veronica. She was gentle, pink and white, with glasses and an obsession for nature. That is to say of *Field and Wood* variety. She was also enraptured by the idea of my poetry, and listened with the patience of a pyramid while I droned away at the plays which I wrote with effortless ease. She said that she felt she had a mission in life to encourage my mind towards 'more intellectual thinking'. (She could, she once said, feel 'the latent stirring'. Of what, I wondered.) Little did she realize that trying to do that was the equal of sweeping up fallen leaves in a gale. But she persisted, sweetly.

Her family, after a spell of this overt intimacy, grew restless. Knowing smiles and nods were the order of the day. I was pressed to stay for meals whenever I cared. A cottage on their estate was suddenly taken in hand, repaired, retiled, repointed, the modest garden tilled. A nest for another 'broody'!

The day that she arrived on her cycle, a thick wallpaper sample book strapped to her pillion, I knew that I would be lost if I so much as flipped open a single page. I could already see that some were slipped with 'markers', ready for my approbation. I dumped Veronica.

The Chelsea Poly opened up again, and I hurled myself into its custody and the arms of my louche ladies in Markham Street, Sydney Street and Jubilee Place. It was much easier, and armed with Dr Lovell's grudging recipe for 'prevention' I felt safe.

Thus, in 1937 and 1938 I drifted pleasantly enough through life on my own particular voyage of self-discovery, retaining at all times my shell, striving to keep intact the anonymity which I had found so useful in the Anthracite Years. It was an excellent shield against hurt or involvement. I let time trickle through my fingers like sand, scattering it recklessly about for my own pleasures. A reprehensible state of affairs.

Living in a cosmopolitan world, like the Chelsea Poly, did not of course mean that I could be totally unaware of the world around me. I knew, in a vague, shimmering way, that unpleasant events were taking place. They were difficult even for me to escape completely, but I don't think that I ever considered, for a single moment, that the dreams which I was so busy dreaming, and stringing around my head, would be scattered by these unpleasant things and left fluttering in the gutter like old bus-tickets in a matter of months.

I had always taken great comfort that there would never be another war. My father had said, over and over again, that his generation had fought so that our generation would be brought up in bucolic peace and serenity. Naturally, as I trusted the quiet wisdom of my father (even if I didn't go along with his ideas on my education), I believed him implicitly. It suited me very well to do so.

Until something went badly wrong in Spain. A civil war had started in the year before I left the gloomy school in the north. I was only aware of this, in truth, because a number of red flags and clenched fists became apparent among the Bunsen burners and retort stands in physics class. (Why are scientists, I wonder, so political?) Some people sang the Internationale in distant corners of the playground, and it was reliably rumoured that three of the masters had volunteered to go and fight.

But for whom, and exactly why, I had not the least idea. I went on contentedly throwing dreadful little bowls and jugs on my potter's wheel in art class. It was, as far as I was concerned, all a matter of alarums and excursions: very Shakespearian.

Of course, I had heard that there was a place called Italy and another called Abyssinia. But both were a long way from Glasgow, and even when Hitler marched into the Rhineland, which was closer, I was as unperturbed as the majority of my fellow citizens, only a few of whom shook their heads gravely and muttered worriedly. I was safely armed with the promise from my father that there would never be another war which could possibly affect me or any member of my beloved family. Foreigners could do as they pleased, but whatever they did couldn't possibly affect us. This brilliant reasoning, which I maintained determinedly until I reached sixteen, gave me tremendous comfort.

I had been more moved by the sight of some collected aunts and uncles sitting motionless round a bakelite wireless set while the King of England abdicated his duties in order to marry the woman he loved. I thought it both romantic and proper; if that's how he felt. I almost sympathized with my mournful aunts, now sitting twisting their handkerchiefs in sodden grief, but I was far more distressed, personally, at the destruction of the Crystal Palace by fire earlier in the year.

So, you see, I *was* aware. Here and there. The hermit crab did not just hide away in his shell and rock-pool; he ventured, occasionally, abroad. However, on my release from the fastness and dourness of the north, I spread my downy wings and flopped about; a fledgling sparrow rather than an eagle. I moved with caution. Which is sensible if you don't know what the hell the world into which you have fallen is all about.

Chelsea led, eventually, to the theatre in the three short years I had of glowing freedom, and there I grew my feathers. Slowly, to be sure, but feathers of a kind. They were hardly strong enough to keep me aloft, but did enable me to get from one lower branch to another without undue panic. I scrambled about avidly. A hermit crab and a fledgling was, is indeed, a strange mix.

But at all times I avoided any form of possession; I was as determined to keep my freedom as a nun her vows. I was equally not to *be* possessive either: an odd fact which has often surprised me when I have considered it. For I have, of course, a sense of *possession*, but *not* of possessiveness. I think that I have never really expected to have anything for long. The Anthracite Years led me to expect nothing to last. It has stood me in good stead all my life: I am romantic to a foolish degree as a man. I will blub easily at a perfect phrase in a letter, a passage which I consider beautiful in a book, an instrument brilliantly played, the sight of wind across a field of standing corn, or Kathleen Ferrier singing 'Blow the Wind Southerly'.

But that is where romanticism ends. With perfection.

There were, I have to confess, a couple of times when romance did blind me to all thoughts of sense and reason. I found myself engaged to my leading lady in a small local rep theatre where we worked. I was never absolutely certain how this happened. Where did my hermit crab shell go? How could I have been tempted from it for long enough to be, literally, caught? I have no idea.

At the time the Germans were overrunning Europe. The retreat from Dunkirk had just taken place. Bombs fell nightly on familiar places. Was it that? Did I lose my cool and control simply because of war hysteria? It is impossible, all these years later, to remember. Perhaps, and it is quite possible, I was

73

simply in love with her, and with the army looming at my side, so to speak, military service was beyond avoidance. (I had tried to be a conscientious objector, at her suggestion, but found that the questions which were asked at a tribunal at High Wycombe were so idiotic that I simply had to abandon her idea.) With the beckoning terror before me, I suppose that I decided, as so many did, to marry before I was thrust into oblivion. She found an engagement ring, and we called it all off after a couple of months when she discovered, to her consternation (and delight), an American pilot in the Eagle Squadron, who offered her the world. Instantly.

So that didn't last long; neither did my distress. I had become involved with another actress who danced better than she acted, and that's not saying much. But she had a splendid body, and did extraordinary things with a long cigarette holder in a skin-tight satin evening dress to Ravel's *Bolero* twice nightly.

One afternoon, ashen and almost plain, she arrived at my digs, in a prim house in Fellows Road, Swiss Cottage, to say that she was pregnant. My immediate reaction was one of gibbering terror.

We were sitting uncomfortably in the large dining-room of the house. Ladies were never admitted to the rooms; Miss Haley, the owner, saw to that. Any meetings were therefore permitted only in the long, drab room, smelling of stale food and sauce bottles, sitting in chairs around the vast table at which we, the lodgers, ate our meals. It was an all-male house-hold, apart, that is, from the owner, who served the food at the head of the table with the dedication and awe of a high priestess at an altar.

'Aren't you going to say something?' said Velma (not her name – she may well be a grandmother today).

'How do you know?'

'I'm late.'

'But it's not possible! I mean . . . well, how? We didn't DO anything.'

'I'm late; that's what I know. And there was that time in the Green Room . . .'

74

'It *can't* be my fault!'

'Then whose is it, I would like to know? All these insinuations . . .'

In a large, sunny room on the second floor at the back, William Wightman had his quarters. I had known him for some years. Older than myself by fourteen or so years, he had been my first counsellor when I made my entry into the theatre. A tall, calm gentleman, with a private income and an immaculate sense of good grooming, he was as unlike an actor (which he was) as anyone could be, and Miss Haley had taken him as a lodger because he, as she said, 'set a tone and has a beautiful speaking voice'. Also, with a private income, he was pretty safe: you couldn't count on bank clerks, or solicitors and school teachers (who made up her regular clientele), for their fortunes ebbed and flowed. She demanded security. William Wightman gave her that.

So pleased was she to have him in her Best-Second-Back that she permitted herself to be persuaded, by him, to take me as a lodger, in a small room at the top of the house, because, he assured her, I didn't behave like 'an actor', although I was gainfully employed at a nearby theatre. So I had a room in which, years before, some wretched kitchen maid must have existed, with a square sink at one end and a narrow window at the other. There was a bed, to be sure, and a midget dressing-table with three drawers. Nothing else. But I was grateful for its spartan comfort, even though I had to hang my best, and only, suit on a hanger from a hook behind the door, and keep my scripts and books in the sink.

Wightman was a wise man, calm, as I have said, unruffled, reasonable, who offered considered, logical advice when asked. He was exactly who I needed at this disastrous moment.

'Hello!' he said affably when he opened his door. 'How nice to see you. Have you come for a cup of tea, the kettle's just on the boil.'

'Something terrible has happened.'

'Oh dear. I *am* sorry. Just let me put off the gas-ring and then you can tell me with no fear of the kettle boiling dry.

75

Such a business.' He turned off the gas-ring and bade me sit down. 'Now. What is this all about?'

'Well, you remember Velma? In the Revue?'

He thought for a moment, fingertips pressed together beneath his chin. 'Ah yes! The girl who danced *Rhapsody in Blue*. Very striking.'

'She also dances the *Bolero*.'

'Most energetic,' said Wightman.

'And she's downstairs in the dining-room and says that she is pregnant.'

'In the dining-room here?'

'Yes. And she's going to have a baby.'

'Splendid! How nice for her. I do hope she's pleased, she was an arresting looking girl.'

'She's not pleased. She says it's my fault.'

There was a taut silence; Wightman removed his fingers from under his chin. 'Yours?'

'She says so.'

'Could it be?'

'I don't know . . .'

'But I mean, what I should say is, are you . . . were you . . . did you. Is it *true*?'

'No! I don't think so.'

'"Think" is perhaps not the word we want today. Do you KNOW?'

'No. I *don't* know. But I'm pretty sure. I mean . . . yes . . . I think so.'

Mr Wightman leant back in his easy chair. 'This is very grave.'

'I know! I know!'

'A serious matter; and you have come to ask my advice. Therefore I shall have to ask you serious questions. You don't seem to me to be at all certain.'

'But I am!'

He leant forward, his face lightly flushed with concern. 'Have you impregnated this luckless girl?' he said.

I stared at him. I'd frankly never heard the word before but understood, in a haze of fright, what he meant.

'No! Dr Lovell has told me exactly what . . .'

Mr Wightman waved an impatient hand crossly at my haggard face. 'Have you made "advances" to Velma?'

'Well, sort of.'

'Have you told her that you love her? That you wish to marry her?'

'No!' I cried in despair. *'Never.'*

He rose imposingly. (He was over six feet tall.) 'I shall go down and have a word with her now. You go up to your room and don't come down until I call you. We must get to the bottom of this business.' He carefully locked his door behind us and I went up the creaking stairs to my attic with its sink and single bed.

It seemed days before I heard his voice calling me to descend. The door of his room was open, he was bending down re-lighting the gas-ring under the kettle.

'Tea,' he said. 'Tea is essential. And I have some oatmeal biscuits here. Chocolate-covered. Sit down.'

I did as I was told, hands clutching my knees.

'Velma has left,' he said, taking his place in his chair. 'She was *very* distressed indeed and doesn't want to see you ever again.'

'What happened?' My voice sounded as shrill as a penny flute.

'She had made a slight mistake in, er, um . . . she has made an error in her dates. She is not actually due to have her, umm, well, it is not normally due until about the 28th. She got things a little muddled, it seems.'

'Thank God! I knew it couldn't be me . . . I knew it . . .'

'But I *do* feel that you have behaved in a most regrettable manner to the poor young woman.'

'How? What have I done?'

'You have, I understand, suggested that your family is very rich. Is that so?'

'Well . . . not really. I mean . . .'

'I rather think that you have.'

'Not *terribly* rich.'

77

'And did you, by chance, refer to the fact that you are in all truth a . . . a baron?'

'I might have done.'

'Neither thing was exactly true. Was it?'

'Well I *could* be a baron – my father told me. We have a splendid coat of arms and so on . . .'

'Which doesn't necessarily make you a noble.'

The kettle started to steam, and the lid wobbled about. Mr Wightman (I was too downcast even to think of him as plain William, or Bill, as he was always called) rose and made the tea with care and precision, found a tin box of biscuits, placed all, with two cups, on the table in the window, and sat down.

'I fear that you have led the unfortunate Velma on with a lot of fairy-tales. In a time like this, when everything is upside down, bombs are falling, and the future is most uncertain, young women, especially one on her own, look for security. I fear that you gave her a false impression of that. Here is your tea, milk it yourself, and there is a bowl of sugar on the top of the little cupboard there.'

'I'm very sorry.'

'So was Velma. And wretched.'

'I'm sure that you behaved very kindly; thank you.'

Mr Wightman stirred his tea steadily. 'I merely behaved in a gentlemanly manner. Which is more, I'm afraid, than you can claim. I think that it is time that you came to terms with life, and with yourself. You are no longer a callow youth – or should not be. Shortly you will be joining the services and going to battle with the Hun, and behaviour of this kind will not be tolerated. I don't think that you precisely *lied*, but you did exaggerate; and exaggeration will get you into serious trouble in life. Poor Velma! She was quite distressed.'

My hands, I discovered, were shaking so much that I slopped tea over the ugly table and had to wipe it up with the sleeve of my pullover.

'Mind you,' said Mr Wightman watching this clumsy operation calmly. 'Mind you, if anything should go, ummm, go

78

wrong, so to speak, in the region of the 28th, you could be in a fearful pickle.'

'Oh God!'

'Ah yes. Just so. Not out of the wood yet,' he said and reached for a biscuit.

The next weeks were hell. I spent them in a state of suspended terror and dread. My whole life, I realized nightly in my narrow bed with bombs hurling down outside, the sink rattling, and the ack-ack guns on Primrose Hill showering the slate roof, inches above my head, with chunks of red-hot steel, could be ruined. I would be a possessed man! With no freedom left, no chance of living my life according to my own pattern. I'd have to marry the girl, be a father, and go to work on the Underground to some hellish office. If anyone would take me.

I never heard from Velma again. And terror gave way to a lethargic relief. I went back to my shell for a time. But I had learned a lesson. I made a vow never to sail so close to the wind ever again. It is foolish, to say the very least, to strike out for the wilder shores of love unless you can swim. And I could not.

So I paddled about in the shallows, until the day came for me to be shunted off, like some stray goods-wagon, on to the main line to the war. Which took care of a great many problems.

It may seem, in this tightly condensed segment of my life, that I had behaved in a highly irresponsible manner. This you could think: and you could be right. But in fact all it was, I am certain, was a sudden, extraordinary liberation of suppressed emotion. After the damped-down existence of the Anthracite Years I let freedom of thought and action go to my head. In much the same way that a tightly corked bottle, when opened, explodes in a cascade of foam and bubbles. To be sure, I spilled a good deal more than I drank, if I may continue with the analogy, but it was harmless and, save for a near-disaster with Velma of the *Bolero*, caused no one any grief.

In the uneasy months before my call-up I kept myself occupied as hard as I possibly could to avoid any kind of involvement emotionally; I do not wish to give the impression that, added to all my earlier faults, I had now become an inchoate lecher, but my interest never waned and had to be controlled by sheer exhaustion.

To this end I worked myself to the bone, waiting at tables in a dingy restaurant in Bear Street near Leicester Square, washing shop windows, those which had not been blown out by blast, playing in the theatre at night and, after that, going on to a subterranean drinking-club to do a perfectly appalling 'act' (which I personally thought at the time was rather good, but was, I have been since told, extremely embarrassing). All this was good for me, in that I had not the least shred of energy, or interest finally, to do anything foolhardy.

It was desperate medicine, but it worked, and by the time I had reached my nineteenth birthday and was ordered to report immediately to Catterick Camp in Yorkshire to be trained as a signalman (God knows why), I arrived there sensibly unattached. A new, very different phase of life began. The callow youth, like so many other callow youths, was off to war, to 'do battle with the Hun'.

*　　*　　*

In the early stages, this consisted of having the Morse code forced into me like castor oil, shooting at tin targets (at which I seemed to be rather good), and chucking hand-grenades all over the Yorkshire Moors. It was not very strenuous or desperately serious, as far as I could see. Not a shadow of the Hun came near as we polished boots, whitewashed coal, cleaned our rifles, and generally found ourselves drifting into a controlled, boring existence. But this didn't last for very long. It was Initial Training. More was to follow.

I had not, to my infinite surprise, been in the least unhappy or surprised by this new, dreary existence. I enjoyed the route marches, the target practices, even the communal life. This might appear to be a strange admission for one who was determined to stay aloof and apart from the crowd. But a crowd is one of the perfect places in which to be alone. I quite enjoyed the warmth of the companionship around me, but went through those first weeks' training as if I had been lobotomized: all I had to do, I was certain, was the best that I could. No more could be expected of me; if I did my best, then life would just continue on its dull, but undemanding, way, and I'd be perfectly secure. Oh! How often I have been wrong in life!

The army, however, wanted me to do a great deal better, and give much more than I was presently offering, so to my dismay, for I had quite settled down into my own unexacting existence, I was hauled out of complacency and bundled off, without the least ceremony at all, to a mud-bog of a camp in Kent where killing the enemy was the main lesson taught – quite apart from killing off what were called 'the slackers'. It was tacitly understood that I was such.

This new existence had absolutely nothing whatsoever to do with life in the dullness, if comparative safety, of Catterick Camp with its greasy NAAFI. In Kent we were wet. And remained wet. The tin huts in which we lived ran with water and there were puddles on the concrete floor which were to remain a permanent hazard to anyone foolhardy enough to crawl out of his bunk in the dark. Which was at least every dawn, and often during the sodden nights to find the latrines. We were cold, muddy and frightened out of our wits. Now the shadow of the Hun was dark indeed.

Around this squalid clearing in a chestnut wood there were assault courses of such devilish invention that I never imagined, for one moment, that I would survive. Death faced me at every instant. Rivers had to be crossed on slippery ropes, sagging low into the racing water so that one got even wetter than ever. Quarries had to be scaled while live bullets whined about one's writhing body, particularly in the direction of one's nether quarters. (The sergeants took intense pleasure in firing rounds at one's backside, missing only by millimetres, to encourage one to climb higher and faster.) There were obstacle courses to follow these pleasantries: tunnels of rusty barbed wire; twelve-foot-high walls of mud-spattered tree trunks to scale; wide water-filled ditches to be jumped. (Should one miss the leap and fall into the muddy water, impalement on a thick wooden spike was probable, rather than possible.)

During this obscene – sweating, sobbing, staggering, gasping – canter, the staff threw fiendishly painful, if not quite lethal, explosives around like children on Guy Fawkes Night, and finally, when this was all over, for in time one reached the last of the obstacles and staggered wearily into what once had been a sweet Kentish meadow, there came the shrieked order to 'Fix bayonets!'

This final piece of gaiety brought the Hun extremely near. Huge, swollen, sagging sacks hanging on a gibbet-like construction of beams were attacked with fixed bayonets to shrill screams from the instructors to 'Thrust! In! TWIST! Withdraw! Get the next bastard!' The word 'Twist', roared at full pitch, was to remind one that one's blade must not get tangled up with a rib or stuck in a breast-bone. Should this unfortunate error take place, you'd be trapped, held fast, and unable to get on to 'kill the next bastard'. He'd very likely kill you; or his friends might. Even I could see the wisdom of that.

But my first attempt at the swollen sacks was rather a mess, which was perfectly reasonable, as each sack (to our slack-jawed amazement) was stuffed with the rotting entrails of cattle, sheep and pigs. The stench was remarkable, and the slithering mess of putrid muck which burst from every thrust one made induced retching and revulsion – the great gobs of jellied blood which spattered one's face weren't particularly pleasant either.

Valiant conscripts keeled over quietly before their swinging 'victims' in a dead faint and got booted hard in their backsides by the instructors. This had no effect on them whatsoever. The 'lily-livered half-wits', as the unfortunate men lying prone in the mud with ashen faces were screamed at, lay as for dead.

This rather barbaric practice of stuffing the sacks with entrails was, I think, eventually stopped. It caused far too many failures among the cadets, and the sacks were decorously filled with sawdust. Which wasn't nearly as much fun for the instructors.

I got through, to my utter amazement, simply because I was petrified that I might not; which would have meant that I would have been 'Returned to Unit', bundled into a draft, and sent to die in North Africa or anywhere else considered in need of replacements.

Another thing came to my rescue, apart from sheer terror, and that was that I had been brought up as a 'country boy'. Most of the others came from towns and cities and had never, as I had, skinned and gutted a rabbit, drawn a fowl, or cleaned a fish. Entrails to me were very ordinary things indeed; I'd first learned to gut a rabbit, for example, at the age of eight. It was a perfectly normal part of my life.

So indeed were mud and rain, swollen rivers and climbing trees. All country stuff. For city dwellers this was a much harder task. A bank clerk, the man in insurance, the shop assistant did not have the enormous advantages which I did.

So by a miracle of endeavour and terror combined, I got through the traps and snares set in the Kentish camp, even though I was unable to swim and suffered desperately, at times, from vertigo. It was suggested that it would 'make men of us' at the end, and that, of course, meant that we should be able to 'do battle with the Hun'.

I suppose that I must have cheated my way through to victory by giving a 'performance'. I screamed and yelled (as commanded) like a crazed Red Indian (this was supposed to instil the fear of God into the most stubborn Hun). I stabbed sack after sack with apparent relish (aware that this item was almost at the end of the course), worried my skinny frame through yards of barbed wire like a ferret, all with a stretched leer of blind panic on my face.

Which no one noticed because it was covered in mud and guts from the sacks. The fear of failure was far greater than the fear of the course. I survived.

There was no residue at all now of Aunt Kitty: of silks and scents and texture; there were no remembrances of Jessie Hammond and her sorry 'thingy', no recall of kith and kin, of Lally and my loving parents, not even a shadow of thought for

83

the Anthracite Years, although they had helped so much to give me the force and determination to survive; and the ambitious lecher had been calmed completely by sheer exhaustion, plus bromide in the breakfast tea-mugs.

At night, in the water-running hut, I would clean my rifle and myself, and when that was done crawl into my bunk with a copy of Surtees or Trollope, and read until lights out, oblivious to anything except the fact that I had managed to survive another day, and that a new one would break to tempt my cunning and resolve all over again.

But I was perfectly contented. I was on my own. And surprisingly fully in charge. The hermit crab had survived intact. There was nothing whatsoever to worry about – except myself.

That's how I liked it.

*   *   *

Not very long ago, a young journalist was interviewing me for a book I had written about a part of my war which took place in the East Indies (*A Gentle Occupation*). He was finding trouble, he said, because he could not 'identify' with the people in the book, the place or the situations. Perfectly reasonable. He was twenty-one; the war had been over for years, I was nearly three times his age. I tried to explain that the title was ironic. This had absolutely no effect on his pleasant, unfinished face at all. I went on, in some degree of desperation I admit, explaining to him that he had no conception of war and would, I sincerely hoped, never have to go through the experience. As if from a distant cloud I could hear my father's voice, many years before, saying the very same thing.

'I honestly don't think that you should worry about this book. It's not your scene, as you say, and it is impossible to explain. War *is*. It's as simple as that. So why don't we just leave it alone?'

'No . . . no I can't do that! I mean, I was fascinated by the book, but I just couldn't believe it. That things like that could have happened.'

I was tempted to suggest to him that there were a number of 'wars' raging about the world at that very minute, but it would have been unfair to have done so because he was a young journalist working for a glossy paper, not a war-correspondent.

'Well, these things do happen, the book is a work of fiction but only up to a point; I would be very distressed if you had to go through a war simply to "identify" with a novel.'

'But tell me,' he said suddenly and urgently, his fork pointing at my chest. 'Do you think that a man has to go through a war to . . . er . . . to crack his balls?'

The baldness of the question didn't trouble me. My reply to it did. What should I say? What, in truth, did I feel? Was it true or false? He settled my dilemma by prodding me earnestly in the chest with his fork and repeating the remark.

'Frankly, yes,' I said. 'Or at least, it was right for me.'

He looked around the restaurant. 'Oh Christ!' he said.

'A war finds one out, I'm afraid. The wheat from the chaff business. But I honestly don't think that it is *essential*; we haven't had a war in Europe, and I am not counting Ireland in this argument, for nearly forty years and it seems to me that your generation is doing perfectly well without one.'

'I am not so sure,' he said. 'Not sure at all. I begin to wonder if people of my age, or a bit older, would even go to fight in a war anyway.' (The Falklands war had not at this time taken place.)

I eased myself out of the conversation and managed to change the subject. But his question has remained in my mind ever since.

I went to Catterick Camp at nineteen; I came out of the war, almost physically unscathed, unlike a great many others, five months before my twenty-sixth birthday, and in those years I had, at last, come of age and grown up. Nothing in life could ever now be the same, and was not. I had managed to get through and I had even, I am ashamed to admit, enjoyed it.

But I was lucky. My war in Europe was not a particularly

comfortable one – I didn't sit about in an office – but I wasn't, on the other hand, maimed, and never personally had to kill a man. Although I know that by remote control, that is by selecting targets for bombing, I was responsible for a great deal of death and destruction. At twenty-three.

I felt no burden of guilt. We were at war and that excuse excused all else. Strangely, it wasn't always the tough-guys who made it; the skinny ones like me, who got sand kicked in their faces by the brawny brigade, often fared better. Perhaps because we were physically at such a disadvantage and *had* to struggle harder to survive?

Bingham-Summers was a case in point. A big, ruddy-faced bully, with a hearty moustache, whose greatest pleasure was to force those of us whom he considered 'drips and Nancy Boys' to play an obscenely stupid drinking game called Cardinal Huff, or Puff, I forget which, determined that he would drink us under the table while he maintained his sobriety and, therefore, his manhood. He landed on the beach on D-Day, dragged himself ashore with a green face (everyone was seasick anyway that morning), dug himself a deep slit-trench, and stayed in it for some days, refusing to come out for any reason whatever. Food was, reluctantly, lowered down to him on a rope, and eventually he was removed by force, screaming and fighting, strapped to a stretcher, and flown back to England. You couldn't, as Lally had so often said, 'tell from the outside'.

The Prawn, as we called him, was on the other hand as wispy a fellow as you could meet. Elegant, fragile apparently, he always changed into his pyjamas (even though at that time we slept in slit-trenches), and wandered about during some fierce night strafing in a Liberty silk dressing-gown crying wearily above the din: 'Oh! darlings! Do stop being so *boring*! You can't see a thing, and it's frightfully late. Pack it in, for God's sake!' Our morale soared at his ridiculous performance. However absurd he may have sounded, he was as strong as an oak and as unyielding. Later we heard that he had got the MC for destroying, single-handed, a persistent machine-gun post which had caused considerable casualties, by lobbing a grenade into the position from a distance of three yards. He lost his arm. But his only comment was that the Germans were so damned pig-headed that he had been forced to take some action. 'They killed a lot of my friends, you know. It simply wouldn't do.'

The strangest people survived, while others went to the wall. There was no knowing who was who until the guns went off for real.

On 15 July 1944 I wrote my first long letter to my father:

... We are in an apple orchard (cider apples, I suppose?) and the farmer is pissed off with us because we have flattened his corn-field for the airstrip and dug slit-trenches all among his ruddy trees.

We are supposed to be the brave Liberating Allies but you'd hardly know that from his sullen face and angry shouts. No one takes any notice of him, of course, we just shrug and wave him away, his wife, an old crone in black, shakes her fist.

You learn something different every day! Life is very interesting indeed. I now discover that tin-hats are not for wearing on your head, they are too heavy and fall off when you run fast, but they are used to protect your private parts when lying on your truckle bed (if lucky!) or over your bum should you make a turn face-down. Very useful idea. Why didn't I think of that before? If you cop one in the head you're a goner anyway, but you wouldn't have much of a life without your privvies!

I feel, at last, pretty well grown up. About time, you'll say. I can hear you! I used to think that being grown up was tearing about Sussex in Buster's red MG with Cissie Waghorn and being terribly sophisticated drinking lagers in Road-Houses whipping down to Brighton. But it isn't that at all, is it? I'm terribly glad that at last I am coming to terms with it all now: a great relief after all the years I have spent TRYING TO.

I never asked for the life which you and Ma gave me. That was your own decision after all, wasn't it? We none of us actually ASK for our lives, but once we are given it, golly! we hang on to it like grim death and take all kinds of precautions, fair and foul, to preserve it, and it takes a bit of a blow-up like this to show just how much it all means to one. Life is pretty cheap here. I mean to keep mine for as long as I possibly can: I'm enjoying it, thanks!

'Coming to terms with it all now,' I wrote!
There was still a long way to go.

PART TWO

CHAPTER

4

I am almost twenty-six.

I'm standing on a platform at Guildford station in a thick fog.

I have just been demobilized.

I have a railway warrant, my ID card, a pocket of small change, fifty Singapore dollars, a 1,000 yen note taken from a dead Japanese, six campaign medals, a cardboard box with my cardboard demob suit and, somewhere on the platform, upended like a bit of Stonehenge, the tin uniform trunk I bought in Calcutta.

All my worldly goods.

Nothing else.

The army has just informed me that I owe them eight hundred pounds because they have been overpaying me for the last two years.

As if that was my fault. As if I had been keeping accounts in the Far East.

I don't know quite how I will be able to pay this back; or when.

They sounded irritated; I suppose that I flustered about.

I have not been back in England since I left for France in 1944.

It is now the fag-end of 1946, and Guildford station offers me not the slightest cheer, or hope.

Delight, which I am supposed to be feeling on demobilization, is drowned in the gloom, and all that I feel is a sense of enormous loss. An incredible unhappiness. All the more incredible because I am on my way home.

The war is finally over.

It's been over for these people on the platform for quite a time: we are rediscovering peace again and I am finding the sensation disturbing.

The mist drifts, veers, wavers. Up the line a blurred pink light changes suddenly to wan green.

A splot of pale colour on grey, damp paper.

The London train is due.

Somewhere a trolley trundles about among the shapeless figures hunched in the pewter light.

A porter is singing. It's an old song; probably an old habit. It isn't funny:

'Pardon me, boy, is that the Chattanooga choo-choo . . .'

I wanted to stay in the army.

I tried to for a time. But an army without a war is as pointless as a car without gas, a party without guests, a bomb without explosives.

And when the war finished, with the great white light over Nagasaki, younger men than I had arrived in bragging good health, with a faint air of superiority, to patronize those of us who had worked to earn the ribbons on our chests.

Which didn't amount to much, really. Endeavour, experience. We were none the less proud of them.

We were called the veterans. With a thin vein of sarcasm in the voices. We called them the newcomers, white-knees, because under the flapping, brand-new, starched shorts, their knees, untouched by any tropical sun, looked like dimpled dough.

I think that we resented their freshness, their superiority as 'new' over 'used'. Foolish no doubt; it was hardly their fault that they had not been old enough to come out earlier. But we resented them all the same, so I packed it in, and came back.

They would always remain 'young'. We *knew*. They did not – and never would, even though there were still a few scraps and scrapings of war left to tidy away.

And we who had known could never be quite the same again.

On D-Day plus four, on the beach at Arromanches, there was a single left leg in an elegant boot, laced above the ankle, drifting around lazily among clumps of weed, a tangle of webbing belts and half a *Reader's Digest*.

Not really a leg. A foot and a shin. No knee cap. No thigh.

The flesh which protruded from the ripped uniform trouser was bleached white by sea-water, trailing little frills of shredded muscle like tiny tentacles.

'The tide brings them around, all these bits and pieces. Funny thing. Yankees. From up the coast at "Omaha". Strong currents about, you don't want to go in for a dip here.'

I didn't.

As I clambered back up the beach through tangles of wire and broken ammunition boxes, gulls wheeled out of the sun like Stukas, feathered on to the rippled sand, stalked towards the bobbing leg with arrogant, watchful eyes, prodded at the elegant boot.

A bell starts clanging, and through the grey the London train surges slowly towards us. The porter is still singing:

'So, Chattanooga choo-choo, won't you choo-choo me home?'

*　　*　　*

'You had a varied war, really,' my father said. 'In our war we just sat in one bloody place for months, in the mud, moving forward or backward now and again.'

Mine was varied all right. I had no complaints on that score. I got about.

'I expect you were pretty scared sometimes, weren't you?' said Elizabeth.

'Some of the time. We all were, we expected that.'

What I had not expected was that almost the first thing I would have to do in action was assist in the delivery of a child.

That's the odd thing about wars. Everything gets so mixed up.

There was quite a lot of stuff flying about, the road was chalk-white in the sun, barred by the shadows of pollarded

The farm. Near Juvisey. Normandy, 1944

elms; my driver muttered: 'Screw this for a lark!' and pulled the jeep into the shelter of a barn wall.

We clambered out and sat in a clump of nettles. It is always wiser to move away from a vehicle, if you can, on account of the petrol tank exploding if the thing gets hit.

A mortar landed in the middle of the road some distance away, sending up a shower of metal, stones and smoke; we crouched low, our faces in the nettles.

'They don't sting if you really grab them,' I said.

'You're kidding.'

Another mortar crumped somewhere behind us; a slithering of tiles from the barn roof, a stink of cordite on the still morning air, and a woman's voice calling.

We looked up in surprise. I had thought that all the civilians had cleared from the area; but obviously not.

She was old, that is to say she was at least forty, in black, with a white and red floral apron, and a man's hat on her head.

Another mortar went over us.

The woman came towards us in a half crouch, running along the side of the barn, her hands open, fingers wide, arms outstretched.

It is impossible to recall at this moment exactly what she said as she reached us; it was in French, naturally, and Norman French at that, and my French was almost limited anyway to 'Oui' and 'Non' and, sometimes, 'Merci beaucoup'. But by signs, and her pulling at my arm, I understood that she wanted me to follow her, so I did.

The barn was part of a farm complex, built round a courtyard. The house was a ruin, tiles, bricks and three dead goats with their legs in the air were scattered about.

Still talking – she hadn't drawn breath since she had grabbed me – the woman pulled me into the barn, where, in the light filtering through the smashed roof, I saw a perfect nativity scene.

A pregnant woman on a pile of hay, another woman kneeling at her side, two dogs cowering. The elder woman spoke rapidly: I understood the word 'anglais' and felt her finger jabbing at my shoulder, to indicate my rank apparently. Then she pulled me towards the two others and got me to kneel at the head of the younger woman lying on the hay who was in labour, and forced my hands on to her shoulders.

I understood what I had to do: hold the writhing, moaning woman down while the two elder ones got on with the job.

I didn't watch much.

The girl screamed and shouted so loudly that I didn't even hear if any more mortars were flying around, and in any case, at that particular moment, I didn't very much care if they were. My cap had fallen off, and the girl under my hands was strong and difficult to hold.

The baby was born amidst screams and sobs, grunts and cries, shouted words of constant encouragement (I imagine) from the two midwives, and an appalling stench of warm excreta. I held my breath for as long, and as often, as I could, and stared into the trampled hay at my knees.

In her struggles the girl's dress, or blouse, or whatever it was, had ripped away and one heavy, milky breast swung loose; her right hand clenched and unclenched; a glint of a wedding ring in the thin sunlight.

It's as difficult and painful to arrive in, I remember thinking, as it is to leave this world.

The midwives grabbed and pulled things about, the girl began moaning, and then was still, all except her head which rolled from side to side, eyes wide like a frightened cow; then she yelled: 'Yeeee! Yeeee!', and one of the women slumped the pulpy scarlet head of a new-born child on to the sweaty white breast of its mother, the umbilical cord wriggling down her body like a length of spent elastic.

I found my cap and went to the door for a breath of clean air.

The mortars had stopped; on the other hand the child had started to cry.

It never occurred to me to wonder about its kith and kin: I didn't think about my own then either.

Everything in my past had been erased from the blackboard of my mind. I thought only of the present moment, and the present moment was all that we really had in Normandy that summer.

All the things which had once seemed to be so important to me, and to my existence, had been ploughed like stubble into the square, hedge-framed fields which were now my life: I walked over memory with heavy boots.

The woman in the man's hat joined me. We looked up at the sky.

There was no sound except for the rattle and clatter of tank-tracks some distance away.

She crouched, pulling me with her, and we scuttled across the cluttered courtyard to the ruined house. There was a vermilion geranium in a pot on a windowsill tangled in a torn lace curtain: gaudy as a whore at a wedding.

Inside an overwhelming smell of dust and soot. Half the room above had crashed down into the kitchen, spilling bricks and lengths of timber across the long wooden table, scattering the chairs like startled witnesses to an accident. At the far end of the room there was a wide fireplace, a tall iron stove with a tin chimney, a long shelf above it on which an avalanche of rubble and dust had fallen among some candlesticks and a plaster figure of the Madonna.

The woman scrabbled about, dislodging pieces of mortar and stone, and finding what she wanted she came across to me, wiping the object carefully on her red and white overall.

She held it out to me in work-cracked hands, blood still packed round her broken fingernails.

A shaft of sunlight which probed through the hole above us glinted on a small glass sphere set on a white china base.

She offered it to me again with impatient upward little jerks.

In the globe a swirl of glass strands. Red, orange, blue.

Like the marbles with which I had once played long, long ago, before the Anthracite Years, at school in Hampstead.

Moving in her agitated hands, winking in the sunlight, they

sparked a lost memory. I understood that this was a gift, for she thrust it into my hands impatiently, nodding with some kind of smile: half frightened, half tender. Then she turned and hurried from the house.

I've still got the globe. It's a cheap thing, the sort of prize you win at a country fair.

It is on my dressing chest. I suppose the baby, if it still lives, is forty years old.

'What was that all about, then? Yells and screams.'

I swung into the jeep beside him, the globe in my hand.

'I've just had a baby,' I said.

'You never!'

We pulled away from the barn wall and drove back to Saint-Sulpice and the airstrip.

'My face is still bloody itchy,' he said.

'It's the nettles; so is mine.'

'It's a funny old war, this,' said my driver.

He was driving slowly so as not to raise dust from the white road.

'The mortars have stopped,' I said.

'We wouldn't be on this road if they hadn't, bet your bloody life. They're just over the ridge up there, in the wood.'

I looked at the glass globe lying in my lap. In the long grasses at the verge of the road lay two bodies in British uniform. On their backs, helmets on their chests, a gag of flies across their mouths, two rough crosses made from twigs at their heads.

'You deliver it, then? The baby?'

'Helped. There were two women there.'

'That sort of thing', said my driver turning left at a narrow crossroads, 'just makes me puke. I don't know how you could do it.' He cleared his throat noisily. 'Sir,' he added as an afterthought.

*　　*　　*

From the early spring of 1944 until the end of the war in Europe in May 1945, Flt/Lt Christopher Greaves and I were joined at the hip as air photographic interpreters attached to 39 Wing of the Canadian Royal Air Force. I really don't remember where we were 'paired off', probably at Odiham airfield, but there we were, an unlikely couple in many ways, but as immutable as Laurel and Hardy, Huntley and Palmer, or Rolls and Royce.

Chris was senior to me by some years, had already had distinguished service in the RAF in Malta, survived the siege, contracted polio, and constantly fell in love with his nurses: he was, later, to marry one and raise a large family. But after Malta, and convalescence, he was stuck with me.

We had a truck which served as our 'office', with a couple of desks and lamps and not much else. In this, plus a jeep, we drove across Europe in the wake of our Forward Recce Squadron who took the photographs.

Being determined young men with great ambitions the pilots had their airstrip as near the front as they possibly could be, dragging us, in consequence, along with them; for we had to be on hand for every sortie flown, ready to interpret.

I have often wondered, and did at the time, how Chris put up with me for so long. We were stuck together in that truck for hours and hours on end, and even when we did manage to get a break, usually when the weather was too bad for flying, we went off into the shattered countryside contentedly and painted. We never had a dispute or row, and remained together in work and in the snatched moments of leisure. We were a good team.

As I have said, the leisure was pretty nearly always in bad weather, which is why the great majority of my paintings had lowering skies, pouring rain and acres of mud and puddles. I never got to paint a sunny day – I rather doubt if I could have done so even if such a day had presented itself. I preferred 'mournful' light.

Chris was a professional artist; I only had the sparse training which I had gleaned at Chelsea Poly in between bouts of fumbling passion at the Classic cinema. But together we painted almost the entire campaign in Normandy, and were made Unofficial War Artists: our work belonged to the Air Ministry and was only returned to us after the German surrender.

At first, after the landings, there wasn't much time for painting anything. The early weeks were, to say the least of it, bewildering, on occasions unnerving. But as the Allied thrust got under way we started to settle in, knowing that we were there to stay until the end which, I was convinced, had to be in Berlin.

On the fortieth anniversary of D-Day, Chris telephoned from his home in the West Country.

'I don't know if you've been looking at telly today?' he said. 'Have you? Do you get that kind of thing in France?'

'All of it. I tuned in for ten minutes and stayed right through until the end.'

'Amazing, wasn't it? What about Mrs Reagan in that awful coat and NO hat! I mean, can you imagine a woman going to a memorial service without a HAT? Damned discourteous, I thought.'

'Oh well . . . it was all a long time ago, Chris.'

'Seemed just like last week to me, but then I'm getting ancient, I suppose. But you know, Pip, it was damned dangerous, wasn't it? If I'd have known how bloody awful it was going to be I'd never have gone!'

Fortunately for us both we neither of us thought much of the danger at the time. Perhaps sheer youth takes care of that emotion, I don't know.

And Chris, who did most of the driving while I navigated, did some extremely dangerous things on our 'off days'. Driving along a wide stretch of open road along a ridge above the still-occupied town of Caen, shells fell behind and ahead of us, sending up ugly bursts of smoke and shrapnel.

'They're getting closer each time,' I said.

Chris was bent over the wheel of the jeep like a crouching charioteer, his cap had fallen off, his glasses glittered in the wet light.

'Bracketing us,' he said through clenched teeth.

Missey, Normandy, 1944

One shell to the back, another to the front, each time the range was slightly altered. And they came nearer and nearer. It was extremely uncomfortable.

'Playing silly buggers.'

'So are we. Can't we get off this road?'

'You should know, you've got the map. I've got enough to d6.'

There was no turn-off; the map shook and flapped, and was impossible to read. I only knew that when the shell behind us and the shell ahead of us landed simultaneously in the one place, we'd be dead centre.

The spectacle, to the Germans below the ridge, must have been amusing – although they are not a race noted for their humour.

But a single jeep belting along a dead straight road, silhouetted against the sky, as if the hounds of hell were after it, obviously proved an irresistible target for 'bracketing'.

A hawthorn hedge on the right of the road suddenly, providentially, was there and Chris swung into a field behind its sparse shelter of thorn and torn leaves.

We crawled out; lay flat in the crushed corn.

The Germans went on 'playing silly buggers' for about twenty minutes and then, mercifully, decided to give up. I couldn't help wondering, with each splintering crash, why they bothered to waste so much ammunition on so meagre and unimportant a target. Perhaps they thought we were Churchill? But in any case the German is always a very thorough creature.

Anyway, they stopped.

In the silence which followed the cease-fire, we crouched our way back to the jeep, inching across the trampled corn.

A group of Canadian soldiers suddenly rose as one man from a high-hedged bank, rifles cocked, mouths open in surprise.

'Where did you come from? For Chrissakes that's Jerry territory!'

'An error in map reading,' said Chris.

'I couldn't read the blasted map bucketing along like that with God knows what flying about. I honestly don't see the point in taking unnecessary risks, Chris, we've got quite enough to take without inventing more.'

'Rubbish.' Chris crammed on his cap and restarted the engine. 'A nice little country run. No need to get fidgety, old boy.'

So I shut up. It was all kids' stuff anyway. *Boys' Own Paper* nonsense.

Nothing to it. And we were still all in one piece.

Bigger and better things were ahead.

Two nights later we all stood in the shelter of the trees in the orchard, rocking and stumbling into each other, as wave after wave of giant bombers roared low over our heads and ripped the heart out of Caen.

We held on to each other, or the scaly trunks of trees. Showers of leaves and tiny apples shook around us as the earth rippled beneath our feet with the shock of the bombs which thundered down three kilometres away. The air trembled and rolled with the sound as if a thousand drums were beating a gigantic tattoo, and the night was drenched in noise, drowning speech or even coherent thought.

We stood, heads bowed, eyes screwed up against the on-slaught, grabbing about for support, like men drowning.

Ahead, through the trees, the whole skyline north of Caen was ablaze with white light, the clear night sky columned with enormous clouds of smoke and earth which barrelled upwards lit from the fires below, appearing to support a vast canopy of crimson cloud above the blazing town. A monstrous cathedral of flame.

With each shuddering blast, which seemed to suck the air upwards and leave us gasping for breath, the trees, in the light of the explosions, doubled themselves as leaping shadows, zig-zagging against the dancing shapes of the tents. In the midst of the fury, a cow, maddened with terror, crashed among us trailing a broken rope at its neck, bellowing with fear, until it tripped in the guy-ropes and crashed to the ground under a sagging canopy of once-taut canvas.

There were no more Germans along the ridge road at Carpiquet to play at 'silly buggers' with a lone jeep: by the next day Caen had fallen and the battle for Normandy was almost over.

It was no time at all, I reckoned, for hermit crabs. All that, with so much else which I had devised for my personal protection, was cautiously set aside. Self-preservation and anonymity were, however, still uppermost in my mind. However, the former now took first place to the latter.

Strangely, I discovered in the first two months of battle that, though I was, indeed, often dry-mouthed with fear (or perhaps fright is a less craven word), at the same time the in-built eye of the observer was as alert as ever: I was curious, anxious to see, to experience, to be aware of the extraordinary things which were taking place about me.

And, in the letters to my father, to whom I wrote every week at least, if not twice a week, I was still 'keeping notes', just as I had done a thousand years ago in the Anthracite Years.

There was plenty of scope.

*　　*　　*

August that year, according to the letters which he had kept for me, appears to have been like a childhood summer: that is to say, eternal sunshine, cloudless, hot and clear.

The sky was always blue, that strange intense blue of northern France, sea-washed, wind-cleansed, limitless, criss-crossed with lazy scrawls of vapour trails like the idle scribbles of a child in a crayoning-book.

In the orchards the shade lay heavy beneath the trees, spiked here and there with emerald blades of grass and clumps of campion.

But everywhere the land was still. There was no birdsong.

Sometimes a bee would drone up and away, or a grasshopper scissor in the crushed weeds of the chalky soil, and then fall silent as if the effort had been too much, in the still heat, or as if, perhaps, reproved that there was no response in the ominous quiet.

No rabbits scuttled in the hedgerows, the corn stood high,

ripe, heavy in the ear, unharvested, and in the meadows cows lay on their sides, stiff-legged, like milking stools, bellies bloated with gas.

Sometimes one of them would explode with a sound like a heavy sigh, dispersing memories of a lost childhood in the sickly stench of decay.

Death was monarch of that summer landscape: only the bee and the grasshopper gave a signal of life, or suggested that it existed. The familiar had become unfamiliar and frightening. A world had stopped and one waited uneasily to see if it would start again: a clock to be rewound in an empty room.

But that comforting tick-tock of normality, of the life pulse, had been provisionally arrested. In some cases it had been stopped for good, for a little further back, towards the beaches, they were burying those who would remain forever in silence.

There was plenty of noise back there: of gears grinding, engines roaring, tracks rattling, metal groaning.

At the edge of an elm-fringed meadow, I stood against a tree watching, curiously unmoved, the extraordinary ballet between machines and corpses, which proved conclusively that the human body was nothing but a fragile, useless container without the life force.

For some reason it had never fully occurred to me before: I had seen a good number of dead men and had, as a normal reaction, felt a stab of pity, a creep of fear that perhaps it could be me next time, but I had become accustomed to them and got on with my own living.

But that afternoon in the shade of the elms I stood watching the bulldozers (a new toy to us then) shovelling up the piles of dead very much as spoiled fruit is swept into heaps after a market-day, and with as little care. Shuddering, wrenching, jerking, stinking of hot oil in the high sun, they swivelled slowly about with open jaws ripping at the earth to form deep pits, and then, nudging and grabbing at the shreds and pieces, rotting, bloody, unidentifiable, which heavy trucks had let slither from raised tail-boards in tumbled heaps of arms and legs, they tossed them into the pits.

Back and forth they droned and crunched, swinging about with casual ease, manoeuvred by cheerful young men, masked against the stench and flies, arms burned black by the August sun.

'Tidying up,' said someone with me. 'One day they will turn this meadow into a war cemetery. Rows and rows of crosses and neat little walks; perhaps they'll erect a fine granite monument, a flagstaff will carry a proud flag to be lowered at the Last Post, they'll plant those bloody yew trees, and relatives will walk in silence through the toy-town precision and order, looking for their dead.'

I remember what he said, because I wrote it all down later, but I can't remember who he was.

Fairly typical of me, I fear.

The words stayed with me for the simple reason that they moved me more than the things which I was observing. The dead lying there in putrid heaps among the sorrel and butter-cups didn't move me at all: they were no more than torn, tattered, bloody bundles. The soul had sped; there could only be regret for those who had loved the individual bodies in this seeping mass: for everyone there had once belonged to someone. That was the sadness.

The absolute anonymity of mass death had dulled grief.

The silence didn't last long – silence in war never does. One gets to discover that very early on.

The ominous stillness which had reproved both grasshopper and bee simply preceded a gigantic storm: Caen fell, the Germans began their terrible retreat to the east. The battle for Normandy was over.

I use the word 'terrible' advisedly, for the retreat, estimated at that time to be composed of at least 300,000 men plus vehicles and arms, crammed the dusty high-hedged roads and lanes, even the cart tracks through fields and orchards, in a desperate attempt to reach the ferries across the river Seine: the Allied armies surrounded them on three sides. We knew that all the main bridges had been blown, so it appeared evident to us that we contained the entire German fighting force in one

Normandy. The Falaise–Trun road, 1944

enormous killing-ground. Tanks and trucks, horse-drawn limbers, staff cars, private cars, farm carts and all kinds of tracked vehicles, anything in fact which could move, inched along the jammed lanes and roads in slow convoys of death.

Unable to turn back, to turn left or right, they had no alternative but to go ahead to the river, providing undefended, easy targets for Allied aircraft which homed down on them as they crawled along and blasted them to destruction: ravening wolves with cornered prey.

By 21 August it was over.

Across the shattered farms, the smouldering cornfields, the smoking ruins in the twisting lanes, smoke drifted lazily in the heat and once again the frightening silence came down over a landscape of shattering carnage.

Those of us in the middle of things really thought that a colossal victory had been achieved. The Germans had been destroyed along with their weapons. There could be nothing left of them to fight, the Russians were about to invade their homeland, surely now victory was ours and the war would finish before the end of the summer?

We were wrong. The people who are in the middle are nearly always wrong. The canvas of war is far too great to comprehend as one single picture. We only knew a very limited part – and even that part was not as it seemed. Gradually we began to realize that the war was not over, that it was going to go on, that the Germans were still fighting, still highly armed, stubborn and tougher than they had been before. Slowly 'a colossal victory' faded from our minds and we accepted the fact that something must have gone a little bit wrong in our jubilant assessment of an early peace.

It had indeed gone wrong. But it was only some years later, when the generals who had squabbled, quarrelled, and bickered all the way through the campaign began to write their auto-biographies, that one learned that, far from a victory, the retreat had been a catastrophe.

By that time it was far too late for thousands of men to worry.

They were laid out in neat rows under white crosses.

What had happened, quite simply, is that the Allied generals, by disagreeing among themselves, had left the back door open to the killing-ground permitting thousands of Germans, and their arms, to escape and live to fight another day.

But we didn't know it, fortunately, at the time.

Standing in the aftermath of violent death is a numbing experience: the air about one feels torn, ripped and stretched. The cries of panic and pain, of rending metal, though long since dispersed into the atmosphere, still seem to echo in the stillness which drums in one's ears.

On the main road from Falaise to Trun, one of the main escape routes which we *did* manage to block, among the charred and twisted remains of exploded steel, dead horses indescribably chunked by flying shrapnel, eyes wide in terror, yellow teeth bared in frozen fear, still-smouldering tanks, the torn, bullet-ripped cars and the charred corpses huddled in the burned grass, it was perfectly clear that all that I had been taught in the past about Hell and damnation had been absolutely wrong.

Hell and damnation were not some hell-fire alive with dancing horned devils armed with toasting-forks. Nothing which Sister Veronica or Sister Marie Joseph had told me was true. Clearly they had got it all wrong in those early, happy Twickenham days. Hell and damnation were here, on this once peaceful country road, and I was right in the middle of it all.

My boots were loud on the gravel, oily smoke meandered slowly from smouldering tyres. Blackened bodies, caught when the petrol tanks of the trucks and cars had exploded, grinned up at me from crisped faces with startling white teeth, fists clenched in charcoaled agony.

Down the road in a haze of smoke stood a small boy of about seven; in his hand a tin can with a twisted wire handle.

I walked towards him and he turned quickly, then scrambled up the bank where a woman was bending over a body in the black grass, a hammer and chisel in her hand.

The boy tugged at her skirts, she stood upright, stared at me shading her eyes with the flat of her hand, then she shrugged, cuffed the boy gently, and bent again to her task.

Hammering gold teeth from the grinning dead.

The boy raised the tin for me to see. It was almost a third full of bloody nuggets and bits of bridge-work.

Waste not, want not.

In the ditch below us a staff car lay tilted on its side, the bodywork riddled with bullet holes in a precise line as if a riveter had been at work rather than a machine-gun from a low flying plane.

A woman was slumped in the back seat, a silver fox fur at her feet, her silk dress blood-soaked, a flowered turban drunkenly squint on her red head. A faceless man in the uniform of the SS lay across her thighs.

I kicked one of her shoes lying in the road, a wedge-heeled cork-soled scrap of coloured cloth.

The woman with the hammer shouted down, 'Sale Boche! Eh? Collaboratrice . . . c'est plein des femmes comme ça! Sale Boche!'

I walked back to my jeep. My driver was sitting in his seat smoking.

'Where do they all come from?'

'Who?'

'Those blokes . . . wandering about having a good old loot. They just go through the pockets, get the wallets, pinch the bits of jewellery. There's a squad of women civilians in all this lot. Gives you a bit of a turn seeing dead women in this sort of set-up.'

Here and there, pulling at the blackened corpses, wrenching open the doors of the bullet-riddled cars, a few elderly peasants clambered about the wreckage collecting anything of value. God knew where they had come from – every building nearby was destroyed, but like the woman on the bank with the boy, they had come to scavenge what they could.

As we drove away the first bulldozers began to arrive to

clear the road. I didn't speak: the sight of the dead girl with the red hair had distressed me profoundly.

I was prepared for people to be dead in uniform, but my simple mind would not come to terms with the sight of a dead woman in a silk dress on a battlefield. That didn't seem to be right. They hadn't warned us about *that* on the assault course in Kent.

We had to pull aside to let a bulldozer grind past; I looked back and saw an old man dancing a little jig. In a fox fur cape.

*   *   *

Chris was kneeling on the grass before a five-gallon petrol can, sleeves rolled to his elbows, kneading a shapeless mass like a baker.

'What on earth are you doing?'

'Don't come near!' he yelled. 'If you light a cigarette we'll be blown to smithereens.'

'I'm not smoking. What are you doing?'

'Cleaning my uniform. Absolutely filthy.'

'So is mine.'

He dredged up a sodden battledress jacket. The smell of petrol was overwhelming.

'Just look at it! Black! Filthy!'

'Is there any particular reason why you want to clean the thing now?'

He looked up at me, dunked the jacket again, did a bit more kneading.

'Thought we might go to Paris,' he said. 'Can't arrive looking like a tramp.'

'But it's not fallen yet . . . they're still fighting.'

'Well, as soon as it stops. Couple of days' time. Seems fitting.'

'But it's forbidden to the British. Only the Free French and the Yanks.'

'Which is damned unfair, we've got every right to be there too, why not?'

On the morning of 26 August, almost before it was light,

we set off in the jeep with the unexpired-portions-of-the-daily-ration, a painted paper Union Jack, which Chris had made and stuck on the windscreen, and a fairly taciturn driver who didn't drink.

'He's essential,' said Chris. 'Teetotaller. We aren't; and liberating Paris should mean a couple of glasses here and there. Got to get back in one piece.'

We liberated Paris: a celebration of the heart in an atmosphere of exploding gaiety and joy.

Driving back to the airstrip, just as evening nudged the edge of nightfall, I realized how wise Chris had been to bring a teetotal driver with us.

We'd never have got back without him.

Teetotal and taciturn he was; indeed he had hardly moved a limb, nor once smiled all day, among the tumultuous crowds of cheering and laughing people. His only comment, which almost brought us to complete sobriety, was: 'These French haven't got no control. Know what I mean? All over you before you can lift a finger to say bugger off – not so much as an "Excuse me". Bloody liberty! Foreigners! What can you expect?'

But he drove safely back through the dark while Chris and I assured each other solemnly that we had spent a really *most* agreeable day. A very agreeable day indeed. Probably the most agreeable day we'd had since the landings. *Certainly* so. A *splendid* day. We decided, after a mumbling silence, that we ought to liberate another city as soon as one became available.

We had our wish granted a week or so later when Brussels fell, and the unexpired-portion-of-the-daily-ration, wrapped in a sheet of the *Daily Mirror*, proved to be a great success in an expensive restaurant on rue Neuve, where our two tins of bully-beef were presented to the room at large on a giant silver salver, sliced as thin as a paper handkerchief, garnished with tomato and cucumber rings, and offered, at our request, to the elderly clientele who accepted with well-fed, but graceful, bows and nods.

The black market, it would appear, didn't run to bully-beef. Yet.

That was early September – ahead lay another city awaiting liberation.

This time we failed disastrously.

There was to be no liberation for Arnhem.

Another catastrophe.

I (seconded to an infantry division) sat in the mud and ice during a long, bitter winter just across the river while the Dutch starved to death on the other side.

This time the catastrophe was obvious. We had no need of the books the generals might later write to explain things. We saw it happen before our eyes, unwilling witnesses to a shattering disaster.

The euphoria of Paris and Brussels drained away. The tough times were back. It was just as well that I was aware of that fact for there was worse to come.

In April, as the last of the snows melted in the larch forests like strips of soiled bandage, we came to Belsen and the first concentration camp: a hideous 'liberation' this time which erased for ever the erroneous idea we had had that 'Jerry is really just the same as us'.

No way was he.

The war ended, for Christopher and me, not as I had somehow always thought it might, triumphantly in Berlin, but while we were sitting on a pile of logs in a pine forest near Lüneberg Heath, drinking coffee in tin mugs.

'Well, old dear,' said Chris. 'That's it. All done; all over.'

I had never felt so useless in my life.

In a letter to my father dated 7 May 1945, I wrote:

. . . It is the strangest feeling imaginable to know that it is over: one just idles about. There are no 'sorties' being flown so no work. And there won't be need of us, *or* our work, from now on. There is a weird vacuum: for so many months now it has been a fourteen or sixteen (sometimes twenty-four) hour day of strain and anxiety. All gone now. The in-built fear that someone somewhere might take a shot at you, or drop a bomb on you, has evaporated. There are still hazards about. Mines, and a band of zealots called Werewolves who are determined to fight on, but, apart from stringing piano wire across the roads thus decapitating one or two unfortunate blokes driving jeeps or motorcycles, they don't amount to much and most of them are kids anyway; about fifteen or so. So we don't worry much.

Jodle apparently capitulated to Ike today in Rheims, and if that is so, that's that. I don't know quite what will happen to me now, it's been a bit sudden in some ways, but I expect I'll be given UK leave and then get shipped off to the Far East. There is still a war there. One sometimes forgets! It'll suit me in a way. I think I'll have a serious try at staying on with the Army: if I survive the next lot of course! I've enjoyed the companionship and the unexpected lack of responsibility. The Army, as far as it can, DOES take care of you, and I'm not at all certain now that I would ever be able to settle down among civilians again. I've got my books, a tent, a servant and a jeep. I honestly don't think I could be happier! But time will tell, it's very early days after all, and I *do* need a job to do. Maybe the planning for the fall of Singapore? It's in the air . . .

*   *   *

They swooped low, swung upwards in a spiralling loop, spun down, and scattered into glossy leaves of a banyan tree, screeching and squabbling as they settled to roost. Aunt Kitty's flights of scarlet birds across an opal sky.

These weren't scarlet – just ordinary green parrots – but the sky was opal, the high monsoon clouds were rising against the darkening sky, washed in carmine, orange, blue and green.

Over the verandah of the Mess, which had once been Tagore's house, peacocks planed down as gracefully and silently as hang-gliders to settle on the crumbling dome of a little temple buried in long grasses, marigolds and zinnias. They preened, bobbed, and fluttered their tails like foppish fans. Raindrops from the last heavy fall edged the leaves of the Canna lilies like diamonds.

Somewhere, from the very back of memory, these sights were somehow familiar. Even to the monkeys who swung through the jacaranda trees baring yellow teeth in hideous grins, defecating in anger.

In the bazaar, across the compound, the sense of texture and

'. . . a little temple buried in long grasses . . .' Bangladore, 1945

scent which she had offered me all those years ago was mine in abundance: silks, cottons, linen, trembling voiles, blazing everywhere in colours far too brilliant for any northern light; and the scents of coriander, mace, clove and nutmeg, of flour and damp hemp, ghee, camel dung and patchouli, swamped the senses.

As the light failed, the wail of flutes and the tapping of drums mixed with the cries of the merchants and beggars, and the high laughter of children trailing kites.

A different world to the one I had left a few months ago, arriving as a Draft of One, to cross India and begin, as I had expected, to join the planning of Operation 'Zipper'.

Only there was no planning because the monsoon had arrived with me; and that meant no flights and no flights meant no sorties and so, workless, one idled through the humid days.

'Difficult to say what they'll do with you,' said Scotty rattling the ice-cubes in his gin-sling. 'No telling really. Once we start off again, after the rains, we might get a clue – you'll probably be sent down to one of the Divisions, I shouldn't wonder. The bloody Japs have got their backs to the wall but they fight like hell.'

'So I have been told.'

'Sub-human, the buggers. For God's sake don't think otherwise. Monstrous people. Don't get taken prisoner. Take your cyanide pill instead.'

Remembering Belsen I said: 'The Germans weren't actually Fairy Twinkle Toes.'

'These are worse. Unfathomable. Savages. Bound four of our chaps with bailing wire into a tidy bundle, head to feet, doused them with petrol and set 'em alight. Alive.'

'Christ!'

'*He* wasn't around at the time; they've no pity, no mercy.' He drained his drink, tipped the melting ice-cubes into a potted palm. 'Should be exterminated like the vermin they are.' He got to his feet, pulled down the skirt of his bush-jacket.

'Want the other half of that?'

I followed him into the Mess.

Three nights later we heard that the bomb had been dropped on Hiroshima.

In the silence which greeted the news in the crowded, still Mess, someone said: 'God Almighty! Now look what we've done, let the bloody genie out of the bottle, we'll never get it back in, never.'

Just for good measure they dropped another on Nagasaki three days after, and a week later the Japanese capitulated. The war was finally over.

If I had felt absolutely useless when Germany had surrendered, I felt worse now. There wasn't a war to fight and I wanted to stay on in the army: I was deeply thankful that I would not have to face the Japanese in battle – everything I had been told by the old hands had horrified me into incomprehension of so barbaric an enemy – but I consoled myself further by my awareness that there would be much to do in the areas which they had occupied and ravaged and in which they had spread their dreadful gospel of hate and vengeance.

Someday someone would send for me.

But they didn't: I was forgotten for the time being. The army had other things to do apart from worrying about one lone captain who wanted to stay on.

In the atmosphere of euphoria and exotic laziness, among the sights and sounds and scents, I drifted into an affair with a woman some years older than myself.

Nan was no starry-eyed girl. Quite the opposite: she knew very well, instinctively, that I was cautious, evasive, unwilling to be trapped. Afraid of possession.

So she played her cards supremely well, encouraging me to read, to write my dire poems, even (time was so heavy on our hands) to write a play, which she carefully typed out for me in the evenings in the now deserted office. She encouraged, flattered, suggested a brilliant future in civilian life, and almost convinced me that I should not remain with my regiment and stay in the army.

She never once, in all the plans which she laid for my future, included herself. Far too clever for that, she was certain that in a matter of time I would come to depend on her for so much that I should find it impossible to break the bond which she was carefully forging.

And the bond, at that time, was strong: we were inseparable, and she was fun. We danced at the Club almost every evening, spent all our time together, rode mules into Sikkim on a three-week trek which I planned could take us to Tibet because I had a great passion to see Lhasa. We never got to Tibet – that was forbidden territory – but at least we saw Everest and lay hand in hand under the stars and the deodars.

As far as our companions were concerned we were 'paired'. I think that Nan believed so too.

I did not. At nights, lying in the noisy darkness beneath my mosquito net, her body heavy in sleep beside me, the scent of 'Je Reviens' on her throat and shoulders, I felt a wrench of panic that I was entering a maze from which there could, decently, be no escape. My love for her was provisional only. I hadn't the remotest idea how to escape from an intense affair which I had helped create only to ease the tedium of my boredom and idleness, and which was now beginning to overwhelm me.

But the army had not forgotten me.

After three months, I was despatched to Java where, Scotty informed me with some degree of relish, they were 'having a hell of a time with a bloody civil war; the Japs surrendered to the Indonesians and *they* won't give the guns back to the Dutch! You'll have a very jolly time, old boy.'

Nan came down to Kidderpore Docks to see me off on the L S T which was to carry me across the Equator.

'It seems very small to cross the Indian Ocean in,' she said. 'A walnut shell.'

'It is.'

'L S T 3033. At least I know what you're in and where you are going.'

'Yes . . . keep your ears open; in case the fishes get me.'

'And you'll write? Remember, after the 27th of next month write to my sister's place. Ladbroke Grove. She'll keep them for me.'

'I will. As soon as I'm settled in.'

Somewhere among the jostling, feverish crowds on the quayside, someone shouted: 'Quit India! Quit India!'; others joined in waving clenched fists in the air at no one in particular.

'You'd better get away, they are starting to get restless. Bloody Congress, bloody Gandhi. Don't get stuck, go now.'

'I will. The gharri's there. Ladbroke Grove, remember?'

'After the 27th.'

I watched her walking straight-backed, but with a slight limp – the strap on her sandal had snapped. She carried it in one hand.

I knew that she wouldn't look back, and she did not.

The bond had been broken.

I turned away as the engine started up, a dull throbbing shuddering up through the metal deck. I went below as a Draft of One: for Java.

*   *   *

At Guildford station carriage doors are slamming. A woman with an anxious look and a paper carrier-bag hurries past the compartment, and the singing porter rattles his empty trolley to the door. Stands there looking up, smiling, waiting for his tip. I fumble among assorted coins.

'All on board. Your gear. Heavy. Full of loot, eh?'

'The Japanese Crown Jewels, that's all.' I give him half a crown.

'Demobbed are you? Happiest day of your life, I reckon.'

'You reckon wrong.'

'Ah.' His eyes narrow, slide across my medal ribbons, badges of rank. 'Singapore, was you? On your trunk. Bombay. All that?'

'All that. And more.'

'Saw you had a nice tan. Expect you'll miss the sunshine. Ta,' he says and goes off singing.

'Until I tell her that I'll never roam,
'So, Chattanooga choo-choo, won't you choo-choo me home?'

But that came much later.

CHAPTER

5

We had crossed the equator in the early hours of the morning; I had set my tin alarm clock for 3.00 a.m. and went up on deck to watch. Some well-meaning idiot at the bar in Raffles Hotel the day before had assured me that there really was a visible line in the sea, and I had laughed, naturally; but none the less set an alarm clock.

To make sure.

And there was. Or so it pleased me to think.

Stars blazed from a jet sky and a half-moon appeared to cast a strange rippling line across the water: it was exactly as if two tides were meeting, riffling together, merging, shimmering in the heavy swell. It satisfied me, leaning over the thin iron rail of the ship.

I liked the idea, even though I knew perfectly well that it could only be an illusion. But then so much of my life in the last two or three years had seemed to be an illusion that one more wasn't going to upset my particular apple-cart. I accepted the line for a 'line', and that was that. I had, after all, *seen* a strange joining of the waters, like the interlocking of fingers, and that is how I would always remember it, and do.

Our snub-nosed LST cut through the phosphorescent waters with an elegant curl of white foam tumbling the wake behind us in folds of gold and silver. Apart from the throb of engines far below my feet, and the soft creaking of a metal stanchion, there was no other sound except the swish and swirl of the sea against the hull.

I felt strangely alone, exceedingly rich, drenched in these sights and gentle sounds with no one in the world to share them, and no one to shatter the beauty by comment and the banality of human speech. That kind of beauty needs no underlining.

It just is. Perfect, complete, rare, unshareable.

Far away to starboard a tiny light flashed with the regularity of a metronome. A lighthouse on the coast of Sumatra, brighter even than the stars.

We slid across the 'visible' line through the glittering night, with the Southern Cross tilted high above, into equatorial waters.

I had come a long way from Great Meadow and the Cottage, from the mud-scented delights of the river at Twickenham, from the grey conformity of the Anthracite Years which had been, after all, the anvil on which my strength, such as it was, had been forged.

I knew that tomorrow all this glory would be memory, which is probably why I spent so much time on that deck memorizing it for ever, imprinting it on my mind so that wherever I went, whatever became of me, as long as I should be breathing and aware, I could remember and in remembering be enriched once again.

My short stay in Singapore during the last two days had heightened my sense of awareness, re-reminding me that life is at best ephemeral, at worst too easily lost and rubbished into oblivion: tomorrow, I knew, I should land on a strange island, wrenched by strife, anguish, bitterness and blind hatred, to take my part as a 'policeman', nothing else, in the bloody shaping of its future.

It seemed to me at the time a pretty daunting enterprise, and unworkable, which so it proved to be eventually, but I had no sense of fear then, or the remotest apprehension: it was a job which I should enjoy somehow, even though I would be forbidden to fire a shot in anger, even to protect myself.

I knew, of course, that it was almost impossible, indeed it *was* impossible, to try and impose law and order on a country hell-bent in ridding itself of colonial rule. I'd seen a good deal of that already in India with the rioting of the Congress Party. If the wretched island to which I was presently on my way wanted its Dutch rulers out, there was nothing, I knew, that anyone, however well-meaning and however imbued with a sense of order and control, could do to stop the surging masses, hysterical with slogans and blood-lust.

In Calcutta one afternoon I had seen the kind of fury that lay just beneath the surface of apparent orderliness when a Hindu youth of about sixteen jumped a food queue and was, there and then, hacked limb from limb in the busy street. There was no quarter, no mercy, no possibility of law or order, no reasoning.

Nan had grabbed my cap and buried her face, trying at the same time to cover her ears so that the screams could, at least, be muffled.

No one tried to help; but then, no one ever did.

We stood trapped in the seething, screaming crowd.

The youth's trunk lay bloodily in the gutter, head savagely battered, hair matted, eyes staring wide in surprise among an incongruous litter of old confetti and orange peel.

It was a fairly common occurrence in those days; mob violence was only a skin's-depth away, and incidents such as this were just the lid rattling on the boiling pot.

Caught in such a situation, the wisest thing to do was to try to ease oneself away as discreetly and quietly as possible; *never* push or hurry; walk slowly.

Capless, I led a weeping Nan through the shouting crowd; her long hair had fallen about her face and shoulders in an untidy cascade, and this probably helped our departure, for we were unrecognizable as officers of His Majesty's detested services by the jostling, screaming horde with its foam-frilled lips.

In India we knew that the fuse was short, the mechanism ticking, the bomb gigantic. When we left, as leave we knew we must, a tidal wave of hatred, violence and heedless frenzy would sweep the great continent, and Hindu and Muslim would only stop to catch their breaths when the killings were done.

The Indian Christians, and the terrified Eurasians, knew this equally well, and begged constantly for help, to be allowed to leave with us when we went, but no one gave a fig for them frankly; no one even bothered to do anything about them.

When we left we'd lower all the flags and quit, and then, as someone said in the Mess one night: 'We'll let the inmates run the bloody asylum, sort it out among themselves – they won't be able to, of course, but let the buggers try if that's what they want.'

It was a sentiment frequently expressed by a great number of men in the army who had come out from Britain to hold India against a Japanese invasion.

It was a negative approach of course – but then India induces negativity.

Standing on the deck that night, now so long ago, I remember being very glad that I had left the country at last; I knew that the official war was over, that the Japanese had surrendered, and that I had chucked my cyanide pill into the sea long since. *That* fact comforted me very much indeed.

I was sailing to a new job as a 'policeman', and if that was the role I had to play, so be it – it was a great deal better than having to fight the Japs, for I knew that if that had been my fate I could never have survived.

I felt pretty certain (wrongly of course) that it would be a fairly peaceful affair; I'd be there to assist in collecting the lost POWs and the Dutch internees (that had been my briefing in Calcutta) and help get them safely home. Nothing to it really – almost a Red Cross job.

So there I stood against the rail, filled with contentment by the splendour of the night all about me, and a feeling that the worst was over, and that I had survived: so far.

I waited until the first thin thread of scarlet day split the night on the portside horizon, beyond Borneo. I was linked with my earliest memories; for these were Aunt Kitty's islands and already, in my imagination, they were half familiar.

I thought.

★   ★   ★

It is true that defeat has an odour.

It meandered through the paint-peeling streets of Singapore like a slowly dispersing marsh gas, lying in pockets here and there, loitering in rooms and corridors, bitter, clinging, sickening.

We docked in Keppel harbour: rusted cranes, a half-sunken steamer, ruined warehouses with hollow, bullet-pocked façades. Military trucks, piles of stores, oil drums, a Union Jack hanging limply from a pole. It was five weeks after the Japanese surrender.

Beyond the wrecked buildings, which lined the dockyard like a row of rotten teeth, the towers, palms and pinnacles of the city struck hard against the intensity of the blue sky; sampans criss-crossed the oily waters like waterboatmen, and birds, strange to me, mewed and cried, swooping low above the churning wake of our L S T.

The day was already hot and humid when I set off through the dockyard to go and see the city which had 'died' so ignominiously in the February of 1942.

A whitewashed bastard Tunbridge Wells – with palm trees.

Domed, arched, turreted, pillared, apparently empty.

Miss Havisham's wedding cake crumbling in defeat and cobwebs after three and a half years of Japanese occupation.

On the Singapore River Chinese life, however went its way in a tidy explosion of activity.

Sampans jammed the muddy waters like the tumble of a thousand dominoes spilled along the winding fringes of the riverbanks.

In Chinatown proper, washing hung from every window and balcony, or from bamboo poles thrust out across the narrow streets; shutters were bleached by years of sun and tropical rains, some had never been opened, others hung like lolling tongues. On the shops, Chinese lettering danced and sprang in scarlet strokes in the brilliant light, and rickshaws and bicycles bounced over the pot-holes in the twisting alleys, tinny bells furiously ringing, weaving through crowds of laughing, playing children, as innocent as butterfly swarms.

Among this cheerful chaos, ramshackle stalls were piled with all kinds of goods, from dried mushrooms and rice to Japanese whiskey and scrawny hens bunched alive, hanging by their legs looking anxious. Everywhere there was the cloying smell of frying oil and dried fish, heavy on the morning air, but above all there was activity and life.

The European quarter was different.

A deserted Sunday afternoon lethargy. Some military personnel here and there, jeeps and trucks revving up, turning, tail-boards clattering noisily in the almost deserted streets, Robinsons Department Store (the Harrods of the East, they said) had been struck by bombs and stared in sullen shock across the silent street with empty eyes: sockets in a scabbed, decaying face.

The city smelled of drains, damp and desolation. The mustiness of a long-closed room. My booted footsteps cracked back in echo in the stillness.

In Raffles Place there was a small parked Austin car with rusted chrome and a flat tyre, and two Chinese men in flip-flops carrying a bamboo ladder.

Far above, in the dazzle of the morning sky, kites planed and swung, coasting in the currents of higher air.

Beyond the cricket club grounds, rutted and worn, St Andrew's Cathedral crouched in abandoned grace surrounded by a filigree of jacaranda and flame trees, as alien and out of place as a swan on the Ganges, and all around the pompous pillared buildings, heavy with swagged stone urns and porticos, stood silent, vacant, blind – their Colonial grandeur humbled as if they too, like the occupants who had been forced to leave them, had also 'lost face'.

I hitched a lift on a truck to Tanglin Barracks and the Club; we drove through wincingly genteel suburbs, past gable-beamed and pebbledashed houses with names like 'Fairholm' and 'The Paddocks', buried now in bougainvillaea and flame trees, the jungle already weaving lianas through shattered verandahs, and thrusting bamboo thickets across long-forgotten lawns and rose gardens.

Some had been used as desperate, hopeless strong-points in a lost battle. Blackened shells, incongruous chimney stacks striking up through charred beams, latticed windows swinging urgently in the stiff breeze which rustled the sword-like spikes of the palms. Some stood in an almost pristine state of suburban elegance, and these, my companions told me, had been used as Happy Homes for the Japanese rank and file; but the sounds of feminine laughter and the whisper of silken kimonos had dispersed into the air as surely as the 'thwack!' and 'thwock!' of tennis balls on the overgrown courts of the 'unconquerable' memsahibs.

In the almost empty bar of the Tanglin Club a friendly Australian ex-POW came over and offered to 'buy you a round, okeydoke?'

Ronnie had a long face and no teeth. 'Rifle butt; I answered back.' His skin was drum-taut over angular bones, his joints, elbows and knees were swollen like melons on arms and legs as thick as drinking-straws, his new jungle green uniform hung on his tall, bony frame like a tent.

'Been here since '42. We arrived just as the bloody place folded up. Great bit of timing. Shoved us up into the rubber and said: "Dig defences", but there weren't any shovels and the English bastard who owned the plantation said we'd be fined if we so much as laid a finger on one of his fuckin' trees. I ask you! The bloody Japs were up the road. Fined! Christ! This was the island that *no one* could touch. It was impregnable. Took me a day to work out what that word meant and by the time I had it didn't bloody matter anymore, it didn't apply. The Empire the sun never sets on they all said. Trouble was they didn't know a fuckin' sunset when they saw one.'

'I thought you had all been repatriated?'

'Yah, we've nearly all gone. I go Wednesday and I tell you one thing, cobber, I won't be coming back, never want to see this sodding country ever again. I just survived, by the grace of God, and next time they can stuff their bleeding Empire.'

'I think they have.'

'I think so too. Good on 'em. When did you land?'

I told him and signalled for the unsmiling Malayan boy in his white jacket and ordered another round.

'Timed it really nice. All over bar the shouting, right? You know there's one thing saved our bacon: those bombs. If you lot had tried an invasion, know what the Japs were going to do? Kill all their prisoners – men, women, kids . . . mind you, they'd been doing their best to do it for nearly four years, but that's what we heard. Wipe us all out. The day they dropped that bomb was the best day that I can remember.'

He spoke quietly, in a tired level voice; there was no anger left in him. 'Only thing is,' he said, pushing his empty glass round in circles on the table, 'only thing I say is, they should have dropped twenty more, wiped the bastards off the face of the earth, because you know why? One day they'll try it again; betcha. All jammed on to those fuckin' little islands. Breeding like rats, they'll be falling off the edges soon, and then what? Plenty of room in Australia, it's dead *empty*. Get me?'

I got him. I was unshocked. The quietness of his voice and the authority with which he spoke of terrible things defused argument.

'Well, not for a while,' I said.

The boy came back with two bottles of Tiger beer and set them on the table. Ronnie began to refill his glass, his hands shook slightly.

'Maybe. Not for a while,' he said. 'If I'm talkin' funny it's because of no teeth, sorry, mate. You stuck here long? Singapore?'

'Leave for Java, day after tomorrow.'

'Good on you. No place to stay: they're all so bloody ashamed here. Lost face you see, and the Malays and Chinks *know* it. Doesn't do to "lose face", it isn't forgotten. Never in front of the natives.'

He sipped his beer for a moment in silence. Put his glass down. 'The men are all right, not too bad, the civvies, I mean.

It's the bloody women, they are the worst, they ran this place. They didn't come here with smiling faces, they came here as bloody rulers. Do this! Get that! Rule Britannia! Christ!'

A small boy with a rubber inner-tube round his middle clambered out of the swimming-pool beside us and came across to the table, his wet hair dripping. He wiped his nose on the back of his hand, pointed to a small dish of rice-cookies.

'Can I have those?'

I pushed the dish towards him and he took a handful, without thanks.

A pale, blonde woman, at the far end of the pool, lying on a li-lo, suddenly sat up in her bathing costume, one arm across her breasts. She wasn't bad, long hair, a drawn face, thin, looking angry and embarrassed all at the same time.

'Jeremy!' she called. 'Jeremy! Come here, I told you not to. They're *soldiers*, come back at once.' A voice as harsh as a cane striking steel: meant for us to hear.

The boy swivelled slowly on his heels and went back to her pushing cookies into his mouth. She said something to him, slapped the cookies out of his hand, lay back.

Ronnie shrugged, sipped his beer. 'See what I mean? Really got a complex, all of them.'

*　　*　　*

Not all of them however: Mrs McCrombie hadn't any complexes whatsoever, at least as far as I could see. If she had, then she hid them quite admirably.

She was sitting on the lawns of Raffles Hotel in a Lloyd Loom chair, wearing a man's khaki shirt and khaki slacks, a red ribbon tied about her short, iron-grey hair, face as wrinkled as a winter apple, eyes as sharp and blue as sapphires, and she smiled a lot.

She was, I suppose, then, about sixty-five or so (old in my youthful opinion). Her husband, David, who had survived the ordeal of Changi Jail, had gone up-country to see what, if anything, remained of the rubber plantations of which he was once the manager, and she had settled for a readjustment to life with friends in a small flat in the city after four years in Syme Road Camp.

'Frankly,' she said, 'I hope he *doesn't* find anything worth saving up there. He's most terribly conscientious of course, but I really have a *terrific* hankering for home – home's in Dorset. Near Corfe, do y'know it?'

'Very well. My father used to paint there a lot.'

'Artist, was he? Oh, we had masses of them. I expect you knew the Greyhound pub then?'

'Lord, yes! Smiths crisps and ice cream soda; shandy when I got bigger.'

'The crisps,' she said, 'with those little twists of salt in blue paper.'

For a moment I realized that I had lost her, she had drifted away, her eyes looking beyond the staff cars and manoeuvring trucks on the carriage drive of the hotel.

Unseeing; a tiny smile trembling.

Suddenly she rubbed her forehead nervously, almost with irritation, adjusted the red ribbon, smiled back at me.

'Sorry. I went off somewhere. It was all such a dreadful muddle here, you know. People *do* behave in the oddest ways in times of trouble. I mean to say, here in this place, they were dancing and playing tennis just as if nothing was happening! The Japs had crossed the Causeway, and we'd pulled out of the naval base leaving it quite undamaged! David saw it. Everything intact. It was madness.'

'Did they really come across on bicycles, the Japs?'

'Oh yes! That's quite, quite true. Hundreds of the blighters spinning along on those dreadful little Japanese bikes. Can you imagine? *We* couldn't. No one here did – we never thought of that, naturally. Bikes! They are, of course, the *most* ingenious people – quite caught us on the hop.' She laughed suddenly, like a dry cough. 'Hop!' she said. 'That's what they did, and that's what we were doing, or they were doing. Dancing. Tennis. Funny. Do you know a dance tune, something called, was it "Deep Purple"?'

'Oh yes. Yes I know that.'

Raffles Hotel. Singapore, 1945

'I hate it,' she said.

A stiff breeze from the sea wrestled with the traveller's trees stuck along the edges of the lawn, snapped the Union Jack on its pole above the façade.

She looked up at it.

'Nice to see it back again.' She folded her arms on the table top. 'We had to kill the dogs. I think that was almost the worst thing really.'

'The dogs?'

'Well, when we realized that it was the end, David and I knew what we had to do; he got the Humber out and we took the dogs to the vet.' She leant forward, her hands cupping her face.

'They thought they were going for "walkies". You know? They adored the car an'all. But of course everyone else had the same idea at the same time. There was a queue of cars simply miles long; people walking too; weeping. So many dogs. All kinds. Tongues hanging out, pulling at their leashes, some being dragged. They were anxious, aware of our grief. Dogs are; did you know? They sense one's anxiety, one's fear, one's distress. Of course you got the odd Jack Russell behaving badly, snarling and jumping at everyone. Terror I imagine – most of them knew what was happening. I know that mine did. Barney was trembling from head to foot, and Rollo, he was David's dog, just stayed close to him, his head jammed tight against his master. He never moved from him. Never.'

She cleared her throat, placed her arms on the table top again. 'Poor people. The vets were dead with exhaustion. Collies, spaniels, Airedales, pekes, all kinds . . . so many – but we simply had to do it; had to.' She sat back in the Lloyd Loom chair and when she spoke again her voice was firm and brisk.

'*You* don't want to hear all these awful things! Too depressing – all in the past now anyway. Gosh!' she said, her eyes sparkling. 'We *were* glad that you all got here when you did! I don't think that we could have managed for very much longer really, things were getting pretty grim. We *were* glad! Oh goodness yes!'

'I'm afraid I wasn't here for the Liberation. I'm on my way down to Java, I only got in yesterday.'

'Well. You know what I mean, don't you? All of you, so young and fresh, so strong; we really never thought it possible towards the very end. There *was* a rumour that they would kill us all. Too many mouths to feed and what to do with us if you had invaded, you know? And then that bomb was dropped; after that it was different. But before, in the dreadful days, goodness what muddles! No one knew what to do, and when the *Repulse* and the poor *Prince of Wales* went down, that was pretty well that. No navy, no air force to speak of, and the Japs were so *much* stronger than we were, thousands of them swarming all over the place. We hadn't a chance. Just caved in, I'm afraid.'

She laughed shortly. Pushed the ribbon about on her forehead. 'Not *really* the sort of thing to tell one's grand-children, is it?'

Long, long after the disaster of the Falaise Gap in Normandy, we learned just what had happened there; and long after my meeting with Mrs McCrombie, and long after I had stood miserably in the fog on Guildford station, I discovered what had actually happened in Singapore, and why the British were so deeply shamed and, as Ronnie had told me, 'lost face'.

Lieutenant General Yamashita, commanding the Japanese forces at that time, was outnumbered by three to one, short of supplies and exhausted. If he had had to hold on and face a counter-attack, he admitted later, he would have lost, and the greatest military disaster in history, as it has since been called, would never have occurred.

But no one knew at the time. And there was no thought of a counter-attack.

Hindsight is a woeful word.

So, as in Normandy, as in Malaya. Those in the middle of things didn't know. Bickering, squabbling, incompetence, absurd snobbery and idiotic arrogance caused the deaths of thousands of men and lost the British their Empire – perhaps not immediately, but the chocks had been kicked away and the ship of state, so to speak, was on the move down the slipway to disaster.

I have always thought that it would have been comforting to think that Mrs McCrombie, and others like her, would never learn the true facts; but if she survived I suppose that, inevitably, she did.

But thousands upon thousands would never know – would never realize that it had all been in vain finally. There are no learned revelations for the dead.

Near the District Commissioner's tennis court in Kohima there is a modest memorial to all those who died in that campaign. It carries a simple message, four lines long:

> When you go home
> Tell them of us and say
> For your tomorrow
> We gave our today.

Who goes now to Kohima?

After I had done my stint as a 'policeman' in Java, I returned once again to Singapore and Tanglin Barracks, waiting for a berth back to England and repatriation.

Many changes had taken place since my first visit. The streets were busy again; Orchard Road was jammed with trucks, cars and rickshaws; ENSA was installed; there were scores of tatty little restaurants 'In Bounds to HM Forces'; people were dancing again at The Happy World; Raffles Hotel stated, on a discreet card, that 'If you are wearing HM Uniform you are not welcome'; and there was a subtle, understated, segregation of Singapore civilians and military personnel in the Tanglin Club, part of which had been commandeered as an Officers Club, where the dough-kneed newcomers (with one Defence Medal up) sat about in their over-starched shorts drinking Tiger beer and gin-slings, talking too loudly; and in the city, Kelly and Walshe's splendid bookshop had opened up again with new deliveries of books from America and Britain.

It was there that I went to find something to read on the long seven-week voyage home. I found just what I needed: a copy of *Gone With the Wind*. As I put out my hand to take it, a neatly gloved woman's hand reached towards it at the same moment.

I instantly withdrew mine, and offered her the book politely.

She was a middle-aged woman, straight-backed, grey-haired, in a blue tussore suit and a blue straw hat, a handbag in the crook of her elbow.

I can see her in this room now – at this very moment.

She turned abruptly away from me, and calling down the entire length of the shop, to a startled assistant, she said: 'Boy! Tell this officer that if he wishes to address me, to do so through you.'

Not everything had changed in Singapore.

*　　*　　*

Major-General Douglas Hawthorn, D S O, was not standing with open arms to greet me as we docked at Tandjoeng Priok. To be perfectly fair he had no idea that I was coming to join his Division.

No one else had either, for that matter.

The place was swarming with people of all kinds and colours, with tanks and trucks, with perspiring coolies, with running Japanese in little squads, naked save for their boots, peaked caps and flapping loin-cloths, with jeeps jolting over the rubbled concrete, with turbaned Indians and tall, bony British military police in crisp green uniforms and gleaming white lanyards. A bewildering crowd scene overwhelmed by the acrid stink of burning rubber and the more subtle, and far harder to identify individually, scent of spices.

With my tin trunk, portable typewriter and a canvas suitcase I stood abandoned in the midst of carnival. Unwanted, unplaced, unexpected.

A military policeman, with a ginger moustache and the disdain of a llama, led me to the office where, he said, with no degree of certainty: 'Someone will sort it out for you.'

The office was sweltering, even at this early hour, and a pallid corporal, with skin as translucent and as pale as a potato shoot, wearily looked up from some files.

'Any idea where they are? Your people?'

'None. I was sent down from Calcutta; told to report to 23 Indian Div. HQ.'

'Could be anywhere. I'm new myself. Calcutta, did you say?'

'Yes.'

'Long way, sir.'

'Long enough.'

'You come in on 3033, did you?'

'I did. She's unloading over there.'

'Dicey trip.'

'Oh. Why dicey?'

'Submarines, sir.' He was rustling papers. 'They say that there are Jap subs all over the place and that some of them don't know, or won't believe, there's been a surrender. Could have been nasty, if you see what I mean.'

'Very. I can't swim.'

He looked up sharply, a paper in his hand. 'Not much point in swimming. That sea is stiff with sharks.' He went to his telephone. 'Got some "gen" here, we won't be long now.'

Two hours later I was still sitting on my tin trunk, wreathed in the fumes of rubber smoke and spices; but any thoughts of Aunt Kitty's magical islands in the Indian Ocean had long been dispersed.

The subaltern who finally arrived helped me load my gear, and started off through the swarming crowds. He was disinclined to talk, but offered the excuse that he had been on night duty, was bushed, and that no one knew I was coming.

As if I hadn't realized this with blinding clarity some hours before.

The sky grew darker as we got nearer the City, the sun floated, an aluminium disc, behind the heavy pall of smoke which hung above the distant buildings like a wavering canopy.

The traffic was intense, the subaltern's driving alarming, the roads pot-holed, swarming with dogs and children, rickshaws and bicycles, sagging electric light cables and heavy trucks pushing through heedlessly; he suggested that I hold on tight.

'Extremists,' he said suddenly, indicating the billowing cloud of smoke under which we now were weaving an intricate, and near-suicidal, path. 'They hit a rubberstore last night, got the oil depot the night before, hacked thirty internees to bits near Bekassi, and you'd better watch out for landmines – *and* grenades. They chuck them about like ping-pong balls, all in the name of freedom. It's not like Margate.'

I wondered why on earth he would have thought I might think it was. But said nothing. I was dispirited enough without this generous information.

A small villa in a suburban street, standing in a long-abandoned quarter-acre was where I finally landed. This was 'A' Mess. It said so on a piece of cardboard nailed to a pole in the front garden.

In a prim, almost empty little room, with sun-rotted lace curtains at the bay window, a picture of a windmill and a canal on one wall, and a rusty tin garden table against another, a silent, but grinning, Gurkha with an embarrassment of gold teeth unpacked my kit, erected my camp bed and mosquito net, and indicated that his name was Goa.

As far as I could comprehend, for we had no common tongue, and it was only by his pointing to himself with his finger and repeating an incomprehensible string of words that I was able to isolate, phonetically, an assumed name, Goa.

Goa he remained for the rest of my tour of duty, and I came to love him dearly. When the time arrived, eventually, for me to leave Java, Goa smuggled himself, and his kit, into my transport to the docks and pleaded to be allowed to come with me to England. He was splendidly smart, his brasses gleamed, his belt was blanco'd, his boots shone, his tears streamed down his cheeks.

By this time, a year later, we had invented a strange form of language which we used together. Anyone listening to us would not have understood a word, but we did. Which is, after all, what mattered.

'No, Goa. No – *Sahib go*. Not possible Goa go.'

For a moment he looked at me in stubborn silence.

'Goa stay along Pip-sahib. Stay along.'

'Pip-sahib go along Britain. *Tikh hai*?'

He suddenly fumbled in the pocket of his battledress jacket and brought out a worn and tattered piece of card. Stuck on it was a photograph of King George and Queen Elizabeth cut from a magazine.

He held it out to me, then turned it towards himself at arm's length, drew himself to attention, and saluted.

'Goa, go. Look-see burra sahib. Burra, burra sahib Brit-inn. Okay?'

'*Not* okay. Not good. Goa not go. Goa rest along Division. Is *duty*. *Tikh hai*?'

He looked at me with such bewildered pain and distress that I felt a lump rise in my throat as large as a fist.

Our 'language' was far too limited to explain why he could not come with me to see his King.

He stood perfectly still, then replaced the piece of card, never once taking his eyes from mine, rebuttoned his pocket, moved one pace back, slammed to attention in his brilliantly polished boots, saluted, turned on his heel, hoisted his kitbag over one shoulder, and was lost in the jostling crowd pushing about at the foot of the gang-plank.

He'd gone. And I never saw him again.

He had been 'allotted' to me temporarily, at first, because he was considered to be hot-tempered, difficult, stubborn – and he was all these things, but we grew fond of each other and respected each other. In some strange way we made a pattern of life together which worked well: he retained his pride at all times while serving as my batman-driver, which must have been difficult for him because he was a fierce, brave fighting man, and it was never his wish to be a servant.

No one else was anxious to have him for the simple reason that he had removed the head of his last officer, neatly, with a single swipe of his *kukri* while the man was asleep. Apparently there was good reason for this extravagant act, for the officer had, in some way which was never fully explained to me, insulted Goa, his bravery, his religion and his race. The whole ugly affair had been hushed up and dealt with discreetly within the Division, for it was well known that Goa was a fair and fearless man, and had shown incredible bravery and courage in battle from Imphal onwards.

The story may, indeed, have been apocryphal, but I accepted it as true. It was far more interesting.

He was proud, funny, devoted to the Division, kind and at all times passionately loyal to his King. He was, I imagine, in his early forties and had a wife and three sons in the hills of Nepal and I can only hope that he got back to them safely in the end.

And forgave me for leaving him behind.

*   *   *

There is a profound difference between being 'alone' and 'lonely'.

I was both for the first few days after my arrival in the Division, stuck in one or other of the three bleak little villas which constituted 'A' Mess. My brother officers were perfectly civil at all times, but there was a clear feeling that I was an outsider among a group of people who had fought together, and suffered heavy casualties doing so, in bitter and costly battles up on the Assam-Burma border, which they had secured against the Japanese.

I knew nothing of their war, they knew nothing of mine in Europe. I spoke English only, no Urdu or Malayan. We had absolutely nothing in common. The problems which they found in Java were not what they had expected at all. It was by no means (as *I* had cheerfully thought on my LST) simply a matter of being a 'policeman' and shunting POWs and Dutch internees back to Singapore and doing, as I had been told earlier, a simple Red Cross job.

It was far graver than that.

The Indonesians wanted to be rid of the Dutch, and freedom from colonial rule: they were determined to get it at all costs, and the costs were awesomely heavy.

Fully armed, by the surrendered Japanese, they harassed the Division at every turn. It is all familiar today – but then, forty years ago, it was a frightening and new manifestation.

Many Indonesians felt that independence would be a disaster too soon, and wanted the protection of their Dutch masters; the main body, however, were determined on complete freedom now, and the main body was the Mass.

Every building was covered with patriotic graffiti screaming for 'Bloodshed or Freedom!', and the blood flowed.

Nightly the explosion of bombs planted by 'extremists' (as they then were called) rocked the city. Machine-guns stuttered and chattered on the deserted suburban streets around the perimeter, fires drenched the starry nights with orange and crimson light, and the crump and crash of mortars and grenades was a familiar sound at any time of the day or night.

There was a lot of Japanese ammunition about, which they had thoughtfully handed around, and a lot of people only too ready and willing to use it against the hated, suppressive colonialists.

This included the unfortunate British, there only to do a humanitarian job before returning home after a long and cruel war. The Division had sustained heavy losses in Burma, and were still to suffer a thousand and a half more casualties before repatriation came in what, they honestly thought, was someone else's affair.

So really it was little wonder that I wandered about feeling like a leper with his bell. I didn't fit, had not been expected, no one knew what to do with me, and quite frankly had neither the interest nor inclination to suggest anything I could do; they were much too preoccupied with the bloody job in hand, which had taken them by surprise as much as it had taken me. No one had expected such an involvement. However, my irritation and despair grew daily.

I had crossed the Indian Ocean in, as Nan had suggested, a

walnut shell, and had arrived, if not absolutely breathless with eagerness to die, at least with a willingness to do any job I could to help. But it seemed to me, in my over-sensitive state, that I was politely rebuffed at every turn and could very well moulder sadly away, forgotten in this distressing existence.

So, I sat about in the prim little room, writing letters to my parents and filling in my journal, or in the messroom in the villa next door. I watched Goa cleaning my brasses, my boots and his *kukri*, read month-old copies of *Punch* or *The Field*, and sometimes looked through the modest, two-sheet, Divisional paper, *The Fighting Cock* (which was the Division's insignia). It contained local news: '28 MURDERED IN DOWNED DAKOTA', and foreign news lifted from radio reports: "VIDKUN QUISLING GETS DEATH!'; there were a crossword puzzle, sports results (local) and, perhaps most important of all as it was to turn out for me, a correspondence column which aired Divisional moans and complaints: 'CIGARETTE SHORT-AGE AT YMCA!'

Lally had always said that the Good Lord helps those who help themselves. I decided to give her advice a try and one morning, after a week of this mournful, useless, isolated and lonely existence, I sat down at the tin garden table in my dreary little room and typed a stingingly bitter letter of sup-pressed anger and complaint, threw all caution to the wind, and sent it to *The Fighting Cock*.

To my absolute astonishment it was published the next day under a banner headline: 'WHY THE BOYCOTT?'

Which was not what I had intended.

Suffused with embarrassment, I thought it prudent to keep to my wretched little room and skip lunch in the Mess that day.

Lally had been right, as it happened.

My life was changed overnight.

Within twenty-four hours I had been given an empty office, right alongside that of *The Fighting Cock* itself, stuck up my trade-plate on the door – APIS – got hold of a desk and two chairs, opened up my portable typewriter (looted in

Hamburg), and settled down to a new, if slightly apprehensive, existence.

There was just one small problem.

No one needed a photographic interpreter. Which is what I was. There were no reconnaissance planes nearer than Singapore; no one was flying photographic sorties anyway because they were all too occupied in flying out the P O Ws and internees.

What, then, should I do? Having made such an unseemly fuss, and drawn attention to myself in a perfectly reprehensible manner, I knew that I had to try and justify myself. I did the only thing I knew how to do under the circumstances: I wrote reams of stories, articles, poems and God only knows what other bits of trivia and bombarded the office next door with them.

My talents were pretty limited, but this was the only way I knew in which to try and join my new Division – it was a case of desperation.

To my intense relief a number of 'pieces' were accepted (the genial editor later admitted that he was short of 'stuff') and in time I started to do so well that I began to write under two separate names: 'Icarus' and 'Bantam'. I can think of no good reason for choosing either name – perhaps I didn't? It is very probable that they were chosen for me. 'Icarus' was supposed to be fairly heavy and have some political comment or content.

One might have called it 'The Leader' if one had been unwise. Heaven knows what it was really: it certainly wasn't political, for I have the political, and historical, knowledge of an aphid, and there was hardly any 'comment', but somehow it passed muster, and by pinching bits and pieces here and there from radio transcripts of foreign news I managed to get by reasonably enough.

'Bantam' was altogether a much lighter exercise, dealing with anything and everything, and in particular large chunks of 'nostalgia' relating to Suffolk fields, Sussex Downs and so on. 'Icarus' and 'Bantam' and I took off.

By this curious method, using *The Fighting Cock* and my Hamburg typewriter as a sort of Trojan horse, I invaded Troy – or, to be accurate, 23rd Indian Division. I was very proud indeed. I had never, in my life, been fully integrated into a fighting Division before. Within a year of landing at Tandjoeng Priok, wreathed in rubber smoke and the scent of spices, I had joined Radio Batavia as an English Announcer, produced an ambitious (and quite unoriginal) revue with which we reopened the Concordia Hall in Bandoeng, fallen seriously (and fruitlessly, as it turned out) in love with my cool lady interpreter-secretary, become editor of *The Fighting Cock*, assuming full power, and, in an act of amazing generosity and patience on his part, become the ADC to Major-General Hawthorn, DSO, CB, and Commander of Java.

You really couldn't say I hadn't tried.

And very grateful I was that in looking after myself the Good Lord had showered me with such amazing bounty.

If life is (as I think it is) a long corridor lined with many doors and turnings, then that first miserable week in 'A' Mess had found me standing at a fearsome crossing. Which way to go? Hopelessness had almost swamped me.

Backwards was impossible (3033 had long since returned to Calcutta anyway). The way ahead was dark with alarming shadows; the turnings left and right were just the same, but did have the advantage of a few glimmers of light along the way – not very many, but just enough to keep the last vestiges of courage flickering in the draught of uncertainty and trepidation.

Hopelessness, at twenty-four, is something one does not submit to for long, so I made my brave turn, wrote my letter of outrage and complaint, drew notice to myself (ill-mannered to be sure, but essential at that time), and with the opportunity which its publication offered me I got down to the job with the only tools I had to hand, the modest gifts which I had acquired directly from my almost forgotten life years before in the theatre.

*　　　*　　　*

143

There was to be a party in 'A' Mess. Someone was going home on repatriation. Any excuse for a party would do in those ugly days.

The General had said that he would attend. Throwing the Mess President and his committee into a state of despairing hysteria. The dank villa was simply that: a dank villa. With trestle tables and board floors.

I offered to decorate it, and did so, with lavish, if inaccurate, murals of the Eiffel Tower, the Place de la Concorde, the Arc de Triomphe and groups of naked ladies whom I stuck all over the place at little café tables under Parisian parasols. From a distance of forty years I find it hard to believe that I could have managed to create an 'Oo! La! La!' feeling of 'Gay Paree' in that awful house, but I do know that I rid it, to some extent anyway, of the ponderous gloom, which at all times prevailed, of a Harley Street waiting-room swamped with the smell of stale curry and fried spam.

The General seemed impressed.

Tall, imposing, no nonsense and a sharp eye.

'You do this business?'

'Sir.'

'Ah. Gather you write for *The Cock*?'

'Sir.'

'Journalist were you? In civvy life?'

'An actor, sir.'

'Oh Christ!'

'Sir.'

'Well, it takes all kinds, I suppose.'

'Sir.'

'Know where I can pump ship?'

'Sir.'

'In Europe, were you? France, Germany?'

'Sir.'

They were dancing 'The Lambeth Walk' with a great deal of laughter and shouts of 'Oi!'.

'Bloody whirling dervishes,' he said.

'Sir.'

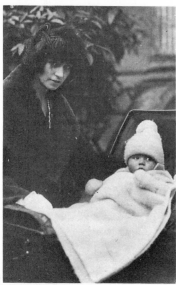

left With Mama, 1921.

below With my parents and Elizabeth, Swanage, Dorset, 1928.

above Some of the 'pretend' kith and kin. The cottage, 1931. Aunt Gladys, Uncle Bertie, Mama, Aunt Coggley, Uncle John, me – apparently smoking a cigarette – Elizabeth in the foreground.

left On the day of my commission, 1941.

below The 'office' truck, Normandy, July 1944.

above On the Hoogley River, Calcutta.
Taken by Nan the day before I sailed for Java,
1945.

left Nan under the deodars, Sikkim border,
September 1945.

below Flt/Lt Christopher Greaves,
Lüneburg, Germany, 1945.

Columbia Pictures

above, left What six months in the Hollywood Dream Factory can do to a boy from West End Lane, Hampstead. Hollywood, Columbia Pictures, 1959.

above, right Ten years later, as von Aschenbach. The first shot on *Death in Venice*, Hôtel des Bains, Venice.

top   With Kathleen Tynan at Santa Monica, January 1981.

bottom   Glenda Jackson and myself on the set, Hollywood, 1981.

top   The presentation to me, by the Teamsters Union, of a pearl-handled revolver (actually a cigarette lighter) on the last day of work. Hollywood Boulevard, Los Angeles, 1981.

bottom   Forwood, Nicholas and Rosalind Bowlby, and Bendo, July 1979.

top   Norah Smallwood on the terrace, May 1980.

bottom   The house and terrace from the east, with suburbia creeping all around, June 1984.

St Andrews Photograph

The 'capping' ceremony, St Andrews University, 4 July 1985.

He followed me up the stairs to the only lavatory, its door decorated with a moderately indecent lady in suspender belt and long gloves, at which he stared for a few silent moments, snorted, and then pushed inside.

I was waiting for him, hands correctly clasped behind me, feet apart, at ease in the right manner, when he returned.

He grunted, rearranged his bush jacket, flicked a fingernail in the direction of my chest as he retied the stock at his throat.

'Five ribbons up, I see. Action?'

'Sir.'

'Arranged all this fandango too?'

'Helped, sir.'

'And her on the door, ummm?'

'Sir.'

He regarded me from beneath shaggy brows for a long moment, pulled his lower lip down with his finger and thumb, then started down the stairs.

I followed him dutifully.

'Know how to sit a table?'

I thought that he had said 'Know how to sit at table', so I said 'Sir' again.

He turned at the foot of the stairs under a giant bunch of inflated condoms which floated above his head in a festive manner; I'd painted faces on them.

'Know any *other* words?'

'Sir?'

'Any other words? Apart from "Sir"?'

'I beg your pardon, sir . . . I was minding my P's and Q's. You are my first general.'

He grinned suddenly. 'I may well be your last.'

'Yes, sir.'

'Apart from all your other talents, lavishly displayed here, I take it then that you have never performed the functions of an ADC?'

'Yes, sir. I have.'

'Have! For whom, if you are not familiar with my rank?'

'Brigadier Wade. North Grampians, sir.'

'Brigadier! Bloody Brigadier! What the hell was *he* doing with an ADC? Brigadiers don't HAVE ADCs, for God's sake!'

'Well, he had me, sir. More of a dogsbody, really, than anything else. Map reading, fixing his appointments, the cars, all kinds of arrangements . . . that sort of thing . . .'

'I KNOW what an ADC is supposed to do. And sitting a table?'

Then I knew what he had meant. At my first effort, two years before, at sitting a table, I had got myself into a muddle about who sat where according to rank and age and the rest of it. We were in a commandeered hotel in Worthing, and the linchpin of the whole evening was a tiresome, but important, ageing Lieutenant-General vaguely connected to the Royal Family. His ADC had advised me, by message, that his General was stone deaf in the right ear and that his only passion was stag-hunting. Which was a great help. Brigadier Wade advised me to sit on his right-hand side and encourage him to talk about stags, and not to interrupt beyond murmurs of awe and respect.

'If you do that he'll tell me after dinner what a damned good talker you are,' he said. Which is precisely what happened.

So sitting a table, I knew, was important.

'I *can* sit a table, sir. We did a lot of entertaining in the Brigade.'

The General grunted, pulled off the folded stock at his throat. 'Too bloody hot for this. What's your name?'

I told him; he looked baffled. '*All* of it?'

'Yes, sir.'

'Something shorter? What brings you to heel?'

'Pip, sir.'

'Pretty silly as well. All right!' He handed me his sweat-sodden stock, ran a large hand through thinning hair. 'Pip, hop off and get me something cool to drink. A John Collins with plenty of ice. And don't lose that!'

He turned about and strode through the leaping and barking 'Lambeth Walk' dancers, leaving me with his sweaty stock which I held with the reverence due only to a fragment of the Turin Shroud.

A few days later I was informed that I was to pack up my belongings and move down to a small villa next door to the General's house in Box Laan.

I was 'on trial' as an ADC.

If the news astonished me, it absolutely overwhelmed Goa.

'It's not sure,' I said, shaking my head to emphasize the possibility.

'*Stay* along him,' said Goa. It was an order, not a request.

Even if the promotion was only temporary, and he seemed determined that it would not be so, his position was greatly enhanced in the Division. For a whole day all one could see of him was a furious polishing, and the blinding flash of golden teeth as he prepared our kit, his *kukri* and a cheap brass photograph frame with a picture of his wife and three small boys.

The batman-driver to the General's ADC was perfectly permissible, in his eyes, and socially he could go no higher; it was a fitting job for a fighting Gurkha.

We moved to the shabby little villa which had one large room downstairs, two bedrooms up and three giggling Malayan girls who were there to clean and cook. Goa arranged his belongings in the garage and was well content, especially when he discovered my pea-green Buick coupé, commandeered from the Transport Pool because we were short of military transport.

He set his hat at a slight angle and drove as arrogantly as if he had Mountbatten in the back.

Things had changed indeed.

We had only one enemy, it seemed, and that was the General's own batman, who was an Indian and who disliked us both on sight; he spent a good deal of his time peering through the shutters on my verandah, or looking across the weedy, bamboo'd garden from their house to mine, through binoculars. It irritated me but I realized instantly that my irritation must never show in front of Goa; fortunately it did not, and his *kukri* remained in its belt round his waist, the Indian batman kept his head, and I, owing entirely to the boundless patience and forbearance of Major-General Hawthorn, managed to keep mine. And my job.

A week earlier life had seemed pretty bleak – the corridor frighteningly long, dark and confusing – but I had found the courage to make a decisive turn at the right moment, and managed to keep on track, mainly because I was determined not to fail, but also because, many years before, in my father's study, I had taught myself to type, with two fingers and a thumb, on his black, upright Underwood.

CHAPTER
6

The transport skidded to an abrupt halt as the first mortar hit a truck some way ahead in the convoy.

It exploded in a ball of smoke and fire.

We were some miles out of Soekaboemi on the road from Batavia, going up to Bandoeng in the hills.

The convoy commander came running through the oily smoke, waving his hands above his head.

'Road-block! Looks as if they'll make a fight for it, take cover!' He ran on waving and shouting.

I knew the drill and left the car like a rocket, throwing myself into a narrow drainage ditch running alongside a banana plantation. I pressed myself into the earth as if I could have pulled it around me like a blanket.

The hermit crab: shell-less.

I lay rigidly still for a few moments. Up on the road I heard feet running, distant shouts, rapid bursts of machine-gun fire, then silence. I looked up and saw, with some embarrassment, Goa walking casually from the car, his rifle held aloft. He slid down the side of the bank into the ditch and knelt upright, close to my prone body. He was humming mindlessly, nodded cheerfully when I moved my head to look at him.

Grinning at my unseemly haste.

There was another splintering crash somewhere on the right, but I couldn't see what was happening because my hands had instantly covered my head and were pressing it deep into prickly grass and smelly mud. However, I could hear the ripping noise of hot metal fragments whipping through the frilly banana leaves, and the 'clonks' which they made as they hit the bodywork of the trucks and cars on the road.

For a few moments there was absolute stillness; no feet ran on the rough road, no one was shouting, no shots were fired. It was the stillness of a held breath. Inches from my face, in the murky shade of a broad-leaved plant, a large frog with amber eyes and pulsing throat sat staring at me unblinkingly.

I looked up again cautiously and was gratified to see that Goa, for all his enviable cool, was also buried face down in the mud, hands over his head, hat lying beside him.

For an instant I thought that he might have been hit by the hot metal shards, but even as I tentatively made a move with my hand to touch him, he looked up suddenly, hands over his ears, grinning gold.

Another mortar sailed across and exploded on the far side of the road. Steel rattled against the transport and the air was thick with cordite and smoke. We ducked again, and I stared at the frog, which had not budged, as a spiral of torn leaves and twigs pattered down about us. A fourth mortar crumped down somewhere up the road, towards the rear of the convoy. They had got our range; I was grateful that I had pitched into the right ditch. Goa grunted, and his grin had gone.

I hated, at that moment, with a consuming hatred, the idiot Major in Calcutta who had summonsed me to my briefing on 'what to do in Java'. He had a red-veined nose, a bushy moustache, little, plump, over-manicured hands which he held before him, delicately clasped together, like a sleek, trim, fat hamster.

It was fairly clear that he had never left Calcutta throughout his tour of duty except, perhaps, to 'take a spot of leave' up in Simla or Darjeeling; he'd probably never even left the fussy office in which we sat under the clickety-clack of his ceiling fan, and he knew as much about Java as I did.

A desk-wallah. India was littered with his kind: they usually ended up with an OBE and a bungalow in Camberley or Cranleigh.

'It'll be pretty cushy, you know. You won't fire a single shot,' he had said, the plump little fingers folding and unfolding like a sea-anemone. '*Not* even in self defence, got that? Consider yourself a policeman, nothing more. Behave with caution and restraint at all times. It is not our quarrel. That's a Dutch problem. It's their look-out not ours, let them sort it out. If they are going through a revolution it's got nothing to do with *us*. All *we* do is maintain order and get the POWs out and home.'

How, I remember wondering, does one 'maintain order' during a revolution without firing a shot. By waving white flags and saying 'Excuse me'?

He saw my look of doubt, which he instantly took for silent insubordination.

'Now, look here! The Supremo doesn't want us to make any *ripples*, get it? Least said, soonest mended, that sort of thing. Just do our job and get out. Leave the Dutch to do the tidying up, it's their affair, not ours, remember that. Any more questions?'

I hadn't asked any.

'Where do I report to? And to whom?'

He briskly told me, handed me a sheet of paper. My Movement Order.

'What do I do when I get there? Am I still Air Photographic?'

He looked at his watch, buttoned a pocket, reached for his cap and cane on the desk beside him. It was time for 'tiffin' at the Saturday Club.

'No idea. You'll soon find out. Replacement, I'd imagine, frankly. We're having quite a lot of casualties, I hear. Quite a rumpty-tum down there.'

Hardly to be wondered at if one was unable to fire a shot; even in self-defence. All his instructions went overboard the very instant, almost, that I set foot on the dockside at Tandjoeng Priok anyway.

During the war in Europe I had never had to use my revolver, which was probably just as well. It had rested comfortably in its holster at my hip, uncleaned and dusty, and was never drawn in anger or fear. In any case, it aimed low, so that when I fired it, as I sometimes did for practice so to speak, it kicked up scatters of gravel at the foot of the target, but did no other damage whatsoever.

Frankly I was far better off with a .303 rifle, but these were not issued to officers.

However, in Java things were different. I quickly learned that my revolver had to be clean, and brilliantly oiled, at all times – and loaded. At the start of my duties, in the first couple of weeks, I even slept with the thing beside my pillow; in a constant state of dread that perhaps I had not applied the safety-catch and that I should be found one morning by Goa like a suicide.

But in time one settled down to life with a loaded gun quite easily, and eventually, as the immediate sense of unrest and preparedness began to slacken and Batavia came more and more under our control, and the 'extremists' pulled out to positions beyond the city, my revolver remained in its holster, clean, ready but unloaded, and even though I took it nightly into my bed like a teddy bear it was attached to its belt, and the bullets were in the pouch.

I fortunately never had to use it.

However, the nights, and often the days, were spasmodically interrupted by sudden bursts of rifle fire, of grenades exploding, and all military dumps or public buildings were still irresistible targets for the restless, angry 'extremists' and supporters who smuggled themselves through the road-blocks into town with ease. And we fired back: chucked grenades, strafed suspicious positions, bombed strong-points, and generally gave as good as we received.

So much for the Supremo's desire that we should not make ripples. We did not.

We made waves.

So much for the hamster-Major in Calcutta sweating it out for his OBE.

He wasn't lying face downwards in a stinking ditch beneath a cluster of rapidly shredding banana trees.

From a distance came the sound of heavy-machine-gun fire, followed by the urgent crackle of small-arms. The machine-guns made a good deal of noise; and then everything stopped again and the silence fell.

I sat up and saw Goa scraping mud out of the buckles of his gaiters with a piece of twig. Another rattle of small-arms fire, this time irregular and further off, as if they were pulling back; I put on my cap and crawled up the side of the bank to look along the road.

Smoke drifted from the truck which had been hit at the beginning of the attack, there was no immediate sign of human life; and then one or two cautious heads appeared along the edge of the ditch, alert, expecting another mortar. All seemed calm; I started to walk along the road, Goa hard at my heels.

There wasn't much to see: the burning truck, a scatter of metal, some charred cloth. Someone gave orders for a half-track to move down and try to nudge the truck into the side of the road so that the convoy could proceed, and I almost tripped over the shapeless lump under a blanket which had been the driver. His five passengers had been carried down to one of the ambulances which were travelling with us.

'Funny really,' said the Scots M O. 'The bastards usually go for the ambulances first thing. They must have misjudged it this time: just a short, sharp, wee attack.' There were bright splashes of blood on the road at his feet; he slammed the doors of the ambulance.

'Buggers,' he said.

The convoy commander came fussing down the line of transport. 'Must get a move on. Come along, don't all stand about . . . we've got to make the harbouring area before dusk and the day's going fast. Come along now! Everybody on the move . . . jump to it, that's the ticket!'

A nanny: we knew that we had to make the harbouring area before dusk, and that he was a man under strain repeating phrases automatically, a reflex action.

As I turned to go back to my vehicle I saw two men start to drag the body of the driver towards the second of the ambulances, an arm fell free of the shrouding blanket, trailing a dark hand in the dust.

His day had gone already.

Windscreens which had been shattered by mortar splinters were smashed out, people began to clamber on board, motors revved up, doors slammed.

Goa had gone ahead and was standing by the staff car adjusting his belt and humming.

'Think you'd better go up to Bandoeng with the advance party,' the General had said. 'Scout around for a decent billet for me. We'll be up there until the place is settled, so make sure we are comfortable and protected, and not in the middle of everyone else. Find a good house, get a lift with the B M of X X Brigade, he's a decent feller, show you the ropes.'

And so there I was, on the Bandoeng convoy with a taciturn Major in a staff car and 'extremists' all over the place.

We started up; ahead one of the half-tracks pulled out into the road and courageously took the lead. We passed the still smouldering truck lying forlornly in the ditch.

It was not what you might call a race for the harbouring area: our pace was that of an ambling camel, and there was a good reason for this – we had to follow the half-track, and the half-track driver had to keep his eyes open for mines which the 'extremists' laid like molehills anywhere and everywhere on the winding road. They were thorough but not very expert, so that the mines were fairly easy to see – as long as the light was right and you hadn't already hit one.

It was not a comfortable, or relaxing, journey and the Major from X X Brigade was an Indian Army regular and disinclined to talk, unless one knew all about horses; but I didn't, so we sat in silence until he took out a mouth organ and, knocking the fluff and dust from it against his knee, began to drone mournfully through a selection of Ivor Novello melodies.

At least that's what he said they were, but I was hard put to recognize much of Mr Novello's music, since he played in one key only with astonishing monotony.

As we climbed, the land fell gently away to the vast chequerboard of the plains, criss-crossed with dykes and raised banks, squared with paddyfields, stands of sugarcane and banana plantations. The water in the paddies glinted in the fading sun and melted away into the far distance in varying shades of blue. From the palest petrol haze to violet and darkest indigo. Beyond, and high above, a shadowy fretwork against the lavender sky, the mountains hung flat-topped with slumbering volcanoes.

It was not really a landscape of the heart: that, for me, was in Sussex, with its soft green woods, and clustered villages, its chalk-scarred downs, and curving fields of plough, creamy with clay, regular as corduroy; its gently winding rivers and streams rippling towards the sea through fields of buttercups and meadowsweet, its crow-crowded elms along the hedge-rows, its white roads cutting through high hawthorn banks under a sky wide, clear and as blue as flax. A far cry from this land beyond the staff car windows.

Clusters of coco-palms stuck up like feather dusters at the edges of burned and abandoned *kampongs*. Sago-palms stood in neat groves, with kanari trees here and there, and flowering bushes of brilliant colour which I had never seen before. But there was no sign of life anywhere. Everyone had fled, and the land lay still, idle, untended.

No white ibex on the dykes, no water buffalo pulling slowly through the paddy fields, no children running; a dead land-scape.

Sometimes a flock of pigeons, or a swoop of bronze-green parakeets, would fly in skimming bounds from tree to tree quarrelling and chattering, and once I thought that I saw a black pig swerve from the roadside and blunder away into the bushes; otherwise everything was still, deserted, and the silence of apprehension fell across the lush, green, watery land like a vapour.

The BM of XX Brigade stopped playing, shook the spittle from his mouth organ on to the floor at our feet.

' "Shine through My Dreams",' he announced gruffly. 'Rather good, what?'

'Fine. Yes. Good.'

'Got a bit lost somewhere there in the middle; difficult part.

But I don't think you noticed, eh? I covered it up pretty well. All by ear, you know? I've got the record if you'd care to hear it one day?'

I was slightly surprised that he should have asked, but thanked him anyway. He started sucking and blowing again. Paused. Grunted. Thumped the instrument hard against the heel of his hand, started off once more.

Goa turned and grinned at me, wagging his head in silent dismay. The moaning sound in the closed car was almost insupportable, and my anxiety began to increase as the light faded gently across the empty land.

We passed a European house set back from the road, the red-tiled roof sagging, fans of black smoke scorched above each window, the shadows beginning to deepen in a thick grove of high bamboo, swaying lightly against the darkening sky.

At least I had the consolation, I thought, that whatever happened next I could at least fire a shot to defend myself. The idiot hamster-Major loomed before me, my hatred blurring his plump, porcine face: all that I clearly remembered of him was his fussy little hands.

Then we all careened to a stop, against the ambulance in front, as a burst of firing broke out once again.

The mouth organ, mercifully, stopped; we leapt out of the car and took cover in the bamboos and a giant datura, heavy with white trumpet flowers.

The firing continued for about twenty minutes, but there were no mortars, and we just crouched where we were, revolvers in hand, Goa kneeling with his rifle at the ready. I thought this was a pretty stupid way of setting out to find the General a house. In time the firing stopped; my knuckles, I noticed to my surprise, were shining white over the butt of my gun. I pushed it into its holster and pretended that I was not shaking.

With a little careful manoeuvring, and rough handling, we managed to disengage ourselves from the back of the ambulance; there was not much damage – one door was stove in, and we'd lost a headlamp and dented the radiator. One of the wounded, jolted cruelly by the sudden lurching halt, began to cry out in pain. A high, sharp, howl: 'Ieeeee! Ieeeeee!' I ran, crouching, along the line of trucks to find the MO.

The shaking, which had surprised me, had also shamed and angered me: it was no way to behave. Running down the open road restored my confidence. If I got hit it wouldn't be while crouching in trembling timidity.

'I think they've scarpered,' said the MO, as a medical orderly clambered into the damaged ambulance with a first-aid sack. 'No one hurt; we were lucky. The shots went wild.'

We eventually got everything sorted out and moved off again at camel's pace, alert, listening for any signs of another ambush; but there were none, and we reached the harbouring area just as night was falling without further incident.

It had been, by and large, a quiet day: only two, short 'wee attacks' as the MO had said earlier.

'I don't know where the bloody RAF got to,' said the BM of XX Brigade. '*Supposed* to patrol this road with a convoy on it . . . I suppose we weren't large enough for them. So damned choosy . . . *Never* there when you need them. I think that I must have dropped my mouth organ.' He was patting his jacket anxiously. 'Have you seen it?'

'No. Probably fell out of your pocket back there in the bamboo.'

'How *could* it! It was in my ruddy hand when we stopped – have a look on the floor, or under the seat, will you . . .'

We found it and he put it into his pocket, buttoned the flap firmly.

'Be absolutely lost without this. Terribly important. Good for morale, what?' He fortunately didn't wait for my reply, but turned to collect his map-case and papers.

A quiet trip, with only minor incidents. One dead and five wounded.

The Bandoeng convoy was often far more costly. We had, in truth, been lucky.

In October, seventeen vehicles, carrying civilians and

POWs, were attacked: the convoy commander was killed, two hundred women and children were taken off by the 'extremists' and never seen again.

By that standard, today wasn't much to write home about.

So I didn't bother; however, two days later we got a three-line mention in *The Fighting Cock* under 'Local Events', followed by a glowing report of a hockey match between Div. HQ and 24th Indian Field Ambulance.

There was no score on either side.

★　　★　　★

If the General's house bore a striking resemblance to the Hoover factory on the Western Avenue I was unaware of it at the time. I don't think that I had ever seen the Hoover factory then: it wasn't until some years later, driving past it on my way to work at Pinewood Studios, that I would feel a sudden pull of memory, and remember the house in Bandoeng. Set on the edge of a high escarpment, overlooking the plains below and the heat-hazed mountain range in the distance, approached by a long tree-lined avenue, across an immensity of weedy grass, long since scabbed with seedling bushes and trees and tufts of whippy cane, it stood in concrete splendour. Compact as a set of shoeboxes, surmounted by a high, square tower (which contained the water tanks), a roof garden with pergolas, arched-trellis bowers and a flag-pole.

Exactly what I felt the General would like: and fitting for his position as the Commander of Java. A 'decent billet' in fact.

Once upon a time it had been white, striking hard against the deep blue of the sky, a dazzle of neo–Bauhaus (plus Chinese) elevations which would have shocked Gropius but delighted me by the audacity of its Sino-Teutonic mix.

It had been built, I was informed, for a Chinese merchant who prudently fled before the Japanese arrived, and it had been left empty during the Occupation. It was now mouldering slowly away in abandoned decay. I was convinced that it could be restored to its former glory, that the General would like it, and, above all, that I could get the job done.

A 'decent billet' for the General. Java, 1946

A 'decent billet' for the ADC

The site was superb; so was the swimming-pool, hacked out of the cliff-face far below, which hung over the plain like an enormous turquoise bidet. During the barren years only nature had been bountiful, creeping across the once-trim lawns, the gravel drives and paths, invading the oval lily-pool before the house, mossing the iron fountain which might have been a Giacometti, but which was not, and smothering the flagged path which led down, across the grass, to a hidden guest pavilion, drowned now by bougainvillaea, a giant datura and a tall grove of bamboos, each as thick as a shin, which I instantly coveted for myself. The whole set-up was perfect.

I could be near the General, but not too near; we would be self-contained, easy to protect and 'not in the middle of everything else', as he had instructed.

I stood, I well remember, in the still heat of the afternoon and watched butterflies as large as saucers flap about the datura with indolent grace, saw birds of astonishing brilliance, and found, under the branches of a giant banyan tree behind the pavilion, clusters of flying foxes hanging like old raincoats, in the diluted light which filtered through the leathery leaves.

There was a familiar scent of wet dog: musty, damp, animal. They watched me with eyes as bright as cut steel: motionless, ears pricked, wings folded about them like the ribs of an umbrella.

Umbrellas, raincoats, wet dogs: the half-remembered sights and smells of distant childhood.

A signal was despatched to the General to say that his house had been found but that a certain amount of work must be done to it before his arrival. The next day I had delivered to me, at seven in the morning, fifty Japanese prisoners accompanied by a sullen officer who never stopped saluting. A tiresome, and automatic, gesture which he, fortunately, discarded.

The General had made his orders on the treatment of surrendered Japanese perfectly clear. They were to clean the streets, and perform all menial tasks required; the officers were to work with the men; they were to double to and from their labours at all times, and if they were some distance from their place of work, which might therefore restrict their hours of effort, they had to start doubling earlier. They stood to attention in five rows of ten, the officer stiff beside them, arms at his sides. Through a Tamil, who spoke some Japanese and had once been their prisoner and cruelly tortured, instructions were given, and their work began.

The house was stripped down and scrubbed, lawns were cleared and mown (with garden shears and pairs of scissors), bushes and canes were hacked up, the avenue of trees pruned and trimmed, the gravel drive weeded inch by agonizing inch, the lily-pool and the swimming-pool restored to their former glory, and two Dutch cannons which flanked the iron gates of the main entrance to the estate were rediscovered beneath years of smothering vegetation and burnished to such a brilliance that they shone like silver and one could easily read the year in which they were cast: 1709.

It took them, in all, I suppose, about fourteen days: at the double.

Which made the General impatient.

They were frighteningly thorough, swarming across the grounds clipping and pruning, uprooting, scrubbing, weeding, raking; pouring with sweat.

I watched them, half embarrassed, half loathing.

Naked, except for their loin-cloths and cotton peaked caps, wearing rubber boots with a curiously separated big toe, they received no quarter from seven in the morning until dusk fell, only being permitted one half-hour in which to rest, drink, and eat a handful of rice and a piece of boiled fish.

As the light began to fade in the sky, just before the sudden hush of sudden night, they were collected together and marched away by their sullen officer: at the double.

It was always a moment of supreme relief to me when they went. I disliked walking among them, being near, smelling the odour of sweat and straining flesh. If I approached them they would instantly cease work and spring upright, nodding and bowing, standing stiffly to attention, or else, which was even worse, they would cringe in humiliating servility, hissing all the while like demented geese, eyes dulled with defeat, mouths wide in grins as fixed as in rigor mortis.

Ugly, abject little men these, who had ridden their bikes across the Causeway and defeated the greatest bastion in the East, who had spread like bubonic plague from China to the borders of India, swamped Burma, Siam, Malaya and the Philippines, who had killed savagely, tortured brutally without a shred of compassion, bound their prisoners like cord-wood and burned them alive, beheaded them, buried them still living, imprisoned men, women and children under conditions, as I had seen, which defied even the most depraved of imaginations, force-marched the defeated to Burma to build an impossible railway where they met their deaths in thousands from disease and deliberate starvation.

How then could I have compassion?

Standing in the blaze of noon watching them at work, their nimble, expert fingers frantically combing the gravel paths for a blade of grass, a crumpled leaf, sweat running into eyes half closed with exhaustion, dribble looping at their chins from slack lips and parched mouths, I could feel no shred of pity.

Embarrassment, after the first two days, drained away: only loathing remained. Superimposed over the vision of these grovelling, bow-legged creatures sweating in the equatorial sun, another vision ran through my mind like an unbroken loop of film, repeating itself continuously. I could see, almost more clearly than the ape-like figures before me, the Circle Stalls, the shabby red plush, the lights dimming in the great chandelier above, and hear, with acutely remembered despair, the words of the song I had so detested long ago:

> 'On a tree by a river
> A little tom-tit,
> Sang, "Willow,
> Titwillow,
> Titwillow . . ." '

*   *   *

The Dutch were proud of Bandoeng, with good reason.

A pleasant town of wide tree-lined boulevards, elegant public buildings and a fine hotel called The Savoy, it was set in the cool hills, some two hundred miles from Batavia, surrounded by neat suburbs of expensive villas and bungalows.

It was also completely surrounded by the 'extremists' who occupied a neighbouring hilltop suburb, or garden city, called Lembang, from which they were able to dominate the entire town and lob mortar bombs and shells indiscriminately into the streets whenever the fancy took them. Which was almost every day.

Making life complicated and dangerous for everyone; and everyone consisted of two brigades, Divisional HQ, plus 45,000 internees and POWs who had fled the camps and hoped to find safety and repatriation.

It was surrounded, under siege and bursting at the seams.

The only way in or out of the town was by road, hence the convoys and the constant patrolling of the RAF, or by air from the one airfield down on the plain at Andir, which we hung on to with grim determination and a constant casualty list.

It is a fact of life that things reach a peak, level out, and then seem to spill away. One is often taken unawares: it happens gently.

Bandoeng was for me the peak: it seemed that I had settled at last into a routine military life. Pleasant accommodation, a good job, a decent boss, *The Fighting Cock* to set up again, plus the fact that suddenly air photographs began to arrive (pretty late but, still, they arrived) from Singapore and now the sign on my office door read 'APIS' coupled with the name of the newspaper in large letters, and the word 'Editor' in becomingly more modest ones below.

The original, genial, editor had been left behind in Batavia to continue with his regular duties, and somehow it fell to my lot to take over his job. Along with the duties of an ADC. I was far from the lost, useless and ignored leper of some months before; there was almost too much to do now.

General Hawthorn was a fighting general; he believed, unlike some of his ilk, that he should be 'up front with the men' and as close to the fighting as possible. He took me along with him.

'Useful, Pip. See how things are at first hand, can't abide second-hand reports, get it all down in the paper as it happens. Be an eye-witness!'

An eye-witness, willy nilly, I became.

He had liked his house; he walked through the high marble rooms in heavy silence. A silence broken only by the crack of his boots on the floor, and the squeal of steel heel-tips as he swivelled around looking at the furnishings which I had collected from among the looted stuff stored by the Japanese in the go-downs by the railway. A fairly theatrical flourish: dressing the set. My held breath was freed by his nods of bemused approval.

'Good stuff. Well done,' and then he had turned and fixed me with his cold blue eyes. 'And where's my golf course?' he said.

My own humble abode caused him to snort with indignation: I had made an error in showing it to him, that was perfectly clear. Although far from pretentious, it was pleasant, with carved teakwood chairs and a large glass coffee table supported by nothing less than an aquarium, bejewelled with tiny fish caught in the river far below.

'Don't think that you are going to sit here on your arse playing a bloody banjo all day,' he said. 'You've got a job to do. *Agreed* to it – I don't want that forgotten!'

It was never forgotten, and there was never time to 'play a bloody banjo' all day, whatever that may have meant, because quite apart from the newspaper, which took up a great deal of time, the drawing of new maps of the town and surrounding area, pin-pointing from the air photographs gun emplacements, road-blocks, tank-traps, and so on, the 'extremists' saw to it that we were fully occupied by what were euphemistically known as 'incidents'.

They were not particularly agreeable affairs.

The Chinese suffered the most at first: their villages were put to the torch with sickening regularity, their people massacred without pity. The indolent, easy-going Indonesians were blind with hatred and bitter, bigoted vengeance towards their more industrious, and therefore more prosperous, neighbours, and burnt and pillaged without restraint.

Through blazing *kampongs*, in the scorching heat from burning bamboo and rattan, among bodies hacked to bits and left to roast and blister in fiery embers, the General and his staff walked in impotent anger. He grew progressively infuriated – I grew progressively more sickened by the sweet stench of decay and roasting flesh which clung to one's hair and clothing and which not even constant washing or bathing would eliminate. But there was little that we could ever do: the 'extremists' melted like wraiths into the sheltering landscape as the victors.

Once I saw what, at first, I took to be the body of a child lying in the swirling smoke and drifting ashes. It moved slightly, a limb twitched, an almost shapeless huddle attempted desperately to rise.

Not a child. A large cat chained to a flaming bamboo post, half dead, but clearly also partly alive. I took it back to the pavilion where, swaddled in bandages, it slowly recovered, nursed by myself and an amused, if reluctant, Goa, until one day, when the bandages were finally removed, a strange beast of extreme beauty stood weakly before us. Not a domestic cat this, a much larger creature with new-growing fur, like a lynx, tufts to its ears, and pads and claws of considerable size.

For some reason, which now I do not remember, it was named 'Ursula'. Although it was quite distinctly male. Although I have forgotten why we named it so absurdly, I did remember a giant ginger cat crucified to a garden fence, when I had seen pain and distress on a human face for the first time. I was to see it again and again in this strange, wasteful and vicious war.

After the Chinese it was the turn of the wretched Dutch colonials. Some, just released from the camps, imprudently made their way back to their homes in the outlying suburbs, trying with what remained of their looted belongings to restart their lives, only to lose them in acts of hysterical hatred and violence.

In a small villa, standing in what had once been a neat garden plot, smothered in a rampant, florid Dorothy Perkins rose, with a stubby palm standing in a circular grass-bed before two ugly little bow windows, just like any other suburban house in Eindhoven or Deventer, two elderly people lay sprawled in their blood, hacked to death by knives and machetes. The woman was lying in the kitchen, on her back, faded blue eyes staring wide with terror, a flowered skirt pulled high above thighs the colour of cold boiled macaroni, mottled with bruises and sores. She had put up a desperate fight, her hands shredded by the knives, her blood sprayed in elegant arcs across the tiled walls. The man lay face downwards in the sitting room, his balding head almost severed from his body, among a tumble of chairs, broken china and scattered gramophone records.

Above us the roof was burning, tiles cracked and exploded in the heat, and printed in crude capital letters across the damp-paper-peeling wall the jeering words: 'TIRENT IMPERLIST!'

The familiar, mindless slogan which was repeated wherever we came across an 'extremist incident' of this type.

This was to be the last of the many events of its kind I was to see: it was in fact the last straw for General Hawthorn.

Three days later an assault was launched on the hill-top estate of Lembang, which fell without very much resistance, and not long after the whole area south of the railway, which had harboured the main body of the 'extremist' group, and their guns and mortars, was cleared. The airfield was secured, and gradually some semblance of law and order was restored to the besieged town and a tremulous normality began to spread.

Shops and restaurants cautiously opened on Bragaweg, the main boulevard among the rubble and ruins of the buildings which had suffered during the bombing and shelling, and people began to start the job of clearing up. The internees, drawn, haggard, at the edge of starvation, were flown out to Batavia, and although there were still furious clashes in the villages along the main convoy route the town gradually eased back to an almost peacetime calm. I no longer slept with my revolver like a comforting, if angular, teddy bear, but kept it close at all times.

The peak had been reached, the levelling out began slowly, things began spilling away, bit by bit.

Little things at first.

Goa was stricken and lay moaning on his bed in the garage of the pavilion with a high fever.

Appendicitis was diagnosed and he was hurried off to casualty and replaced by a grim, unsmiling, unspeaking Gurkha called Kim, who found being a 'servant', even to the General's ADC, much below his dignity. He made it perfectly clear, from the start, that all he intended to do was to call me at 5.30 a.m. with a mug of tea, roll up my mosquito net, pull up the bed, clean any boots or belts or cap badges, and clear off.

Until the next day, when the same routine took place. In silence.

I took my meals down in 'A' Mess, the pavilion began to lose its attractions under fine coatings of dust, the fish died in the aquarium, the water became as thick as asparagus soup, and Ursula got fed only because I managed to scrounge bits and pieces from the Mess cooks.

My interpreter-secretary, Harri, complained daily that the place was beginning to show distinct signs of neglect.

'I haven't time to *dust* bloody furniture!'

'Well, give me something to do it with and I'll try. And we must throw the dead fish away, they smell.'

Harri was ravishingly beautiful: long legs, long hair, long neck – a sort of Modigliani creature; she detested housework and wasn't very good at it anyway.

'How long does it *take* to have an appendicitis?'

'Oh, I don't know. About three weeks . . . something like that.'

'Perhaps you ought to move back to "A" Mess . . . until Goa is better? Ummmm?'

'I can't take Ursula to "A" Mess, for God's sake!'

'So you keep in this place, this silly place, just for a wild cat?'

'I *like* this silly place; I *like* to be on my own. Not in "A" Mess.'

'You could be murdered by extremists, they can get into this house easily, all on one floor. Aren't you afraid?'

'Yes.'

'Well!'

'I stay here. I like it here. The grounds are patrolled day and night, and things are quiet now.'

She would begin humming under her breath, a sure sign of irritation, tossing her hair over her shoulders, thumping the cushions on the teakwood chairs with such force that dust spiralled up in clouds to resettle gently on the furniture which she had already made a brave attempt at dusting.

'Things are changing. You will see,' she said.

'What things are changing?'

'Ah ha! Things. You should look carefully. People are going away; new people are coming. The white-faces from Holland, the new boys. Soon you will all go, back on your repatriation, the Dutch army will take over.'

'You are so bloody sure! I suppose you've seen it all written in your loony old Tarot cards . . .'

'Oh! You are in a mood. I hate you in a mood. You are impolite. I will not speak to you while you are in your mood. You cannot see what is evident.'

But I could see. And I had seen; and the fact that she was reminding me that we would all be leaving disturbed and distressed me: I had no wish to leave.

And so we bickered, like any other couple who have become physically and mentally close to each other, affectionately

169

aware of each other's frailties and weaknesses. I had, for some time, convinced myself that I was deeply, permanently and irrevocably in love with her.

She put this notion of mine carefully aside, refusing to acknowledge it, accepting it merely as an emotional reflex which every man suffered during a war. She never for one moment, I know, took me as seriously as I took myself. She would smile shyly, shaking her head slowly from side to side as if she had heard it all long ago and many times, that she found it touching but just a little wearying.

However, she always listened to me tolerantly and let me argue with myself. I knew hardly anything about her, for she never offered information about herself or her past life. I knew only fragments which, like stalks of corn in a harvest field, I gleaned diligently.

But they didn't amount to much: I couldn't have made a quarter of a loaf from them. She once said that she was 'diluted Dutch', and when I pressed her, in laughter, for an explanation she flushed and said that she had a maternal grandmother who was Indonesian but a 'pure Dutch father: he was tall and very fine to look at'. Although this combination gave her great elegance and grace I knew, instinctively, that it distressed her profoundly.

I didn't even know exactly where she lived, or if her family had survived the Occupation. From some scattered corn-stalks I deduced that they had not; but I never asked, and she refused to speak more of them. I knew that she had a 'pleasant room with a nice Chinese family' in the Chinese Quarter but I was never allowed to go there with her, and when I dropped her off from work sometimes, at her insistence it was always vaguely some streets away from the house where she lived. She was determined to keep her private life apart from her life with me, and the Division. Harri was a 'loner' in every way. Something which I understood perfectly.

'You tell me that you do not like to be possessed, or to possess! Neither do I. So that is why we are beautifully matched. We understand each other very well,' she said.

But sometimes I was not altogether certain that we did.

'People, you know, Pip, always want to know too much about each other, and when they do, then they get bored with them and throw them away like an apple core. Finished! It is much more *enviable* to be like us; isn't it?'

I would agree because I was unable always to follow her logic. Her attitude to me, as the months went by, was at all times generous, loving, warm, lightly mocking, affectionate, sometimes half impatient, half amused, but always tolerant of my gaucheness and my sudden enormous leaps of enthusiasm or deep plunges into black depressions.

She managed me very well, and we laughed together, and, more important perhaps, we were capable of spending long periods of time with each other in complete, comforting silence, without need of speech.

A contentment.

Sometimes she would sit hunched forward, her elbows on her knees, chin in her hands, hair tumbled across her eyes any old way, looking unblinkingly into space. And when I asked her where she had 'gone' to, or of what she was thinking, she would suddenly laugh, as if caught hiding, pull her hair behind her shoulders, and shrug.

'Oh. Thinking. Thinking of a million things.'

'Was I among them? The million things?'

'No! Goodness no! Sea shells. Sea shells on a beach that I know. Thousands of tiny shells, the sand so white, the water so clear, little fishes darting like arrowheads, so swift, so sure. No pain anywhere, no fear. All peace.'

'I know those shells.'

'You do? So many different kinds.'

'Some like emerald snails? Like vermilion fans? Like long cases to keep your spectacles in? I know, I had some once in a basket, it was made of palm leaves.'

'From where?'

'From here. Somewhere near here. When I was very small.'

'Pink shells, tiny as the nails on the hand of a new-born baby, delicate, small as small, transparent; starting to die.'

'To die?'

'A new-born baby commences to die from the moment that it leaves the womb, didn't you know that? We are only alive in the womb. When we leave it we begin the process of death.'

I would laugh because I didn't, then, comprehend what she meant, and she would laugh with me, to oblige my ignorance.

'You are mad, woman!'

'I am mad, yes. How good! Mad people are sometimes happy, I think.' And she would fall silent once more, thinking again. Back to her shells.

I was intrigued by these silences, by her laughter which was rich and full-throated with delight, and which did not arrive often. I liked her distance, her reticence, her sense of the idiotic and ridiculous; her mischievous grins which, I knew, would never be explained to me. Above all, perhaps, I admired, as well as loved, her coolness and her bravery, for we had been caught together in ugly situations from time to time during the worst of the shelling and she never faltered in her courage.

She spoke perfect English, French and Malayan and, because she had been a prisoner of the Japanese (shut in a lightless cell for one year as a punishment for some 'conduct which was anti-Nippon' as she said), she also spoke a little of their hideous tongue.

Unlike Nan she never, at any time, spoke of a future: as far as she was concerned there was no future, only the present, living moment. There was certainly to be no future for us: Harri was not, by any manner of means, a 'broody'. She had absolutely no intention of nesting anywhere, and certainly not in England.

'I would die there! My goodness me, yes! I would *die*, you know. And you would have to see me wearing shoes and stockings and terrible big coats; maybe even a hat! And you would be very bored of me, you know, because I would be weeping and sighing for this high blue sky, for the scent of spices, for the millions of shells on my white sand. And I would always have a cold, which would be very unattractive.' I let her chatter away, for I was quietly convinced that when the time came, the ultimate moment of choice, to stay or to come away, she would come with me.

I may have a modest ego, but it has a loud voice.

In this instance, however, it did not prevail.

When the time came, the ultimate choice, she was far more stubborn than I, partly because she knew exactly what she wanted from life and I, at that time a newly minted twenty-five, did not.

In any case, I lost out.

★   ★   ★

A letter to my father: Batavia, 24 June 1946.

. . . only hope that this reaches you in time to cancel the Air Mail Edition [of *The Times*, which he had sent me weekly]. I shall be on my way back to the UK in a matter of weeks now, end of August certainly, and the OM [the General] is on his way back for some conferences at the WO [War Office] so there won't be anyone left here to appreciate the paper! The other chaps, in any case, riffle through it and *only* read the bloody Sports pages!

I know that I should be feeling elated and terrifically happy at the thought of coming back, like the others here, but, frankly, I rather dread it. I'm not being the ungrateful son, believe me! I long to see you and Ma again, but I have got terribly habituated to this sort of life, Army life I mean, and especially with this Division.

But there we are. We all pull out of here in November, I gather, for the job is done and there seems to be no need for us now: India is being handed back to the Indians and I expect after that they'll *all* start clamouring for Independence, just as they did here: so there won't be any need of the Army because there won't be an Empire to run. We'll feel the draught when the time comes! The sun is really setting! God knows what I'll do in UK. It's a gloomy prospect, but there is no point in trying to hang on in the Army as I thought. But what do ex-Officers DO? No one wants to bother about ex-Service people, once we've won the blasted battles for the stay-at-homes they forget all about us. Look what they've done to Churchill, for God's sake! Surely the most dishonourable, ungrateful, behaviour ever given to a Leader. There is still the prospect of that prep-school in Surrey that X suggested I might go to, but I really don't think I'm up to being a teacher yet! I've only just started learning myself.

I won't, by the way, be bringing the cat with me. Which may or may not be a relief to you all! He was ready to be brought down from Bandoeng last week, but got wind of the cage I had had built for him, and jumped through the windows and sat staring at me balefully from a safe distance. They eventually caught him, bribed him with a chicken, got him caged safely to bring him down on the Rear Convoy (I had to fly down here) but they ran into an ambush fifty miles from here and in the banging and crashing he managed to escape and fled into the forest.

So that is that. I mind very much: but perhaps it is better that he returns to the wild, as long as some gun-happy Indo doesn't shoot him for 'sport'. Oh well . . . Batavia is hot and noisy, changed a lot in the months: it's heaving with traffic and people, and is almost back to normal. There are even tea-dances at the Hotel des Indes with 'dancing to The Pickler Brothers Dance Band'! Dear God . . .

*   *   *

I never mentioned Harri, it seems, in the letters that have survived from that time. Not a whisper of her name.

A week or so before I was due to sail to Singapore she just disappeared, and, although I eventually managed to trace the exact house in the Chinese Quarter where she had her room, no one would admit that she had existed, or that they could speak English. They nodded and smiled, arms folded, impassive faces shaded by their wide coolie hats. I couldn't very well storm the house, and all the shutters were tightly closed. The place seemed deserted, the gate into the bamboo-fenced yard wired up. So I left.

The day before I was due to sail, clearing up the office, taking down the maps and emptying the files, I discovered, set at the far edge of my desk, a blue cut-glass bowl which I had never seen before. It wasn't very big, just big enough to hold three vivid sunflower heads.

There was a folded note stuck under the base; it read: 'These two colours go well together. Adieu.'

'Adieu' sounds far more final than 'Goodbye'.

A farewell party was given for me in 'A' Mess that evening; a lot of farewell parties were taking place in those days, for men were beginning to gather like October swallows, awaiting repatriation and the long, happy voyage home. I got pretty drunk on Japanese White Horse whiskey sitting in a deep, plush armchair under a pepper tree in the garden.

We had stripped out the main rooms of the house to make more room for the dancing. The garden, in consequence, looked like a village fête jumble sale. I sat maundering away under red and orange fairy-lights strung in the trees, and bored everyone witless who would listen to my sad story about being the odd man out and not wanting to go home at all, but to stay on. Naturally everyone thought I was as high as a kite, which I almost was, and took no notice.

I moaned away to myself in sullen despair, the 'loner' suddenly alone in a crowd.

The laughter and the scratchy music from the wind-up gramophone only compounded my misery. I was sober enough to realize that the evening was almost over-happy, that people were laughing and talking with an edge of hysteria to their voices: an hysteria born of relief that the end was in sight, that the fighting had stopped (as far as they were concerned anyway), that a new life was about to begin – and they had got through.

Some were taking their new wives with them; laughing, sparkling-eyed girls who had worked for us in the offices at HQ, but who had only the vaguest idea of what England or Europe might be like, and who would have to face the grey north, and new habits and customs in places like Swindon, Manchester, Macclesfield or Croydon. I didn't, at that moment, envy them.

No high blue skies there. No scent of spices. No million little shells scattered along the white sandy beaches . . .

A group of three came wandering towards me, arms round

each other's necks, glasses in unsteady hands; they stood swaying cheerfully, their voices unmatched, unsteady, loud with drunken happiness.

> 'Oh! *When* there isn't a girl about,
> You do feel lonely . . .
> When there isn't a girl about,
> You're on your only . . .
> Absolutely on the shelf with
> Nothing to do but play with yourself . . .'

One of them leant forward and patted my head, I ducked his hands, and they laughed, turned, and roared back into the dancers . . .

> 'When there isn't a girl . . . AROOOOUND!'

★   ★   ★

We sailed in the *Oranje* for Singapore on the evening tide. I was completely sober by that time, but wore dark glasses to conceal the massive hangover which was still apparent in the hoops of mourning under my eyes.

I had said an unsteady, almost gruff, farewell to the General earlier in the day, and was wretched as he himself seemed to be.

'Did a good job, Pip, thanks. I put you through it rather, didn't I? But you came through damned well . . . really very grateful. Good luck.'

I had saluted, about-turned, left his room.

Standing at the foot of the gangplank, saying a last farewell to those who had come down to send me off, we talked lamely together; the usual useless words used at departures.

'Give my love to the Albert Memorial when you see it, if *it's* still there, eh?'

'Be on my way in a month. If you would just telephone Suzanna when you get time? I did give you the number?'

'Yes . . . you did.'

'You have got it? Speedwell 2345?'

'Got it, Bobbie.'

I looked past the jostling soldiers, sailors in their whites, the hurrying, laughing girls in batik sarongs, calling and waving up at people on the upper decks.

Gulls swung and swooped about the ship.

She might, possibly, have come down.

Perhaps standing quietly in the shadows by the go-downs? She'd be bound to wave, if she was there.

But I saw no sudden turn of a familiar head, no long hair swinging in the evening light, no white shirt, no grey cotton skirt – her 'uniform' almost – no slender arm raised in farewell.

I shook hands all round, turned to mount the gangplank. Then I saw Goa.

*   *   *

A postcard to my father dated Singapore, 2 September 1946.

This is THE Raffles. Need I say more? When I get home and have my letters published (!) I shall use this as an illustration. Off to lunch with some old friends I re-met here. It's torrid, dull, I am hotter than a snowball in hell. Must away to have a shower. Have only been able to draw $\frac{1}{4}$ of my month's pay! So you'll have to forget silk and gold, all I can possibly bring back as a present is myself! I'm awfully sorry . . .

Seven weeks later, in the fog on Guildford station, it was all over.

The mist drifted, veered, wavered. Up the line a blurred pink light changed suddenly to wan green.

A splot of colour on grey, damp paper.

The London train was due.

the film
ation is
e is still

n WOOD

:ombine
rial shot
f travel-
hing the
e back-
era. By
MATTES
re used
e DUPE

FRONT
avelling
used in
rinciple
ally and

direc-
o direc-
was his
e Lady
g and a
him to

bull-fighter Carlos Arruza. After his own script for *Two Mules for Sister Sara* (1969) had been, against his wishes, assigned to Don SIEGEL, he returned to Hollywood and the Western with *A Time for Dying* (1969).

BOGARDE, DIRK (1921–), British actor, made his film début in *Esther Waters* (1947). For some years he was popular as a romantic lead in films of little substance, but he also played more interesting and varied roles, including young delinquents in *The Blue Lamp* (1949) and *Hunted* (1952), and a suspected homosexual in *Victim* (1961). *Darling* (John SCHLESINGER, 1965) gave him a strong and sympathetic role, but his increasing versatility and skill became particularly evident in films directed by Joseph LOSEY: THE SERVANT (1963), *King and Country* (1964), *Modesty Blaise* (1966), and ACCIDENT (1967). His close association with VISCONTI, in *La caduta degli Dei* (*The Damned*, 1970) and MORTE A VENEZIA (*Death in Venice*, 1971), has perhaps been less happy, leading to a degree of self-indulgence.

BOGART, HUMPHREY (1899–1957), US actor, appeared in films from 1930. His first real impact was made in *The Petrified Forest* (1936), repeating his stage success as Duke Mantee, and for the next five years he was identified with the

The years between were gently occupied.

PART THREE

CHAPTER
7

In New York, yesterday's snow hillocked down the length of Park Avenue in varying shades of soot, charcoal and pewter. The sky was zinc-coloured, when you could see it, the giant buildings melting into low cloud and a heavy flurry of fresh snow.

The doorman heaved the last of our baggage into the trunk of the car, slammed it, accepted my ten-dollar bill, and, turning away, said: 'Have a nice day.' I almost thanked him. But remembered that the phrase was as impersonal and uncaring as a belch.

At Kennedy Airport the — Building was high, spacious, surgically clean, almost empty at this early hour in the morning. Cold, functional; glass and cement. A candy store with journals and Snoopy toys, a self-service restaurant, the check-in desks, two signs baldly marked 'Men' and 'Women'.

No social niceties here. From the shoulder.

The check-in clerk was polite, efficient, middle-aged and smiling. He arranged a window seat, stowed the bags, handed me the boarding cards.

'Super-Executive Service,' he said admiringly, as if I had made it socially or won a cup. 'You go right up there, along to that gallery, you see? Then you ring the bell at the door of the Super-Executive Class lounge and they'll take real good care of you, so have a nice day, now.'

Two tall steel doors set into a steel wall. A tiny, discreet bell at the side. I pressed it and the doors opened silently into a cavern of simulated leather armchairs, each attached to a telephone for the last-minute business calls executives always make, a jungle of glossy green plants, a small bar already, even at 8.30 a.m., in full swing, a mixed smell of hot coffee and Bloody Marys. There was a scatter of elegant women in New York black; inelegant men in shirt sleeves, braces yanking up plaid trousers two inches above their shoes.

Bells were ringing, deals were made, a woman took a crushed Yorkshire terrier from a bag, rearranged its bow, kissed it, stuck it back again.

At a small reception desk beside the doors, an obese woman in a careful wig, net-covered and sparkling with rhinestones, was stapling papers.

'Your Cards, please.' She didn't look up through her lozenge-shaped glasses.

I offered the boarding cards and our tickets.

'I said Cards,' she said with a flick of impatience and began dialling a number on one of the telephones squatting before her like a hatching of multicoloured toads.

'What card? I'm sorry . . .'

'Super-Executive Class. Helen? Helen, honey, do you have news yet on Mrs Aronovich? She didn't show yet? Oh. You don't? Well, maybe she didn't make it, the snow, traffic . . . I'll get back to you.'

'I'm afraid I haven't got a Super-Executive Card,' I said.

The obese woman replaced her receiver patiently. 'Then you can't come in here. You do not have the right.'

'But I'm *flying* Super-Executive Class. The check-in clerk told me . . .'

'That's not my problem, what the clerk told you. If you don't have the Card you don't belong here.' She was busy looking through a list of numbers in a notebook. 'You haven't done the mileage. Right?' She started to dial briskly. 'It stands to reason. Okay? Oh, Joanne? Joanne, don't bother about Mrs Aronovich. If she makes it just before we board that'll be just fine. Sure, I'll take care of her. If she checks in with you before I see her, call me? Sure thing . . .'

She hung up; and looked at me; for the first time. 'I'm sorry. You don't have our Card, so you don't have the mileage.' She took a pencil and scratched the back of her head under the wig, then folded her hands together like a pair of stuffed gloves. 'If you want to stay here it'll be eighty-five dollars. That's the fee. Right?'

I began to collect my hand baggage, my manager, Forwood, lifted the briefcase and his coat. The woman picked up the telephone again and started to dial with the pencil.

'Have a nice day,' she said.

Down in self-service, among the glitter of stainless steel and cellophaned packets, we sat at a long empty table, bare save for a bottle of ketchup and a jar of mustard, drinking weak coffee in half-pint paper cups. The only other people present in this impersonal, lifeless, sterile world sat across the way; they were elderly, tired. The woman wore a shabby cloth coat and a brown woollen hat like an inverted pudding basin. She wept quietly into a paper handkerchief.

The man, huddled in a crumpled raincoat, touched her hand from time to time across the table, murmuring to her in a pleading voice in Polish. She kept shaking her head, wiping her eyes, staring blearily at an unopened plastic-wrapped sand-wich on the table before her.

It was a sorry change from yesterday's splendour of the flight from Paris on Concorde.

But that was already a different world; and very far away.

*　　*　　*

On board a squad of hostesses waiting to greet one. Cosmetic smiles, severely cut uniforms, double-breasted jackets, skirts shiny at the seats, crisp collars and ties. A bevy of minor matrons. Name-badges over the heart informed one that we had a 'Margie', a 'Barbie', a 'Tracey' and a 'Cindy', who was, she assured me while taking my coat, 'All yours for the trip; hope it makes you happy?'

The shabby suburbs of New York swung away and tilted far below, rapidly lost to sight in low cloud and flurries of driving snow.

'And now,' said Cindy, handing me a fairly grubby card,

'here's the lunch menu. You take a look at it and I'll be right back . . .'

The lunch menu had *Dinner* printed quite distinctly at the top. Not a bad one either: Hors-d'Oeuvres, Cornish Game Hen and Wild Rice, a Maine Lobster, Prime Beef 'Texan Style'. A comforting wine list: Château-Lafite, a white Bordeaux, Moët et Chandon.

It would do, I thought. At the bottom of the card there was a small print of the Arc de Triomphe. Beneath this, elegant script suggested that *'When In Paris, It's "The Holland-House-Hotel"! Right In The Heart Of The City Of Light!'*

The date in the far right-hand corner was three days before.

'I have a distinct feeling,' I said to Forwood, 'that we are presently returning to France.'

He looked over the top of his glasses. 'Why?'

'It's the 16th today, but this menu is for dinner on the 13th.'

'Ohmygod!' cried Cindy. 'They screwed it! This is the Eastern flight menu for Paris, France. We're Domestic today!'

A fuss of blue-clad women hit the Super-Executive cabin like a hockey team without sticks. Suddenly a butch lady, who could quite possibly have been the referee, broke away from the menu-retrieving throng and pushed her way up the aisle swinging a narrow basket holding three upright bottles. The sign over her left breast stated that she was 'Mary-Jo'.

'Red,' she announced, handing me a plastic beaker. 'Or do you want the white, or the champagne?' From the shoulder all right.

I asked for champagne: it was warm, sweet and Californian. I took a careful look at the bottles while she filled Forwood's beaker.

'You know, this isn't *French*? You really shouldn't call it champagne,' I said with residual charm.

'We do *here*,' she replied. Without any.

'It might be wiser not to argue,' said Forwood quietly. 'I'd do it their way, or else they'll get annoyed. When in Rome . . .'

'I wish to God I were.'

Somewhere over Maryland the menus got sorted out and

186

Cindy spent much of her time on her knees before two gentle-men in the seats in front of us. She was being very attentive – she had no option, as neither of her passengers could speak, or read, a word of English and came, it would appear, from Korea or Vietnam. Or maybe just Hong Kong.

The nodding heads, the flashing gold in the teeth, the smooth, flat Piaget watches on each immaculately cuffed wrist, eyes slitted by the fixed smile, gave them away as the In-scrutable East. And rich with it. Unhappily they decided, with many a nod and a leer, to have 'Prime Rib of Beef Carved Before You', which meant that Cindy had to crouch on the floor with a knife and fork and a chunk of meat on a wooden board, hacking away and muttering 'goddammits' each time a piece of Prime Rib slid to the blue nylon carpet. She stood before me a few moments later, wiping her hands on a cloth.

'You want the Appetizer, right?'

I didn't, particularly. I wasn't even hungry, but I had been so overwhelmed by her performance with the Prime Rib that I agreed meekly.

Not to do so seemed churlish.

It was, when it arrived and was set on the pull-down table, a small roll of rubbery substance in a diluted tomato sauce; it swung idly around in its plastic bowl like a specimen in medical class.

It had no recognizable taste whatsoever; Forwood watched me curiously without touching his.

'So? Can you cut it?'

'Just. I think it's fish. There is a faint, lingering flavour of synthetic fish, nothing more. Perhaps formaldehyde . . .'

Forwood placed his fork on the little table beside his untouched dish. 'Never eat fish of any kind on a flight. Imagine two hundred people with diarrhoea.'

I imagined them and ate no more.

'Fish!' Cindy was wide-eyed with surprise. 'What do you mean, fish?'

'Well . . . that's what it tasted like. I don't think I'll bother.'

She took up the soiled menu and read it rapidly. 'The Ap-petizer is chicken. It says so, right here. Chicken.'

'Quite the fishiest chicken I've ever eaten.'

She looked at me with hostility. 'You're funny!' she said, collected the two dishes, and went away.

I didn't see her again, at least not with food, which was probably just as well. If I did happen to catch her eye during the flight, she turned quickly away with a toss of her head. An insulted hostess, who had been 'all yours for the trip', cruelly rebuffed.

Mary-Jo eased past me a couple of times, doing her best to ignore me, but failing when confronted with my outstretched arm and the plastic beaker thrust almost into her stomach. She refilled my beaker reluctantly each time, but did her best, like Cindy, to keep her distance, and if it hadn't been for the Koreans, or whatever they were, in the seats in front I'd very likely have crossed America parched as well as starved. They drank like desert survivors.

The heart of the Middle West lay 35,000 feet below us, stretching away into a haze of light and infinity. It lay as chequered and as flat as a giant's tablecloth: not a curve, not a wood or forest, no winding river, no hedgerows, no irregularity – everything at right angles, with, here and there, a small cluster of buildings round a farm, a tree for shade, drowning in an immensity of space.

It was clear to see that the people who lived in this vast area of land and sky could never adjust to confinement of any kind: during the war American prisoners from this wide land curled up in their prison camp bunks, their faces to the walls, and died in sleep. One understood perfectly well why: the lack of space, of sky and wind, of distance, did the killing.

But even from so many thousand feet above, the monotony appalled one; there were hours and hours of it to cover before Kansas gave way to Colorado.

Across the aisle a tall, balding man sat bolt upright, fists clenched, safety-belt buckled, stiff with apprehension, still wearing his galoshes which he had omitted to, or dared not, remove. He had been in this state ever since take-off, during which he uttered high piercing cries, like those of a bird trapped in a net, his eyes tightly shut. He watched the activity in the cabin with glazed terror, wincing in anguish at the smell of the food, the pouring of Mary-Jo's bottles, at the masticating gentlemen from Korea eating their Prime Ribs with the relish of starving cannibals; and now and again, exhausted by the smells and sights around him, he stifled moans of despair, and stared ahead of him at the back of the seat in front, but he never once relaxed his clenched fists or slumped into exhausted repose. During the whole length of the dire in-flight movie he, very sensibly, looked at his knees, occasionally closing his eyes in misery.

As we began to reach the two hundred square miles of housing density which constitutes the city of Los Angeles, he suddenly made a surprising, and desperate, lunge towards Mary-Jo, fumbled for a plastic beaker, and indicated, with animal grunts of distress, his need for refreshment.

'You want red, white or the champagne?' said Mary-Jo, but he rolled his eyes in agony, so she shrugged and filled his glass, and turned to me, the empty bottle clasped by its neck in her strong fist like a hanged cat.

'You want to see this label, real good? Napa Valley C-H-A-M-P-A-G-N-E from California. It is the greatest place in the whole wide world for wine, just let me tell you. We even shipped our vines right across to you Europeans when yours all got the pest: right? We saved Europe one more time. So when you lift a glass of your fancy stuff over there, just you remember that it is *Californian* wine you are drinking.' She dumped the empty bottle into the basket.

'I'll remember,' I said.

'You just do that,' said Mary-Jo triumphantly, and stamped down to the galley.

'There seem to be some contradictions in her argument,' said Forwood. 'But let it pass, we're coming in to land, I think.'

Below, the scrubby desert, grey-pink in the afternoon sun, began to disappear under the hideous agglomeration of back-to-back ticky-tacky houses each with its own blue square, rectangular, oval, kidney or circular shaped swimming-pool.

The 'Fasten Seat Belts' sign flashed up. The man across the aisle groaned, let his plastic beaker fall from a now nerveless hand; his chin sank to his chest, his eyes closed.

The two Koreans looked intently at their Piaget watches, compared times, nodded approvingly: we began our slow descent to International Airport.

*   *   *

The Call from the Coast.

For millions upon millions of actors, singers, dancers, musicians and anyone even remotely concerned with entertainment, or having the least pretensions to being in Show Business, the Call to Hollywood is the burning, enduring dream. From New York to Tacoma, from London to Paris, Berlin, Amsterdam, perhaps even Moscow and Leningrad, certainly, as I know, in Bombay and Sydney, they wait: longingly, yearningly.

Even my own mother, in the year that she was married, heard the Call for which she had waited so long, only to be forced to let it go unheeded when, packing with alacrity, she was halted in euphoria by a bewildered, and extremely stubborn, husband. Her heart was broken, and the searing wound of disappointment never fully healed; she carried the scar all her life, and we, as her family, endured it for all of ours.

Once upon a time (I don't know if they still stand today), there were rows of wooden posts all along the beach from Santa Monica to Malibu, each with a telephone attached, so that out-of-work actors lying supine in the smoggy sun might call 'in' to their agents to see if the great moment had arrived for them, or pray hourly that the post might ring with the Call.

I never heard that it did.

Hollywood, where after all the commercial cinema began in a barn in an orange orchard on a dusty road which became Sunset Boulevard, the street of dreams and shattered illusions, is still the Mecca for actors all over the world. The dream is absolute, it is almost never lost; the tragedy being that while some *are* called, very, very few are chosen.

Yet the myth persists. Fame and fortune, in that order, lie at every corner, on every street and parking-lot, in every drug-store or greasy-spoon 'Ethnic' restaurant.

They know, with blinding faith, that one day the Call will come; they are certain that they will be ready to take it, and after that the rest will be plain sailing. Patience and de-termination will pay off with their name in lights, a star on the door of the dressing-room, a swimming-pool and servants, a Cadillac, furs, orchids, Dom Perignon for breakfast, their name in the papers, adulation in the streets, and as much cocaine as they can possibly sniff.

They know, without any doubt, that it has happened before: a ruby has been found in the mud, diamonds in the shale, gold in the desert – why, then, should it not happen for them? The player is admirable in his optimism, courage and tenacity. And of course it *has* happened – someone has been 'spotted' on a bar stool, washing down a car, driving a truck, crossing the screen in a crowd scene, selling shirts in a department store – certainly it has happened, or happened *once*; so it can happen again.

What is forgotten, or overlooked, is that when they do reach the mountain peak of fame and glory, it is the staying there which is the toughest part: it tears the nails, breaks the back, destroys the soul, empties the bottles, kills illusion, and can finally erase the last shreds of reality and personal dig-nity. The slide down is bitter, and no one waves goodbye for there are thousands eagerly waiting to take the vacated seat, and in the hysteria of the rush the loser is crushed by the weight of numbers, callous with ambition. Some, a lucky few, manage to survive – but it is a brutal, often dishonourable, battle.

At the end of the war with Japan, Hollywood came 'shop-ping' to replenish its local talent with fresh blood from Europe. Britain was the main market-place because of the language.

Conveniently, people spoke English. In a short time Hollywood and its major studios stripped the British studios of many of their top players.

James Mason, Deborah Kerr, Stewart Granger, Jean Simmons, Michael Wilding and others found that the Call was irresistible.

After years of wartime privations they were ready and eager to bask in the sun, to dive into the swimming-pools, to accept the vast salaries offered, to enjoy the peace and the plenty of California, not to mention the vigorous, exciting, highly skilled industry which had exploded with astonishing power during the years of war and had cornered the world market – now their talents would be spread far and wide, not just confined to a weary, battered, strike-torn Britain sliding into socialism and bleak with continuing restrictions.

Who could possibly blame them? Mecca had never beckoned so enticingly, nor so successfully.

So they left, but in leaving they made space for newcomers to fill.

I was one of the lucky ones.

The Call first came for me early in 1947 when I least expected it. I had no yearnings in that direction and hadn't even considered that it might be a fact of life.

What was a fact of life at the time was that I still owed the army some eight hundred pounds in back-pay, and hadn't the least hope of paying the debt. I had managed to secure a few jobs in television, at that time just starting up again after the war, and eager to employ anyone who would work. The pay then, as now, was not going to make me rich, but it did enable me to put down a deposit for the rent of a one-room flat in Hasker Street, and with all my wealth contained in a large Oxo tin, my demob suit kept ready for 'interviews' (the trousers pressed nightly beneath my mattress), and on a steady diet of Weetabix and Kraft cheese I was beginning to face up to the realities of peacetime.

Without, it must be confessed, a great deal of enthusiasm.

However, owing to one appearance in a television play I

was approached by a major Hollywood studio, at that time 'shopping' among the left-overs in London, and told by a bird-like, bright-eyed, tough middle-aged woman that the 'world could be your oyster', as she put it graphically, on the one condition that I placed myself entirely in their hands and worked myself to death. If I signed the contract which she had before her on her desk in a splendid office on Piccadilly, I would be required to move – directly to Mexico, or perhaps it was New Mexico, I wasn't certain then and still am not, where I would learn Spanish. After three years 'under wraps' and, presumably, with a perfect knowledge of the language, I would be 'reimported to the States' under the name of Roderigo Something-or-other, given a house in Pacific Palisades and a car (I remember that this was to be a Volkswagen to emphasize my foreignness), and gradually, through small parts at first, I would be 'built into a major star . . . if only you let us do the whole construction deal, and give us your trust. We *know*; don't forget that . . . we've been building stars since Noah left the ark.'

'Who would I be in the end?' I remember asking.

'Our major import from South America. We've got English, French and a German, and a South American is important for that particular market.'

'What *part* of South America?'

She looked irritated suddenly. 'I don't know what *part*. How do I know? That's not my job. My job is to get you signed. I guess it depends on the kind of accent you acquire. But you get to speak Spanish: not Portuguese, that's a no-go market . . . we stick with Spanish.'

'And what else?'

'Well . . .' She looked suddenly shy, for the first time, tapped her writing-pad with a pen, smoothed out the 'regular, seven years plus options contract' awaiting my signature. 'Well, we have to see how it goes, right? If you make the grade; what impact you have on screen. We have ways of finding that out, naturally. *If* you make the grade. If you *are* star potential for an audience in, say, San Diego or maybe even in Dallas, if they

193

like the "sneaks" we'll screen, we'll really go to town.' She looked up at me, her black eyes slightly hooded.

'And then what?' I said.

'Then you get married. You'll see the contract list of the girls we have and all you have to do is pick the one you really like and we'll fix the rest.'

'Oh.'

. The hooded eyes suddenly opened wide with a glint of panic. 'You aren't *already* married?'

'No.'

'That's great. Fancy-free.' She sat back in relief.

I tried to explain, as politely as I could, that I did not wish to go and live in Mexico or even in New Mexico, I didn't want to learn Spanish, be 'under wraps' for three years, or marry a lady on the studio contract list.

'Listen.' She picked up the contract, struck it crossly with the back of her hand. 'This is a great opportunity for you! We have literally queues of people waiting for this chance – thousands. The studio takes all the risks, not you! We pay you all the time you are studying, we pay you *all the time*! You can have the world if you want it. As long as everything works out right. The marriage doesn't have to bother you one bit. It's routine, that's all. You get to choose the girl, we have a slow build-up of publicity, then a fun marriage and lots of publicity, so you get well covered world-wide – maybe you could even go to Europe for the honeymoon . . . and that's all. Nothing to it.'

'But it's still marriage.'

'Sure it's marriage. We are an honourable studio, for God's sake! But you don't have to stay married, you can split after a year or two . . . if that's the way it goes, you just have to put a face on things. Think of Louella and Hedda! Think of the gossip if you were single! You'd be ruined, so would the studio. It would lose you, the money, the *time* and its reputation. You want that?'

'I don't want any of it.'

'But what have you got to lose?' she said in exasperation. 'Who are you, anyway?'

Who indeed?

An out-of-work, 26-year-old ex-Captain, saddled with a burdensome debt for having had the extreme privilege of serving his country in the cause of democracy. That's who I was.

Walking through Green Park in a heavy snowfall, I realized that my demob shoes were leaking, that my feet were both wet and freezing, but also, which was far more important, that I was not about to be shipped off to Mexico, learn Spanish, drive a Volkswagen, or marry anyone on a studio list.

I had made that perfectly clear.

I was, when all was said and done, still my own master, even if the money in my Oxo tin rattled mockingly like the sound of distant maracas.

There were to be other Calls during the years which lay ahead of me, but they were ignored, except for two which proved to be minor disasters and convinced me that to be a biggish fish in a small pond was a great deal better than being a dead fish in an ocean. Each time the Call sounded I said 'No', and the money always doubled alarmingly – but I stuck to my last and made do with a more modest, but far happier, life.

However, here I presently was, coming in to land at Los Angeles for the first time in twelve years, perfectly well aware that I had heeded the Call yet again but that this time things would be different.

Why does one always think that 'this time it'll be different'? I suppose because one never finishes learning in life.

But I had considered the script with care; the star was Glenda Jackson, whom I greatly admired and with whom I wanted to work very much, the director a young and brilliant Englishman, Anthony Harvey; the money was reasonable, the time absolutely right.

January is a brutal month here on the land. Los Angeles would be no bad place to spend three weeks of the winter, it was time I heaved myself out of my comfortable rut and went out into the world again. I might even enjoy it; I was pretty sure I'd be happy: the idea of working on a good script with a superb actress pulled me out of apathy, rekindled the old excitements and challenges, filled me with eager curiosity about working in Hollywood once again now that I had reached the sensible, balanced age of sixty and could, I hoped, cope with any problems which might come my way – what, I thought, as we made a perfect touch-down and trundled along the runway, could possibly go wrong?

Plenty could – and plenty did.

*　　*　　*

Anthony Harvey sprawled comfortably on the over-stuffed settee in my hotel suite.

'*Thrilling!* That you are here at last. Really *marvellous*, quite thrilling: it all begins to feel real. Glenda won't be in for a couple of days; her father died suddenly, you knew that?'

I said that I knew that, but that I had decided not to wait about in New York but get across to California, lose my jet lag, and begin to feel my way around again.

'Marvellous! Absolutely thrilling, *thrilling.* And we are shooting the whole thing on film, not tape – so don't think of television, think of cinema! It'll be TV in the US, but a real movie in Europe and the rest of the world. We must not even consider that it's a television film. Cinema, remember it's *cinema*!'

Perhaps our very first error.

The story, at this stage called *Pat and Roald*, was the true history of the appalling tragedy which struck the writer Roald Dahl and his actress wife, Patricia Neal. During work on a film in Hollywood she had suffered a massive stroke and had become, to all intents and purposes, a vegetable.

Only Dahl's determined, desperate cajoling, bullying and fighting got her through and brought her back to life, eventually.

They had been friends and neighbours of mine when I had lived in Amersham, and when the subject had first been offered to me I immediately telephoned them to ask if they had agreed to the film being made and had accepted myself and Glenda to portray them. They were shattered that a film was to be made of their private life, but they had no option other than to let the project go ahead: a book had been written, with their permission, about the whole tragedy and thus they were, as they were firmly reminded, in the 'public domain'. The film rights of the book had been sold and they were helpless, and powerless, to stop the film.

However, they seemed relieved that Glenda and I were playing them – at least we were serious players – and Roald was reasonably pleased with Robert Anderson's very sympathetic and un-Hollywood script: they generously gave us their blessing.

'We won't look much like you,' I told Roald. 'But at least we'll do our damnedest to honour you both and to keep any sensationalism out, that'll be our main job. But the script is good, that's why I even considered such an impertinence.'

'Don't, for God's sake, let them tart you up in Savile Row suits,' he said. 'I'm not that kind of chap . . . you know that.'

I knew that, and assured him that I would cart all my old jackets, flannels, cardigans and knitted ties out to Hollywood, and if I couldn't actually look like him (he was to begin with over a foot taller than me), I'd try to 'represent' him satisfactorily. He very kindly offered to 'jot down some things I remember from that time, things I said and did, which might help you'. And I had left for America with a fairly clear conscience.

The cardigans and knitted ties were now spread over the suite for Harvey's, and the wardrobe master's, approbation, when the telephone rang. Harvey answered it: there was a brief pause and then he erupted into roaring fury.

The room shook, the wardrobe master stood stunned, I sat crouched in a chair, stiff with alarm, the storm roared and rumbled and reached tremendous crescendos of rage. Then he slammed down the receiver, his face crimson with anger. Shaking, he crashed back on to the settee, his head buried in his hands. We waited in silence for him to recover.

'What's wrong? Glenda . . .?'

His voice was muffled by clenched fists when he spoke. 'No. No. The script. The script. Our glorious script! It's too long!'

'Too long? How can it be too long? It's the script we all agreed to shoot, isn't it?'

'It was, it was. That was the script girl. She's just read it through with a stop-watch, timed it to the tenth of a second. It's thirty minutes too long!'

'But how *can* it be? We start in three days ... why didn't they know that long ago? Why only today?'

'They only hired the script girl today ...'

'How can the script girl possibly time a scene which we haven't even played yet!'

He looked up with a haggard face. 'As it stands it won't fit the time slots for the commercials, it'll run over.'

'But you said we were shooting a film ... not a television film.'

He shook his head wearily. 'They are making cuts. Making cuts. It's too long.'

We looked at each other in despair. I knew, and Harvey and Forwood knew, exactly what this meant. We would be getting rewrites every day on pink, yellow and green pages, the script would be hacked to bits to fit the commercial breaks. Although I had never made a film for commercial television I knew perfectly well that it was far more important to sell hair-spray, shampoo, deodorants or aspirin than to sell the film, and that under these present circumstances we couldn't hope to make a main feature film at all: we would be forced by the sponsors (a new, and dreadful, word to add to our vocabularies) to bow to their selling time. All ideas of a movie, the bait on the hook which we had all so naïvely swallowed, must be set aside.

I had only been back in Hollywood for two hours and nothing, it seemed, had changed one jot since I had left it twelve years before – it was the same old place: the town of deceptions.

Forwood broke the silence which prevailed, the wardrobe master continued quietly folding away my shirts and ties.

'I think it probably *is* a bit too long. It might be good to have a few cuts . . . if they are carefully done. I shouldn't give up hope yet . . .'

'But WILL they be carefully done?' cried Harvey in despair. 'Thirty minutes is thirty minutes, a hell of a long time on the screen.'

'Well . . .' said Forwood with his customary reasonableness. 'If they cut it about to such an extent that it is no longer the script which Dirk and Miss Jackson agreed to shoot, then they can, I imagine, pull out.'

My heart sank: more battles ahead. Perhaps I had made a dreadful mistake after all; I should have stayed quietly in France and got on with writing. I really had no appetite for any more film fun. I'd had years of that form of exhaustion.

'Let us wait until Miss Jackson gets here,' said Forwood. 'She'll have something to say about this, I feel certain.'

When Glenda eventually arrived she was far too exhausted to say anything after a gruelling flight from Birmingham, via London, directly over the Pole to Los Angeles. She came down to my suite the night that she arrived in a pink candlewick house-coat; she said it was her dressing-gown and did I mind? I didn't; and perhaps it was. Her face was white with fatigue, her eyes pulled through to the very back of her head like upholstery buttons, but all her faculties were splendidly intact. It was our very first meeting – we had never even spoken on a telephone together – and it was a miraculous, instant joining.

My failing courage soared; with this person at my side I'd be able to fight all the bloody sponsors, producers and script girls.

I thought that I passed muster as well, for as she was walking down the hotel corridor with her small entourage after a happy, and even relaxing, hour in the suite I heard her say: 'Well, he *seems* all right, doesn't he?'

I felt braver than a lion.

* * *

I needed all the courage I could use during the next three weeks. The first two days were fairly calm: we settled down to work on location in an elegant house out in Pasadena, where the main body of the filming was to be done. This necessitated getting up at 5.00 a.m. in order to get out to the location and begin shooting at 7.30 a.m.; we worked through, with half an hour for lunch on the spot, until seven-thirty in the evening. A tough schedule.

There was no let-up; Glenda and I were, apart from three children, the two main characters and were in every scene – those which remained of the once-rich script, which was treated rather like a chicken carcass: defleshed of much of its 'meat', crushed, beaten to fragments, and stuck in the stockpot. From the tattered remains of Anderson's work we retrieved as much as we possibly could that was nourishing, and Harvey, true to his word, shot the whole thing as a film, in long takes, with low-key lighting and a sense of 'documentary work' rather than glossy Hollywood.

Screams and cries from the Office.

The results, after five days' shooting, were deemed to be too dark and 'unseeable'. Harvey's 'gritty' and 'grainy' method (these two words were his favourites, apart from 'thrilling') caused tremendous concern and alarm.

Fine, it was argued, for a big screen in the cinema, but hopeless on a small screen twenty inches in width. The sponsors couldn't see anything when they looked at their sets, but were entranced when they saw the material projected on the big screen. Which was precisely what Harvey had intended. A movie, not a TV film.

We came unstuck: everyone came unstuck. While the performances were genuinely praised, the lighting was considered disaster. Fire the cameraman, fire *everyone*, then get lots of 'run by's', that is to say establishing shots of the locations, 'so that they'll know where they are when they see it in the Middle West'.

How *they* saw, understood, empathized in the Middle West was the key to everything. No one really cared all that much what anyone thought on the West Coast or even on the East Coast: the people who lived down on the giant's tablecloth, over which I had so recently flown, were the arbiters of all taste.

They were the people who would buy the goods which we advertised on television. They were the profit. If they should grow restless, become bewildered, bored or disturbed, and turned, in consequence, to another channel, the loss to the sponsors would be incalculable – come what may, we had to keep their attention; therefore, if they couldn't 'see' us they would turn the switch and no one would buy the deodorants, the sliced bread, the shampoo, the lavatory paper ('So Soft, So Soft, Softer Than A Sigh. So Kind To Your Skin'!) or the aspirin.

In order to hold this vast audience, and it was vast indeed, things had to be simple, people must be able to 'identify' easily with everything they saw, above all they must be 'involved', and it stands to reason that you can't be involved if you can neither see nor hear.

A turn of a knob on a television set is as lethal to commercial television as a button pressed in the death chamber.

So, flood the film with plenty of light – no half-tones or shadows – so that people will see. Use simple words which they will understand, have no subtleties in playing that get in the way of 'the direct approach', have no pauses for thinking – there isn't time for thinking, and pauses can make an audience restless, anxious or bored – and as a further added restriction the name of the Lord must never at any time be used in vain. No 'My God's!' Or 'Goddammits!' No God at all.

As most of our story was set in a hospital, concerned a massive brain haemorrhage, and necessitated a good many incomprehensible medical terms and distressing sights (Glenda spent half the picture lying flat on her back, bandaged like a mummy with tubes up her nose and stuck into her arms, only able to communicate by animal grunts and cries), we were on a pretty sticky wicket from the start. But we stuck firmly, determinedly, to our intentions, in spite of daily screams and thumping fists and the repeated demands that everyone should be sacked. Except for Glenda and myself, who were constantly lavishly praised, even though, apparently, no one could see what we were doing.

It was a battle for banality against quality, and it raged unabated. People were frequently fired, removed from the set by physical force in the very middle of shooting a scene, something I had never witnessed in over thirty years of film making (but there is always a first time), and the crew, with good reason, grew more nervous and despondent; and each day brought a flutter of coloured pages indicating scenes 'cut' or 'trimmed'. None of this made for a happy atmosphere, but Glenda and I hung on grimly. We were passionate in our work together and had no intention of throwing in the sponge. Or towel.

We all knew, from the work on the set and the support from the whole crew, that we were salvaging something from the tottering edifice, enough at least to make a reasonable, if compromised, movie.

Harvey stuck doggedly to his original plan of a cinema film: we worked long and exhausting hours, sometimes shooting as much as ten or twelve pages in a single day, where the norm in my experience was never much more than a page or two at the most, so that what we actually got *on* to film could serve as a main feature film for theatrical release in Europe and the rest of the world, but could be cut about for television and the Middle West, the theory being that when it was completed eventually there would be enough footage in reserve for the cinema.

That was the theory; it was exceedingly hard to make it fact.

There was never any possibility of Glenda and me pulling out, as Forwood had once envisaged – we were too deep in, too fond of the loyal crew who were bending backwards to help us achieve what we all wanted so much, too involved, anyway, with the original story and the excitement of playing together. There were some heavy-hearted evenings in our hotel restaurant in Pasadena when we sat, exhausted and drained, before plates of dreary little fish in breadcrumbs, known as sand-dabs, which were about the only thing on the menu which we could eat in our exhaustion, wondering how we could manage to survive the next day – seeking, at all times, acceptable compromises for television; and for ourselves. Not easy.

One evening the telephone rang in my rather tatty suite (it was like cheap digs in Newcastle). Forwood answered it, fully expecting it to be another member of the crew who had reached breaking-point calling to apologize for quitting. This had happened two or three times already, and always caused me keen distress, but it was Tessa Dahl, the eldest of the Dahl children, who had been extremely hostile to the whole idea of a film about her parents' private grief, and about the invasion of her family's privacy.

I was certain that she would have something disturbing to say; we had never met or spoken before – doubtless she had bad news of some kind.

But she had not. She said that she had been cajoled and persuaded to see a good piece of the completed filming in the hope, perhaps, that she would publicly change her objections to the making of the film and might therefore provide some useful and 'positive' comments for publicity.

But she had made no sound during the projection, nor did she move a muscle, contenting herself with a polite, but non-committal, 'Thank you', and leaving the theatre in silence. She immediately telephoned her mother, then staying in Martha's Vineyard, to tell her that what she had seen had overwhelmed her and that she now whole-heartedly approved. Her mother, Miss Neal, suggested that perhaps she should call the actors concerned and tell *them*; so she called me.

'It's really all right?' Relief suddenly gave me new strength.

'It's more than that. It's fantastic, really wonderful. If you want to know I went along to have a laugh – but I couldn't. I thought that I'd be able to send the whole thing up as a bit of terrible Hollywood schmaltz, but I was simply stunned. I wanted to burst into tears, only I knew that I was under observation, that they were waiting for a good response from

me to leak to the Press – you know what I mean: "Tessa Dahl
Sobs At True-To-Life Movie", that kind of thing?'

'That kind of thing. I know.'

'So I didn't move. I just sat there. It was tough; but amazing.
I was only twelve when that all took place; I didn't really fully
understand what was happening, but now, because of you and
Miss Jackson, I know just how wonderful my parents were,
how terribly brave, how hard Roald fought to get my mother
through – I'm so grateful, will you tell Miss Jackson that I
think she is magnificent?'

'Well . . . why not tell her yourself. She's in this hotel . . .'

'No. I can't do that. I'm too ashamed. I made a fuss about
this film being made, I didn't want her to play my mother, I
didn't think that *she* was beautiful enough, but she is. She IS
my mother.'

Tessa Dahl saved the film from disaster, that is to say she
saved us all from moral collapse. It had not been far off, but
her encouragement was tremendous: we got a new wind, new
courage, new strength and we fought even harder than before,
which was just as well because the battle got tougher; Tessa
became our talisman. If Tessa Dahl thought that we had got
things right, and she ought to know, then to hell with the
Middle West.

Eventually, with half the film safely 'in the can', we finished
work late one night in a heavy desert mist, everyone streaming
with flu caught, we all were quite certain, from the redundant
hospital in which we had been working and which had been
stripped clear of everything except germs.

I got bronchitis in the last three days and lost my voice
completely: stuffed with cortisone, in order to shrink the vocal
cords in a hurry, I managed to croak my way to the final shot.
Glenda survived intact – she is not the sort of person to
succumb to anything trivial – and we all said sad farewells in
the swirling fog.

The second half of the film was to be shot in England, but
not until the summer, when Glenda had completed the run of
a new play, *Rose*, which she was taking to Broadway. The

film was put on ice until June, the American crew were miserable that they would not be able to finish the job, and we were equally saddened that they were to be left behind after the tremendous encouragement which they had given us, determined to get us through the disasters. Never, indeed, have so few owed so much to so many.

The Teamsters – the truck drivers and car drivers – members of the toughest union in America, had become our greatest supporters, admiring the way we worked and the determination to stick it out no matter what. On that final evening they made a presentation to Glenda, myself and Forwood of three pearl-handled revolvers, in the form of cigarette lighters, as a token of their regard. We were very much moved.

With heavy hearts, in spite of all the problems, we went our separate ways, Glenda to New York, I to France to await the Call, not to the Coast this time, but to England and a rose-embowered cottage in Hertfordshire for the second half of the film when Glenda was free.

*　　*　　*

To England in June: a new director in Anthony Page (Harvey had other commitments in America to which he was bound), a little less hectic atmosphere and continual help from Roald Dahl, who wrote copious notes for me on a great many things about which he had forgotten, or perhaps banished from his mind during that desperate time, which were immeasurably useful.

Glenda worked daily with a voice therapist who helped her to invent a manner of speech which, while comprehensible, suggested the inarticulate manner of speaking which a victim of a paralysing stroke would use; it was distressing but appallingly real, and we finished on a dull, wet English summer evening, comforted by the fact that we had made a film as authentic as possible to its origins.

It opened in America (as *The Patricia Neal Story*) in December to quite sensational reviews. Glenda and I were praised

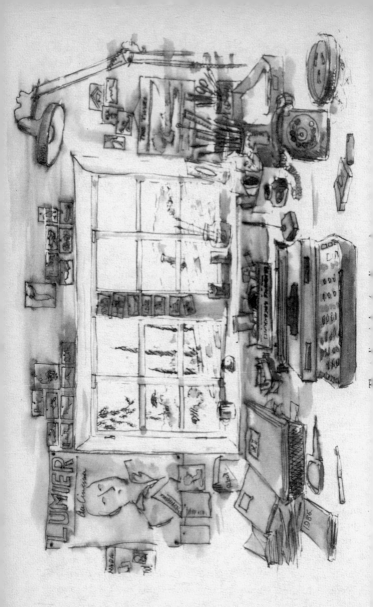

extravagantly; so were Harvey, Page and Bob Anderson. The telephone rang almost daily with calls for interviews from newspapers and journals, some as far apart as Quebec, Hawaii, Florida and New York. It was prime-time coast-to-coast, and the movie of the year on television.

Or so you'd think.

We finally reached the peak of euphoria when it was rumoured that Glenda and I were each nominated for an Emmy, the television equivalent of the cinema's Oscar, and, perhaps best of all, news came that it was all such a success, the Press had been so enthusiastic in their praise, that the movie version, re-titled *Miracle of Love* (well, you can't have everything) was being hurried into Los Angeles cinemas to qualify for the Oscars in April.

I sat about up here in the olive store where I work, bemused and happy, reading through plays and stories in a search for something else for Glenda and me to do together because everyone insisted that we 'were a really great team' and we both wanted to get on with something else while the iron was hot, so to speak.

But the iron cooled rapidly.

The ratings came in. I don't exactly remember what they were, but they weren't any good: not 50 per cent, not enough to make us a success or to make us a smash hit. The Middle West, that giant's tablecloth, had turned off after about fifteen minutes to look in at a popular series called *Hart to Hart* which starred Robert Wagner, whose wife, Natalie Wood, had died tragically in a drowning accident only a few days before. The Middle West, it was suggested, was curious to 'see how Bob looked after the tragedy; how he was taking things'.

The fact that the sequence of *Hart to Hart* was probably made some time before Natalie died, and that Robert looked just fine and was managing very well indeed, made no difference.

The Middle West stayed with the show and we lost out, on the ratings. Then I understood the colossal power of television to make or break.

The telephone stopped ringing, no one got an Emmy, and the movie version, if it ever really existed, slipped quietly into oblivion.

Was it honestly as simple as that? Was more than half the population of America really so concerned about poor Robert Wagner? Or was our film, perhaps, too painful, too distressing, too 'gritty' and 'grainy'? Did the hospital, bandages, drip-feeds and inarticulate speech put them off? Was I too bullying or too British? The imponderable questions remain imponderable: only the harsh facts of the ratings provided the glaring truth – we'd flopped.

But there was never the least feeling, in my mind, of doubt or regret, that I might perhaps have made a false move in pushing wide the open door in my corridor which led directly to Los Angeles and the cinema again. I had enjoyed the experience enormously, learned a great deal, and even if a lot had been hellish much more had been sheer delight.

The greatest pleasure, without question, had been working with Glenda Jackson – it was one of the highest peaks in my career as an actor – as strong as teak, as pliable as plasticine, as professional and dedicated as any actress I had ever worked with. We joined together seamlessly, and the work we did was stimulating and exciting – it didn't really matter what happened left and right of us: when we were together, united in a scene, we were absolutely isolated by performance.

We hardly discussed the roles we were playing – there was no need. We knew who we were, and matched each other's emotions and responses exactly. There was never any heavy breathing, head beating or 'anguishing', as they call it, about 'motivation' or 'who' and 'how': we'd got that together long before the cameras rolled.

Sometimes I know that our set behaviour bewildered the crew, obviously used to a different style of playing: we'd sit around on the set, waiting to be called to work, talking and laughing, discussing books or music, people we knew, places we had been, anything and everything; none of it profound or deep, just light, easy – to the onlooker perhaps even casual.

208

And then we would go directly into a scene of almost Shakespearian tragedy, dark, desperate, wrenching: which often brought tears, and applause, from the crew. A response which astonished Miss Jackson.

'But why? What's the matter with them all? I mean: REALLY!'

There was nothing wrong with them: they were just not accustomed to this form of playing; the (apparently) instant leap from one world to another caught them quite by surprise, they were at a loss to know how we had performed this act.

What in fact surprised them, truthfully, was the sudden release of 'actor's energy'. A different thing altogether from mere 'energy', which is physical. 'Actor's energy' is both mental and physical, it is the life force behind a performance; without it a performance can be adequate, acceptable: but lacking in lustre. Nothing is worse than a dull actor – far better to be a bad one: at least a bad actor may have some interest but a dull one has absolutely nothing.

Many actors have 'actor's energy', but most don't know that they have, or how to use it, and spend a good deal of their ordinary energy frittering it away. It must be cherished like chastity, guarded, husbanded, kept gleaming and bright, and the only possible way to do that is by concentration. Concentration so intense, so hard, so deep that it causes almost physical pain. Sitting on the side-line, chatting about, say, Proust, or perhaps China, or the best way to make corned beef hash, we would none the less be concentrating subliminally on holding the 'actor's energy' so intensely that I swear had someone touched us they would have found that our bodies were tense and trembling as if we had the palsy.

The physical and mental release after playing a scene perfectly, or as near perfectly as one can try to achieve, is so draining that it often feels as if one has just played an exhausting game of squash.

Sweaty, breathless, weak-kneed, drained, limp from effort spent. And, really, that's how good playing should be: like an exhilarating game of squash.

It seldom is.

But when it is, an audience will react instantly; the experience disturbs, excites, and involves them completely.

As Tessa Dahl had seen for herself, Glenda had the uncanny power, as some of our great actresses in the past have had, of being able to transform herself from a shaven-headed, inarticulate, shambling vegetable-woman into a creature of glowing beauty. It never ceased to amaze and move me to watch this happen. It occurred before one's eyes, not through tricks of make-up or lighting. It was instant and extraordinary and came directly from the gut, the repository of nearly all an 'actor's energy'.

No one can possibly be taught how to do this, there are no short-cuts, it doesn't come free in the actors' acting kit; it is a far from liberal gift, based on absolute truth and complete belief in the person one has become, and on concentration. 'Being' and 'believing' unshakeably are the essentials for the cameras – not 'pretending', as is so often supposed.

The camera, with its cruel lens, can often shatter the most carefully prepared performance. If there is no belief or truth behind the work it is photographing, the whole thing goes for nothing. No lustre, no impact.

It is therefore not so surprising that the crew members were moved to applaud; it was an instinctive reaction of a group of people identifying instantly with what they saw before them; they had been removed from the immediate world and transposed to a higher plane of experience. They were observers no longer; they were *sharing*.

Which is, after all, exactly what acting is about, and always has been.

It was not so surprising either that, after a full day's work at high pitch, there were never glamorous parties or suppers in the evenings: there was absolutely no residual energy left, 'actor's' or the other, for that kind of frivolity. The batteries had to be recharged come what may, so that 'delivery' was assured for the next day; even if the recharging took place before a plate of breadcrumbed sand-dabs in a dreary hotel dining-room.

But sand-dabs notwithstanding, and all the rest of the miseries right and left, it had been a wise decision to push open the door in the corridor; even if the film had tragically been lost, I had gained immeasurably in many other ways.

It was eventually shown on British television one New Year's Eve by a commercial station who apparently decided that New Year's Eve was a perfect time to get rid of it.

There would be no one at home to watch it, and no one was, as far as I could ever find out.

They were all extremely occupied in their own personal revels or pushing each other into the fountains in Trafalgar Square.

It was a bitter blow to us – but that was that.

It all might never have happened.

*   *   *

I have always firmly believed in taking one hurdle at a time in life.

And taking it with caution.

I see no point in trying to clear them all at one go: the whole lot can so easily fall and bring one crashing helplessly down among them. Far wiser to take it slowly than to break one's neck at the very start (you usually get there in the end); in any case, I have such feeble co-ordination that I can only ever really manage one thing at a time anyway – so it's a case of *force majeure*.

The first hurdle, in this instance, was the Hollywood shoot. Apparently I had cleared it and survived. The next hurdle, the English shoot, was so far ahead in time that I really could pay it no heed, and sitting in the calm splendour of an Air France jumbo jet I had absolutely no desire to try. Here there was no Cindy with her chicken Appetizer, no Mary-Jo with her three-bottle basket, no petrified traveller across the aisle jammed into his galoshes, just peace, and a caring young woman in a silk dress replenishing my glass with discretion and skill.

I was going home to France at last.

We roared out into the night skies from International Airport, leaving the city far below in a slight drizzle, a myriad of winking lights for as far as the eye could possibly see: green, crimson, blue and gold, a casket of jewels strewn far and wide as if by a wilful child. We swung over the Pacific and climbed high above a lone lightship rocking gently on the swell, its beacon lamp bobbing idly, an incandescent lollipop, then we banked sharply and turned inland towards the dark immensity of America.

It was the last I saw of Los Angeles.

Wheezing and coughing, croaking like a tree-frog with acute bronchitis, stuffed to the gills with cortisone, I was none the less comfortable and relaxed at last, relieved that the first leap had been accomplished.

My work seemed not to have suffered from the four-year lay-off since *Despair*, which pleased me, so the more minor hurdles, ones which I could almost step over really, could now be considered under the soothing influences of wine and a moderately high temperature.

At home the proof copy of my second novel was awaiting my urgent attention, and there was a cover design to plan. Norah Smallwood, my publisher, had written to say that she felt it should be 'something as gay and filled with sunlight as a child's painting. Perhaps we could consider a kind of *faux* Dufy? Think it over.' So I thought it over, mulling it about for a while.

But then the pond was ready for mucking out, the waterlilies were ready for dividing, there were new roses to get in before the end of the month – we can plant late in Provence – and somewhere, pinching my blurring consciousness like a too-tight shoe, the first lines for the opening chapter of a new book were arranging and rearranging themselves in different patterns.

I managed to get the opening line fixed in my head before I fell asleep. It was not the full line, only the first five words in fact, but five important ones none the less:

'I am an orderly man.'

That seemed to me a good start: the other ninety-five thousand could follow on later.

When I was just a bit less tired.

One thing at a time.

CHAPTER
8

When Aunt Kitty went 'a-voyagin'', as Mrs O'Connell often told me, I don't suppose that she minded – it is far more than probable that she liked it, for the First Floor Front of my father's house was pretty gloomy. I didn't find it so, at three or four, but she was, it would appear to me now, in constant search of somewhere better. And she found it, of course, in the islands where the beaches were of white sand glittering with a million tiny shells.

However, that is *one* thing I did not learn from her.

The best part of 'a-voyagin'' for me is always coming home. The supreme moment, I suppose, is when the taxi from the airport turns into the track towards the house, winds up through the terraces and the olives, a dog capering in welcome, the sun, on this particular occasion, shining hard on the frost patches under the walls, gleaming on the water of the pond, throwing the shadows of the cypress trees across the smooth grass at the back of the house like long pencils.

Then the car stops, the doors slam, the luggage is humped from the boot, greetings are called to Henri and Marie (who have been guarding the house in my absence), the dog arrives breathless with delight, a stone carried in his mouth as a welcoming gift.

I'm home again.

I do not immediately enter the house but, fatigue temporarily dispersed, eyes sharpened by the brilliant winter light, go to take stock of my land; to see what has happened to my private world since I left a month ago. Forwood deals with the trivia of household problems within, and I walk over crisp, springy grass, breathing clean air into lungs still foul with the soot of cities and the haze of paraffin from the flights.

Nothing very much seems to have happened anywhere.

In February spring is only about to begin, the land stirs slowly, almost reluctantly, as one does waking from a deep, relaxing sleep.

The daffodils under the willow are thick with fat green buds which thrust from scattered tufts, like green-gloved hands, among the rough grass, brown with last year's leaves; there are lambstails on the hazel, clumps of arabis sit white in the sunlight, tight snowballs on the gravel and in the cracks of the terrace, the first primavera and pansies fill the pots and tubs which in the summer will dazzle with scarlet geraniums and the brilliance of lobelia, a much despised plant used mainly as bordering in public gardens but which here riot in azure glory from May to November.

Otherwise the land is still sere and ice-burned: a few cautious anemones indicate where the drifts will later spread across the terraces, scillas cluster in the shelter of the stone walls, braving the frost, the first celandine, down by the cess-pit run-out, look like green enamel buttons scattered on the banks of the ditch, and the early coltsfoot star the rough ground by the bonfire site, bold on their single stems.

Above, the sky is achingly blue – in the summer it is white with heat, but in winter the mistral washes the air, the winds are sharp and cutting, and the hills are revealed in sharp clarity, every rock and fissure, every crag and boulder, every stunted pine holding hard to the barren limestone. The silence is so intense that the hurdy-gurdy noise made by the guinea-fowl down at the Miels' farm comes up clear and distinct; so do the sheep bells tonkle-tonkling somewhere down beyond the wood.

It is still here. So still that summer guests complain that they cannot sleep because of the silence.

The silence of childhood; of the ramshackle cottage on the Downs which Uncle Salmon long ago offered us as a second home, and which became, for me and for Elizabeth, merely

The house from the west

'home'. Nothing else. Everywhere else was 'the other place'. And so I had come full circle, to the stillness, the sheep bells, much as I had heard them on Windover Hill, the guinea-fowl gobbling as they did at Court Farm, the wind wuthering in last summer's dead grasses.

After Los Angeles, New York and, more recently, Paris, the silence sings for me and I am once again 'within my skin'.

Down by the pond, which I had had bulldozed years before out of the shale and rock, the fish lie still; a pair of toads tumble lazily together in the ugly waltz of copulation and a lone hen-toad threads her ropes of eggs in long slippery strands among the brown stalks of the water-iris, as busy as a basket-weaver.

Below her, in the crystal water, the first bronze buds of the water-lilies have begun pushing through the silt. Elizabeth brought a root of these for me from her pond in her garden at Angmering. She wrapped a chunk in damp paper and stuck it in her wash-bag. Now, after more than a decade, the chunk has increased alarmingly and the dividing of the roots will have to begin before the pond is smothered with the big green plates which these tender bronze buds will become by April, if I don't get into the water pretty soon.

Life is starting again: no doubt of that.

Another season is about to commence and I am here to see it. After sixty years each spring which arrives is a glorious bounty, and is not to be taken for granted. Standing under the giant olive at the edge of the pond I am suffused with content-ment and relief; until I remember that this new season will once again deny me the sight of my father clambering up the hill, easel under his arm, canvas in one hand, whistling to the dogs, coming up for his lunchtime beer.

My mother's feet will not be heard clacking across the tiled floors which she so disliked. 'How you can *live* without carpets I simply don't know! *So* uncomfortable.' Her idle humming won't be heard under the vine when we open the wine, and Labo and Daisy were not leaping beside the taxi as we came up just now – and never will again.

This season will be without some familiars.

Daisy died just before Christmas, a not very good boxer bought on impulse from a pet-shop in Cannes, and Labo, who sought me out fourteen years before in Rome, a slum dog riddled with worms, his foreleg smashed to pulp, insisting on my company, had apologetically haemorrhaged while I was washing up just before I had left for Los Angeles, and died in my arms.

Fourteen years of a shared life lay buried under a rosemary bush in the *potager*. He would not be present when I lugged the lily roots from the pond this time. It was a particular job which he enjoyed for it entailed smells and muck and, as often as not, a bite at a gasping fish which I sometimes, accidentally, chucked out with the silt.

He was a street dog and hated the country. Smells were all. He really only liked filth.

Once he had caught and killed a pullet (chicken was his favourite food) and I had tied the stinking carcass round his neck as a punishment. He was killing them off daily after all; something had to be done. He ate the lot with relish.

Visconti called him 'Poverino', which in English means 'poor little fellow'.

Poor little fellow, my foot.

He was as sly and deceitful as a pickpocket, and I loved him with all my heart.

Fourteen years of life; and over a decade with Daisy. The deaths of the dogs were the hair-cracks in the fabric of my complacency, but, as is usual with hair-cracks, their warning was not immediately apparent.

Forwood called from the terrace, and as I turned to walk back up the slope from the pond I suddenly noticed that all the shutters were closed on the house, save for the one pair over the room where Henri and Marie took their meals; this was quite unusual.

'All right?' I knew that my voice carried uncertainty.

'No. Not at *all* all right. Henri's ill. Very ill. We'll have to get him home right away.'

'What's happened?'

'I don't know. How do *I* know? Marie says he's been getting slowly worse ever since they arrived. The doctor has been, they don't know what's wrong.'

Henri and Marie had come to run the house, wash and cook, during my first three years; they had suggested that they were much younger than in fact they were, but loved dogs, were loyal, and had splendid references; I finally retired them to a small flat with a balcony down in the valley. They came to 'mind the house' whenever I left it, enjoying what they called a 'little holiday in the clean air of the hill', but this time when they had arrived it was clear that Henri was unwell.

He was vague, stumbled a bit, was slow to recognize words. Marie, indomitable as ever, swore that 'the change of air will do him good, the doctors have said so'. Nothing would persuade her otherwise.

The decline had been swift.

He sat slumped in his armchair, chin on his chest, hands in his lap, as if for dead. Somehow, I don't honestly remember quite how, Forwood and I half dragged, half carried his dead weight down the stairs and into the car; Marie had packed and stood watching in silence.

Henri moaned softly to himself: 'Oh God! My God! What has become of me, what has become of me?'

We drove to their flat. The strong neighbour who lived opposite was out, so we had to carry him up two flights of stairs, his arms trailing, head lolling, then Marie called a doctor and begged us to return, for we had left the house untended. We drove back through the lanes, too tired, too sad, to talk. The late sun starting its slide down behind the mountains, the sky fading from blue to lavender, from lavender to saffron.

At the gates to the track the new boxer, Bendo, a replacement for lost loves, hurried up beside the car, leaping the low stone walls, turning back from time to time to be assured that we were following, and when he was certain his anxiety gave way to pleasure and he tore off to find a stone as a welcoming gift.

It was a rough homecoming.

*   *   *

In May the water-lilies sat among their green plates like shining porcelain cups, as well spaced and set about as a nursery tea-table: the winter-work had been justified, and in time.

On the terrace, the roses which I had managed to plant into their pots before the end of March were already fat with buds; the orange tree by the front door was beginning to scent the mornings with its bridal blossoms; wallflowers and columbine had invaded every rough corner; the wistaria hung presumptuous purple tassels round the window of the olive store; and Henri died.

The funeral was in his local village church. There were no relations, no children, no one close, for they had no one.

I picked a bunch of roses from the garden and we drove down to their village and waited in the early morning – it was not yet nine o'clock – at the square. The church bell began to toll for the dead, that solemn, rather tinny, deliberate Clong! Clong! Clong!

A girl hurried into the baker's and hurried out again with the breakfast bread, a small boy rode across the cobbles on his bicycle, lifting his small rump from the saddle with each shuddering bump as he hit the kerbstones.

The hearse swung into the square, wine-dark, flowerless.

We watched the coffin being carted, with not much delicacy, into the dark door of the ancient church; there was no sign of Marie.

A few people, perhaps five or six, straggled in behind Henri, neighbours from the flats; all women.

Inside, the church was cold, dusty, dim, neglected. The village was predominantly a Communist community and the Mayor was allowing the church to decay deliberately, 'phasing out' religion.

I sat at the back, near the door, on the hard wooden bench. The tiled floor was cracked, the walls, scaling with wet crumbling plaster; there was a smell of damp wool, leather from the bindings of mildewed prayer books scattered here and there, of varnish and rust. On the walls, grimy marble plaques set into the mouldering frescoes of the Stations of the Cross. Christ had lost his head in the *Scourging at the Pillar* and his feet and shins in the *Crucifixion*.

On one plaque, a name, a date – 1916 – a place – Verdun.

On another, three Italian-sounding names; their ages, between twenty and thirty-one; a date – May 1943.

Deportation. Buchenwald. Germany.

Neglected reminders of the agonies of France which had reached down even to this small place.

There was a scattering of people now among the pews, perhaps not more than twelve of us, plus Henri in his wooden box (pine, because it was cheaper) on bare trestles standing before the shabby altar, two candles guttering in the wind from the open doors, an altarcloth, plain as a winding sheet flapping and rippling like laundry on a clothesline.

Beside me on the wall a glass bead wreath hung crookedly, the words '*Ave Maria*' worked in dusty violet silk; beside it, a headless saint, hand raised in a fingerless blessing; and the iron pipes, which once must have provided some form of heating in this cheerless place, had long since cracked and leaked emerald moss in broad fans across the crumbling stonework.

The bell continued to Clong! Clong! Clong! somewhere above us; I took the bunch of garden roses and placed them on the coffin, about where, I judged, his chest must be.

People turned, looked over their shoulders, coughed, nodded, returned to their glazed study of the guttering candles.

Henri, with his silly chuckle, his boyish good humour, his love of beasts and birds, his pride for the land from which he had sprung, his extreme clumsiness, his 'moods', his terrible slurping when he took his soup, his pleasure in, and knowledge of, his tiny cellar with its modest rack of bottles, his relish in a piece of good Saint-Nectair cheese – all these things, and the mortal remains of him, were bundled up in a shoddy box before us, under a clanging bell.

'Oh God! Oh my God! What has become of me?' he had sobbed as we carted him down the stairs.

Well, this is what had become of him, boxed up under the bells and a bunch of Grand'mère Jenny roses.

There was a shuffle of sound behind us and Marie, leaning heavily on the arm of the neighbour across the hall, came down the cracked-tiled aisle, as the priest came through a little door by the altar, youngish, in a white surplice with neat lace cuffs, a small book in his hands.

He waited before Henri, rocking gently on his heels, lips pursed, as Marie was led, rather than shown, to the front pew.

She was bowed, no longer upright now, wearing a blue wraparound cardigan which I had brought her once from Marks and Spencer's, a grey stuff skirt with a drooping hem, elastic stockings. On her feet, beige plastic sandals from Monoprix; on her head a widow's cap in cheap black lace.

A short service, the priest laconic; there were no acolytes to swing his censer so he did it, almost irritably, himself. Little puffs of smoke meandered in the damp air.

We were on short means here – very different from the chapel at the convent in Twickenham, the glitter and the glory, the soaring organ music and the flying Christ, the viridian and crimson, the rustle and bustle of Sister Veronica's grey habit, the clatter of her rosary, the overwhelming scent of the incense which, once, long ago, I had been permitted to swing in its silver censer, puffed with pride and reverence.

I'd like to have done it for Henri, even though I knew it was all nonsense, that it really didn't matter and that it could no longer comfort him now. That dead is dead, and that bodies are bundled and tumbled by bulldozers, left to rot in tiered bunks in Buchenwald, exploded into bloody fragments in Verdun, or bound, doused with petrol, and burned alive beneath frangipani trees.

Henri, I reckoned, was neat and tidy where he was.

When the service was over, Marie was assisted by her neighbour and began the cruel walk, past her husband of fifty years, towards the open doors. Her face was gaunt, wrenched with tearless grief, ashen with cheap powder, her lips a startling scarlet weal.

A lipstick, as far as she was concerned, was red. And red was red.

As she drew abreast of Forwood and me sitting in the gloom, she half raised her head for a moment, and saw us.

She smiled the smallest smile of gratitude, suddenly stood tall, removed her arm gently from that of her neighbour, and walked out into the sunlit square, the rough wind teasing her widow's cap.

They shouldered Henri out of the church, the roses wobbling dangerously so that I removed them and when he had been rolled into the wine-dark hearse replaced them on his chest. They drove him out of the square, down the road to the new cemetery. And, as far as we were concerned, that was that.

Dead is dead when all is said and done. And all had been said, and all had been done. If a door had shut quietly behind me in the corridor, I confess that I was not immediately aware of the fact: it is sometimes just as well that we do not hear the closing, and the turning of the key.

I remember, driving home that morning, thinking how wretched it was that Forwood and I were the only kith and kin that they had had. Finally your life ends and you are left with only your last employers as mourners, apart, that is, from a handful of kindly neighbours.

However, my own desperate search for kith and kin to attend my funeral had finally come to nothing.

Aunt 'Coggley' Chesterfield, who had tried to teach me to spell: 'There is no "e" at the end of "potato", darling. You keep sticking "e's" where there are none. How many "s's" are there in "necessary"?'

Uncle Bertie, who had removed my tonsils and who swore to keep me alive while so doing; his laughing wife, Aunt Gladys, pink of nails, blond marcelled hair, silk stockings on elegant legs; and Aunt Celestia with her nicotined fingers and damp cigarette butts; Uncle Salmon, who had given me 'George', the tortoise, and opened a new world for me through an ancient cottage in a Great Meadow; Aunt Yvonne, who had, literally, pushed me on to a stage for the first time in my life; and Granny Nutt, and garden-proud Uncle Arthur whom I let beat me at croquet.

And my parents.

All of them had gone long before I had had need of them to mourn me. But they had not altogether gone, and Henri, I was pretty certain, was now about to jostle his way among them on to the backcloth of my life before which I performed my modest show with those of the cast who remained: Elizabeth and George, my brother Gareth, his wife Cilla and their family, Forwood and, without question, the ever-constant Lally.

She was still 'on stage' with us.

Valiant, strong, brave of heart, and of soul, she had sent me a picture postcard of a palm tree from Torquay a few days before.

Here for my little annual holiday, dear, with my nice friend Mrs Hutchings who can drive a car. So that's good, isn't it? Coolish at the moment but it'll cheer up because I have brought my bathing-costume. May have a dip after tea-time, the water is hot in the hotel pool! Whatever next!

Remembering her card, the day was suddenly brighter; I no longer heard the Clong! Clong! of the bell.

But I hadn't heard the closing of the door either.

*   *   *

After Henri and Marie had, reluctantly, been retired, Soledad came to do 'two hours a day, six days a week'. She was a sturdy, bright-eyed young woman, who arrived on her *moto*, a two-year-old daughter strapped into a seat behind.

She looked about the house, in silence. The principal reason for this being that she was a Spanish immigrant and spoke almost no French. However, she made it clear that she would not work in a house where there were women; I assured her that she would not be troubled by her own sex and she agreed to try it out, for a month.

That was in 1972, and she is still here today.

The giddy idea that two men could run, single (or is it double?)-handed a house and twelve acres very soon faded in a scurry of irritation and helplessness. I can't cook an egg; and practically not even boil water – Forwood agreed to do the cooking (he was good at cauliflower cheese and could grill a chicken). I was to be the scullion, preparing the vegetables and doing the washing-up.

I frequently thought that I had got the worst of the deal.

Madame Bruna, the mason's wife, did the 'heavy laundry' and I stuck the teacloths and underpants in bushels of Persil and hung them on the line.

It really wasn't very satisfactory: cauliflower cheese becomes wearisome, and I got bored cleaning the oven, and the land, of necessity, became neglected. So Soledad was engaged, and after she had decided to remain and take things in hand she was called 'Lady', and 'Lady' she has remained.

I reckon that she is known right across the world now, from San Francisco to Delhi, for as soon as it was possible we stripped out the staff flat, converted it into a guest suite, and opened, what seemed to us all, a small *pension*. Suspicious, at first, of strangers in 'her' house, she quickly warmed to their odd habits and over the years became as indispensable to them as she is to me.

Although there was hardly any common language (after all this time she is far more fluent in French) she managed very well, and most especially with Elizabeth, to whom she became devoted.

Without a single word in common, they would screech together, laughing and whooping in some strange form of invented Esperanto, and when I was away for a long seven months working on two films, back-to-back, Elizabeth and George came to mind the house and Lady and she became even closer, especially as Lady was pregnant and had little 'turns' from time to time. She eventually had a rather severe one and was sent home on her *moto*, bouncing down the track, her crash-helmet rocking, blue smoke spurting from the noisy

225

exhaust, and an hour later gave birth to a son – almost on her kitchen floor.

She was back at work, up the track on the *moto*, three days later, earning Elizabeth's undying admiration and affection.

And so it was; a household had formed that was altogether satisfactory, held together by Lady, who took the teacloths and underpants, and sundry other pieces of washing, and did it all properly.

Like rinsing them.

Perhaps, apart from Elizabeth, her favourite guest in Tart's Parlour, as it became known because it was a smother of English chintz (fat roses and lilac), pink shaded lamps and an elegant Eugénie chair, buttoned tightly and braided in silk, was Norah Smallwood, who came to stay every year with a leg, foot or an arm in plaster, for she was accident prone and very frail, and Lady enjoyed the shocks and surprises which accompanied Norah on her visits.

I first saw her sometime in the early seventies in the pages of a glossy magazine in an article on 'Women in Power' or 'The Silent Geniuses', or some other idiotic editorial heading. It was a small photograph of this, I gathered, elusive, mysterious, extraordinary woman, who almost single-handed, it implied, ran Chatto and Windus, the publishers. I was suitably impressed because, though small, it was a photograph of great elegance. Norah appeared to be swaddled in a sea of silk cushions. She had a fine patrician head, a slightly mocking smile (she detested the Press and loathed being photographed), an air of luxury and, distinctly, breeding.

It was well known, even to me, that Chatto and Windus were *the* publishers, the most respected, the ones with the most impressive 'list' of authors, the most desired by all writers. If Chatto accepted you it was the highest accolade; whether you were accepted or not depended entirely on this woman. She had the power of life and death, as it were, over a book, and she very seldom made an error.

It was not in her nature to do so.

The next time I saw her, some years later, was standing at

the door of her own office, slim, tall, chic in a white silk shirt
and a coral wool skirt, her white hair set and groomed, a tiny
pearl in each ear, her eyes sparkling, her voice and movements
brisk and unfussy. In her hands she held two copies of the first
book of mine which she had agreed to publish, and she
demanded, in a firm voice, which colour binding I preferred?
The blue or the yellow?

I was too overcome by the sight of my own book, in whatever colour of binding, to properly answer her, so she chivvied
me off to the Garrick Club for luncheon. I was pretty overcome
by her as well. Awed is a good word.

We had reached, by this time, the Christian name level.
Although it still slightly embarrassed me to call her 'Norah'
she obviously had no compunction in calling me by mine. We
had written letters to each other during the writing of the
book, but only in the latter stages. At first the letters were
signed by someone other, and only when we got down to
selecting drawings (mine) and photographs, and when I had,
in some way, 'proved' myself to her, did she finally sign her
own letters; and, in time, she dropped the 'Smallwood' and
signed herself simply 'N'.

Our first meeting, at the Garrick, seemed to satisfy her that I
did not eat peas with my knife, talk about the cinema, or pick
my nose at table. Her relief was frankly obvious: she had no
knowledge of an actor's life and feared, I'm certain, that I
might be swathed in chinchilla, smoking 'hash'. That I wore a
sober suit and tie, had washed behind my ears, and spoke the
Queen's English (even though I found it difficult to write it
correctly) reassured her, and we began to relax together; I
think that our friendship was finally sealed at the supper party
which I gave at the Connaught on the day of publication.

It was a carefully seated table; I had ordered what she called
a 'scrumptious supper' (of six courses) and a splendid claret
with which she could find no fault. My training as an ADC,
and understanding of 'sitting a table', had paid off admirably.

Norah, a corking snob in many amusing ways, was agree-
ably impressed by 'her writer'.

227

Once, some years later, when I had the temerity to suggest that perhaps she was 'a bit of a snob', she had smiled at me wistfully, touched a pearl in her ear, twisted it thoughtfully – an old habit of hers.

'Well. I don't really know. I've never thought much about it. I know that people *think* I am; but if it means that I only tolerate the very best in things, you know, like ... well, Colette, perfectly fried eggs and bacon, an Auden poem, Sienna in the autumn, the best of *anything* ... then I suppose that I am. I can't abide mediocrity, ugliness, cheapness ... I can't bear slackness in word, deed, writing, or in people. Behaviour is terribly important to me. Grace, good manners, kindness, a striving to attain, to be better. If that's being a snob then I suppose that I must be – and I so *detest* "snobs"!'

Her first visit to the house here was curious for many reasons.

Lady had bashed herself into a state of near exhaustion polishing the floors my mother so detested, the house was filled with flowers, white and green for the white-and-green room. Tart's Parlour shone with hours of waxing, the pillows were plump and fat and daisy-scattered. The view from the windows, across the wooded hill to the valley and the sea, and the ragged line of the Estérel range, soft against the sky, caught Norah's voluble breath and stilled it. She stood in silence, filled with joy at the beauty before her.

In the evening we sat around the burning logs in the stove, and began to 'discover' each other. She admired bits and pieces in the room, and then apologized for so doing.

'But *do*! It's splendid that you admire the Portuguese dishes ...'

'My father always said that one must NEVER admire anything in anyone's house, that it was the height of bad manners, just as it was to speak of the food at a meal ...'

'Your father sounds very strict, Norah? Surely to admire one's host's choice is a compliment?'

'Not to my father. It was an impertinence.'

Later, a glass of framboise clutched in her arthritic hands,

228

she spoke about 'fillums', as she called them, slightly disparagingly.

'I never go, you know . . . oh, I used to years ago, with the Bloomsburys for fun. We used to go and see all those rubbishy things made by a man called Cecil Someone.'

'B. de Mille?'

'*Cecil.* I don't remember the "B." . . . Perhaps. But we used to sit and laugh like anything at all the ghastly mistakes. You know, the Bible all the wrong way round, and silly ladies with sillier faces speaking Yankee in Egypt and Palestine or wherever.'

'They gave a lot of people a great deal of pleasure.'

'I suppose so,' she sighed. 'I wish they would *read* instead of looking at all that nonsense; can't be good for them.'

'Have you never seen a French film? *Un Carnet de bal? La Règle du jeu? Casque d'or?*'

'Oh yes . . . sometimes I got taken along by one of my writers to the Curzon, and we saw a foreign fillum . . . they were MUCH better. Much. Intelligent, too. Oh, quite different. I loved *them.* But really the cinema and that awful television thing are such utter rubbish.'

'There are sometimes good things to watch.'

'I never do. Unless forced.'

'You were watching television when you saw me.'

'Oh! Absolute fluke. My hosts were glued to the damned box all day watching sport and when they put the thing on AGAIN after dinner to watch something they called a "replay" I nearly went mad; so I got up and turned the button to see if there was ANYTHING other than a crowd of men kicking a ball about, and I got your programme, talking to that nice man.'

'And I'm very grateful indeed. It's because of that desperate gesture that I wrote a book and we are here together tonight, isn't it?'

'Correct. But it was a fluke, a lucky fluke, but that's all.'

I refilled her glass.

'I'll sleep tonight,' she said. 'I never sleep, these wretched

229

hands keep me awake. You've noticed them, of course? Like seal's flippers. I did have pretty hands, I was very vain. My punishment, I suppose.'

'Are they frightfully painful?'

'Frightfully. I'm stuffed with pills all day. Don't do much good. A glass of wine or a stiff whisky does much better. If you see me wearing my table napkin wrapped round my fist, take no notice. It's just pain.'

'You are wearing one now.'

She looked at it in surprise.

'So I am. Brought it down from dinner I suppose. It was pretty hellish for a while. Now.' She changed the subject briskly. 'I *did* see a really splendid fillum some time ago, I think the young Graham Greene forced me. A fillum of a novella of Thomas Mann's . . . of course I was very suspicious, you know how they always fudge that sort of thing, but it was quite magical, absolutely wonderful . . . not *quite* Thomas Mann. The director person had stuck in some outside stuff, but it all seemed to work. Now that was one fillum I saw three times! *Death In Venice*. Did you see it? Do you get those kind of fillums here in France?'

'I was in it,' I said.

There was a long, still silence; a log settled.

'*Death In Venice?*'

'Yes . . . Thomas Mann.'

She unwrapped the table napkin, looked into her glass, wrapped the napkin round her poor, knobbled fist again.

'But what were you? There was only an old man and a rather beautiful youth . . .'

'The old man. I played von Aschenbach.'

Norah's eyes were steady with disbelief.

'I saw it three times.'

'And each time it was me.'

'Well . . .' She shook her head. 'It didn't look the L E A S T bit like you,' she said.

*   *   *

This first visit was a test-case. Friday to Sunday was all that she would spare. She was not about to take a risk and find herself perhaps trapped in marble jaccuzis, swimming-pools, Le Corbusier chairs and, perhaps worst of all, wall-to-wall television.

She wasn't; and relaxed gratefully.

Her real reason for coming, apart from testing the ground, was to collect the finished, and edited, typescript of my second book, and to ensure that I did a cover design for her to take back to the office for Monday morning.

A rather hefty demand which, fortunately, I was able to manage.

'I know', she said tartly, 'that there are only supposed to be twenty-four hours in a day, of course, but I manage to make mine last thirty-six at least.'

And she seriously expected lesser mortals to behave in the same way; even with twelve acres to tend and tables to lay and food to buy, dogs to feed, and all the rest of the trivia of life. Having 'discovered' me, helped me to write, encouraged me to work until I dropped, she would not take slackness, as she called it, as any kind of excuse.

The ground tested, and found acceptable, the food tasted, and declared 'scrumptious', the knowledge that she need not trouble to conceal the agonizing pain which she suffered practically all the time, the delight in what she called 'conversation' after dinner on the terrace, or by the fire, the fact that there was so much to discuss and plan and that she had taken my new career, for that is what it was beginning to seem to be now, firmly in hand, brought her to the house every year and, now that she knew its pattern, she stayed longer and was a demanding, but wonderfully rewarding, guest.

She was also a fearsome responsibility.

Her poor skin was as thin as tissue paper from all the drugs which she had to take to lessen her pain. The least knock, scratch or bump, even the touch of a leaf, could cause instant, and alarming, bleeding which nothing would staunch until the

231

wound healed, and every time she went off into the garden, heavily gloved, with secateurs and a box, to potter about dead-heading whatever caught her knowing gardener's eye, my heart was in my mouth. But the light songs she sang, trailing sweetly across the lawn, or from behind the bay hedges, gave me infinite pleasure, and usually reassured me that she had not come to grief.

One morning I took her breakfast into her bedroom. She was, as she always was, wide awake, sitting up among her pillows, looking through the open windows to the hills.

'Didn't sleep?'

'Until three. Never after three, the pills wear off. Anyway, it's getting light by five, so I open the window and breathe in this delicious air. It's like being on top of a mountain.'

'You almost are. It's four hundred metres high here.'

'I wish the bed was.'

'The bed was what?'

'Higher. You see, lying here I just *can't* see the hills . . . come and sit where I am; by the pillow. You see? The bed is too low, or the window too high; something.'

'What should I do, Norah?'

'Well . . . would it cost a frightful lot to *lower* the windows?'

'Frightful. The wall is a metre thick, it's been like that for 400 years.'

'Pity. Never mind. It would be nice, but very spoiled of me. Is that fresh orange juice?'

'Pressed by myself. As promised.'

'I loathe that tinned stuff; how good you are.'

Two months later I bought a pair of brass beds, copies of those in the Paris Ritz. They were higher; and the next time she came she lay in delighted glory, looking at the hills, the sea, down to the vineyards in the valley, frail and content among her pillows. It was well worth it to me.

We were neither of us, of course, unaware that in the world of publishing there were murmurs of dissent, even derision. I was teacher's pet, and the fact that my name as a film star had helped to get my work on to the best-seller lists did not please those who were still struggling to get published at all.

'Of course,' someone once said to her, 'we know that you are biased, Bogarde can do no wrong in your eyes. It's dangerous, you know.'

Norah's reply was sharp and to the point. 'He's making money for the firm, that's all I care about.'

Her personal judgement was being questioned, and she would not accept that. Her judgement, as far as she was concerned, had been justified. I did my best for the rest of my time with her to honour that belief.

★   ★   ★

Lady gave a soft cry of despair when I told her that Henri had died. Her hands went to her face to cover instant, rather facile, tears.

'And Marie?'

'Very sad, and very lonely.'

'Better that she dies too, poor thing.'

'Oh I don't think so . . . in some ways it might be almost a release for her now, and she has no intention of giving up. She's coming to lunch on Tuesday.'

'And when is the big party, for the Festival?'

'On Wednesday. There will be fifty people at least.'

She threw her duster into the air and caught it; inexpertly. 'Where will you put fifty people?'

'At tables under the olive trees – it is May after all.'

'And if it rains? It always rains for the Film Festival.'

'It won't.'

It didn't. The rains, which indeed had been looming over Cannes all week, suddenly veered away, and the day broke brilliant with sunshine for the party to honour David Puttnam, his director Hugh Hudson, his actors and their various appendages for *Chariots of Fire*, which had been the British entry the night before.

We'd borrowed trestle tables and little folding iron chairs

from the mayor and set them up under the trees among the buttercups. Scrubbed wood, peeling green slatted chairs, dappled sun: very informal, very Renoir, very, I chose to believe, French.

Madame Rolles, a formidable lady from Alsace, did the catering (someone said that it was 'criminally over-catered', but this wasn't going to be a bridge roll affair) and her son, resplendent in white coat and tall chef's hat, served an apparently never-ending, and starving, crowd of laughing, relaxed people.

Everyone had turned up except one who declined because, he said, he was not going to be 'patronized by a bloody film star'. His absence, however, was hardly noticed; which might have irked him.

No sooner had the tables and chairs been folded down and carted back to the village for the next Old Folke's Supper than Lady was up in Tart's Parlour scrubbing the white carpet and polishing the wood in preparation for Madame Petit-Bois's (the nearest she could get to 'Smallwood') yearly arrival.

This year Norah hobbled in. Ugly bandages on her elegant, crane-slender legs: the result of a careless collision with a coffee table some weeks before. So, sticks and footstools again, and the village nurse daily to dress the wounds and to complain to me, privately, that 'Madame is dehydrated! She is all skin and bone! She has no fluid in her! You must make her drink water, litres and litres of water, or she'll die . . .'

Trying to force Norah to drink litres of water was about as absurd as trying to force an elephant into a barrel.

'Silly woman! She's mad! I *detest* water. I drink lots of my wine, lots of lovely tea. Dehydrated! Absolute bosh!'

'I only passed on a piece of medical information and advice.'

'Stuff! Now . . .' She changed the subject swiftly, for she detested talking of her ailments, thinking, I suppose, that if they were not discussed they would go away. 'Now . . . what have you written? Anything to show me? Should be.'

I handed her the first chapter of *An Orderly Man*, which made her laugh and which she accepted 'as a start'.

'When can you get down to things? I'd say pretty soon frankly. That wretched fillum Festival is over now, so there is nothing in your way, is there?'

I looked across the terrace down to the acres of mown, unraked hay, thought of the weeds flourishing in the *potager*, the gutter which had to be painted, the pots which had to be fed and watered, the small bunches of grapes already forming on the vine above our heads, which had to be removed before they grew too large and their weight brought down the iron trellis.

Nothing in my way but work.

'I'll start, surely, when I get back from England next month. I've still got half the film with Glenda Jackson to finish, remember.'

She took up her wine and sighed with impatience. 'That dratted fillum. They do get so in the way.'

'Three weeks, that's all. Then I'll be back at work, I promise you. But I've got to earn a little loot, you know, darling: books don't exactly match the movies in money, unless you are a Frederick Forsyth or a Dick Francis, and I ain't either, as you know.'

She knew perfectly well: she was scrupulously fair, but not over-indulgent, as far as money was concerned; she didn't believe in cosseting, as she called it, her writers and, sadly, her ideas of money were based strictly on pre-war standards.

'I think that you may well do comfortably with *Voices* (*Voices in the Garden*). I think it's your best novel so far really: the Meringue-Hats will go for it, but I'm not certain about the Young. It's a book about class, you see, and the Young have rather dismissed class; such a pity . . . they won't understand "your people", I'm afraid. Don't believe that they exist. All this business of "identification". Really it's *too* boring.'

'Well. Let's wait until September, when it hits the shops. Then we'll get an idea. And this time no publicity, no promotions in Bradford or Birmingham, above all no chat shows. Never again.'

She took a sip from her wine, eased her leg on the footstool.

'You may regret it, you know, it made a lot of difference to the last three books.'

But I knew, in spite of her undoubted concern, that she was secretly relieved. A true Scot, the last bill for my expenses at the Connaught during promotion had caused her to rock slightly on her Ferragamo heels with horror.

'My dear! This is a year's salary for some people!' she had cried. 'Couldn't you take a *room* next time? With friends? You must have lots of friends in London who would be delighted to let you have a *room* somewhere.'

I had argued that I simply couldn't do promotional tours of the punishing variety which she, in part, had organized and which she was almost insistent that I should do, even though I might bleed to death in the doing of them. Reluctantly, she was convinced that I had to have hotel service to fulfil my job and help sell her wares, as well as my own. But it always rankled.

'Norah! Think of the money you'll save this time. All you have to do is take a little advertising in one or two of the better papers and sit back and see what happens. No Connaught bills, no car hire, no trains, no planes . . . easy.'

'Do you know the cost of a "little advertising" in the better papers today?' A fat Provençal blue bee swooped in under the vine, she ducked, it swung out into the breathless morning. 'I'd like to get this' – she wagged the chapter at me – 'on board as soon as you can manage really. I'd like to have it "in the house" at least by, well . . . let's say March. Can you try?'

'I can. Certainly. You're pushing me a bit – you've always said "Take your time" and "Don't hurry". Why the pressure?'

She placed the chapter on the table beside her, the wine glass on top, lay back, closed her eyes.

'I think that perhaps I'd better tell you something. I wasn't going to, but . . .'

'Something not very good, is that it?'

'Well, not very good for me. No. I think I'm going to pull out of the firm in March. Retire me'self.'

I sat mute with surprise. This. Of all things.

'I've been there a long time, you know. William IV Street. Not getting any younger either, and this pain is really pretty fearsome.' She opened her eyes wide, looking up into the leaves above; not at me. 'I think that it's spreading, the arthritis. Into my hips . . . and perhaps my legs . . . a frightful nuisance but there we are. Time for someone younger to take over the ship, frankly.'

I was so stupefied with shock that I could think only in banalities. 'Have you someone in mind? You must have?'

'Oh yes. I've been thinking about it for a long time. I'm a woman, but I managed to run that firm pretty well for a long, long time. I'd like another woman to take it on. I've got my eye on her. Very bright, clever, sharp, very, very ambitious, tough as anything and strong. Just as I was when I was young. Lots of guts: I had those too. Keep this to yourself, it wouldn't do to let it out yet.'

'I'm unlikely to telephone the *News of the World*.'

'The *Bookseller* would appreciate it much more, my dear, I assure you!'

'No fear . . .'

'So if you can get this . . . what's it to be called? *An Orderly Man*.' She squinted at the chapter, held it to the light. 'Good title. Don't change it. Have it under way so that I can get it all set up and "in the house" before I . . .' She placed the pages back on the table, lay back. 'By March anyway. On board by March. Try?'

'I'll try. Promise.'

Nurse Humery's car turned into the track below in a cloud of pale dust.

'Here's nurse. The bandages all in your room?'

'All ready,' she said. 'What a bore it all is, really.'

I knew the anguish that this decision had cost her: the restless, pain-filled nights which forced her to reach such a conclusion, the rage against her body which had given up so long before her brilliant, sharp, inquisitive mind, the cruelty of forcing her own retirement.

Chatto without Norah was unthinkable, even to me who

237

had been with the firm for only a few years; she was the core of it, the heartbeat, the very life; she had seemed to be as permanent, as solid, as dominating and unshakeable as Nelson's Column beyond her office windows, and the fact that she was, after all, merely human and full of all the human frailties we know I had overlooked.

As I walked across the grass to meet Nurse Humery, I heard, this time quite distinctly, the whispering creak of hinges swinging uncertainly in the wind of change which was riffling along the corridor, and I resolved, there and then, to get down to work on the new book as soon as I humanly could so that she should have it 'in the house', and in her hands, before she closed her door.

★   ★   ★

Although Henri's death, and the uneasy awareness of Norah's possible retirement, were not exactly hurdles over which I 'could almost step', for they had come harshly and out of left-field, so to speak, I had somehow managed to take them in a clean leap without coming to absolute grief in a tumble of emotions: somehow I was given extra strength for the unsuspected effort and got over.

The main hurdle, and one which I had expected for a long time, and not without trepidation, was the English shoot; but that, as I have said, went pretty well, all things considered, and although it was a pretty high hurdle, and dangerous, that too was cleared, mainly owing to Glenda, who slipped effortlessly back into her role of 'Patricia Neal' after a three-month absence on Broadway just as if she had never been away, and held my hand tightly.

Mainly, too, because of the excellent British crew who, smaller than the giant one which we had used in Hollywood, nevertheless coped smoothly with, to them, a brand-new production, and who were far less liable to 'fuss' or intimidation.

'I wanna rostrum!'

'Okay, guv. Rostrum it'll be.'

'A ten-foot, maybe twelve-foot rostrum. You got that?'

'We have, guv.'

'And set it right here! Right where I'm bloody well standing. Here! See?'

'Got it, guv.'

'What's that tree thing?'

'A tree? Nah, guv, not a tree. It's a *bush*. A rose bush.'

'What kinda rose bush. Special?'

'Very, guv. Oh, very special.'

'We can't clear it away? It's in shot. Right in shot! I want the camera right on top of this rostrum and I wanna pan it right down this road-place and that fuckin' rose bush is right there in the way. Get rid of it.'

'It's a *Tudor* rose, guv. Can't move it. Heritage. All that.'

'Tudor? That is?'

'Elizabethan. Real English.'

'That so? Well . . . Hey! Mike? That's a Tudor rose, right? So *linger* on it when we pan across, right? Atmosphere. Then speed up and catch the car as it passes, you got that?'

One dog rose was spared for another English summer.

Whereas in Los Angeles everyone on the set seemed to be forced to 'jog' everywhere, even while eating their tuna sandwiches, the British just took their time, in the traditional British manner, and in spite of constant shrill screams from the Office caused by uncomprehending exasperation (for they did not fully understand the way that the British work, and why, indeed, should they?) everyone had their bacon sandwiches, their tea-break, their sit-down lunch-break, and another tea-break at four o'clock, with a 'snack' coming up about five-thirty. It was reckoned by the Office that we lost two hours' work a day, which I am certain is a grave exaggeration, but where time is money, exaggeration becomes truth. We worked to union rules, which in consequence made for a calmer, less frenetic, happier atmosphere. After a few days everyone got sorted out and settled down, and in spite of inclement weather we crammed in the work (all those bacon sandwiches for energy) and sometimes shot until last light at about eight-thirty in the evening.

And then, suddenly, it was all over. No slow wind-down, no gentle easing of the stress, just a cheerful call: 'Okay, boys . . . that's it. It's a wrap. Thank you one-and-all.'

Together, after we had shed 'Roald' and 'Pat', and sent their garments off to wardrobe for packing, Glenda and I sat in the grounds of a hospital near Wendover in my trailer, a Guinness for a 'strengthener' on the formica table between us, before we attempted the long journey back through the traffic to town.

We looked pinched and tired, and we were. Listless; and we were.

When a player has been wound up to a high pitch of emotionalism for any length of time the sudden ending of work comes as a physical, and mental, shock. One is drained suddenly: the adrenalin is still flowing but now there is no need for it, no receptacle in which to store it, so that it seeps and dribbles away leaving one weak and void.

A stoked-up engine, boiler roaring, steam billowing; stuck at the buffers.

'Well.' Glenda started to collect her hand-grip, a book, a half-eaten apple. 'That's it. Off we go, that journey back to Blackheath in all this traffic is just what I don't need. At this time of night.'

'You shouldn't live at the end of the world.'

'It's got a lovely garden. You should come and see my garden.'

'I feel I've been shooting for months.'

'Three weeks, love. I mean it hasn't been all *that* long.'

'Feels like it. I wonder if they'll pay us?'

'Pay us. What do you mean?'

'It seems to me that I don't get fully paid for the movies I make, I can't think why.'

'You got paid for the first half, didn't you?'

'Yes. And expenses. Expenses on this side too, but there's a deferment, and deferments have a habit of not getting paid.'

'Well I've been paid all I'm owed. So they tell me.'

'For the whole deal?'

'I don't know! You *are* suspicious! Listen to you!'

'I still haven't had my deferment for *Death in Venice*. I got twelve thousand quid for that and not a sou extra. We're still in debt, five million or something, and the movie only cost about *two*, so I don't know . . . you have to believe what they tell you because no one is bright enough to work it out. Including me.'

'As far as I'm concerned, I'm paid. That's all I know.'

'I've got a written guarantee that they'll pay me for this piece of the action. Signed and sealed it is.'

'Fancy. I haven't got anything as grand as that.'

'Forwood fixed it up in L.A. My contract wasn't exactly "in order", as they say.'

'Wasn't it?'

'Was yours?'

'Never saw it. I imagine so.'

'Be sure, then. It's not much good "imagining" 150,000 dollars. I need it now.'

I wasn't far wrong, and I didn't get it right away. At the time of writing (July 1985) there is still a modest 50,000 dollars owing and the roof has had to wait – it hasn't really been dealt with since 1641. It's about time something was done.

But, one thing at a time.

There was a book to be written.

*   *   *

My Muse had wandered off again in the most maddening way: she does this frequently now, leaving me sitting here in the olive store staring glumly across the sloping tiled roof of the woodshed towards the three cypress trees (there were four, but one was torn away during a particularly fierce mistral), the little wooded hill beyond and a tall stump of an olive, straight, sturdy, as unbranched as a Doric column. It is fourteen feet high and has been peasant-pruned. By that I mean that it had simply been ruthlessly cut to promote new growth; olives are pruned every twenty or so years.

Usually M. André, who is a magician with olives, and cares for their beauty as much as I do, clips away gently, cutting out the dead wood, always leaving the basic shape of the tree standing in trimmed, lace-like splendour. He never savages them, but, alas, he retired a few years ago and no longer comes.

The stump of which I write was butchered years ago, and has never put out more than a collar of leaves half-way down its trunk, the top of which is as round and smooth as a breadboard. This is the direct result of peasant-pruning: they care not a fig for the aesthetic splendour of their trees, but only for the harvest. Which is absolutely understandable. And the trunks, which they hack down, fetch a vast price on the market, where the wood is used for hideous pepper-mills, salad bowls, cheeseboards, egg-timers and sundry bits of tourist kitsch. So pruning means harvest; it also means money.

My neighbours on the west boundary (alas! I have neighbours now to the left and right of me) had their grove savaged to such an extent that the land resembles Passchendaele. They have been assured, naturally enough, that 'in three years, the trees will be just as they were; but healthier'. I know that nature has an amazing capacity to heal: but how she can possibly regrow in three years limbs which took perhaps twenty or fifty, even eighty years to evolve beats me.

And of course it doesn't happen like that at all: what *does* happen is that, though the trees never fully recover from the savaging, they do, eventually, start to look like moulting feather dusters, and then, about three years or so later, the gnarled trunks resemble rows of broccoli staggering up the hill. Of course, in years to come, they will *appear* to be trees again. But, frankly, who has so much time left to await the miracle?

As I sat looking at my mutilated column I noticed a movement on the breadboard top. Sitting in the late sun, preening and brushing, upright on his hind legs, so that he could give full attention to his toilet, was a fat, bright-eyed vine-rat washing his cream-yellow weskit. I don't know the real name for this species; we call them vine-rats simply because they forage among the grapes and don't resemble at all those scaly tailed, ugly black rats of the streets and markets. This breed has a fair pelt, enormous round ears, bright eyes, a yellow blaze on its chest and coral-pink feet. It is altogether pleasing to look at in the warmth of September as it rustles through the vine overhead searching out the ripest 'framboise' or dusty-green 'muscats', and causes no revulsion in the timidest heart; it's more like a squirrel than a rat, anyway.

There he was, occupied in the sun, grooming himself with such intensity that he was unaware of the weasel which was creeping up the olive stump. A red streak of danger, arrow head, tail flat to the bark, hidden from the rat by the frill of leaves which wreathed the column a foot or so below him.

Then the sudden dreadful fury of the two tumbling, writhing forms. A horrifying dance of death on the breadboard: red and cream rolled together in turmoil, the squeals of the rat, perfectly audible from my vantage point, the looping, writhing, leeching shape of the weasel gripping tightly to the creamy throat of his victim, until it suddenly went limp, blood spilled like scattered rubies, and the weasel dragged his prey, jerking now in death, down through the collar of leaves into the long grass at the foot of the stump and out of sight.

I watched this fandango of sudden destruction mercifully unaware that in actual fact I was like the preening rat in the sunlight, all unsuspecting. I did not know then that weasel-time would creep up on me suddenly and bring an end to my tranquillity. I suppose that I thought the peaceful, easy life could go on for ever, really. That nothing now could mar the simplicity which I had worked to achieve.

It has always been a failing of mine: I really should have learned by this time. Shadows would fall across the childhood fields, and the hermit crab would be forced from his too tight, far too snug, shell, to become as vulnerable as a sprat on a griddle.

But for the moment, for that caught instant watching from the olive store window, I was unaware, and the shadows of the future, when they fell, fell lightly.

At first.

CHAPTER
9

They arrived uninvited and unwanted, just in time for tea.

Margaret, whom I knew, and her friend, whom I did not know, nor wished to know, but who radiated relentless charm and an overpowering determination to be instantly friendly and overtly familiar.

Not my style at all.

Uninvited guests are a particular hate; 'dropping in' something which I find personally unforgivable. But when it happens, and it doesn't frankly happen all that often, one is forced to put on a performance and 'pretend' goodwill; good manners usually ease the moment.

'I *knew* that you'd be furious,' Margaret said in a low murmur. 'But Netta is very tough indeed. When she wants something she goes at it until she gets it: we were passing the house and I just happened, unthinkingly, to say that it was yours and she simply insisted that we came up the track. I do feel *awful*. Really.'

Silently I decided to buy a padlock, aloud I said that it really didn't matter, I wasn't actually working at that hour, that it wasn't her fault (of course it was, the idiot; why not just drive on?), but that there were only biscuits, no cake, for tea.

Netta Wynn-Gough, broad of hip, and teeth, tall, scrubbed-faced, came up gaily on to the terrace: she had gone off on her own to 'have a look round the place', with Bendo.

'We, that is my husband and I, Derry – he's Navy, and NOT "wavy" I might add – were offered this place simply years ago, long before you bought it, but it was quite hopeless. A wreck. And the price my dear! Quite potty! The land had gone to hell, there was a car on blocks in one of the rooms, and no telephone! There was nothing one could do with it: *nothing*.'

She named a price far in excess of anything I had paid and announced that I must show her 'simply everything'. 'I'm *so* curious!'

Well, I didn't as it happened; I managed to avoid that tour, and we had an uneasy tea with supermarket biscuits while Mrs Wynn-Gough chattered on endlessly about what *she* would have done with the garden if it had been hers, and spoke of all the plants I *should* have planted, using only their Latin names, which irritated me because I don't know the Latin names for anything.

'I do see,' she said cheerfully, 'that it is a perfect place for a "recluse", I mean, no one could possibly find it unless they were in a helicopter.'

'You weren't in a helicopter.'

'Ah, no!' she said, with what I suppose she imagined was a roguish smile. 'But sweet Margaret here knew the way, so that was splendid, and I was *so* interested to see how you lived up here in your stronghold.'

'Well . . . it really isn't a stronghold, exactly. There is no moat, no drawbridge, no portcullis, I don't pour boiling oil on people from the ramparts, and, as far as I know, I'm not a recluse. I don't live in a cave exactly.'

Suddenly all eight items seemed instantly desirable.

'Well, shall we say a hermit crab then? People in the neighbourhood say you are,' she said with stunning tact.

'I don't go about in the neighbourhood so I can't understand why people should say that.'

'Just because you *don't* go out! No one ever sees you, do they?'

'I really haven't the least idea: I've spent most of my adult life being stared at by strange people so that I have cultivated deaf ears and a sort of blind eye, it's the only way that I can survive.'

'What I find so extremely odd,' she continued remorselessly, 'is that an actor, of all people, should try to be a hermit crab anyway! It's so contradictory. I mean you all love showing off on the stage and so on. Wallowing in all that adoration and those awful fans. I mean to say, it's not like a hermit crab at all, is it? If a hermit crab did that sort of thing, you know, went about showing off, he'd be eaten alive in no time, wouldn't he?'

She appeared not to realize that she was as voracious as a killer shark herself. The crassness of her conversation, if that is what she considered it to be, was wearying: it was quite obvious that she had never seen the house before in her life, with or without non-wavy Derry. It had never been for sale before I bought it, it was not a ruin, no car had stood on blocks, and she had, as she had let slip, forced poor unwilling Margaret, now sitting in abject silence, to bring her up because Margaret knew the way and had made a careless remark.

Sheer curiosity had spoiled an afternoon.

The 'hermit crab' part of her conversation was boringly familiar: I always get it, and the 'recluse' and the 'stronghold' bits, too.

I admit to the hermit crab, as you are well aware, but she did not know of the Anthracite Years and the reasons which had forced me to fashion my cover. Neither are people like Mrs Wynn-Gough remotely aware that most actors are hermit crabs by nature. The pulpy flesh within being the true creature, the 'shell' the role which they play on (and sometimes off) the stage or the screen.

An actor is entirely his own instrument. Whereas a painter has canvas, paint and brush to come between himself and his observers, the musician his violin, cello, piano and, at a pinch, his electric guitar, the writer his pen and his selectivity, an actor has only himself to set before an audience: naked and available, even if he be festooned with Falstaff's padding or an astounding variety of putty noses and padded hump-backs.

Discarding his protective shell he is, indeed, completely vulnerable to the sharks who will as often as not eat him alive 'in no time'.

But then those are the rules of the game: he is therefore

246

forced to grow a shell. The almost desperate determination to avoid the Netta Wynn-Goughs of this world, and their ilk — the mundane, the dull, the envious and resentful, the unfulfilled and untalented (and they seem to me to be legion) — literally forces one to become what *they* choose to call a 'recluse' out of sheer self-preservation.

And all that this really means, in the final analysis, is that one tries to avoid direct contact with them as much as is possible for they exhaust, demand, give nothing in return, are supremely self-satisfied, unaware, complacent and patronizing, and, apart from all these little peccadilloes, they are (worst of all things) *boring*. They almost force one to concede that Sir Walter A. Raleigh, who died in 1922, was bang on target when he wrote:

> I wish I loved the Human Race;
> I wish I loved its silly face;
> I wish I liked the way it walks;
> I wish I liked the way it talks;
> And when I'm introduced to one
> I wish I thought *What Jolly Fun!*

At the car, Mrs Wynn-Gough laughed a happy laugh.

'Well, now that I've managed to winkle you out, so to speak, we won't take "No" for an answer, you must come along to us for a glass of sherry on Friday: we have open house every Friday; lots of terribly amusing people, and Derry will be *so* curious to meet you. He encouraged concert parties like anything during the war when we were in Mombasa. You'll have lots to talk about: just let me have your telephone number and I'll give you a tinkle on Thursday to give you directions up to our place.'

I stared at her in glassy silence.

'I really don't remember it, I'm afraid.'

'Your telephone number!'

'Quite forgotten it.'

'I see,' she said, getting into the car. 'A recluse — and rude with it.'

She seemed unaware, as they always are, that she had been pretty bloody rude herself.

I didn't bother to tell her that I can't stick sherry either.

*　　*　　*

Within my acres up here on the hill I normally have no need of the carapace which I have carefully assembled about me over the years. I am free, in my own little rock-pool as it were, and, apart from the unexpected and unwanted arrivals of outside predators, I feel perfectly safe and relaxed.

The hairline cracks in my complacency, such as the deaths of the dogs, don't for the moment alarm me, for I was almost unaware of them. However, shadows are things which one can see creeping across the landscape; you can't duck those, cannot be unaware. They show.

During the first few years up here, life had been pretty well serene, give or take minor ailments, household disasters and the havoc caused to the land by the unpredictability of the weather at such a height, just below the snowline. The land then was all unfenced, the fox and the badger free to roam at will from field to field as they had always done; but in time changes began to take place which I could not possibly ignore.

The peasants in the valley gradually began to sell off their land and their old houses, moving into the high-rise blocks nearer the town. The jasmine fields, the *rose de mai* and the vineyards were gradually abandoned to thistle and burdock, and one now seldom saw, in the early mornings, before the sun was too high, industrious figures culling the blossoms in the fields below.

It was a harsh life, however romantic it may have appeared from a distance, and now that the essences were made synthetically, and the rose petals were cheaper to import from Turkey, the peasant who had toiled for centuries on his land in the valley found it was less back-breaking, better paid and far more comfortable to work at the check-outs in Monoprix or Carrefour, to attend the petrol pumps in the many new garages, or to work on the big building-sites which were starting to ring the town: you couldn't ignore them either.

Splendid Edwardian villas were torn down and in their places huge blocks of flats, looking like slabs of marzipan cake, rose high above the butchered trees of ancient gardens. The old peasant houses were abandoned, sold to rich Dutch, Danish and German buyers who stripped them out, tarted them up, and laid out lawns and 'patios' where once chickens and ducks had prodded and poked about in dusty yards. The jasmine fields, the fields of *rose de mai*, the artichokes and the vines fell into the hands of speculative builders from London, Paris and Düsseldorf (and almost everywhere else) and were smothered with neo-Provençal villas, each with its swimming-pool, standard lamp-post, wishing-well and barbecue chimney.

The gentle days were torn asunder by the groan and whine of machinery ripping out the new foundations, and the song of Provence, if there ever had been one, was no longer that of the golden oriole, the blackbird or the nightingale, but of the cement mixer and the bulldozer.

Times were changing – and changing rapidly; as Madame Miel said sadly one morning when I took down the kitchen refuse for her goats: 'You can't turn your back for a week here now! It happens so quickly, and they are destroying the very things they all come down here to enjoy! The silence and the beauty! The world is crazy.'

Crazy indeed: suburbia was spreading all about us.

Each new villa had, naturally enough, at least two cars to sit in the garages, or to jam the narrow lanes; each villa, of necessity, had an Alsatian or a fierce Dobermann pinscher to guard the hideous property from intruders. The Alsatians and the Dobermanns roamed the terraces at will, fouled the land, savaged the dogs, and scattered the fox and the badger to distant places up in the hills.

The birds began to leave, too: for the hedges and sheltering brush were destroyed, and crazy-paving or chain-link fences took their place; a nightingale, for example, will only nest in thick scrub three, or less, metres from the ground . . . there was no room now for the nightingales. Transistor radios and lawn mowers took over.

The time came, therefore, when I, with a heavy heart, was forced to fence in the land and erect a high wooden gate at the foot of the old track. The ugly chain-link fencing glittered all around me like barbed wire, but it did, at least, keep out the Alsatians and the Dobermanns as well as the *folles*, as we called them; these were strange women who found their way up the track in high heels (in the heat of July even), see-through dresses and black frilly underwear, who claimed that they were either 'journalists' or else that we had had imagined assignations in the past or, at least, hoped-for ones in the future. Lady got fed up with locking herself in the house against their abuse but I was always given warning of their unwelcome approach in good time to hide like a criminal.

It was altogether very tiresome, but the fence and the gate did give me some chance of privacy, and thus the 'recluse' became, over the years, far more of a recluse than he had ever wished to be: the first shadows had begun to fall.

In time, however, the fence was smothered with bramble, rust and old-man's beard and was hardly noticeable, the ugly villas were screened by 400 olive trees and a desperate planting of bamboos and poplars along the lower border of the land, and although I felt that I was in a cage, after the freedom to come and go at will, it was an acceptable cage, and, like everything else in life, one grew accustomed to new routines: like locking the gate with padlocks.

For centuries there had been a short-cut through the land down to the lower road and the little chapel on the hill opposite, and this short-cut I insisted must remain, so a gate was built at the top of the hill for Madame Miel to get down to her farm from the village without taking a two-kilometre trudge; and the three old ladies, who tended the chapel, could still make their way, bent in black with broad straw hats in the summer, and knitted caps in winter, to their duties, which consisted of getting the chapel prepared for Easter and Christmas Eve services, clearing out the swallows' nests, and decking the modest altar with wild flowers in old baked-bean cans, and seeing to it generally that the place was cared for.

A view from the terrace

Time caught us all out eventually.

One by one the old ladies in black died off, the penitents' chapel, consecrated in 1189, crumbled quietly into decay and, in a few months, became only a silent relic frequented by village wooers in the spring and summer, or by hunters in winter who, unable to find anything much to shoot, now shot each other, and lit fires for warmth on the cracked tiles of the chapel floor below the abandoned altar.

Madame Miel began to find the haul up to, and down from, the village too much of an effort, gate or no gate, and securing a tinny 'deux-chevaux' for herself drove, with excruciating caution, round the lanes to her farm; so the gate at the top of the land was locked for ever and the large padlock, and wide-linked chain which held it, fused into a rusty lump: a warrior's head by Elisabeth Frink.

From the end of September until the beginning of May the telephone seldom rings, and no one comes, welcome or un-welcome, until the sudden little burst of short-life, which is Christmas.

This lasts only a couple of days in France and is a holy celebration more than a five-day bloat, as it has now become in England, and after it is over everything sinks back into deep winter torpor, the snow falls, ice sheets the pond, bitter winds rattle the shutters and howl under the roof tiles; evenings by a blazing log-stove are long and it seems almost impossible to remember that one had ever walked barefoot across too-hot tiles on the terrace, or sat exhausted with heat under the dense green of the grape-hung vine, grateful for the stillness and the coolth.

Then the spring arrives and the 'recluse' raises the portcullis, lowers the drawbridge, and welcomes the cherished invaders who arrive with the swallow, and the cuckoo.

The house is filled with laughter, conversation, music and sunlight.

Sheets are changed like minds, towels replaced, soap re-plenished in the bathroom, Tart's Parlour is littered with coat-hangers, tumbles of suitcases, shoes and other people's clothing.

In the kitchen, there is food that has been carted up from the car in prodigious quantities, wine and beer fill the fridges, ice is made; bowls and jars are crammed with flowers, dishes brim with peaches, apricots, cherries and nectarines, according to the month, and down on the iron rail by the old circular water-tank which once watered the long-lost vineyard the swimming-pool towels flutter like circus banners.

The water-tank is about thirty feet in circumference and six deep; every year I clear it of rotting leaves and water-boatmen and paint it a virulent blue, and it serves very well as a swimming-hole. It is called, with some affection, the Hippo Pool, because all that one can really do in it is wallow.

Essential in the blistering heat of July and August.

From where we sit, sprawl, stand, or lean from windows, the world all below is still strangely very much as it looked when the little chapel was consecrated. The hills have not altered, the land holds its contours, the new villas are more or less hidden, or covered with plumbago and wistaria, even the dreadful modern industrial city, lying in the plain like a pile of discarded pink and white shoeboxes, twelve storeys high, takes on an almost romantic aspect hazed as it is in the glaze of the heat, glowing in the firefly-nights like an Aladdin's Cave.

The fox and the badger have returned, through the holes I left in the fence, at the entrance or exit of their trails; the little owl, the hoopoe, the golden oriole and the nightingale are back too, because my fenced-in area is now an official and registered refuge both for them and for myself; the nightingale, in early June, sings hard in his thicket down by the cess-pit outlet, frogs agree with each other in the pond, '*Quaite*, *Quite*, *Quaite*, *Quite*', a genteel bickering in the still evenings pre-saging, perhaps, rain tomorrow.

There isn't much that I can complain of for the present.

In late August the thunder-heads begin to rise silently above the hills, the cicadas chatter frantically in the crackly bark of the olives, dragonflies swing and zig-zag over the rushes in the pond, the grass lies dry, golden, crisp as straw. On the vine the grapes have swollen, red and amber-green, gorged on by wasps and the dreaded *frelon*, one sting from which can send you to your doctor, two to the local hospital – and three (so I am assured by the local dustman, who has lived here for seventy years) will kill a horse.

It is wise, therefore, to be prudent in August under the vine.

In the evenings the sun begins its slow decline into dusk just a little earlier.

Summer is almost spent.

Down on the trampled beaches the holiday-makers start to pack up the sun umbrellas, tanning lotions, beach balls and beach bags, lash the rubber dinghies to the roof-racks of their cars, and begin the weary bumper-to-bumper journey back to the grey cities of the north.

Trains are crammed with travellers standing in the corridors waving forlorn handkerchiefs in farewell to the deceptively clear blue sea as they speed along the coast to turn inland up the Rhone Valley, until – perhaps? – next year.

It must seem a very long time to wait.

In the neo-Provençal villas the shutters go up, the burglar alarms are set, the Alsatians and Dobermanns are crated and despatched home, the garden furniture is stacked under cover for the winter ahead, and the narrow lanes, all at once, become quiet again, and as they were.

There are sudden flash-storms which break the stifling air: swift, wrecking winds which tear the last of the plants in the terrace pots to shreds and scatter the petals of geranium, nicotiana, petunia and roses like cheap confetti across the wind-driven tiles; and then the rain comes – drenching the crisp, baked grass, cooling the fading evenings – and, quite suddenly it always seems, the house is strangely quiet; rooms which echoed with laughter and argument are still – so still that standing alone in the middle of the Long Room one can hear, perfectly distinctly, the drip! drip! of a tap in the guest bathroom.

Everyone has gone.

Down by the Hippo Pool a tumbled bathing towel: yachts and seagulls gaily scrambled.

A pair of sunglasses forgotten under the mulberry tree, bum-dents on the fat upholstery of the terrace chairs: the marks left by a body which has now become only memory, no longer vibrantly physical.

It induces a feeling as strange and as unsettling as that of finding, in the washing-machine, a lipsticked glass and realizing with an acute sense of loss that the person who drank from it last is now already perhaps in New York, San Francisco or London: worlds away. Has there ever been laughter here? Did we talk? Did someone sing, argue about a play, a book or Francis Bacon? Was there life? Did ideas form? Was theory disproved? Was there Mozart, Bach or Gershwin?

Where are the voices which soared with joy as bodies jumped into the Hippo Pool? The cries of pleasure from nephews and nieces, Brock, Rupert, Sarah and Mark, from Rosalind and Nicholas, Penelope and Roddy, Kathleen, Capucine, Glenda, or Elizabeth and George? All gone now, spread through the waves of time, lapping at the edge of memory like a lazy sea, flip-flopping on the sandy beach of a lost summer.

This was negative thinking: negativity, like tears, never does anyone any good, and I had a book to write.

And a secret to keep.

Norah's decision, if such it really was, to 'pull out in March' weighed as heavily with me as bricks in the pockets of a drowning man.

In that early May, when last she had been here, I had taken in her breakfast as usual and found her standing at the open window of Tart's Parlour, her thin nightgown fluttering in the morning breeze, the little silk scarf which she always wore about her shoulders pulled tight in anxious, crippled hands; her head bowed.

'What is it? Norah! What's wrong?'

'A magpie! Down there on the grass.' Her face was taut with distress.

'Dearest Norah! The place is *full* of magpies, all the birds are back again . . . the place is full of magpies: you could call it *Domaine des pies* . . .'

'What's that?' Eyes sharp.

'Oh . . . literally translated: "The Domain of the Magpies".'

She shuddered visibly, pulled the scarf tighter round her shoulders. 'I *must* see another. I simply *must*. Not one; never just *one*!'

'Well, look out again, I bet you'll see fifty . . .'

'I wouldn't dare. I'm flying back to London today . . . and you know the rhyme I suppose?'

'No.'

She crossed the room on bare feet; settled into her Ritz-copy bed again. 'You *do* spoil me. Scrumptious croissants. Black cherry jam . . .'

'What rhyme?'

'This *is* fresh orange, isn't it?'

'You know it is . . .'

She was fiddling with a tea cup and strainer and didn't look up. 'The rhyme? Oh, there are many versions; the one I hate is:

> 'One for sorrow.
> Two for mirth.
> Three for a death.
> Four a birth.
> Five for silver.
> Six for gold.
> Seven for a secret . . .'

She looked up at me quickly, a half smile, tea strainer pointed at my heart.

> 'Ne'er to be told!'

'I promise. I may be dim-witted, you know, but I can keep a secret, I spent years of a war keeping them.'

'Can't imagine how they trusted you.'

'There are six magpies strutting their stuff down on the grass now.'

'Six. That's for gold, isn't it? So that's all right. Except that *you* saw them, not me.'

'You were too chicken.'

'I assume that's American slang for "cowardly"? Well, I was
. . . but it'll bring *you* luck, anyway.'

Standing on the deserted terrace, the evening light dying,
the cypress trees black against the distant hills, I wondered
what on earth I would do without her advice. Who would
help me over the high hurdles of writing which I felt unable to
leap? Who would assist with the essential 'patching', with the
'needlework' which my unskilled hands and brain would need?
Who now would encourage, cajole, bully, sometimes praise,
and always lift a flagging morale? I was pretty certain that I
would never be able to manage on my own.

The light had almost gone, I started to gather up the garden
cushions and cart them into shelter.

It was still only the end of August: I had just seven months.

My moment of vivid panic faded with the last of the light. I
reminded myself to go up and turn off the dripping tap in the
empty guest room.

*   *   *

Before they were playing 'Jingle Bells' and 'Holy Night' in
Monoprix I had completed the first four chapters of the book
(*An Orderly Man*) and mailed them to Norah, who accepted
them without alteration (she never altered anything I ever
wrote – but had a hell of a time with my paragraphing and
punctuation) and asked, rather plaintively, when the next ten
would be ready. 'It's difficult, you know, to judge a book on
only four chapters, but this does "feel" good. If you don't
have those beers at lunch I am certain that you could write all
afternoon, you follow?'

It had been a bone of contention between us that I could
write, clear and fresh, only in the morning, but that after
twelve-thirty I was drained, and needed my glass . . . after
which all afternoon work was dulled, and in any case the land
had to be tended, so the book waited until my head cleared,
the hay was mown, and I could go back to the olive store at
five-thirty in the afternoon to correct and revise and, as often

as not, rewrite. And I was damned if I would break this rule even though I sometimes thought that she was right.

By mid-March, just before she retired from William IV Street, she had ten complete chapters on her desk and the book, lacking only two, was securely 'in the house'. She was greatly pleased and liked it, bullying gently for the final two.

It had been a struggle to get as far as I had; not only because of winter work on the land but because, to my growing consternation, I realized gradually that Forwood was not in his usual good form: something was wrong, and something, he finally confessed, had been wrong ever since we were doing the English shoot the year before. He had said nothing about this at the time because, as always, the 'film comes first' and even though I was sometimes aware, during the shooting, that he was more tired than normal, less interested generally, I put it down to sheer boredom and pushed any nagging fears behind the bastion of work.

'I just haven't any strength now; I suppose it's age?' he said one morning while I was having my beer.

'Better see Poteau. Let him check you over.'

'I think I might.'

The last thing that Forwood ever considered was going to a doctor. This acceptance was a certain sign that all was not as it should be, and the hairline cracks of complacency widened; if he was concerned about himself I had cause to worry. But I was not, at that time, particularly alarmed.

I was sixty-one now; we were no longer the same people who had arrived on a hot July morning more than twelve years before; people grew old, strength did give out. Together we had worked the twelve acres of terraced hillside in all weathers, mowing, raking, carting, burning, tending the trees, the terrace and the lawns which had been created around the house from the tussocky, abandoned land, and were now as green and smooth as baize.

Apart from a couple of wandering Arabs who had carted boulders and rocks about and rebuilt the fallen walls of the terraces, the rest was entirely up to us to manage. It was hard work by any standards; it was also back-breaking, and the fact that it was impossible to leave the place untended for so much as a week, let alone a month, kept work at a constant peak of activity; only in the dark months of winter was there any respite, which is why I started to try and write a book in the first place: it filled in the time.

But now we had a Socialist government in France, a great deal of New Broom Sweeping went on, and one of the first things swept away were the wandering Arabs who, for a pocketful of francs, and a few bottles of iced water during Ramadan, would sweat their guts out carting rocks about and generally doing the heavy work. Everything had to be re-gularized: no more moonlighting, no more under-the-counter francs according to the hours and the work done.

I could no longer afford the prices charged by the local 'experts'; nor could I afford their social security stamp money.

So twelve acres of land were entirely in the hands of two elderly gentlemen, and with only *one* pair of hands I knew that the land could be lost.

It was something we had often discussed in the past. At forty-nine I was optimistic, or fat-headed enough (have it which way you wish), to think that although the time *would* come when so much land could not be handled, when it would become a kind of albatross about our necks, it wouldn't be for a while.

It would happen 'one day'. No shadows then. Just 'one day . . .'

Well, it seemed that 'one day' had arrived, or if not it was snapping at my heels like a chivvying hound.

So, blood tests were taken which proved negative, pills prescribed which proved useless; and although nothing 'un-pleasant' was discovered, Forwood felt not the least bit better, a warning light had flickered on to remind us, if we had forgotten, that we were mortal, and that twelve acres of land were already too much to handle.

But tension, to some extent, had been relieved, and I battled on with the final chapters, the afternoon work was eased a

259

good deal, and I did a 'bit extra', leaving Forwood to cope with lighter work and lighter machines.

In May again Norah arrived in Tart's Parlour for the holiday which we had planned she would have to help ease the hurt of her retirement from Chatto – it was something which she had kept in mind during her bleak last weeks in the shabby little office in William IV Street which had been so particularly her own – but she arrived in pretty good spirits (the break had really not quite hit her) to correct and edit the now completed typescript of *An Orderly Man*, the last book we would do together.

'I had hoped to hang on until you'd got six under your belt: a nice round figure, don't you think? However, five isn't such a bad record, so I can't complain . . . and you are on time, and Iris [Murdoch] is almost ready with hers so at least I go out, as they say, with two damn good books, and I'm still on the letter-paper, somewhere. Down at the bottom as a "consultant" or something. Doesn't mean a thing of course, but it's better than being scrapped absolutely. Now,' – she took up her typescript, pencil in hand – 'you've used the word "sagging" in four places on one page . . . delete three, I suggest?'

We worked together through the warm spring days on the terrace, she gay, alert, relentless, arguing, bargaining, snapping sometimes, as she always did when she was 'editing'. It was fun, exhausting, instructive, and we 'put the book to bed', so to speak, in three days of intensive work, whipping out extraneous words, reparagraphing, deleting pieces which, although they delighted me, alarmed her by their threats of libel. But the book was finished and in her hands. As she had wanted.

One evening, while I was lighting the stove, she suddenly said: 'Is Forwood quite all right?'

'No. Not really. I don't know what's wrong, but something is . . . and now that this is all finished, the book, I think we'd better get over to London and get him looked at. Do you know a first-rate chap? I've been away since '68. Out of touch.'

Naturally, with her many medical problems, she did: and fixed an appointment.

From then on it was a gentle slide: all the way down. Weasel-time was creeping up the tree-trunk, and I was caught almost, but not quite, unaware.

To London, then, and the diagnosis of 'a very slight form of Parkinson's: it's NOT Parkinson's, you understand, but related. It can *all* be dealt with by a very good pill.'

And, to our joint relief, it was: one hurdle over.

The second, as in all good races, was not far beyond; paces only.

A hernia.

Dr Poteau had been long retired by this time so new advice in the area had to be sought. It is far easier to discuss one's symptoms in one's own tongue – having mastered, almost, the vocabulary needed to deal with plumbers, electricians or cess-pit cleaners and the intense complications of the French tax system was not enough. Medical terms are bewildering in any language, describing one's ailments subtle and very compli-cated, especially in French where a simple word like *fatigue* can, when incorrectly applied, cover anything from 'weariness' to 'a stout pair of walking shoes', and *fatiguer*, different by only one letter, *could* mean that you are boring someone witless or merely tossing a salad. You have to be careful. Errors must be avoided at all costs. One must make the greatest efforts to speak precisely and, even more to the point perhaps, listen with extreme care and attention.

The hernia was diagnosed by a new young doctor Forwood approached one morning in the village shop. He had only recently arrived in the area, had a very pretty, pregnant wife, and rented a pleasant house at the end of the lane. He also spoke excellent English. A young doctor, and an English-speaking one at that, seemed to be the very best solution to many problems: he would know the latest drugs and potions, and would be fresh from training and up to date in his methods.

Just what was required.

Patrick and Solange became very good friends; they were decorative, amusing, young above all, and excellent company, and Patrick, perhaps not perfectly trained in the bedside manner yet, but gentle anyway, spread confidence all about him.

For a little while things seemed to go on an up-stroke.

Okay, a 'form of Parkinson's' and a 'very mild hernia' were boring, and caused problems, but they could be coped with.

I started the mowers. Forwood pushed them around. We got used to it in a short time because we had to do so: I couldn't take on all the mowing myself and write a book. I carried in the heavy stuff from the shopping expeditions, and took the dustbins down to the wooden gate at the end of the track: with patience and understanding, all would be well.

And was: until Forwood started to lose weight rather too rapidly.

In the Long Room one morning Patrick said the word one least wanted to hear.

'Cancer.'

At this stage it was only a 'possibility'; at any stage it was undesirable.

So, more tests and X-rays at the local, excellent, clinic, and after a number of anxious days of waiting a negative report. *Not* cancer, as feared, merely a 'polyp in the lower intestine'.

Anxiety falls away like armour-plating, leaving one light-headed and light in body. There is no great euphoria, I have discovered – one has been too frightened, too exhausted, too tensed for that. There is just a slow, calming spread of relief, and no one gives champagne parties to celebrate. You simply thank whatever Fate may be in charge of you and get on with the life which has, apparently, been returned.

In the middle of all this a film, in the form of a book, had arrived for Glenda and me to make together: we liked it, and were assured that there was enough money, that a good script would be forthcoming, plus director, and that we would start shooting in the January of the following year. I had gone ahead with discussions because until we were quite certain of

262

the medical facts it seemed foolish not to – it was also good for morale to have an alternative thread of thought, even if the thread, at the time, was exceptionally slender. I also started a new book based mostly on the trip I had made to Hollywood a year earlier when I was able to go, for the first time ever, to places into which I had never ventured before, simply because on my first visits to Hollywood those areas were considered either 'unsafe', 'black' or 'unsmart'. One didn't go, I wasn't taken. So I never got to them. On this last trip things had changed a little, and I went off and discovered an area of Los Angeles (and a forgotten cast of lost Europeans living there) which I had never come across before. I discovered a strange bigotry, hatred, hysteria and racial intolerance which was new and disquieting. To lose the chance of writing it up seemed foolish, especially as it is essential to try and exist normally during a period of excessive stress.

Barium meals, blood tests, X-rays and all the rest took their places sensibly in my mind as I started to plot and plan and work out a construction line for the new book.

The land foundered . . . if land can do such a thing – the grass grew longer, the walls became slightly ragged, the energy behind the extreme effort required to maintain it was low, to say the least – but on the surface, to the unobservant eye, it looked not very different. Just a bit blowsy. Not yet neglected, but not quite cared for with passionate love.

There wasn't much strength left over to give it that now.

Things could have been a great deal worse, it had to be faced. A new film ahead of me, a new book, in a new 'style', well on its way, and as soon as we got to London in January the polyp, which naturally was ever-present in the darkest recesses of the mind, would be 'nicked out', as Patrick had so eloquently said, and everything would be back to normal again. Or as near normal as we now could ever be, give or take a 'mild hernia' and a 'very slight form of Parkinson's'.

The fact that the first script of the new film was a disaster didn't cause me a great deal of surprise, or Glenda for that matter, who is hard to surprise, anyway – and we were assured that a new writer would be brought in, that the money was still all there, and that a splendid director had been chosen whom we would both like very much. (We did, as it happened, greatly. But he was whipped off the project to do a far bigger job, just before the end of the year.)

However, after more than sixty films I was pretty well undismayed, and still – idiotically – trusting, and rather gratified to think that I had already got six chapters of the new book finished and ready to take to London in January when the film – surely? – must go as planned.

The night before I was due to leave, packing a large suitcase for the three months' shoot, with a wretched Bendo hanging around, hounding – or is it really 'dogging'? – one's footsteps, aware that something unpleasant for him was in the air, the telephone rang to say not to come over, there *was* money for the film – but there *wasn't*. What does one make of that kind of inane remark? You either have the money or you haven't, especially one week away from shooting, and with Glenda already half-way through fittings for her wardrobe.

I was more concerned, frankly, with getting to London and seeing that Forwood had his polyp removed.

So we left anyway; the whole thing, at my end – guardians for the house, accommodation booked at the Connaught, appointments made for hospitals and doctors, and so on – was all too firmly arranged: I couldn't pull out, even had I wanted to. In some odd way I felt secretly convinced that as soon as we got to England things would fall into place somehow.

And they did.

But not quite as I had expected.

*　　*　　*

I was fidgeting through a battered copy of *Country Life* in the waiting-room of the London Clinic: a small dreary room, chairs round the sides, a table with old magazines and a sad-eyed Pakistani lady sitting opposite me.

I don't know what month the *Country Life* was, I don't even remember what year it was, but I do remember a church, a river and daffodils on the cover: the trivial detail which imprints itself on the mind when one waits for a medical diagnosis.

Suddenly, a whisper of starched overalls, a woman at my side, half kneeling, her hand on my arm. She was small, dark; a gleam of glass beads at her throat, the edge of a flowered print showing at her neck.

'Now *please*! Don't be distressed, don't panic!'

I closed *Country Life* carefully: I had not the slightest intention of doing either.

'It's bad news,' she said, quite unnecessarily.

I got up and replaced *Country Life* among the pile of tattered magazines on the table.

The Pakistani lady placed her hands together, bowed her head towards me with a sweet smile of sympathy; I said: 'Thank you', and turned to the overalled woman hovering at my side impatiently.

'If you'll come along with me? I'm afraid that Mr Forwood is rather, ummm, rather upset.'

Mr Forwood was, apparently, quite the opposite: he was lying on an inspection bed, in a short blue paper shift, a cup of tea and a biscuit in one hand, his other comfortably behind his head, smiling wryly.

'Well then,' he said.

'What's up?'

There was a tall, pleasant-looking young doctor in the small room and a red-haired nurse.

'Well, apparently it's a bit more than *just* a polyp . . . not quite as simple,' said Forwood.

'The sooner it's dealt with, surgically, the better,' said the young doctor. 'He'll be a lot better without it, I assure you.'

The nurse smiled kindly, took Forwood's empty cup, and she and the doctor left.

For a moment we looked at each other in silence; somewhere in the street below a car blew an impatient horn three or four times.

'Go and have a word with him, will you? While I get

dressed? They took photographs, I think, and I'm not certain that he's told me all I'd like to know. You have a word, will you? Try and find out. They are all so secretive – after all it is *my* bloody polyp . . . or whatever it is.'

In the hall outside, men were repairing the ceiling, there were dust sheets draped everywhere, and perfectly ordinary, healthy people clambered about on step-ladders repairing pipes or electric wiring, banging and joking, pulling things about.

The young rugger-bugger doctor was extremely pleasant; he was drinking a mug of coffee when I reached him behind a cluttered desk.

'I think that Mr Forwood is a bit uncertain about what he's actually *got* – I'm pretty good at disinformation, if that worries you . . . but if you could perhaps let me know?'

The doctor picked up a small bundle of Polaroid photographs.

'Help yourself. Take your pick. But take a look at this one first: may give you some idea.'

A black photograph with, dead centre, a sulphur yellow blaze of vicious light.

An evil starburst, brilliant, flaring; deathly.

'Well, not a polyp,' I said.

He shook his head. 'No. Not a polyp, I'm afraid.'

'Odd. Everyone has checked the X-rays – the French doctors, the London doctor . . .'

'Doesn't always show up on an X-ray. Easy to miss.'

'How long can it wait?'

'*Not* long. A day or so . . . soon as possible, frankly. Sorry, it's bloody bad luck.'

An immense sense of calm swamped me.

Now that I knew for sure, now that the weeks of uncertainty and strain were ended, dissolved instantly by the blatant, brutal, vicious yellow blaze in my hand, I knew exactly what to do and how to do it. I was grateful, also, that we were in London and not sitting, all unaware, up on the hill miles from anywhere: now at least there was a chance.

If you have a chance you can deal with anything. Or try.

'Well, what did he say?' Forwood and I were walking down to the street, rather than talking together in the lift with others around us.

'Didn't really say much, honestly. I saw the photographs . . . looks to me like a sort of abscess-thing. Obviously the sooner it's removed the better – no wonder you've been feeling so wretched for so long.'

No wonder.

Four days later he was filling in his rank, name and number, and various other military details requested, on a buff form in a small grey room in the King Edward VII Hospital for Officers, naming his son Gareth next of kin, but giving me full authority to take charge.

Gareth and I walked down Marylebone High Street in the bitter winter Sunday, across a deserted Oxford Street towards the Connaught.

'I'd better tell you quite frankly that it is cancer – Pa doesn't know that *yet*, but he's not an idiot,' I said.

'Is it malignant?'

'Don't know. Can't say. But the photograph I saw was not friendly. That's all I can tell you at this moment.'

'So it's a matter of crossing fingers?'

'That's it. In one.'

At the Connaught I stripped out Forwood's room and repacked his suitcase; couldn't afford that now, it would be at least a six-week haul, and severe, stringent economies had to be made immediately.

The film had collapsed like a wet paper bag the week before – so had the money, my expenses and its director.

With an intestinal 'problem' . . .

* * *

The week before – how far away it seemed.

It had started reasonably well: London was arctic, the plane on time, the luggage intact; the Connaught suite (modest because I was there to do a modest film, with matching expenses) crammed with spring flowers, and gift-wrapped

267

bottles to welcome one back, not just to London, but to the start of a new film after some years away.

It was all very jolly and comforting.

I started work almost immediately, with costume fittings at Berman's, who had dressed me for a great many films and plays for more than thirty years, and discovered, to my pleasure, that according to Phillip Link, my cutter, I had only put on two inches round the waist in all the years.

'Beer bloat' Norah would have called it. Rightly perhaps.

I chose a selection of shabby suits and tattered shirts, old shoes and battered hats (it was a battered-hat, shabby-suit part), and although there was always a faintly queasy feeling that there *was* no money to make the film we carried on in that idiotic way film-people do, confident that all was well, certain that, whatever happened, we were bound to start work on the appointed day: too much had already been set up to pull back now.

Glenda liked her costumes, her wigs and almost everything else; except the script: which was, after five rewrites, still a mess. A curate's egg: bits good, bits bad. We were fairly convinced that we would get it all together eventually, 'on the floor'. That fatal phrase which has been used so often in the cinema and brought so many films to grief. You can't (or very seldom can) get it right 'on the floor'. It doesn't work that way. But we always hope it will; it's a survival complex.

We had a new, exuberant, determined director who threw optimism about him like a happy reveller with a sack of confetti at *mardi gras*. We were smothered in his confidence and happiness. If *he* felt like this, why, then, should not we?

For some reason we didn't. Unease lay just below the surface like a quicksand, but I have made so many films under these same circumstances that I was not dismayed. I'd walked planks across quicksands more often than most players – I was sure I could do so again, conveniently forgetting that I had often slipped neatly off, and drowned.

I confess that I did have a slight gut twinge when I overheard someone suggest, at Berman's, that my costumes should 'not be altered or refitted for the time being'. We were only days from the start.

A pretty clear suggestion that the money *wasn't* there, and was far from secure; but I battered along with the happy director daily, up in the little suite among the spring flowers, trying to wrestle the script into some kind of shape.

There were, of course, other pleasures.

Suppers and luncheons, visits to the cinema and the theatre – things I missed in France, where all the films were dubbed and there was no theatre; anyway, in my town.

I went to Drury Lane to see *The Pirates of Penzance* in a new American version, desperately hoping that the hideous theatre ghost of the Anthracite Years in Glasgow would be laid for ever: and it was.

I went to see *E T* in a cinema whose audience was obviously on the verge of acute starvation, for they crammed themselves with food, to right and left of me, from the start of the advertising to the end of the main credits; and beyond. They slurped tomato soup through paper straws from half-pint plastic cartons; removed onion rings with fastidious fingers from their McDonald's, scattered them under the seats and over my shoes.

'Too many onions,' a woman in thick glasses and an Aran-knit sweater said.

'Probably horse, not beef, anyway,' said her companion.

'Eric! You've put me off . . . you *are* rotten . . .'

Finally, ten minutes into the film, they threw their litter under the seats, and crunched and crumpled it under their feet.

'Eric! Hanky, dear,' she said.

They started to clean up.

Did Mr Spielberg know that this was the audience for whom he was making his film? Why, in the name of sanity, was I making one myself if this is how our work was now accepted? They shut up after a while, and finally, in floods of tears, held on to each other like survivors on the raft of the Medusa, sobbing helplessly.

A perfect example, if example was needed, of a Television-

Trained Audience. Contempt and indifference, and then facile emotion. A frightening new breed; anyway to me.

No wonder people had stopped going to the cinema. It was no longer a pleasure. Who wants to watch a film in a litter of plastic, and the stench of fat-saturated foods?

But there were happier compensations to this cinematic gluttony. Norah, in her pretty flat in Vincent Square, was definitely one of them.

Brown bread and butter, scones and honey, Earl Grey's tea, a blazing fire, the plane trees in the square whipped by a sleety wind and the first bound copy of *An Orderly Man* in my hands.

'And the six chapters of the new book are *werry, werry* good,' she said, stretched out in her deep armchair in orange slacks and an Italian sweater.

'Werry good.' Sometimes, when she was making a strong point, she used 'W' instead of 'V' and it never ceased to amuse me, and impress me, because I knew that her emphasis was indicative of her enthusiasm.

'I just wish the firm were going to print it. It seems terrible to me. A neat *six* books . . . it would have been perfect. *I'd* have said "Yes" in a shot.'

'Well the firm [Chatto] haven't exactly invited me to stay: I haven't had a letter, or heard a word from them, in the year since you retired, so I feel it's better I go elsewhere. If I'm lucky.'

'But surely John? You've been writing to John, surely?'

'Oh yes. Of course . . . but only about *Orderly Man* . . . business, that's all.'

'What's your *agent* . . .' – she paused heavily on the word – '. . . going to do: she's a nice gel, very tough, very competent, you're in good hands, so I suppose she's got plans for this?'

'Pat [Kavanagh] is going to auction it. Next week.'

Norah sat bolt upright staring at me as if I had kicked her cat or vomited on the carpet before her.

'Auction it! It isn't even finished! You're a chapter short! You can't auction – *filthy* word – an unfinished book! It's madness.'

'Well . . . that's what's happening. Sorry. You asked and I've told you. I'm on my own now, I have to do as I'm advised by Pat and I reckon she knows what she's up to.'

'A pretty gel, *very* bright indeed, but to auction an unfinished book seems to me to be verging on insanity. When can you finish it?'

'It's blocked out. I know where I'm going. I'll get down to work as soon as the film is over and I'm back home. April . . . sometime about then.'

Norah sighed resignedly, offered me another scone, put a log on the fire. 'Things are changing' was all she said. 'I suppose I'll never come into the twentieth century, will I?'

I walked through the gathering dusk from Victoria, up across Green Park, where years ago I had scuffed my way through deep snow in wet shoes having refused fame and fortune in Hollywood, back to the modest suite in the hotel and the smell of white hyacinths which Joseph Losey had sent with 'Welcome! Next time it's with me.'

We had tried to work together for years, but there was always the same old problem. Money. We were neither of us any use to the 'box office', in fact we were famously known as 'risks'. So there wasn't much point in any 'next time' – I was certain there never would be, and there never was, alas. But the hyacinths and his thought comforted me.

Forwood was on the telephone when I arrived, replaced the receiver.

'They've fixed an appointment for the polyp business on the 8th . . . so we'll have to hang on until then, film or no film, and go back about the 10th . . . all right with you? I mean, if the film folds, that is?'

'What I'll do is accept the National Film Theatre Lecture. They have offered to pay my expenses here for two or three days, so if the film goes down the drain we can still hang on here until the 8th . . . it won't cost us much that way.'

Glenda came to lunch the next morning, uncertain, on edge, feeling, I could detect even before she said so, pretty certain that there was no money for the film and, what's more, that there never had been or would be. We ate an expensive lunch in light gloom, and when I saw her to her car in Mount Street to drive back to Blackheath she made me promise that if I heard any news I'd call her instantly. I promised.

I had only just got back to the hotel and up into the suite when the phone rang to say that our exuberant, optimistic, happy director had collapsed and been taken to the London Clinic with 'abdominal complications, probably serious'.

Glenda, by that time, could only have been going through Grosvenor Square . . . there was no point in calling her in Blackheath for at least half an hour or more.

Forwood and I sat in a fairly dejected mood. No money – we had expected that; but a 'probably' serious illness for a much respected and liked director was something else. What could that mean, now?

Agents and producers arrived; the suite was filled with fretful, worried executives. Yes, they *had*, finally, got the money, but the director was ill . . . and the production would have to be delayed until April at least. Maybe longer, depending on the seriousness of his illness. Would we postpone, Glenda and I?

Glenda, when I finally reached her, listened in silence and then, with a resigned sigh, agreed. We'd delay until April.

But I knew in my heart that the stuffing had gone out of us both.

The film had now been put on the 'back boiler', so to speak, but it was equally true to say that we had gone off the· boil.

It had all dragged on too long: the 'on-off' business of the money had lowered our enthusiasm. Trying to raise a million pounds to cover the *entire* cost of one film, including our salaries, the sets and costumes, the crew, locations and our now unhappy director had irritated and depressed me.

I knew, very well, that some players received two or three times that amount as their salaries alone in dollars for playing almost supporting roles in some turgid war or Bible extravaganzas. To have to haul about, almost with a begging bowl it seemed, from company to company and, indeed, country to country (for they had tried to raise money even in Los Angeles), to finance a film in which someone of Glenda's stature was to play, infuriated me.

The fact that I was 'box office poison' because of the 'intellectual films' which I had made, and which did not attract a mass audience, did not faze me. I had made those films from choice, and I'd had a pretty good run for whatever money they earned me, which wasn't very much; but to think that the two of us, so recently apparently nominated (even if we didn't win them) for the Emmies in the States, praised for 'the two best performances of the year' in New York, and generally swamped with hysterically enthusiastic hype, couldn't get ourselves hired to make a small, amusing *British* movie filled me with despair.

Even though the scripts had been a problem, the book from which they were written was excellent, and there *could*, in time, have been an acceptable screenplay. More despairing indeed even than that was the unhappy fact that there *still* was no money, in spite of firm assurances to the contrary, but it seemed that the sudden collapse of our bustling director had come at an opportune moment: it gave everyone more time to go on looking for elusive funds.

Shortly after this, the pound fell so low against the dollar that it was essential that Glenda and I had our contracts completely redrawn; the deal we had agreed, months ago now, made no sense at all.

So, as far as we were concerned, the film was off for good. I determined that, for the few days left to me in London while we awaited Forwood's operation, I'd fill in the time by seeing some shows, meeting old friends, ordering books from Hatchards for the long winter evenings ahead, do my National Film Theatre Lecture and an 'in-depth' interview for the BBC, and then, when all that was over, clear off back to sanity and peace up on the hill, leaving the miseries and uncertainties behind.

Just chalk it up to experience, and forget about movies

from now on in. I'd return to the olive store, bruised, but intact.

Three days later I was sitting in the waiting room of the London Clinic fidgeting through an old copy of *Country Life* . . .

CHAPTER

10

DIARY

Monday, Feb. 14th '83.

Walk to Edward VII in bitter cold. Buy champagne-splits, toothbrush, soap. F. wants a bath. No soap provided, apparently.

Back to Connaught: interview with rather smooth young man, pleasant, and possibly friendly, but won't know, as usual, until I see his piece printed. Many a slip between Interview and Article. Take the risk because it is for *The Times*.

F. asked for a print or picture to have on wall of his rather spartan room. Wants a 'Country scene: fields and things, summery: something I can tell myself stories about while I'm lying here. You understand?' I do. But where to go? Probably Medici tomorrow.

National Film Theatre Lecture. Theo Cowan collects me early at four-thirty. Show sold out with no advertising, which pleases me, but am still terrified. Good audience, clever, alert, good reception as far as I can make out, on stage for two and a quarter hours, which seems quite long, but as always am far too nervous to register anything.

Norah there, John Charlton and wife Susan, Olga (my French agent) comes from Paris, Margaret Hinxman, Gareth F. and many others. All have drinks in gloomy black Refreshment Room, but feel happy all went well. Olga Horstig Primuz amazed, and moved, by the long clip shown from *Neal Story* which closed show. She can't imagine why it has never been shown as a film; it looks fantastic on Big Screen.

I can't imagine why either. Ho hum.

Tuesday, Feb. 15th '83.

Hospital late, 10.45 a.m. because of incoming calls anxious about F. Amazing how news gets about. But comforting so many people care.

Walk to Medici. Fairly hopeless really. Flower prints, Burmese ladies, Chinese horses, and masses of Rowland Hilders. Finally unearth print of *A Somerset Field* for five quid.

Hospital staff wonderfully kind and helpful. Sister Hilda Ford and I stick print on wall at foot of F.'s bed with some kind of awful sticky chewing-gum stuff I've never seen before. She assures me that it won't mark wall or print.

Elizabeth calls in afternoon.

'Do you want me to come up to town? Bit of company?'

Worry about her own family obligations in Sussex.

Say 'Yes'.

'Good. If you'd said "No" I don't think I would ever have spoken to you again. I'll stay at Sarah's [her daughter] flat.'

Walk back to hospital in evening. Taxi fares too much, and exercise will do me good. Fairly safe from recognition. If people don't *expect* to see you in a place they don't see you. Simple. Passing Miss Selfridge, however, a whole window, it appeared, of young women started screaming and waving and jumping up and down. Maybe they thought I was someone else? Will buy tweed cap at Purdey's tomorrow for safety.

Watch an hour of dire television. God! They say the French are bad. Bed ten-thirty with this diary.

Wednesday, 16th Feb. '83.

D-Day for F.

Pat Kavanagh calls early to say she has made very satisfactory deal for *West of Sunset* minus its last chapter. Slightly overcome, but very cheered, couldn't have happened at a better time. All I have to do is finish final chapter: they say they will wait until May–June. They'll be lucky.

Elizabeth arrives 12.30 a.m. Brings mimosa for F. to 'remind him of home', it instantly goes into tight black balls in the heat of his room, but is a very kind thought. We wait with F. until his pre-med injection at two-thirty.

Sally Betts [my typist] suggests I write final chapter in hotel while I am stuck there: says she knows my handwriting after all these years and can easily cope. A very generous offer, but I don't see myself making the effort yet.

Hospital at 6.30 p.m., sit in library and wait for 'Prognosis'. Read one sentence of the book I have brought with me fifty or a hundred times.

Surgeon extremely pleasant, kind, serious, aware. Get full details. Malignant growth. But certain, almost, that he has removed it 'cleanly' and nothing has spread. If all goes well he suggests that F. will be mowing and 'doing all those chores he dislikes in the garden' in a year. *If.*

Wait in F.'s room until he is brought down from Recovery (8.15 p.m.). Very pleasant matron offers me coffee or tea and biscuits. I decline. She says: 'You *do* know what to expect in here, don't you?'

I assure her that I do. Pretty good at hospitals after five hospital films (the *Doctor* series) in a row, plus *The Patricia Neal Story*.

F. zonked out, very small in large wheeled bed, lots of tubes and bottles, drips and feeds and saline solutions or whatever they are. Help nurses (all young and super) to hang bottles and untangle tubes. They say no point really in hanging about because he'll be 'out' for hours yet.

Take my overcoat and in passing foot of his bed raise my voice in full theatrical projection. 'Well. No good hanging about, Sister. I'll be off now.' F. suddenly opens his eyes, smiles, zonks out again.

Call Gareth F. and reassure him as far as I can, call Margot Lowe (F.'s oldest and closest friend) in San Francisco. She says: 'You need money, or you need me? I'll get the next plane out, be with you tomorrow.' Am very touched, tell her I'll call when I know more details. At moment we just wait.

I think that nurses should be paid a thousand pounds a day.

Thursday, Feb. 17th.

Hospital at 10.30 a.m. F. very doped but aware. Discomfort, prefers sleep.

I go with Elizabeth and Sarah to Covent Garden Market. Elizabeth so proud of new Market you'd think she built it herself. But a market is a market. Kitsch, pottery mugs, second-hand clothes, Japanese junk, tinny jewellery ... but fun anyway, and not *like* London.

Drinks and sandwiches at The Globe. Super Victorian pub almost unchanged; jammed. A Guinness at ten bob rocked me slightly! Walk back to Connaught taking in the National Gallery. Elizabeth ravished by the Sargents: particularly the family group of the Sitwells. Lots of Impressionists I'd forgotten were here. Amazed, and very curious, at the amount of young people present. Punks, Rockers, red hair, green hair, Mohican hair, shaved heads, but all informed, sensible, interested. Hopeful signs? Buy a dozen postcards of Vuillard's *La Cheminée*.

Hospital: F. okay, fed up with physiotherapist who thumps him all the time to try to get rid of some phlegm in his lungs, residue of the cold he arrived with; otherwise all well.

Friday, Feb. 18th.

Walk to hospital. Reckon I'm saving between £8–12 a day. Easy walk and pleasant. First snowdrops in Manchester Square and a blackbird singing this evening from some scaffolding. Dear Sir: Is this a record?

Woman at crossing in Oxford Street waiting for the lights says: 'Excuse me, were you Dirk Bogarde?' I say no, sorry. Not me. Perhaps it's the Purdey cap?

Tea this afternoon Norah. Crumpets and roaring fire. She

has cut her hand on a rusty nail in a piece of firewood. Oh, Lor' . . .

Saturday, Feb. 19th.

Dull. Bitter. Walk to hospital. F. stronger, more alert. Buy enormous tin of candies for the nurses, all of whom are incredibly kind and caring. Nurses should get two thousand pounds a day. Not one. Cold starting, I think. Bugger.

Lunch Elizabeth and Sarah at very noisy restaurant (their choice not mine) at end of Kings Road. Ear-splitting noise, plates crashing on tiled floor, food fairly oily, masses of Sloane Rangers, 'Hooray Henrys' plus 'Hooray Henriettas', with too many children, all shouting and eating pasta. Proof they've all 'done' Italy at some time, I suppose. Rupert [nephew] and pretty girl, Portia, arrive for coffee. Three bottles of wine. Elizabeth insists on paying with her Barclaycard. Never had one in her life before . . . showing off! Cost a bomb too, silly girl.

Rupert drives me back to Connaught in clapped-out car, very fast, very expert, a really super chap, at least six foot four. Where does he get the height in our family of 'ordinary measure'?

F.'s room massed with flowers like a mobster's funeral parlour. Remove most into the corridor, he'll suffocate. Stay longer than normal: a good sign.

Boaty Boatwright, Diana Hammond, Kathleen Tynan call from N.Y. A lot of love flying around.

Meet Kathleen Sutherland in Hall. Sad, growing old. She was so vivid and glamorous when she taught me fashion design at Chelsea Poly in '37–38. Misses Graham terribly and says she is just waiting to join him. Why did he have to go first?

No answer to that.

Monday, Feb. 21st.

Hospital gives way this a.m. to TV. I do live-by-satellite interview with some chap on a chat show in Australia.

'Why do you do those awful chat shows, you always swore Never Again,' someone asks.

For £500 is why.

Telephones from Charlotte [Rampling], Rosalind [Bowlby], Glenda, [Jill] Melford and others offering meals, drinks, comfort, affection. Grateful and glad.

F. off his 'drips' and, more to the point, the hated cathoda (or however you spell it). Take him walk up and down corridor, first time out of bed: corridor crammed with crawling ladies and gentlemen in dressing-gowns with nurses at their elbows. A little like the Promenade Deck on the *Queen Elizabeth* but not as much fun.

Terrific improvement, however; last Wednesday was Op-Day.

We will have to return [to London] every six months for 'checks'. A slight blow. I am anxious to get home, try to finish chapter, and begin to sell up the house. It seems clear that the future must be nearer help. Not London, I hope. Maybe Paris. But whatever, it's farewell to the hill. Sod it.

F. could come out on Sunday for 'a couple of hours only'.

Tuesday, Feb. 22nd.

Still freezing. Hospital early, but take taxi because I'm a bit late. Driver flatly refuses my fare, 'Because you have given me and my wife so much pleasure for so many years.' I'm very touched: there are some really splendid people in this town, it's just the people they vote in who are such sods. Sign his autograph book for 'Mavis'.

Forwood stronger, but still pretty fragile. Says that on the lunch menu today he could have 'African Beef Stew'.

What can it possibly be? Elephant, buffalo, giraffe? The mind is dazzled.

Wednesday, Feb. 23rd.

In local shop for fresh fruit. At counter elderly man, frail hair combed like membranes over bald head, regards me with worry and distinct unease. I look at the broccoli avoiding his gaze. Recognition, I can see, is struggling hard while he chooses my Comice pears. Calls younger assistant (28?) arranging pyramid of wilting cauliflowers.

'Is it HIM?' asks Membrane-Hair.

Younger one looks at me with intensity of a scanner. I continue to look at broccoli and Golden Delicious.

'Nah,' says younger man. 'Might have been, years ago, but *not* now.'

Chastened I take pears and go to check-out; hear sudden cry behind me: 'Yeah! It *was* him!'

Make for Davies Street quickly. Age! Oh, Lord!

Thursday, Feb. 24th.

Clear out mass of dead flowers into sluice room. Nurses rather pushed this morning so offer to help F. bath. A bit of a struggle, but quite funny, and stitches are out, clean as a whistle, which is why bath permitted.

Lunch with Charlotte at Claridge's. Pretty suite, very glamorous, terrible food. Charlotte lovely, cool, superbly dressed, calm. A pleasant lunch therefore, the food, with such elegance beside one, doesn't seem to matter.

Am amused, in retrospect, that the only person who has not recognized me in London, in one form or another, is the concierge at Claridge's.

Saturday, Feb. 26th.

Lunch with Molly Daubeny in her elegant house in Victoria. Buy vast bunch of expensive freesias and have super lunch (smoked salmon and turbot cooked by my hostess) in exchange. A loving friend for almost forty years: it's important to keep your friends, thank God I have.

James Fox, amazingly, comes to dinner in evening. First time we have met since '67. Unchanged, a little more adult (but there was room for that) and a moustache which makes him look like a Camberley subaltern. He swears it's for a film. I hope so.

Sunday, Feb. 27th.

Car to hospital to collect F. All nurses, and most of staff it would appear, on steps to wish him well.

Drive him back at four-thirty. Weary, but pleased that tomorrow he'll be out for good. Best day for a very long time indeed.

Monday, Feb. 28th.

Last day of this fretful month. Buy framed prints (*Hay Wain*, etc.) for hospital rooms, with matron's approval ... leave hospital in flurry of affection from nurses. F. clearly very well liked, *and* admired, in Ward 1.

Flowers galore at Connaught. From Sheila Attenborough, Daph Fielding, Melford, Forwood family, among others. He rests in the afternoon, I go to Royal Academy to see Cimabue Crucifix. (Okay if you like relics, I suppose.)

We discuss, gently, prospect of selling up in France. It is suggested that we might have to come back to England. Many hurdles to jump before that.

Wednesday, March 2nd.

Hounded practically all day by Press who want statement on David Niven (ill in the Wellington). I don't know David Niven, and wouldn't speak to Press anyway even if I did. Strange race, journalists, strange country; hounding a dying man to the grave.

Thursday, March 3rd.

Walk with F. very, very slowly 'round the block' (Grosvenor Square). But he's stronger. I walk all afternoon round the Serpentine. Brisk, sunny day. Masses of people about, not one English voice among them. It's like Central Park.

Saturday, March 5th.

Day of triumph! F. walks round Serpentine with strength and a stick and enjoys the air, the Brent geese, and the snowdrops in the Dell.

Sunday, March 6th.

To Royal Avenue to see Joseph Losey. Old, gross, weary and worried. He offered two suggestions for possible movies we could make but both are dreadful. He doesn't know what to do next and misses Paris (where he had been living for some years) bitterly.

'No one knows who I am here any more. They *all* do in Paris. And I know who everyone is there. London is different; it's changed entirely; new trends and new faces. I'm a stranger *again*.' A terrible sadness.

I think of myself and my probable return to this strange, to me too, city, and dread the thought, so tune out. Joe suddenly wonders if we could make *Lotte in Weimar* with Peggy Ashcroft and a script by Harold [Pinter], but I suggest that Harold probably a bit too busy and famous for us now. However, agree, because he looks so miserable, but am forced to ask 'When?' to which he, naturally, can give no answer.

Monday, March 14th.

Elizabeth and George arrive to accompany us to airport and home. She will do the housekeeping, George the land which has been neglected for so long. I'll need help. Wheelchair, stick and the rest of the paraphernalia. Forwood valiant and brave; anyway, it's better than walking at terrible Heathrow. I push him and no Press near because we are flying Air France. So that's a relief. Flight on time, easy, specified seats (booked in advance . . . why *can't* you on 'The World's Favourite Airline', B A?) and land at Nice about four. Fine spring rain, car waiting, arranged by Arnold (my ex stand-in for many years) and we drive home with anxious, and not very good, driver who is terrified of the narrow lanes, sounding horn at every bend.

Marie-Christine [guardian] has meal ready for evening, house spotless, flowers in Long Room. All smells of strong 'shag' (her husband rolls his own cigs) but all serene. Bendo slightly hysterical. Settle F. and then discover that I have left his suitcase down at the airport. Typical. I'm so bloody *capable*. But we are back at home.

For the time being, at least.

*　　*　　*

In June, when the big fig-tree down at the end of the track was breaking leaf, the roses in the pond-bed were at their peak, and the neglected terraces flowed with lush green grass, moving in the morning air just as I remember that it did years ago in Great Meadow before the hay harvest, I put the house on the market discreetly (even Lady didn't know), and sold it twenty-four hours later to a pleasant Belgian couple with two children and another on the way.

It was, they said, exactly what they wanted: no changes, no alterations, everything to be left just as it was. They even suggested that I simply pack the clothes and personal pieces and pictures and leave the place to them, as it stood.

This I had to refuse: it had taken years to collect all the clutter together which made it so, apparently, attractive to them, and I might need it again somewhere else. It was agreed that they could take possession in September–October.

We'd have a final summer on the hill.

The following week was spent with the firm in Cannes who had moved us in on that fateful day long ago (fateful because

The house from Chapel Hill, with the terraces

the English packers in London had smashed practically every piece to bits), and would now crate us up and move us to their depot in Paris until I knew where I wanted to settle.

I had absolutely no idea where to go: I only knew that a six-monthly medical check, and the possibility that something might go wrong at any time, meant that I had to be within an hour, if possible, of London at all times. It is no delight to be seriously ill, or ill at all, in a foreign language, and although I knew from experience that there were splendid hospitals, and excellent doctors, in Nice, Nice was almost as far away in the end as London.

How could I close up the house and just leave it? The place was seething with wandering Yugoslavs, Arabs and out-of-work youths who would have stripped the place bare in a few hours for drug money, and there was no one near enough to notice if they did. What would happen to the wretched dog? Couldn't cart him to an hotel in Nice ... How could I, who had hardly ever thought for myself, deal with so many problems? No 'recluse' was I now: the hermit crab was suddenly shell-less − you can't take full charge of your life skulking away in protective camouflage.

I'd been spoiled over the years by Forwood, who shielded me from anything which might remotely disturb the work I was doing for the cinema. Every bill, contract, script, family problem, household worry, letter or tax demand had been in his capable hands.

Now there was no cinema − that door in the corridor had swung shut it would appear − the door which had opened into the world of writing cast the only light down the unnerving length, filled with worrying shadows. But it did leave me enough light to see which way to walk, which was just as well, frankly, because now, all of a sudden, I was Leader.

Although, as I have said, I have always had a reasonable sense of 'possessions' I have never believed in 'possessiveness', so that once I had made the unhappy decision to sell it was firm and definite and there was to be no looking back. It had been a good time − probably the best time of my adult life −

286

and it had come at the right moment. If it had to end now, then so be it: I really couldn't complain, everything has to come to an end someday, however much we believe in 'ever after' and all that rubbish with which the frail human consoles himself by reiterating from childhood to tomb – which, as the song says, 'Isn't so long a stay'. And, in any case, I have never believed that anything can last – this was the one useful legacy, I suppose, apart from strength, which I gained from the Anthracite Years – so I am seldom taken by surprise.

I had, however, not quite reckoned on the effect this positive action of mine might have on a sick man.

While I was hustling about planning what to take and what to leave, what garden furniture to dump, what statue to remove, how a skip could be got to the house so that I could strip the olive store of the junk which I had accumulated over the years – while in fact I was trying to work out how the hell to clear from a place which I loved with all my being, I had overlooked the main cause of the upheaval.

Forwood grew more and more silent, more crumpled, greyer by the day. I had hardly noticed, so involved was I.

He said little – we had after all discussed this move logically and in detail for some months – but the psychological effect on him was disturbing. It reached a point one morning when, sitting under the vine for a breather (I had begun to sort out books in the olive store), he suddenly said: 'Are you *sure* that we are doing the right thing? Where shall we go from here? An hotel in Paris? To London and the greyness? I mean, if we tried *hard*, couldn't we manage to stick it out here? Do what we could with the land, let the rest slide, but try and hang on?'

The same afternoon I called off the sale, to the consternation of the unhappy Belgian family, and settled for a tougher existence, determined that whatever the risks were which I would have to face I'd face them here, on the hill.

Forwood began to recover almost immediately; it was strange to watch. So, I must confess, did I, for I had no idea where we would settle – there had been the floating plan of an hotel or an apartment in Paris (half an hour, give or take a bit, to London) or even, in final despair, renting a small house somewhere in the Chelsea area, while the furniture gathered dust once again in a warehouse.

I knew perfectly well that a 'small house somewhere in the Chelsea area' would cost me more than I had in the bank and would finally kill me off with claustrophobia, having lived for so long at an altitude of 400 metres with a green mountain-top beyond the kitchen sink and the whole of the Estérel range outside my bedroom windows.

So we stayed.

Naturally the hard work on the land had to be curtailed: two strong men with big machines, and far fewer years than I, dealt with the waving grasses on the terraces, while I worked the easier stuff around the house, and Forwood, with care, managed his lawns and long walks; and although the place would never again be 'impeccable', as it was once called locally, it was tidy, safe from fire and tended.

Somehow we'd manage.

I went back to work, finished off the missing chapter of the new book, mailed it to Sally, and started to plan the cover for my new publishers.

Things were, almost, back to normal again, or at least one did one's best to make it seem so.

It was the only way to play the game after all.

* * *

DIARY

Saturday, December 31st '83.

Misty morning with light sun later. Gentle, and soft. Attenboroughs for supper to see the end of this disturbing, and almost disastrous, year.

The end of a year in which F. might have copped it but didn't; owing to care and wonderful skill. October 'check' (his first since op.) was successful all round.

An Orderly Man made the best-seller lists, I did a couple of episodes of one hour each in a marathon twelve-week French–Japanese 'cultural' TV series, *History through the Louvre*, with Charlotte [Rampling]. We won't measure up to K. Clark, but it was fun in an exhausting way. Weeks of homework on ancient Greek and Roman sculpture, plus the Flemish School of painters. *West of Sunset* ready for publication in March, and the land has not, as I so feared, reverted to 'savage heath' after all: we have managed to cope very well and had a bumper (200 kilo) olive crop, so that's not bad.

Another year ahead now. Orwell's 1984. Well, face it with high hopes and flying flags. To show my trust have started new novel (am I *really* quite neurotic?) and had timid try at start of autobiography four. Like novel, so far, best. Have to keep working somehow, and with No Cinema I am stuck with writing. I should be so lucky. At least I am pushing like a soap salesman at every door, along the corridor: I may well be astonished by what I find; but, as Colette says: 'To be astonished is one of the surest ways of NOT growing old too quickly.'

I'll go along with that.

*   *   *

There was astonishment all right.

In January I was summonsed down to Cannes and, in an imposing suite in the Carlton Hotel, invited to become President of the next Film Festival.

My first reaction, as always, was blind panic, my second to thank them and to ask for twenty-four hours to 'check my dates'. I had to keep the 'six-monthly medicals' in mind.

I telephoned Olga Horstig Primuz in Paris, who cried: 'Accept immediately! It is a great honour, actors are seldom asked to be President!'

I then called Losey in London, for he had been President once and could, if he felt like it, help me. I was not altogether certain what the President's duties were.

'Why you? For God's sake!'

'I don't know why me: probably scraping the barrel.'

'They must be.'

'I gather you are in one of your "mean" moods?'

'Just weary. It's a terrible job. *Terrible*, Dirkel.'

'Can you give me any helpful suggestions?'

'Say no.'

'Well I might say yes: I might like it.'

'You'll hate it. No one could *like* it. But insist on a private car and driver at all times for yourself, a suite of rooms — NOT a bedroom — and a translator to be at your side night and day if needed.'

'Thanks. Did you hold your Jury meetings in French?'

'Did I hell! That's why you'll need the translator.'

'I think I'll manage.'

'Have a translator anyway. Insist. He'll get you out of all the shit that hits the fan, and plenty will.'

'You've been a great help, Joe. I'm jam-packed with confidence.'

'Don't think that it's just a question of going to the movies three times a day and having fun. It's bloody hard work. Take pens and notepads, make your notes after *every* screening — otherwise you'll forget whether it's Sunday or last July. Any idea what films they'll shove in?'

'No. Nothing firm yet . . . there is talk of, *perhaps*, *Under the Volcano*.'

There was a silence from Joe.

Some years ago we had had a series of discussions about me playing the Consul for him, and I had been bitterly distressed when he, behind my back and without telling me at *any* time, decided to play a Celtic actor known for his extravagances and with whom Joe had become infatuated. I was 'dumped', and we did not speak to each other for some years. Then the breach healed: he lost the film anyway, and the rights reverted to the Mexican Government, who asked me to play the Consul. Without Joe. I accepted; but there were, shall we say, script and director problems, so that faded away too. No skin off anyone's nose finally.

'Well,' said Joe. 'That should make you happy.'

'What are you doing next?'

'I am doing a film with a lot of naked ladies in a Turkish bath.'

'Well, that should keep *you* happy.'

His laughter was tired, beaten, joyless.

'Turn down the President's job, Dirkel . . . it'll kill you.'

I accepted it.

'We want you to try and restore the dignity to the Festival which it has sadly lost over the last few years' I was told at my first 'briefing'.

A difficult job indeed. Joe's words were in my ear: 'Why you? For God's sake!'

The Festival had fallen on sad times. Once a glamorous occasion, it had now become a rather tacky affair, a film market attracting a host of unattractive customers, porno films, bums and tits, dope and drugs. The glamour had begun to fade, and the big stars, such as there were, stayed away. And, what was far more to the point, the film-makers kept their best films out of the Festival – its increasing (perhaps apocryphal) reputation for splitting the vote, juggling of the Jury votes, and general under-the-bar-counter chicanery to suit individual interests had frightened off many serious studios and directors. The American market wanted value for the money which they had lavishly poured into the coffers of Cannes in the past. It was openly suggested to me that a 'good film' had no chance of winning unless, as the saying went, a 'wallet was placed on the table'.

I felt rather like a member of the Salvation Army: I was in for a battle to save lost souls indeed. How to restore dignity to a crumbling Festival?

With a good Jury, honour and the discipline of a British Sergeant-Major? Perhaps it could work that way?

One other part of my briefing alarmed me.

The Jury was not to vote for anything overtly political. No emotional hysteria as there had been for Wajda's *Man of Iron*. Whoever went to see *that*? We were to choose films which would please a Family Audience, not ones which would appeal to 'a few students and a handful of *faux* intellectuals. Family Entertainment for all the world markets'.

My heart sank. Shades of the old Rank days. I began to think that I was not the right man for the job, for I had long ago deserted 'Family Entertainment', and catered, with the work I did, solely it would seem for precisely those 'few students and a handful of *faux* intellectuals'.

However, my Jury, when the time came in May, was superb. Serious, caring, no one at all frivolous. I began to assume my Sergeant-Major figure and we attended the first solemn meeting, in a heavily guarded room, sitting at a long table with bottles of mineral water, notepads and sharpened pencils, as if we were at a major summit meeting. Secrecy, we were informed, was the key to the whole business. Not a word must be leaked out at any time. The Press must be avoided by all Jury members, and the final results of our deliberations would be announced by the President, only, on the last night of the Festival from the stage of the Palais where it would be sent round the world via Eurovision. This was part of the new formula to 'save the reputation of the Festival'. Before, the world Press had always had the results 'leaked' to them so that they could reach their readers with the news well in advance. Now they'd have to wait (breathlessly, it was assumed) for the last night and the first announcement.

All very well so far: secrecy was to be paramount, we all nodded and agreed and swore to be as monks and nuns, and took our vows.

But I had discovered, quite by chance, that the chic, and pleasant, woman who was there to translate for those members of the Jury who had no French, and who would be present at *all* our meetings and *all* our deliberations, was married to an American executive who represented two major American companies and was presently in town.

It seemed to me wiser, without impugning the undoubted integrity of the lady, to have someone with us who had nothing whatsoever to do with the cinema or the Festival. I asked for a teacher from the Berlitz School of Languages, or anyone else they could find, who would be impartial. A young lady, who translated for lawyers and doctors in the town, was found. She stayed with us for the whole two weeks.

It was my first (unpopular) stand against any 'errors'.

It was not to be the last.

We worked hard; we debated long hours locked in private rooms, haggled, discussed, argued, and finally, sometimes just before midnight, got our results ready. They were, at all times, a majority vote: that is to say seven or eight out of the possible ten. And there was no split vote at any time: if that seemed to be happening I insisted that we sat on and went over it all again until we had one clear, majority agreement.

Our results, on Best Actor and Best Actress, threw Authority into confusion. It was appalled, demanded who the players were, even asked what films they had appeared in. Since each and every film had been selected by themselves I felt that they really should know, and we stuck even more firmly to our decisions. They were official; they *had* to accept.

The last day's voting, for all the films, the Hommage and the coveted Palme d'Or, took place in a heavily guarded villa some way out of Cannes. We had outriders and police cars with flashing blue lights everywhere, and were locked in the villa all day until our results were read to Authority.

We eventually reached our decisions just after six in the evening – the announcements were to be made, on the stage for the television and to the packed audience, by seven-thirty. We still had to change into dinner jackets and get back into town: there was little time left.

Authority arrived to hear our results. I read them out in a firm, clear voice.

There was a horrified silence.

'What about the American films? There are no American awards?'

'No, none.'

Consternation and dismay. We sat perfectly silent at our huge round table.

293

'For *The Bounty*? There is nothing? It is not *possible*!'

'No votes at all.'

'For *Under the Volcano*?'

'Alas, I'm sorry . . .'

'You have not read the rules correctly, Mr President!'

I nearly, very nearly, took a punch at the speaker.

'I have read the rules correctly. We have followed them *precisely*. These are our considered and unanimous judgements.'

'You think that this . . . "*Paris, Texas*" is Family Entertainment?'

'We think that it was the best film submitted to us for judgement for the Palme d'Or.'

'And the Hommage! Why to Satyajit Ray? He is not here in Cannes!'

'No. He's in hospital in India with a serious heart complaint. This Hommage is to him for all the films, and entertainment, which he has given the world.'

'You *can't* do that! What about John Huston?'

'Nothing for John Huston.'

'You must give *him* the Hommage . . .'

'We have already given the Hommage to Ray.'

'Huston is here, in Cannes. He has come especially for the Festival, he has given us *Under the Volcano*! He is a very old man, he has travelled many, many thousands of miles, six thousand miles he has travelled to be with us. *Six thousand!*'

I sat mute, staring at my pile of votes; at the list which I would have to read out in less than an hour.

Suddenly a member of the Jury said, in a voice flat with hours of discussion, his pencil pointing at the heart of Authority: 'Listen: you do *not* win the fucking Palme d'Or for *travelling*!'

Astonishment indeed. But the verdict of the audience was tremendous, the applause and cheers for every one of our decisions was deafening – we grinned at each other with exhausted, happy relief.

We had, we hoped, restored a little dignity to the Festival. Only one compromise. No 'wallets on the table', all above board and honourable.

At the lavish supper which always ends the Festival in the pillared halls of the Carlton Hotel, the Jury and I sat together like a happy, weary group of schoolchildren.

Exams over, holidays ahead.

Madame Anne-Marie Dupuy, the formidable, enchanting and tireless Mayor of Cannes, came to thank us for our 'splendid work' on behalf of her city, and just one courteous member of Authority added his congratulations, suggesting that the evening had been a triumph.

Early the next morning I stood on the rain-drenched balcony of my hotel as a team of gardeners ripped out the wallflowers and primulas from the flowerbeds below and replaced them with fuchsias, petunias and geranium. Instant-Gardening for the Summer Season.

The Festival was over.

As I left to drive home in the rain a card from Olga was handed to me by the doorman.

It was quite simple, very gratifying.

Saturday.

Mon cher Président:
I am sorry to have seen so little of you . . . but work is W O R K, and I have the impression that you have done a *wonderful* job . . .

There was no note of any kind from Authority – and there never was to be any note, not even to say 'Adieu!'

I had a shrewd feeling, somehow, that I would never be asked back.

*   *   *

Four weeks later, Patricia Losey, Joe's wife, telephoned one morning to say that he was dying. It was very sudden: a matter of days not weeks.

I was not, in some curious way, surprised. Perhaps I had subconsciously expected the news: his extreme sadness, weariness, disillusion and disenchantment were acute to a distressing degree the last time we had met and discussed, almost hopelessly, the possibility of doing *Lotte in Weimar*.

I telephoned at noon the next day, on a sudden impulse, to inquire how he was. His secretary, Victoria Bacon, answered: 'Well; have a word with Patricia . . . she'd like to talk to you.'

'I don't want to trouble her really; you can tell me . . .'

'No, honestly . . . Patricia is right here; we're just having a mug of coffee together –' She broke off suddenly.

There was a sound of scuffling, a door slammed, something fell.

Victoria was back on the line, her voice quick, alert. 'Call you back,' she said and hung up.

She returned my call in twenty minutes.

'He's gone,' she said. 'Isn't it strange? Just as you telephoned they called down for Patricia and she was with him. It's so odd that it should have been you. Do you think it could have been telepathy or something?'

It could have been – I don't honestly know. All I do know is that I had a strange compulsion to call at that precise moment – I could easily have waited until the evening. But knowing Joe as well as I did it would not have surprised me if, somewhere along the wavelengths, he had summonsed me: and I had obeyed.

We had known each other for over thirty years, thirty years of an 'imperfect friendship', imperfect only in that neither of us really *fully* understood the other and didn't trouble to do so. What we knew we liked well enough, admired and even loved, so that was sufficient.

I didn't know, or care, what his politics were. He laughed at me for my ignorance, and upbraided me for being a-political: 'It shows that you have no *real* thinking brain,' he used to say cheerfully. He didn't even like my life-style, although he greatly enjoyed some of the benefits which it brought him. He disliked 'servants' and 'aristocrats', as he called them, but made use of both at all times when he could. The 'aristocrats' he despised, just as he did 'servants'.

He was often distressingly rude to waiters, and maids, my own staff and anyone whom he considered to be 'subservient'; on the other hand, he was unable to do without them and enjoyed luxury to a disgraceful extent, expecting at all times only the best. He was jealous of people, courageous, he envied, was affectionate, caustic, rude, and quite capable of being devious if it so suited him. As I well knew. But whatever the faults, there were glorious compensations and nothing, finally, ever managed to break the deep affection, and respect, which we had for each other.

So. Joe had gone; Visconti, the Emperor, had gone; Cukor, who had perhaps taught me more about screen acting than any other director – he too had gone; and Fassbinder, the gentle, sometimes astonishing, genius-victim of a troubled and tortured childhood, had killed himself in his crummy flat. He too had, alas, gone.

It seemed to me that June morning, kicking a pebble down the track for a leaping Bendo, that the 'gathering' had begun.

*　　*　　*

As I walked into the ward I could see her, down at the far end on the right. She was lying half out of the bed, head down, arms trailing on the floor.

The bed beside her, where an ashen girl had lain unconscious for the last five days, was empty, the blankets neatly folded at its foot.

I called her name as I reached the empty bed and she looked up instantly, raised her arms, as thin as broom-sticks, to embrace me.

I leant towards her and kissed her forehead.

She smelled sour: the wound at her stomach had seeped through the dressings and soiled her nightdress.

'Darling!' she said. 'How lovely. I *knew* you'd come; get that chair and sit down.'

'What were you doing down there? Brushing the floor?'

'Resting. Getting the blood to my hands, what blood there is. I think they've drained it all away, I'm so feeble.'

She smiled weakly, her eyes sunken, hair straight, lustreless, grey: only the two little pearl earrings appeared to have life in the dull light of the ward. The woman in the far bed, a cheery person in glasses, nodded towards me with a bright smile, went on reading the *Sun*.

'She's *very* nice,' said Norah. 'They all know who you are now, of course; impossible to pretend it isn't a fillum star who comes to see me: aren't they extraordinary?'

'Where's your neighbour, the girl?'

'Oh. They took her away last night. Died, I suppose. That's the trouble with a public ward, you know everything that goes on, disagreeable business.'

'Well it's your fault. You insisted on National Health, not private.'

'Too expensive! Anyway . . . I hardly had any choice this time, darling, it was a near thing.'

Just before I had left France for the September 'medical check', Rosalind had telephoned to say that Norah had collapsed with a perforated bowel and had been rushed to hospital. They thought, at the time, that she was 'stable and all right'.

We had planned to dine together the night that I arrived in London, but instead she had telephoned the hotel and asked me to go and see her as soon as I could.

'Are you allowed visitors already?'

'I'm in a little curtained cubicle thing . . . you can come any time.' Her voice was frail, but the old Norah was lurking just below the surface.

She didn't, considering the seriousness of her operation, look too bad; she was bright-eyed, weak, but greedy for the smoked salmon sandwiches which I had brought her and which she ate almost before I could unwrap them.

'You are good to me! And fresh orange juice in a champagne bottle! How delicious.'

'Especially pressed at the Connaught. There must be a full pint there.'

'What a business it's all been.'

'What happened, for heaven's sake? You sounded absolutely splendid when I spoke to you on Tuesday.'

'I *was*! So odd. Then this terrible thing happened. I'm *werry*, *werry* lucky you know. They say they got me just in time. I was on the brink! Don't you love the way doctors speak? "On the brink"! *Honestly* . . . did you bring the photographs of the garden you promised me?'

She leafed through them with professional skill, admiring the roses and the lilies, the view of the pond and the yellow iris, one I'd especially taken for her of the view from Tart's Parlour and had had enlarged.

'Oh! How lovely! How I wish I were there . . .'

'How long, do you suppose, you'll have to be stuck here?'

'About a week . . . I hope. Then back again in six weeks for another operation which I simply dread. My guts, you see,' she said with a grim smile, eating away at her smoked salmon sandwich, the size of a postage stamp, 'are in a bag by my side, so for God's sake don't sit on the bed, will you?'

The elegant, fastidious, patrician creature with her guts in a bag at her side in a public ward.

'They are wonderfully kind to me. Nurses are marvellous. But I don't K N O W any of them, you see? As soon as you get used to one she's whisked off somewhere else or goes on 'leave'. It's disconcerting really. And all the young doctors are different every morning. Keep asking my name and what's wrong with me. Unsettling.'

'When you get out, then what?'

'Ah, that's the problem. I can't go back to the flat: all those stairs! So I think I'll go down to Betty in Kent . . . she spoils me marvellously, and I can have a tiny apartment to myself and the local nurse can come in . . . we'll manage.'

But it was not to be like that.

I went to the hospital every day and one afternoon discovered that she was no longer in the little cubicle, but in a different ward, on a different floor, and was looking a great deal less well. It was a busy ward and very full. As I arrived they were wheeling an ashen-faced girl towards the bed beside her, putting up screens; there was quiet bustle and rustle everywhere.

Norah smiled, as she always did when she saw me. 'There you are at last,' she said.

'Moved you?' I said, sitting beside her, my back to the bed-making behind.

'And you found me. I was, apparently, in the wrong place. They want me in a ward so that they "can keep their eye on me". *Too* silly . . . no one seems to bother much anyway.'

The table across the foot of her bed was crammed with jars of flowers of all sorts, a few from gardens, others from expensive shops looking like hotel arrangements. The water in some was scummy, the flowers wilting, there was a faint smell of decay.

'They really have so much to do, poor creatures, they can't go around changing the water in my flowers . . . I don't like to ask them: they get quite snappish, you know.'

'How are you today. Mouldy?'

'I *look* mouldy, you mean? I feel bloody, frankly. Something's gone wrong.'

'What's gone wrong?'

She did look 'mouldy' and untidy and distressed.

'Well. One of the nurses, I don't know which one, gave me a purgative. I mean, can you beat it? A purgative with my guts where they are?'

'But why?'

'I don't know why. I complained to one of the interns this morning and he was very rude. Wagged his finger at me and said: "You *do* carry on, old girl" . . . I was so angry.'

'Well, I suppose they are rushed off their feet here . . . it's pretty well crammed.'

They had finished with the ashen-faced girl, removed the screens; she lay rigid beneath tight sheets and blankets, her feet poking up under them, like a Crusader's wife on a tomb.

'I hadn't been "carrying on" as he said, I simply told him that I had had the most dreadful time all night, terrible pain . . . I simply couldn't help myself . . . I had no control . . .'

'You are still in pain?'

'Yes. Fearful gripes . . . I don't know.' She brushed her hair helplessly with the back of her hand. 'Anyway, the intern went away, read my chart thing of course at the end of the bed, and then came back in a fearful state and said I should NEVER have been given the whatever it was. I ask you! I knew it was wrong . . . anyone would know. He was very apologetic . . . but the damage has been done. I feel *awful*.'

A tall, rather hefty nurse arrived at the bedside, the menu list in her hand. 'Tomorrow's lunch . . . what do you feel like, dear? Want to look or shall I give you a few suggestions?'

'I feel like death, frankly; give me a few suggestions.'

'Well, there's soup, three kinds: spring vegetable, mushroom or tomato . . .'

'I really don't want anything . . . just some bouillon. Or Bovril? Is there Bovril?'

'You must eat, dear,' said the nurse, and looking across the bed at me she said: 'She's being *very* naughty, you know. Simply won't eat, and that won't get us well and strong will it? I'll come back in a couple of ticks; think it over. There's a good girl.'

Norah looked at her receding back as she went down to other beds. 'They treat one like a monstrous child. Maddening. I really CAN'T eat custard and prunes or boiled cod and spinach . . . I can't eat anything.'

'Shall I nip out and get you some smoked salmon sandwiches, very tiny, thin, from the Connaught? It wouldn't take a moment really, the car is waiting.'

She shook her head wearily on the crumpled pillows. 'I can't eat, darling . . . I'd rather you stayed, don't go . . . stay with me. How's Forwood?'

'He's okay . . . the tests are all negative.'

'Thank God for that. I am glad. Do tell him . . . give him my love. All my love.'

'I wish to goodness you'd let me try and get you into Edward VII . . .'

'No . . . no . . . don't fuss about me. Of course I *could* go

301

there: widow of a serving officer . . . but I don't think I could face the moving about. It would mean an ambulance and so on . . .'

'Let me try?'

But she refused point blank. The stuffing, as she said bitterly, with that odd twist of black humour which surfaced from time to time, had 'gone out of her'.

'Anyway,' she said, 'so many of my friends would have to be told, they all come to see me here . . . it would be frightfully difficult to tell everyone I'd changed and then, of course, there might not be a free bed.'

I could see that she was still playing, vaguely, with the idea of a move.

'I could call your friends . . . it wouldn't take long.'

'Take years! I have so many, they really are too good. Jerry, and Betty, Laurens, Iris, Grania, Amanda, dear Christopher . . . so many.'

'Too many. Sister says that you have far too many friends and that they exhaust you.'

'She's quite, quite wrong. They are my lifeline.'

I started to get up, she grabbed my arm urgently.

'Don't go! Stay . . . can't you stay a little longer?'

'The car's waiting. I've got to go all the way out to Twickenham.'

'Twickenham? What delightful friends do you have in Twickenham with whom I cannot compete?'

'It's a sort of, I know you hate the phrase, but it's a "sort of" memorial service for Joseph Losey. He hated all that rubbish in churches, ageing knights reading eulogies about him who had never even been to see his films. So we're having an end of film party for him on one of the stages at the studios, where he was most happy. Everyone is coming. Just to have a drink and a sandwich, to remember him.'

Norah was silent, she twisted one of her pearls. 'It's a splendid idea. Much better. Will you come tomorrow?'

'I'll come tomorrow, promise. No smoked salmon; sure?'

She smiled a sweet, lost, tired smile . . . as frail as a thread of fading light. 'No smoked salmon, darling. Kiss, though?'

As I walked through the long ward, two people were coming towards her with a large bunch of flowers, looking around at the beds.

'Ah!' said the man. 'There she is . . . right at the end.'

*   *   *

It was the next day that I saw her from the door of the ward half hanging out of the bed, the thin arms trailing on the floor, her head down. The deterioration had been extraordinary overnight: I was alarmed and distressed by the haggard face, the circles under her eyes, the sunken look, but we had talked and she smiled a little and I got over the hump of the moment of shock.

'I wonder if you'd be an angel . . . there's an envelope there, on the table under the flowers somewhere . . . I haven't been able to read any of my letters. People write but I'm too exhausted to read them. But the envelope . . . a long one . . . not square . . . can you find it for me?'

I found the envelope under a jar of dying asters: a list of pencilled names scribbled down its length.

'Here you are; but let me get your pillows right, they are all squint and squashed.'

'They don't have time, you see.'

I pulled her gently towards me, she lay against my body as I leaned over the bed as light as a fledgling sparrow. I turned the pillows, restacked them, plumped them up, eased her back.

'There you are. Better?'

'Much. There's a pencil somewhere . . . I'm being a bother . . . a blue one, can you find it?'

'What are you up to? Making a will, or a shopping list?'

'Not a will . . . not that. Did it ages ago, but there are some people I perhaps forgot. I want the flat stripped out and auctioned; everything. Except my pictures and a few little bits and pieces. So I make a note of the names of the people I want to go and choose something before they chuck the lot out . . .

you know how lawyers are, so slow, takes them ages to do anything. Just something to remind them of me.'

'Norah! Really . . . you've got plenty of time for that, come on now.'

'Must do it while I remember, they take so long, the lawyers . . . must see it in print. Amanda. I must remember my Amanda, she's been a saint . . .' She wrote slowly, in her clumsy hands, the blue pencil wobbling with effort. 'Just a tiny re-membrance, that's all.' She handed me the envelope and the pencil. 'Put them back under the flowers, will you. Then I'll know where they are. They will come and tidy everything up every minute of the day. There's a Philippino gel, a real devil. Everything goes into her waste-bucket.'

She lay back on the pillows as transparent as egg-white on a windscreen. 'You go tomorrow?'

'On the nine fifty-five Air France.'

'Lucky old you. I wish . . . I wish . . .' She looked out of the big windows at the far end of the ward. 'When do you come back, then? Next "check" I suppose? Six months?'

I lied easily. 'There's a fillum on the way. Script's not right yet but I've said that I'll come over in October . . . about four weeks . . . and see how things are going.'

'Oh! October! Autumn . . . your hated month. All those dreadful colours you dislike so much.'

'Bonfire colours. Awful. I'll be able to come down to Kent to see you.'

'All the trees will be russet . . . like my hair used to be. Years ago . . .'

'In October, then . . .'

She turned suddenly and took my hand. 'You didn't tell me about the Losey thing at Twickenham. The memorial business. Was it fun?'

'Great fun. Everyone, well, nearly everyone, came. Lots of champagne, sandwiches . . .'

'If they ever had one of those terrible things for me . . . memorial services, you promise me faithfully that you'd never go, would you? Without me?' She was smiling lightly.

'I promise. Not unless you are by my side.'

She laughed, turned back to the windows.

'It's raining. Don't get wet.'

'I'll be back. In about four weeks. All right?'

'Lovely. Simply lovely.'

I leant down and kissed her on the lips.

'You know, I do happen to love you, very much indeed.'

She pressed my hand with both of hers, her eyes suddenly alive, bright with pleasure.

'I think that I *do* know that,' she said. 'I've got that on board.'

I walked quickly out of the ward and I didn't look back; or ever see her again.

★   ★   ★

I'm almost sixty-five.

I'm sitting on the platform, stage left, of the Younger Hall in St Andrew's University, Scotland.

I am shortly to be awarded an Honorary Degree of Letters.

Why? You may well ask; it'll raise a few eyebrows. It already has.

I don't give a fig about that.

I'm wearing a fine black satin cassock with wide cuffs. All down the front there are bright yellow buttons; these designate 'The Arts'.

I'm scared to death. I am not used to any form of academic life, and never expected to become a part of its rituals.

We were 'robed' a little time ago. A cheerful affair, like a changing room at a football match. Dons and tutors and graduands struggling into their gowns and hoods, the new boys, like me, being assisted by uniformed gentlemen of charm and distinction, who know exactly, after years of experience, just how one should be correctly dressed. And buttoned.

White bow-tie, the dark suit I bought to wear in Cannes for the Festival, a beating heart. You can hide that with clothing – but you can't stop it thudding under your shirt.

Then the procession. We walked in solemn state, two

abreast, I too dry-mouthed to do more than smile weakly, led by liveried gentlemen carrying on high trophies and emblems of gold and silver. Tremendously serious, very moving, humbling.

Through proud crowds of singing parents and family members, mouthing the Latin words of the Gaudeamus, and then past the serried rows of singing students, all, I hoped, as anxious as I felt.

And so I sit up here, on the stage, so to speak, a captive audience below me. I can think a bit: there is nothing that I have to do for the moment.

All these young, unlined faces before me! Life has not yet printed its cruel map upon them, on their brows and cheeks, nor pulled down the corners of their mouths, creased their eyes, thinned their hair.

How I envy them their youth; how proud I am that I am there among them. I'm well aware that they have been sweating out their hearts for three or four years to reach this supreme moment in their lives, while I have idled through without the least thought of academic reward.

It's funny, sitting here in my leather chair, gowned like a clown with my yellow buttons, that when I was first asked to accept this honour, and it's an honour I never dreamed of, I thought it was a student hoax.

'No hoax indeed!' the Secretary of the Senate scribbled in his own hand in reply to my cautious acceptance.

I remember (sitting here, watching the Chancellor take his place at the 'altar') that I, puffed with pride, telephoned Norah with the news and only stopped when I had got to 821 of the code: she had died three weeks before.

I hung up, and looked out of the olive store windows to the oaks turning russet on the chapel hill. She'd have been 'werry' pleased, I think, that I am to be honoured by Scotland's most ancient university, founded in 1411; thirty years before Joan of Arc was burned at the stake in Rouen, and many, many years before Columbus discovered America. It's pretty clear to me that they don't chuck honours and degrees about like ping-pong balls. Which makes my situation all the more astonishing.

It would have pleased her, too, because it would have proved that her 'judgement' was not at fault, and that was something about which she minded greatly. Her life was books, words and her writers – she cared for little else. She always insisted that she 'published writers' as well as publishing books, and she at all times loved, bullied, cajoled, supported the people who came within her world. She gave beginners encouragement, often a start, always a chance, and by a sudden switch of a television button she had given me mine.

It would appear, therefore, from this wondrous moment, in this softly rustling hall, that her judgement had not been misplaced: her 'writer' had been accepted. It might have amused her, wryly, that while she had received her doctorate from, what they call here, a 'municipal university', I will get mine from so ancient and hallowed a place. But I never knew her to be envious or resentful of anything.

I'm thinking all this to stop rising panic: I hope that I appear laid-back and cool.

They are calling on the first degree students. The Chancellor stands tall and splendid in black and silver, John Knox's cap in his hand.

I wish that Pa and Ma were here.

She'd have cried beautifully, with enormous care, so that her mascara didn't run. Pa, I reckon, would have scratched his head in amused bewilderment thinking of all the money he had spent in the past to try and educate me against my will.

Look where ignorance has got me today, Pa!

I'd like Forwood to have been here too: after over forty years of care and counsel he'd have been pleased as punch, but the journey, and the standing about, and all the social business would have been a bit too much for him; however, I'm not entirely alone – Rosalind has come with me to be my 'minder'. I'm really not absolutely used to doing it all for myself. Yet.

I can see her, right up there in the front row of the packed gallery. Very pretty, blonde. Very straight-backed, very proud, very much a 'Smallwood product', for she was trained by Norah and became one of her 'gels'. So it's fitting that she is with me here today: a direct link with the past and this extraordinary moment. She started work with me on my first book at Chatto's; now she brings me ineffable comfort.

A linking indeed.

I know that behind me, in ranks rising high to the ceiling of this splendid hall, sit the dignitaries of the university in their varied cassocks, gowns and caps, but I know equally well that behind them, far, far away, and only in my mind's eye, is the backcloth massed with the faces and figures of the people who brought me here, providing the support I need for the modest performance, without words, which I shall shortly be required to make.

When I kneel before the Chancellor, as soon I shall, I will know that they are all about me, watching somewhere in the cosmic atmosphere.

★   ★   ★

DIARY

Friday morning, July 5th '85.

It's 3.35 a.m. and I can sleep no longer. They say that as one grows older one needs less sleep. Perhaps it's true?

I'm writing this at the oval table in the bow window of my opulent suite in Rusacks Hotel overlooking the 18th hole of the oldest golf course in the world. It is already quite light. I had forgotten how short the nights are here.

I've got two fat armchairs, settee, coffee table with a wobbly leg, a vitrine full of tarnished silver cups for long-forgotten matches played on that course below, a vase of dried leaves and grasses on the mantelpiece, the colour of mashed turnips, a large, dark print of anemones in a bowl, parchment lampshades hanging high on the ceiling.

There is a thick sea-mist and I cannot see the waves, only hear them sighing lazily along the beach, and only then when I open the windows. Close them because it is bitterly cold.

Last night was fun. Graduation Dinner with tables at herring-bone angles, a piper to play us in. Me at top table with silver candelabra, apricot roses, crystal and silver. Very elegant, rich apparently, established. Scowling scholastic faces in heavy gilt frames on the panelled walls, stained glass, speeches, a loving cup passed from one to another. Altogether moving, ancient and perfect. Kindness has overwhelmed me all day.

Later the Graduation Ball, in a giant chiffon-draped marquee on the lawns. A Tissot painting. Girls in long dresses and tartan sashes, some of the men in the kilt, the rest in tails with white buttonholes. Everyone young and gay, and alive, and I an unbelieving part of it all.

Walked home to Rusacks with Rosalind through a silent St Andrews. I suppose, after so many centuries, the town takes all this in its stride? I can't, quite, yet.

This morning – or was it yesterday morning? – a television man said: 'Doctor van den Bogarde, would you move a wee bittie to your right . . . you're too far apart for the camera.'

I turned in surprise to see which of my relatives it could have been.

I *am* a mutt. I'll get used to it.

Perhaps back to bed: it's so damned cold my fingers are white.

Across the brilliant green of the 18th sacred hole, coming wanly through the mist, a young couple, she in a long dress trailing a negligent scarf, he in crumpled tails. They are wandering slowly, her head on his shoulder, through the meandering spume and fine rain, arms around each other.

In no hurry. Life before them. Or is it only breakfast? Which they are serving at four o'clock.

No matter: a new day has begun and it is as beautiful a way to see it start as any I can imagine.

A billow of mist rolls in from the ocean, drowning the ancient Club House, swirling across the pampered green below, dimming the light about me.

The tarnished cups in the vitrine look like lead; the chairs, the settee, the wobbly-legged coffee table become dark looming shapes, like fat scattered cushions; and the dried grasses on the mantelpiece are ghostly, still, spiky as sticks of incense; the lamps above me hang in shadow, shrouded in the gloom.

It's *very* cold; back, I think, now to bed. The maid is bringing tea at eight o'clock.

*　　*　　*

Perhaps, in that ethereal light, if I had heard the distant whisper of a scratchy wind-up gramophone, the rustle of a silk kimono, the clinging scent from a small leather powder puff, I might well have been persuaded that I was back where it had all begun for me: in Aunt Kitty's room.

INDEX

312

FOR THE BEST IN PAPERBACKS, LOOK FOR THE

In every corner of the world, on every subject under the sun, Penguin represents quality and variety – the very best in publishing today.

For complete information about books available from Penguin – including Pelicans, Puffins, Peregrines and Penguin Classics – and how to order them, write to us at the appropriate address below. Please note that for copyright reasons the selection of books varies from country to country.

In the United Kingdom: Please write to *Dept E.P., Penguin Books Ltd, Harmondsworth, Middlesex, UB7 0DA*

If you have any difficulty in obtaining a title, please send your order with the correct money, plus ten per cent for postage and packaging, to *PO Box No 11, West Drayton, Middlesex*

In the United States: Please write to *Dept BA, Penguin, 299 Murray Hill Parkway, East Rutherford, New Jersey 07073*

In Canada: Please write to *Penguin Books Canada Ltd, 2801 John Street, Markham, Ontario L3R 1B4*

In Australia: Please write to the *Marketing Department, Penguin Books Australia Ltd, P.O. Box 257, Ringwood, Victoria 3134*

In New Zealand: Please write to the *Marketing Department, Penguin Books (NZ) Ltd, Private Bag, Takapuna, Auckland 9*

In India: Please write to *Penguin Overseas Ltd, 706 Eros Apartments, 56 Nehru Place, New Delhi, 110019*

In Holland: Please write to *Penguin Books Nederland B.V., Postbus 195, NL–1380AD Weesp, Netherlands*

In Germany: Please write to *Penguin Books Ltd, Friedrichstrasse 10–12, D–6000 Frankfurt Main 1, Federal Republic of Germany*

In Spain: Please write to *Longman Penguin España, Calle San Nicolas 15, E–28013 Madrid, Spain*

In France: Please write to *Penguin Books Ltd, 39 Rue de Montmorency, F-75003, Paris, France*

In Japan: Please write to *Longman Penguin Japan Co Ltd, Yamaguchi Building, 2–12–9 Kanda Jimbocho, Chiyoda-Ku, Tokyo 101, Japan*

PENGUIN BESTSELLERS

Is That It? Bob Geldof with Paul Vallely

The autobiography of one of today's most controversial figures. 'He has become a folk hero whom politicians cannot afford to ignore. And he has shown that simple moral outrage can be a force for good' – *Daily Telegraph*. 'It's terrific . . . everyone over thirteen should read it' – *Standard*

Niccolò Rising Dorothy Dunnett

The first of a new series of historical novels by the author of the world-famous *Lymond* series. Adventure, high romance and the dangerous glitter of fifteenth-century Europe abound in this magnificent story of the House of Charetty and the disarming, mysterious genius who exploits all its members.

The World, the Flesh and the Devil Reay Tannahill

'A bewitching blend of history and passion. A MUST' – *Daily Mail*. A superb novel in a great tradition. 'Excellent' – *The Times*

Perfume: The Story of a Murderer Patrick Süskind

It was after his first murder that Grenouille knew he was a genius. He was to become the greatest perfumer of all time, for he possessed the power to distil the very essence of love itself. 'Witty, stylish and ferociously absorbing . . . menace conveyed with all the power of the writer's elegant unease' – *Observer*

The Old Devils Kingsley Amis

Winner of the 1986 Booker Prize
'Vintage Kingsley Amis, 50 per cent pure alcohol with splashes of sad savagery' – *The Times*. The highly comic novel about Alun Weaver and his wife's return to their Celtic roots. 'Crackling with marvellous Taff comedy . . . this is probably Mr Amis's best book since *Lucky Jim*' – *Guardian*

FOR THE BEST IN PAPERBACKS, LOOK FOR THE

PENGUIN BESTSELLERS

Cat Chaser   Elmore Leonard

'*Cat Chaser* really moves' – *The New York Times Book Review* 'Elmore Leonard gets so much mileage out of his plot that just when you think one is cruising to a stop, it picks up speed for a few more twists and turns' – *Washington Post*

The Mosquito Coast   Paul Theroux

Detesting twentieth century America, Allie Fox takes his family to live in the Honduran jungle. 'Imagine the Swiss Family Robinson gone mad, and you will have some idea of what is in store . . . Theroux's best novel yet' – *Sunday Times*

Skallagrigg   William Horwood

This new book from the author of *Duncton Wood* unites Arthur, a little boy abandoned many years ago in a grim hospital in northern England, with Esther, a radiantly intelligent young girl who is suffering from cerebral palsy, and with Daniel, an American computer-games genius. 'Some of the passages would wring tears of recognition, not pity' – Yvonne Nolan in the *Observer*

The Second Rumpole Omnibus   John Mortimer

'Rumpole is worthy to join the great gallery of English oddballs ranging from Pickwick to Sherlock Holmes, Jeeves and Bertie Wooster' – *Sunday Times* 'Rumpole has been an inspired stroke of good fortune for us all' – Lynda Lee-Potter in the *Daily Mail*

The Lion's Cage   John Clive

As the Allies advance across Europe, the likes of Joe Porter are making a killing of another kind. His destiny becomes woven with that of Lissette, whose passionate love for a German officer spells peril for Porter and herself – and the battle for survival begins.

FOR THE BEST IN PAPERBACKS, LOOK FOR THE

PENGUIN BESTSELLERS

Illusions   Charlotte Vale Allen

Leigh and Daniel have been drawn together by their urgent needs, finding a brief respite from their pain in each other's arms. Then romantic love turns to savage obsession. 'She is a truly important writer' – Bette Davis

Snakes and Ladders   Dirk Bogarde

The second volume of Dirk Bogarde's outstanding biography, *Snakes and Ladders* is rich in detail, incident and character by an actor whose many talents include a rare gift for writing. 'Vivid, acute, sensitive, intelligent and amusing' – *Sunday Express*

Wideacre   Philippa Gregory

Beatrice Lacey is one of the most passionate and compelling heroines ever created. There burns in Beatrice one overwhelming obsession – to possess Wideacre, her family's ancestral home, and to achieve her aim she will risk everything: reputation, incest, even murder.

A Dark and Distant Shore   Reay Tannahill

'An absorbing saga spanning a century of love affairs, hatred and high points of Victorian history' – *Daily Express* 'Enthralling . . . a marvellous blend of *Gone with the Wind* and *The Thorn Birds*. You will enjoy every page' – *Daily Mirror*

Runaway   Lucy Irvine

Not a sequel, but the story of Lucy Irvine's life *before* she became a castaway. Witty, courageous and sensational, it is a story you won't forget. 'A searing account . . . raw and unflinching honesty' – *Daily Express* 'A genuine and courageous work of autobiography' – *Today*

FOR THE BEST IN PAPERBACKS, LOOK FOR THE 🐧

A CHOICE OF PENGUIN FICTION

Maia Richard Adams

The heroic romance of love and war in an ancient empire from one of our greatest storytellers. 'Enormous and powerful' – *Financial Times*

The Warning Bell Lynne Reid Banks

A wonderfully involving, truthful novel about the choices a woman must make in her life – and the price she must pay for ignoring the counsel of her own heart. 'Lynne Reid Banks knows how to get to her reader: this novel grips like Super Glue' – *Observer*

Doctor Slaughter Paul Theroux

Provocative and menacing – a brilliant dissection of lust, ambition and betrayal in 'civilized' London. 'Witty, chilly, exuberant, graphic' – *The Times Literary Supplement*

July's People Nadine Gordimer

Set in South Africa, this novel gives us an unforgettable look at the terrifying, tacit understanding and misunderstandings between blacks and whites. 'This is the best novel that Miss Gordimer has ever written' – Alan Paton in the *Saturday Review*

Wise Virgin A. N. Wilson

Giles Fox's work on the Pottle manuscript, a little-known thirteenth-century tract on virginity, leads him to some innovative research on the subject that takes even his breath away. 'A most elegant and chilling comedy' – *Observer* Books of the Year

Last Resorts Clare Boylan

Harriet loved Joe Fischer for his ordinariness – for his ordinary suits and hats, his ordinary money and his ordinary mind, even for his ordinary wife. 'An unmitigated delight' – *Time Out*

BY THE SAME AUTHOR

The first two volumes of Dirk Bogarde's bestselling and highly acclaimed autobiography:

'An irresistible writer ... every dialogue, every voice rings true' – John Carey in the *Sunday Times*

A Postillion Struck by Lightning

With superlative skill and power, Dirk Bogarde evokes his early life, from the idylls of childhood to his arrival in Hollywood.

'What emerges ... is a whole life. Whole in the sense that the sensitive, shy, brilliant human being called Dirk Bogarde speaks to you as you read' – Dilys Powell in the *Sunday Times*

'Really remarkable, a childhood brilliantly recalled ... his exact pen-and-ink sketches are almost unbearably nostalgic' – *Daily Telegraph*

'Romantic, modest, funny' – *Guardian*

Snakes and Ladders

The years from the Second World War to the making of *Death in Venice* – spellbinding years in which Bogarde transformed himself from the matinée idol of the 'Doctor' films into one of the finest screen actors of our time.

'Beautifully written, extraordinarily observed' – Sir Peter Hall

'His books are in a different class from the ghosted, pedestrian or anecdotal memoirs which so many stars of stage and screen produce' – Margaret Drabble in the *Listener*

'A work of art from a very gifted writer ... vivid, acute, sensitive, intelligent and amusing' – *Sunday Express*

And a novel:

West of Sunset

'It wasn't an accident, you know. With Hugo. It was deliberate. He drove into that truck quite deliberately in his white Maserati ...'

Set amid the gaudy wastes of Los Angeles, *West of Sunset* is a savage, funny and romantic story from a novelist at the height of his powers.

'Very engaging' – *Observer*